Praise fo *Stolen Grace*

"I couldn't put it down, and am aching not only to re-read it, but to instigate reading it with a group or book club where I can challenge others to deliberate their own life tenets through the engaging storyline, shocking plot turns, and surprising conclusion. Five exhilarating, thought-provoking and courageous stars!"
—*The Book Enthusiast*

"A very dramatic, spellbinding, and out of the box success for Ms. Richmonde!! I LOVED every minute of it!!"
—*Kawehi Reviews*

"I was literally biting my nails while reading this book. As always, Arianne Richmonde's writing is in a league of its own. Lyrical, beautiful, intelligent, with perfectly drawn complex characters."
—*New York Times Bestselling author Nelle L'Amour*

"If you are looking for a story of romance that will take your soul on a voyage of discovery and deep analysis of the important things in life, Stolen Grace is definitely a novel you are destined to read."
—*Tami Talbert*

About the Author

Arianne Richmonde is an American author who was raised in both the US and Europe. She lives in France with her husband and coterie of animals. As well as *Stolen Grace*, she has written the international bestselling contemporary romance, The Pearl Series.

STOLEN GRACE

by

ARIANNE RICHMONDE

Mendacity. You know what that is? Lies and liars.
Tennessee Williams
Cat on a Hot Tin Roof

1

Sylvia

"So you're definitely going to Los Angeles then?" Sylvia asked. She knew what the answer would be but the words still tumbled out of her mouth. She needed to break the silence which had been festering in the air all day.

Tommy's eyes swept over her, and she wished she wasn't wearing an apron. *Not the glamorous Sylvia I married,* is that what he was secretly thinking? Sylvia used to feel so graceful, so elegant, but now it was as if that grace had been stolen from her, snatched from inside her like the Devil taking someone's soul.

"Yes, of course I'm going," Tommy answered, his British accent sounding more clipped than usual. He was leaning against the fridge, drinking a beer.

Sylvia fumbled with the apron knot and untied the strings, but then didn't take the apron off. What was the point? He watched her as she wiped the table. His gaze still affected her, still made her heart flutter, even after all these years of marriage.

Tommy's lips curved up just slightly, perhaps a small attempt to cajole her into believing that he was doing something worthy. He added, "What makes you think I'd pass up an opportunity like this? I'll make more money in two weeks than I have all year."

They were standing in the roomy kitchen of their Wyoming log home, a soft May breeze wavering through the open backyard door, the grassy scent of an almost-summer lingering with the sweet smell of apple pie. Sylvia was baking. She never baked. She hoped that it would, in some way, fix things. She abandoned cleaning up the mess of flour and globs of dough, and focused her eyes on their huge kitchen window and to the landscape beyond. She observed a moose in the distance, its curved muzzle bent to the ground, droopy lips foraging for food, its antlers flat like a doubled-clawed hat. By September those antlers would be massive—over five feet across—then the creature would shed them in winter.

Winter—she dreaded that time of year. When early wet snow would freeze and cattle couldn't break through to the grass. The mud—boots on, boots off—heavy coats and gloves to brace the hissing wind. Then the howling Wyoming wintry nights would sneak up, Sylvia's breath puffing faintly warm in the icy air. The hardships of country life were not what she had signed up for, not what she had left New York City for.

She looked back at Tommy and studied his beautiful, dark brown eyes; it was hard to gauge his expression. Flecks of golden afternoon sun lit up his face, making his sandy hair blonder, his defined jaw softer. Was he telling the truth, she wondered? Was it really just a job offer and no more? A part truth, yes, but *the truth*? She doubted it. She wished she didn't feel the pit of her stomach pine with emptiness—then it would be easier.

Easier to watch him lie.

It was a shock when she had realized, just six months before, that Tommy could be duplicitous—the awful discovery that the kind, trusting man she married had changed. She'd never snooped or pried, had always taken his word for everything, but she began to snatch his Smartphone whenever she could—her hands trembling, fumbling, searching for snippets of evidence while it lay like a potent, dark secret on a table in the bathroom or kitchen, with only minutes of spying time before he came back into the room.

But Sylvia, green as a sapling trying to push through a mass of bramble to a blue sky, had worn herself out, and now she was trying to make things better. Hence the pie.

"So how long will the job last?" she asked, trying not to sound too despondent.

"I told you. Two, three weeks. Depends on the weather and stuff," he replied, standing strong, his legs assertively astride, all six feet, two inches of him. This very same stance could make her go weak with butterflies. If she allowed herself. Right now, her armor was on. Would she, she wondered, trust him again? Enough to let herself feel that all-encompassing love once more?

She brushed her hands on her apron. "But it's May. You'll have guaranteed sunshine in LA at this time of year."

"Yes, but you never know."

"No, you don't ever know," she muttered. *Funny thing, sunshine,* she thought. *One minute you have it and the next it's obstructed by a storm cloud. Unexpected—out of the blue, yet with a faint hope that it will vanish . . .*

Sylvia glanced at Tommy again. Grace's painting of Mrs. Paws, the neighbor's white cat, was just to the right of him, stuck on the fridge door with a magnet. A reminder. What the hell had he being playing at, jeopardizing their family life, risking losing her and Grace? Temptation by way of Facebook, the modern-day Jezebel? *Ugh!* She turned her eyes again to the window to hide her resentment. *That time-wasting Internet addiction. The thief that was swamping people's lives, robbing people of their creativity. Robbing relationships.* There were some people with a thousand so called "friends" usurping tangible, flesh-and-blood friends. Real feelings. Touch, smell, humanity. The cyber world was making children insensitive (all those violent video games), and husbands and wives unfaithful. Her old school friend Bob, for instance, who just a month before, had been dumped like a hot brick. His wife had reunited with an old flame from college. With a click of a button, she fell in love all over again, leaving her husband an empty, bitter man, fighting to see his children.

Sylvia's internal ramblings pattered on in her head. *Love like fast food. Want to find an ex? Type his name in the Facebook search bar. Want to hook up with that pretty girl you saw at a party? Bingo, there she is. Ask her out, why don't you? You could even find her on Twitter. Easy, no phone call necessary. Just send a message. Tweet, tweet.*

"So it's a fashion shoot, you told me?" she asked with a faint smile. "Do you know who the models are?"

"Not really."

"Not really? What's with the *'really'*?" She turned back to the window. She didn't want to see Deceit, with a capital D, on her husband's face, but still, she couldn't drop the conversation.

"I got sent a couple of photos of some girls but nobody's been chosen yet."

"Who chooses? You or the magazine?"

"Both, I suppose."

"So *she* isn't part of the parcel, then? Or is this whole trip an excuse to see *her?*" *There, she said it.*

He let out an exasperated groan, walked over to the kitchen table and sat down. "Of course not! This is a *photography* job—they need a model for a clothing line. It has nothing to do with her, she's an actress."

"No, she isn't." Sylvia wanted to add that the girl was a *wannabe* actress, that she'd never had a professional acting job. Hadn't even been to drama school. A wannabe actress who fancied herself as a model, posting photo after photo of herself on Facebook, so men could drool over her. But she and Tommy had been through that tired argument already, so Sylvia held the tip of her tongue between her teeth to stop herself from lashing out.

As if reading her thoughts, Tommy mumbled, "Give the girl a break; she's embarking on her career, she's only twenty years old."

The sting. *Young. Fresh. Desirable. Could practically be her daughter.*

"Exactly. Only twenty. A baby. Didn't that make you feel odd, Tommy, and *old*, to be obsessing about a twenty-year-old? You do realize that she's a *female*, don't you? Right now, all she has to worry about is which pair of heels she has to wear, or what make-up, because she's only *twenty*, for Christ's sake. If you actually started having a relationship—"

Tommy banged his fist on the table. His empty beer bottle toppled onto its side, rolled to the edge, but he caught it before it smashed to the floor.

It made Sylvia stop herself mid-sentence. She would have continued . . . *She'd be just like me, nagging you, finding fault, being disappointed* . . . but she was glad for the interruption. The sound of her own voice reminded her that she was turning into the kind of woman she swore she'd never be; the nagging, picky, ball-busting wife. She and Tommy had become the type of couple she used to despise, that snipped at each other over inconsequential nothings, who went to bed feeling angry without a kiss to make up for it—the sort that couldn't be bothered to have sex anymore because it seemed like just too much effort after a long day. Besides, she needed to put on a happy face for Grace. It wasn't fair on their daughter to be fed her parents' marital breadcrumbs.

Tommy stood up with a jolt and said, "Look, we've *been* through this, Sylvia. I told you I wasn't going to have contact with her anymore, and I'm not. Please can we drop this whole *Bel Ange* thing? You have to trust me, darling. *Please.*" The please was a begging sort of please.

Tommy laid his arms around her. He was warm—Sylvia loved that about him. His feet were like hot water bottles in bed, his touch generous. Yes, he'd always been that way, even when he'd obviously been fantasizing about other women. Because sniffing about on Facebook, looking at pretty young girls, was as good as looking at porn, wasn't it? She took a deep breath and counted to three—she needed to dispel that grudge and allow the warmth of her husband's arms to engulf her. The seesaw of emotions was driving her crazy. She leaned into him and her stomach pooled with longing. It infuriated her that Tommy turned her on so much when she still couldn't trust him.

Umm, he smells so good, she thought, inhaling the odor of his neck and remembering just one of the reasons why she had fallen in love with him. Sun. Earth. The faintest smell of sweat; not acrid but masculine. He always smelled of whatever he had eaten or done. Today he must have been outside in the fresh air—he smelled of wood. She loved his natural smell—the beautiful, sensual and masculine man he was, he simply didn't need any sprucing up to make him more attractive.

"Please promise you won't put that poison all over yourself again," she whispered.

He laughed. "Eau de Cologne isn't poison, Sylvia."

Despite her disappointment in him, Sylvia couldn't help herself; she yielded completely to the firm hold of her husband and pressed herself against his strong, hard chest. His solidity made her feel momentarily safe. Perhaps if she held on tight enough her insecurity could melt away. It felt good—*he* felt good.

But her inner-voice reminded her that she mustn't let her guard down.

It had been that insidious after-shave that started the whole episode six months earlier. She'd always told him how she hated him, and men in general, wearing scent of any kind. Why cover up your natural odor when you smell so incredibly attractive? Like dogs, really, rolling in manure—convinced they smell fabulous when they don't. After-shave, Eau de Cologne, fragrance, eau de toilette—whatever—it smelled like a cloying lie. When Tommy took that last trip to LA, six months before, he had bought some at the airport.

After always having smelt of grass and sun, of . . . Tommyness, he stank of a pungent, sickly TV commercial. He reeked of a lie. A stinkingly-sweet lie. After he returned, Sylvia discovered what that lie was. She'd glanced at his public post on Facebook:

Phew that was a long ride home, and then a comment from a woman she didn't know, that read: *It was great to see you.* Then his remark below hers, written in French, *Avec plaisir, bel ange.*

Sylvia remembered how her heart felt as if it had, literally, been stabbed. Who the hell was this "*bel ange?*" Tommy wasn't the type to go round calling people "darling" or "love" or "honey." *Bel. Freaking. Ange?* Her palms glistened now with sweat—remembering how she felt—as if she would black out, blood rushing to her disbelieving head. He'd never called *her* a *beautiful angel.* At least, not in forever. And yes, "*bel*" *ange,* not "*belle*" ange, as she had supposed. An angel, Tommy had explained, takes the masculine in French, even when referring to a woman. *Ugh! Thanks for that tidbit of information—because if the bel ange isn't me, why the hell would I care?*

Reminding herself about all this made a rush of adrenaline surge through her. She pulled away from his embrace.

"You promised you'd fix the faucet," she said coldly. "It's still dripping and it's really bugging me." She turned her back on him and stared out of the window again, back to the safety of her loneliness.

For the past year and a half Sylvia felt the ache of Tommy's distance. He'd cuddle her or put his arm around her but he'd stopped saying, "I love you." Compliments were saved for rare occasions. Sylvia realized that he had fallen out of love with her like a man bored with his out-of-date computer or car. Yet she found herself making excuses, putting it down to the monotony of their life, living in the deep Wyoming countryside, the tough winters, the stress of having a five-year-old without the paychecks to support their daughter with ease. Yet Sylvia's gut told her something was pecking away at their marriage and the Bel Ange was the cause.

No, the Bel Ange was not the cause. Tommy was.

Sylvia shifted her stare away from the view, leaving the moose to his foraging, and she looked back at her husband.

Damn, he's so annoyingly handsome.

He must have felt her gaze boring into him because he stopped what he was doing and looked at her. She noticed hope dancing in his beautiful, sable-brown eyes. They still glittered with warmth, despite her frost. She heard herself sigh again, and she wondered how long she would keep this up. Punishing Tommy with her barriers.

Punishing herself.

The telephone rang, jarring her from her inner monologue. She glanced at the caller ID. It was her father.

She broke into a smile and picked up. "Hi Dad." She hadn't realized that the Bel Ange pitter-patter of negativity in her head had been making her mouth turn downwards. She wanted her father to believe everything was perfect with her world—didn't want to pile him with her burden. Every time she spoke to him, she sensed his fragility. "How are you doing? Is Melinda still with you?"

"Yes she is, and it's been such a treat to have her here. When are you coming to stay, sweetheart?" he said down the phone. "I know, I know, it's not the right moment—Grace is still in school—but soon, I hope. Make it soon, honey. I miss you."

"I promise. Or you could come here." *I miss you,* her dad just said. He rarely spoke those words. Sylvia's heart pinched.

"Michigan to Wyoming is a long way for an old man, honey."

She laughed nervously. He was right. He was getting older—he wouldn't last forever. It still made her sick to her stomach that she hadn't seen her mom before she died. Grace had come down with a fever so Sylvia wasn't at her mother's deathbed. Guilt lapped at Sylvia daily like a gentle wave—never too rough to unbalance her, but a constant reminder. She felt a twist in her chest but said gaily, "Oh please, so not old. Your aim is still the best out of all your golf friends."

"What friends I have left." He chuckled. "The pickings are slim."

"Yeah, sorry about Jim—that's so sad. I sent flowers. I wanted to call Susan but—"

"How's little Gracie?"

"Bigger every day. You'd be amazed. So grown up and frighteningly smart. She plays with Tommy's iPad, you know. Records her voice, draws pictures, makes paintings—well, virtual ones. She's even learned to download books for her library of animal stories."

"Well she's a smart kid, like her mom. And beautiful, too."

Sylvia laughed. "Grace is the opposite from me—she must take after Tommy. She's so techy, Dad. So precocious for a five-year-old. She's showing signs of a brilliant mind. But maybe that's just because I'm her mom I think that."

Sylvia wondered if it was because of Tommy's influence or because of her daughter's genes. She half listened to her dad chat on about his day, and remembered how united she and Tommy had been during the whole Grace adoption process. The trips to India, the research they'd done about her origins. Grace was originally from Kashmir—hence her startling, golden-colored eyes and soft, gentle features—her little nose and her heart-shaped face that melted Sylvia every time Grace looked at her.

Sylvia remembered how picky the agencies and countries had been with prospective parents, but how she and Tommy weathered the storm together, always a team, vying for the same goal: happiness. Creating a family unit. Finally, she had accepted the fact that a biological child just wasn't their path in life. Tommy swore he didn't care and championed the adoption all the way. The Indians had insisted upon the couple having been married five years. She and Tommy qualified, but the paperwork, the traveling, and all that twisting scarlet tape had been arduous, but the second they set eyes on Grace, they knew it had been worth every minute of the ordeal.

But now their perfect family unit was fragmented. They'd have to fight equally hard to win it back again.

"She'll do well at school, mark my words," Sylvia's father went on. "You lucked out, honey."

Sylvia snapped back to attention. "We sure did. She's my moon, my stars, and my sun."

"That's how I feel about you sweetheart," her dad told her. "I love you, honey."

"I love you too, Daddy."

"I'm putting Melinda on, she's right here. Bye, Sylvie, honey."

"Bye, Dad." She rolled her father's loving words around her tongue. *I love you. I miss you.* Those words rang sweetly in her ear. He had taken her by surprise and Sylvia could feel her eyes well up. She'd managed not to even hint about Tommy. She watched her husband out of the corner of her eye. He was still fiddling with the faucet.

Melinda's voice had its usual upbeat, bouncy ball tone. "Hey cuz."

"Hi Melinda," Sylvia said into the receiver. "So glad you're there. Thanks for making the effort. I feel so guilty living this far away. Wish we could visit Dad more often."

"Well don't feel badly. Uncle Wilbur's doing just great. It's just a short plane ride from Chicago for me. No big deal."

"Well thanks, anyway, for taking time off work. How long are you staying?"

"I have to get back tomorrow. Deadlines. There's this report I have to do."

"He's lonely without Mom, isn't he?" Sylvia felt guilt gather like thick molasses in her throat.

"Yes. But, hey, that's life. He has the country club, he has his friends. How about you, Sylvia—everything okay now with Tommy?"

Tommy was still there in the kitchen, his ears pricked up, probably. That was, if he truly gave a damn. "Well, you know," Sylvia answered, twirling a lock of her thick blond hair.

"Still pissed? Sylvia, it's been over six months, hasn't it? And remember, he never actually *did* anything."

Sylvia cradled the telephone to her ear and slipped out of the kitchen. She made her way through the large hallway of their log-lined house, and into the guest bathroom. She sat on the lid of the toilet seat and contemplated her reflection, sidelong in the mirror. Those telltale lines. She plucked a lone gray hair from her temple, while still hugging the telephone between her ear and shoulder.

Getting older was no picnic.

Melinda went on, "You can't milk this grudge forever. Marriage is about forgiveness. All he did was flirt, give the guy a break." *Trust Melinda to tell it how it is,* Sylvia mused. *No bullshit; straight to the point.*

"It's . . . just . . . he's going off to LA so the whole thing is coming up all over again, you know . . . feelings. I've been so insecure about myself lately."

"Oh please, with your looks?"

"I guess I'd never dwelled on our age difference before and . . . well . . . I just don't—*trust* him."

Sylvia relayed to her cousin the ramblings in her head that were still eating away at her, but admitted that it hadn't even been the young girl's fault (the "Bel Ange"). Sylvia—her mind working like a detective at the time—remembered how she had clicked on this Mystery Woman's Facebook page, after she had made her discovery that Tommy was in contact with her—this beautiful doe-eyed stranger. Sylvia sent the girl a friend request. To her surprise, the Bel Ange complied. Sylvia was in. They were Facebook "friends" ("Keep your enemies closer.")

Her stomach churned again, recalling how it made her feel at the time. She remembered drawing her hands up to the edges of her eyes and feeling the faint ridges of her thirty-six year-old crow's feet, as she perused the girl's online photos.

Marie, she was called.

She was breathtakingly beautiful. Worse, she seemed aware of her power. Sylvia had pored over dozens and dozens of her profile pictures: the young woman looking off into the distance, her bedroom lids half-hidden by the sweep of thick, maney hair. Full lips slightly parted, a hint of sexual innuendo, coupled with a schoolgirl, "but you can't have me" innocence. Provocatively sweet.

Lolita.

Tommy hadn't been the only one to drool over her photos; she had reams of male fans. Beneath the lovely pictures there were comments—Tommy's the keenest of them all. Accompanied by hearts, his read:

> *Ravishing, Marie. You're a real stunner, that's for sure* ♥ . . . and:
>
> *Yet another gorgeous photo, your charm and talent are beguiling* ♥ and:
>
> *Amazing! Wow, Marie, that would make a fabulous album cover. Eat your heart out American Vogue! You really are superb, so classy, with a naturally profound look in your beautiful eyes – so rare, so unusual. Where can I buy the poster? LOL.* ♥♥♥

"*Profound?*" Sylvia sniggered. "Talent?" As if being pretty was a "talent." She remembered flicking desperately through more online photos, with messages that seemed like they'd been written by a teenage boy, not Sylvia's thirty-two year-old husband.

> *Yes, yes and yes!* ♥ And *I have a fabulous idea for a project, Marie, can't wait to tell you all about it.*

The messages, Sylvia saw from the dates, had been piling up for over a year and a half. There were about thirty of them. These were not private messages but public—right there on Marie's main page for anyone who was her Facebook friend to see. The comments had begun around the same time Sylvia felt her marriage had started flaking apart. Like filo pastry. Crumbling into little morsels, still there to taste, but fragmented. Separate. No longer one whole.

"But Tommy loves you so much," Melinda offered, her telephone voice irritatingly positive. "He's not going to jeopardize your marriage. Or Gracie. You should be more confident."

Sylvia wet a sponge and started cleaning the bathroom sink. Cleaning, scrubbing. She used to be so glamorous, and now look. And yes, she *had* always been confident about Tommy. Then. He'd been crazy about her. The Bel Ange had been a wake-up call, an alarm bell screeching in her ear. Sylvia smiled at Melinda's encouraging words but then caught sight of herself in the mirror and her smile faded. "I know I should be more forgiving, for Grace's sake if nothing else."

It was true what Melinda said, though. Tommy hadn't slept with the girl, hadn't—as far as she knew—even kissed her. But the intention was there. The mental betrayal. Still, she needed to get over it.

"You don't want this silly Third Party saga screwing things up again," Melinda warned.

Sylvia looked into the mirror again and pushed her shoulders back. *Grace. Poise. Stand tall, woman!*

Melinda was right. Tommy had been Sylvia's second chance. The Third Party saga *had* messed up her life when she was at college. Sylvia's then boyfriend, Lance, had kissed another girl. So she, in retaliation, kissed another boy. Lance was devastated. He got drunk and spent the night with a girl called Judy Merchant, a senior. So Sylvia did the same with a fraternity boy. The irony was that Lance was so sozzled with vodka when he was in bed with Judy Merchant, that nothing happened. But the damage had been done. Sylvia broke his heart and the relationship was over. They both had broken hearts. All for nothing. All because of that silly kiss with the first girl. Sylvia didn't want history to repeat itself. What's more, she had a child to think of now.

"You're right, Melinda. Listen, I have something in the oven."

Melinda rippled with laughter. "That, I really believe!" Then she said in a serious tone, "Why are you shrugging off this conversation, Sylvie?"

"I swear, I'm not kidding, I'm baking an apple pie."

"Okay, so you really are trying to make things work between the two of you?"

"I'm trying, yes."

"Well good for you!"

"Bye," Sylvia said. "Send a kiss to Aunt Marcy, will you? And give Dad a big hug from me. Thanks again for spending so much of your vacation time with him."

"A pleasure, my dear. Go, go. You have your apple pie to think of and that drop-dead gorgeous husband of yours. We'll speak soon."

Sylvia sauntered back to the kitchen, feeling momentarily uplifted by Melinda's belief in Tommy. *Yes, she could do this.*

Grace skipped into the room, one of her teddies tucked under her arm, his mangy torso, poor thing, devoid of legs. One arm clung on—forlorn but loved. Sylvia heard her say to Tommy, "Don't you know that Mommy likes your natural smell, Daddy?"

Sylvia laughed. *Doesn't miss a trick, that one.* Her daughter was hugging the solid legs of her beloved dad, clinging to his trousers with her tiny nails. Those small five-year-old hands were such a marvel, and Sylvia pitied Tommy for missing out on even a week of their growth. It seemed like yesterday that she was a baby and now she was a proper person, a separate entity who had her own vision of life.

Grace pummeled her dad's rock-hard legs. "Why do you have to go away, Daddy? You promised we'd go to the river and swim. You *promised!*"

"We will, Bunnykins, we will. When the water's warmer. And we'll do some fly fishing, too. But Daddy has to work. I'll bring you back a present from LA."

"What's LA?"

His arms were clasped about his little girl. "It's a place, darling. With lots of palm trees and a very blue sky."

"What present will you get me?"

The edges of Sylvia's lips tipped up. She loved that word, "present," instead of gift. Grace had picked up British expressions from him, the cadence of his voice, the lilts, the inflections. Sylvia wasn't sure of all the nuances of the tiered English class system, but Tommy was well spoken. Educated, too. He'd got a double first at Cambridge University in Engineering and had been head hunted for a job in Silicon Valley as a techie, deep in the world of IT. That's what brought him to the States. Then he moved to New York, where they met. Sylvia still didn't understand *exactly* what it was he did back then, but she knew that only super-smart people had those kinds of jobs.

She observed him, hugging Gracie. Yup, he was smart, alright—not so smart to not be caught by her, though. *Women's intuition always wins in the end.* But in other ways he was a genius. His job title had been something like, "Oracle Designer." Sometimes he'd spout off about this program or that—a clever new app—but she wasn't on his level when it came to technology, and found it hard to concentrate on what he was saying. She knew the basics but had always switched off with anything that reminded her of a math class. Switching off—a terrible habit she wished she could break. She still hadn't even changed her cell. What was the point? Her life in Wyoming was so simple; she really didn't need to be checking e-mails and Facebook on a Smartphone every five minutes.

Sylvia observed her daughter cling to her dad with such devotion, she felt ashamed for harboring suspicion. Tommy was a wonderful father—surely he wouldn't risk their family life?

But the Bel Ange thing made her wonder if he felt incomplete, if he was secretly wishing to sow his seed, father a biological child

15

of his own. The threat of a young, fresh twenty-year-old, ovaries pumping away, had made Sylvia more vulnerable than she believed possible, and she felt Tommy had betrayed their child, even though he had not seen his fantasy through.

Yet Melinda was right. In reality, he had *done* nothing except take the young woman out to lunch one time, promising her a portfolio of free headshots. But Sylvia's unwavering trust was betrayed, her puppy-dog faith broken.

That St. Valentine's Day duplicity was still a half-open wound. She never wore red anymore even though he loved her in red. She'd punished him, by kicking him out of the house. Punished him for making her feel like a fool in her red dress, make-up, and heels. She remembered how much she had toiled over that intricate, Valentine dinner of Milanese chicken, how she'd chilled the pink champagne, and laid the table with her late mom's white damask tablecloth, and decorated the place mats with glittery, crimson hearts. Tommy seemed nonchalant about the whole affair. Not uninterested, but disinterested, as if he had no part to play. After dinner, he was using his iPhone, and the next day, despite Sylvia's threats and tears from the weeks before, she saw that he had used his phone to send a goddamn message to the Bel Ange. (That darn Facebook again—public, for all to be read as if he subconsciously wanted to be caught. Who knew? Maybe he'd been sending private messages as well?) It was nothing romantic, just an "*I'll call you soon, take care, Marie,*" but still, that was it, as far as Sylvia was concerned. She, standing in uncomfortable heels for his benefit, too cold in her thin red dress, while he was busy thinking about someone else, the egg dripping down her Valentine's Day face.

Now Tommy was back. She'd forgiven him for his schoolboy, mid-life crisis crush.

And now she was baking apple pie, wasn't that proof enough? They were a family, and she was prepared to endure the bumps along the path of marriage.

For Grace's sake.

And her own, if only she could shed that hurt the way a snake sheds its skin.

Sylvia turned off the oven, took out the pie, set it on the table, and breathed in the homey aroma. She looked out the window but the moose had moved on. It was lonely living in the middle of wild, Wyoming countryside. Sylvia assumed her love of the red-ochre-colored hills, the sweep of valleys and creeks, the blue-ribboned rivers, and skies bigger than God, would last forever. But she reminisced about her old life in New York, sparkling with friends and parties. Trips to art galleries, delicious take-out food, buying shoes for shoes' sake that now clustered up closets, unworn.

She often wondered when it was, exactly, that she and Tommy had made the decision to sell their Brooklyn apartment. Was it that one Christmas when they were drinking eggnogs by the fire in Saginaw with her parents, when her mother was still alive? Or the summer afterwards, crammed onto Jones Beach, clawing for their patch of sand? Whose idea had it been to cash in the profit from the apartment and sink it into an environmentally friendly log cabin in Wyoming? Hers? Tommy's? She asked herself that now, as she stared into space—into the never-ending view. Sylvia had a talent for decoration and had made their humble apartment a showpiece, but restoring a house in the countryside was a different story. They had not reckoned on the toil that eco country living would demand. It had all seemed so romantic at the time; moving to the heart of Native America—the two of them leveling out the garden and building their year-round greenhouse for their organic vegetables.

But the novelty wore thin. They ran out of stamina. The eco-friendly heating system had left them shivering. The furnace broke. It was freezing (they'd bought the house in summer, wide-eyed as they were). The snow fell thick, and the wind, like a howling wolf, yowled relentlessly about their chilled ears—so strong even Tommy, with his heavy frame, could sometimes lean against it, his weight supported.

Sylvia's horse fantasy was pushed aside. The stables that came with the property stood empty. Just paying the bills was tough, never mind supporting an expensive equestrian hobby. Tommy had once been handsomely paid working in IT. She, too, made a good income from her job as a theatrical agent in New York. Yet both of them decided to turn their lives around, to live at one with nature and explore their creativity. Lord knows, she'd read enough movie scripts. She knew the format. She could write one too. Why not? And Tommy had always dreamed of being a photographer. They packed it all in, packed it all up, and drove out West to rolling skies and nights the color of indigo. They could live like cowboys, fulfill their dreams, and then sell the house in a few years with a nice chunk of profit if things didn't work out. They could always return to their old jobs in New York. Or even start up afresh in California.

But neither they, nor the world, saw the recession like a sly fox waiting to pounce. Neither knew the extent of elbow grease a rural place demanded—the extra costs like a new septic system, the plumbing, and replacing the fire-hazardous wiring. Sylvia had imagined that Tommy (with his hardy, worked-out physique) would be the consummate Fixer-Upper and embrace chopping wood for the greedy stove all winter. She was wrong. He grew tired of their project; even the knotty pine doors and cedar-lined closets ceased to thrill him. The twenty-two feet cathedral ceilings that made them whoop with joy when they first set eyes on the house now spelled out C.O.L.D in cruel capital letters. The wrap-around porch made of redwood decking no longer held the most beautiful view on earth, because when December came the view was home to icy-tipped mountains that gnawed their bones with a walloping wind.

Then spring and summer would arrive and life was blissful again. Wild flowers sprinkled themselves like daytime stars across the hills, skies sang deep blue, and sparkling rivers were brimming with trout. But the joy all this brought was tempered by the Big

Winter Threat lurking around the corner. Pretty summer days were interrupted by frosty visions of what was to come around again. She, Tommy, and Grace were caught in a never ending eddy, round and round they went as if they were in a little canoe looking out over gushing white water, stuck by the danger around them. If they sold, they'd lose every penny. They'd sunk all they had into this house. Besides, where would they live? They'd have to start from scratch and rent again. But there weren't any jobs anymore, how would they make the rent? Tommy's salary was history. So were the jobs. The IT world moved so swiftly, with thousands of wiz-kids jumping aboard the train every month that, even at thirty-two, Tommy seemed like a dinosaur. And he'd been out of touch, out of circulation. Getting another job, even with a pay decrease, was not an easy task. The theatrical agency Sylvia worked for had been bought out by one more powerful. Many of her old colleagues had been fired and her contacts were now spread thin.

Sometimes, she dreamed of her little family moving to Europe but Tommy wouldn't hear of going back. Besides, the dollar was as weak as "an ex-Marine Colonel dying of cancer," he said. Once a force, it now grappled to survive.

She and Tommy had also been a force, and were now grappling to survive.

So they soldiered on. Perhaps this disillusionment was what had caused the Bel Ange fantasy to hatch. A distraction, like looking at porn or sports cars. Living in a two-dimensional daydream world. Something to ease the stress for a thirty-something male who'd bitten off more than he could chew.

Grace needed him, though. And Sylvia too. Although she hated to admit it. Even with her armor on, she still felt butterflies flutter inside her when Tommy looked at her. She remembered how he licked a raindrop from her cheek one time, passion dancing in his eyes.

Love like that can't just disappear.

She wondered if he sensed that she still had faith, that he still made her stomach flip-flop. She knew she was repelling him—frost on a winter lawn. Yet she needed him, wanted him close. Her head was telling her that the only reason she desired him was because they were a family, but even if Grace weren't there, the truth was that Sylvia was still in love with Tommy.

Painfully in love.

But there was that niggling feeling inside that one day, he would just get up and leave her for good. The only thing keeping him there for the moment, she feared, was his love for Grace.

2

Grace

"Will you get me an Xbox, Daddy?" Grace cried out. She was sitting on the pine table in the kitchen, wildly swinging her legs. She looked at her dad, who was leaning against the handcrafted hickory cabinets that he had helped the carpenter make, her shimmering eyes expectant. She gave him her biggest smile. They were discussing the "present." Grace knew she needed to seal the deal before he forgot, or became distracted with something else. She cocked her head and blinked her lashes.

"No, no Xbox, honey," Sylvia interrupted. "Please don't get her any more stuff like that, Tommy, and no video games."

Grace pouted. Her mother just didn't *get* it. "But I *like* video games, Mommy," she said, her voice rising on the word "like."

"Daddy can get you some paints, *real* paints that you can touch and mix with water. Not just virtual, iPad paints."

"You'd be surprised," Tommy said, "what digital artists can achieve with iPad art apps. Don't knock it, Sylvia."

"What's virtual?" Grace asked.

Sylvia put on some oven gloves and took out the pie. "It's when you can't touch or smell something, when you cannot feel it with your hands."

"But I can feel Daddy's iPad with my hands when I paint and draw." She looked up at her mom, widening her amber eyes.

Sylvia set the pie on a hotplate on the kitchen table. "Well, honey, I guess that's true, but now we're going to take those cute, artistic, itty-bitty little hands of yours that can paint and draw, and wash them before you eat this apple pie." She lifted Grace from the table and set her on her feet.

"Yummy!" Grace loved apple pie, although she was pretty sure that this was the first time her mother had ever made it. Grace never ate the doughy parts, though, just the juicy, apple bits. Her dad called her "Putty-Tooth" when she wouldn't eat her crusts. Sometimes, he was the "Great Bird Ziz" who would come with his big, wicked beak and snap at her bottom or her arms. She loved the Great Bird Ziz, although occasionally it could get out of control and she'd beg for her dad to return to normal. Grace knew it was just his big hands pretending to be a beaky, child-eating bird, but still.

She stood on an upside down crate by the sink, as her mother washed her hands. She felt the warm, soapy water running through her fingers, and her mom's big palms massaging the fat wide bits below her thumbs as the gushing water flowed from the faucet. She liked seeing the different colors of their hands together, too. Hers and her mom's, like white chocolate and caramel.

As her mom pat-patted them dry, Grace thought about something she had been meaning to ask for ages. "Mommy, what is God? My friend Joey says that God is dog spelled backwards so he must be a dog but you always use a capital letter when you say God's name. Why does God get a capital letter?"

"Good point," Tommy said. "That pie smells good."

"Because" Sylvia said, "there is only one God. At least in America that's true. Where you came from—India—there are lots of gods."

"Like Ganesh, the elephant god?"

"That's right," Tommy answered. "And Hanuman, the monkey god."

"A capital letter is a big letter, right?" Grace asked.

"Exactly. Like when we were writing Grace the other day for writing practice, and we made a big G," her mom replied, serving out some apple pie on a plate for Grace.

"Our God *is* a dog," Tommy piped up, "and God is a tree and a flower. In fact, God is all the trees and flowers and grass and animals of the universe."

Grace bit her lower lip and thought about this. It didn't make sense. "But if I pick a flower does that mean I'll kill God?"

Tommy laughed. He went over to the refrigerator and took out a beer.

"No, of course not, sweetie, God lives forever," her mom explained, tying a napkin about Grace's neck. "Careful with the pie. Blow on it first—it's hot."

"Oh." Grace considered this some more. "But if God is everything and he is a dog and a rabbit and a flower and a tree, then that means he is you, Daddy, and you, Mommy, and—"

"That's correct," Tommy said, and winked, "very observant. God is in everything good."

Grace took a big spoonful of pie. The apple part, not the crust. She saw her mom smile, but this God thing was serious. She needed answers. How could God with a big G be everywhere at once? Wasn't he too busy? Grace had been told about brains, that each creature, each human had a brain, and that would mean God would have millions and trillions of brains because every brain was His and that, in fact, to be so on top of it all, God must actually be a computer. But if He was a computer, he wouldn't have a real live brain at all. And if God was living inside a rabbit, did that make him think like a rabbit? Or want to make millions of babies the way rabbits did? She wanted to ask this but was worried her mom would stop smiling. Not about the rabbit part but about the computer part. She'd ask her dad later. He'd understand.

Grace thought of another problem: "Mommy, when's your friend coming to stay?" She didn't want the friend to steal her Mom-Time.

"That's right," Sylvia said, walking over to the sink. "I forgot to tell you, Tommy, Ruth is coming to stay for a couple of weeks."

He took a swig of beer. He still hadn't sat down at the table. "Ruth?"

"She's Mommy's Skype Friend," Grace explained. "The one she talks to about *Writing*," (yawn, yawn). "I've seen her. She looks like a weasel."

Sylvia doused a pan with some dishwashing liquid and began to scrub. "Ruth does not look like a weasel, sweetie. You *loved* her when she came to stay a couple of years ago."

"I can't remember her. But on Skype she has eyes the color of poop!" Grace thought of all those *long, BORING* conversations they had. Stealing her mom away from her.

Sylvia laughed but shook her head. "Such nonsense. Ruth is very attractive, actually. She's fun."

"Well I was away when she last came to stay," Tommy said, "so I wouldn't know about her eyes. It's true though—you do Skype a lot. How come she didn't come last summer to stay?"

"She's been living abroad. In Dubai. That's why I thought it would be fun if she came to visit now—she left her job, so has some free time. It would be nice if we discussed our projects face to face for once, instead of always online."

"Well you do seem to have a lot to chitchat about," Tommy said, taking another gulp of beer.

Sylvia stopped her scrubbing. "It's nice to get feedback." She gave him an angry smile. But dipped in sugar, Grace thought.

"What's feed back? Is that the food you give to horses?" Grace asked, her expression earnest.

Sylvia's lips curled into a grin. "No honey. You give horses feed. Feed*back* . . . is . . . how would you describe feedback, Tommy?"

"When a band plays and there's all this noise from the amps and stuff."

"Tommy, *please*. Don't complicate things."

Grace saw her mom's Cross-Face scowl at her dad. She hated it when she looked like that—the Wolf Face. Her dad didn't have a Wolf Face. He had another kind of face. It was the Naughty Dog Face. It happened when he told fibs. Like that time he promised to take her to the movies but he forgot and bought her Reese's peanut butter cups instead, and he thought that was okay, which it wasn't. *A deal is a deal.* Or when he mixed powdered milk with water and put it in the fridge, pretending it was real milk. She knew he was a Naughty Dog sometimes, and she knew he'd been a Naughty Dog with her mom. Something to do with Facebook.

"Can I start my own Facebook page?" Grace asked, forgetting the feedback question.

"Of course you can, Bunny," Tommy said. "We can do it today as I'm off tomorrow. So what time's Ruth coming, Sylvia?"

Sylvia took off her apron and laid it on the back of one of the kitchen chairs. "I don't know about Facebook for a five-year-old, Tommy. I mean . . . no. Just, no."

"Please, Mommy!"

Sylvia shook her head and said, "I synchronized it with your flight so I don't have to make two trips to the airport. I'll drop you off and wait for her. Only half an hour, or so. Gracie and I can get some lunch there."

"Can we get a burger at the drive-by?" Grace didn't know why she was even asking this question. She knew it would be a "no." It was always a no. No to Facebook. No to burgers. Her mom was against Intensive Farming and believed that cows must be free in fields and eat grass, not grain.

Sylvia gave Grace The Look. The Don't Be Silly look, the Watch Out or I Could Get Cross look: one eyebrow raised with a flicker of a smile on her lips.

"Just kidding!" Grace said. "I'll get a giant-sized bucket of greasy popcorn instead."

"Quite a sense of humor you've got going there, little lady," her mother answered with an I'm Smiling but It's Not Funny look. She now turned her attention to sweeping the floor with the funny broom that looked like it belonged to a witch. The old-fashioned kind, made of real straw.

"So how *was* it again that you and Ruth met in the first place?" Tommy asked, winking at Grace.

"They met on Facebook!" Grace cried, wondering if the Facebook part would make her mom's Wolf Face return.

"Yes, that's *right,* I almost forgot," her dad said with a grin.

"Drop it, Tommy," Sylvia warned.

Grace knew that the Facebook bit would get some sort of reaction but she still wasn't sure why. Why was Facebook such a big deal?

"So *you* can meet strangers on Facebook," he quipped, "and even invite them to stay in our house, yet I—"

"You *know* it's a different situation, Tommy. I don't go round asking to be friends with strangers just because they look good. Anyway, the fact is that Ruth and I *didn't* meet on Facebook. We met when I was trying to find someone to help Dad after Mom died. I sent out an e-mail to friends asking if they knew anybody. She was a friend of a friend of a friend. And then we both did that writers' workshop together, she came to stay here, and we became very close."

"Same deal as Facebook, people start out as strangers and then become friends. What's new? That's what life is. It's just that Facebook has a way of making it happen faster." He was smiling as he spoke.

"She's not a *stranger*. And we really bonded. We chat all the time on Skype. I know lots about her. She's lovely. Really warm." Sylvia started scrubbing another pan so hard that Grace could hear the pan squeal out in pain.

"Tell me about Ruth's background again?" Tommy asked, more seriously now.

"She went to Yale, and Harvard Business School. Worked as a banker. I'm not sure exactly what she does, some sort of consulting work. She was sent to Dubai by one of the big banks but hated it."

"So is she going to work at one of the banks in New York now?"

Sylvia started to dry the pan. It was so scrubbed it shined silver. "Said she saved up 'pots of money' and is now taking time off to write her novel—wants to take a break from work. I think she's really clever. Lived in Europe, speaks perfect Spanish and Portuguese. Grew up in Brazil."

"That's right; I remember you telling me that."

"Anyway, she's really well traveled; she backpacked around Asia, too. She's half Cuban, half Brazilian, I think. By blood anyway. But totally American. She's interesting. Just separated from her boyfriend."

"But she doesn't have kids, right?" Tommy asked. "Or are they all grown up? She's in her forties, isn't she?"

"No kids. After the banking job, she went to Mexico to a specialized IVF clinic to have her eggs frozen, but then she and the boyfriend broke up. All that money she invested and then her boyfriend left her. And there were other complications."

Tommy dipped a large spoon into the apple pie, Great Bird Ziz style, not bothering to get a plate. "I bet. How old is she, anyway?"

"Forty-six."

"Forty-*six?*" he exclaimed, nearly choking on a full mouth. "I know women can get pregnant naturally at that age, but isn't she a bit past her sell-by date to be having her eggs frozen and the whole IVF thing?"

Sylvia hung the pan on a rack. It swung in the air, back and forth, on its hook. "Ruth's in great shape. It was her last chance to have a baby."

"I'll say."

"Don't be such an ageist, Tommy—she's a very *young* forty-six. I mean, look at Sandra Bullock. She's pushing fifty and she looks amazing. Better, actually, than a lot of women in their twenties." She glared at him, and went on, "Anyway, Ruth and her boyfriend split up, so now she has nowhere to live. She's doing a sort of tour, visiting friends this summer before she buys a place of her own with all that money she saved from the finance job. I thought it would be nice if she stopped here for a couple of weeks, you know, while you're away. Thought we could do our own sort of writers' workshop. It'll be great, She can give me feedback on my half finished script, see if I'm going in the right direction, and I can give her feedback on her novel."

Grace watched her parents' Ping-Pong match. That Feedback word again. What kind of food *was* feedback? Why did she want to give food *back* to people all the time? And the frozen eggs thing. All this talk about food. She'd find out what it all meant later when her mother was in her Sweet Mood, when they'd be all cozy together, later at Story-Time tonight, when she'd be tucked into bed with a cup of warm milk.

3

Tommy

Tommy had his bag packed. A year or so ago, he would have felt pained to leave Crowheart behind, but today his heart leapt. A break would do him good. This rustic lifestyle just wasn't working out. It had been fun at first, but subjecting himself to being Earth Man for years to come, chopping wood all winter, was the last thing he wanted. He'd done everything he could to please his wife, but it wasn't working. He'd tried, yearned to make her happy, but he couldn't do it anymore; be her "happy barometer," the one responsible for her equilibrium. He needed to make new plans for his family, for himself—he needed to get them out of this rut.

As he stood in the kitchen drinking a Guinness, he watched Sylvia as she half-leaned against the table, chopping vegetables. Her tall frame was slightly stooped. She'd changed. The only thing he'd ever noticed about her height before was her grace, her elegance. She had always carried her shoulders erect, her golden head held high like a dancer. He'd always been struck by her beauty—she was still beautiful, but different. These days, she had a sad look to her so much of the time. Never with Grace—she was an amazing mother. But with him.

He wondered if she even loved him. Certainly not the way she used to in the beginning, when she laughed at his jokes and marveled at things he'd say. She used to think he was clever, dynamic. Now she was bored by him. Unimpressed. Obviously. He sensed that she was judging him, dissecting him all the time. Grace coming into their lives was incredible—he loved that little minx—but Sylvia had become distant toward him, as if she already had all the love she needed by way of her child.

Sylvia dressed badly now. Slobby jeans and ugg boots. In New York, she looked like a movie star every day of the week, even Sundays. She had her hair done, wore heels, short skirts, make-up. He remembered he used to think of her like a sparkler—fizzy, blindingly bright. Sexy. But now it was as if she just didn't give a damn. He'd heard Grace refer to that nonchalant look she wore as her "Ground Dog" face, and Grace was right. It was as if a switch was turned on (or off). Sylvia would be playing with Grace, all smiles and joy, and then he'd walk into the room and she'd don a deep, hurt expression as if he'd wounded her in some way.

There she was now. Chop, chop, chop. She was always in the kitchen, doing chores. He didn't want her to be that woman— sweeping, chopping, scrubbing bloody pans. She was better than that. He wished he could afford to get help. He felt emasculated. He wasn't earning enough money to support them. Sylvia's father had been helping them out the year before and the more he did so, the more distant she became. They hardly had sex anymore. If they did, it was as if she was doing him a favor. She'd say, "I know we haven't done it for a while so feel free to come whenever you want." e.g., *get it over with as soon as you can.*

So no wonder he'd got tempted. Because Sylvia didn't even seem to notice. All she appeared to care about was being a mother. He felt expendable like some piece of dirty laundry tossed aside at the end of each day. Had he fixed this? Had he fixed that? Could he do dinner tonight?—she was feeling tired. She was always tired, lackluster. She never laughed at his jokes anymore; she tuned out when he talked about his passions. Photography, for instance, nodding her head in agreement with a glazed look in her eyes. Distant. Absent. Even disdainful, in a passive, supposedly benign way.

He needed time for himself. He needed to get his identity back. He used to be a player earning a hefty income. And he'd jacked it all in for "creation," for a peaceful family life. But the price he was paying was high, when what he was getting on his return was proving to be cheap, shoddy. Like a new piece of equipment you long for but once you've tried, you want to take straight back to the store because the ads for it were better than the product.

Rural life was not for him. Evidently not for Sylvia either. It was hard to be creative when you were broke. But he was trapped in a catch-22. Skint. Out of a real job. Neither creating nor earning— lost in a sort of purgatory.

And he wanted out.

Sometimes he thought of taking his family to England. But what a mess his country was turning out to be. Unemployment, crime, schools either insanely expensive or too dangerous to attend. No, he was over the UK. His home was here, in America. Still the land of opportunities, if you worked hard and luck was on your side. Maybe, just maybe, this job in LA would pan out.

Right now, he felt creatively homeless.

All this "Bel Ange" and Facebook guilt crap Sylvia was throwing at him was just making it worse. He hadn't *done anything* except take the girl out to lunch that time, but his wife was acting as if he'd sold his soul to the Devil. He might as well have fucked Marie for all the fuss it caused.

And on some days, he wished he had.

4

Sylvia

Sylvia and Grace were at the airport, waiting for Ruth to arrive. They'd already seen Tommy off, and for some reason it was Sylvia who cried, not Grace, when she saw him turn the corner and disappear through Security.

However, the prospect of having a friend to stay for a couple of weeks was exhilarating. Sylvia had nobody to chat with apart from her husband. There were some friendly women about, it was true—they'd been welcoming, and she liked them, but they had nothing particularly in common with each other. Not really. Unless you called living in the middle of America's wilderness something in common.

Sometimes she'd hook up with a neighbor and they'd go horseback riding when Grace was at school. They'd chat about this or that, but Sylvia had gotten used to her sophisticated, New York friends who traveled the world, and who could talk about art or literature with her. Ruth was like that. During their Skype calls, they'd discussed the structure of novels and scripts. Points of view, character, what made someone tick, and why. She knew Ruth valued her judgment as an armchair critic and editor. Sylvia could spot faults quickly. Easier done, of course, with somebody else's work. With her own screenplay she'd got completely stuck and was half tempted to chuck the whole thing out. Figuratively speaking. She, like everybody else, wrote on her laptop, addicted to spell-check, just like any writer. Writing a movie script had been a dream but it was far harder than she'd imagined it would be to complete. How could a hundred and twenty pages be so tough? But it was. If it was that easy, she guessed, everybody would be at it.

She missed her job, though. She thought it would be a relief to no longer play nanny cum psychotherapist to her actor clients who were so needy and self-centered. But they were also fun, often a bit eccentric and creative, and she missed them. She'd go to first nights at the theatre, movie premieres; they'd review scripts and sit in dark bars talking about the Method or the craze for hand-held cameras, and they'd show her brilliant short films shot on iPhones. She pined for all that now. Although, having Grace did make up for it. Her daughter was just as entertaining as any of them, and smarter, too. Grace's little mind never stopped clicking away, asking questions, dissecting possibilities. She made Sylvia alert. Grace wouldn't let her get away with bland explanations. Thank God for that, she thought, *or my mind would be marshmallow by now.*

"Mommy, why doesn't Ruth have a home?"

Sylvia swallowed the last of her lunch at one of the airport ca-fés. Grace was sitting on a chair too big for her, swinging her legs excitedly, and slurping freshly squeezed orange juice through a straw. She'd begged for a soda but to deaf ears.

"Because she split with her boyfriend, honey."

"But why did she live in her boyfriend's house? You told Daddy that she had *pots* of money. She could have her own house."

Never misses a trick that little girl. Grace had a point, though. Why hadn't Ruth bought her own home yet? Why wasn't she house-hunting this summer instead of visiting friends?

"Maybe because she's a free spirit, sweetie, she didn't want to tie herself down."

"With rope?"

Sylvia laughed. "It's just an expression, Gracie, a way of saying something. It means not getting bored with the same thing. I remember when I was a little girl though, your age, and a friend of mine got dirt all over her skirt and she said that her mother was going to 'kill' her. And I said, '*What with, a knife or a gun?*' She just meant that her mom would get very cross with her because she'd got dirty." Sylvia realized she'd said too much, forgetting her daughter was merely five years old. "Have you had enough to eat, honey? Would you like a brownie now?"

"No thank you, Mommy, I'm full."

Sylvia took in a deep, satisfied breath. She had raised a polite little angel, she gushed to herself. An adorable, perfect child. "Come on, Gracie, let's go and find Ruth."

Ruth was more glamorous than Sylvia remembered. She was wearing a straw cowboy hat, her skin tanned golden, her dark hair long and unruly. A smile stretched across her friendly, open face. Her eyes lit up when she spotted Grace, and Sylvia felt a wave of relief, knowing that she was having a friend to stay for a while. A real friend, with whom she had so much in common.

"DO YOU STILL think Ruth's eyes are the color of poop?" Sylvia asked as she tucked Grace up in bed, later that evening.

"No, she's pretty. And very nice. I like her. *A lot.* I do remember her now."

Sylvia walked over to the bedroom window and looked out. The stars fell thick in the blue-black sky and the first crickets of the season chirped in the high grass, even though it was still only May. She drew the curtains.

Grace pouted. "But you took so *long* to come up and read me the Two Bad Mice!"

"That's because we have a guest. Guests need to be treated with respect and made to feel welcome."

"Well Pidgey O Dollars thinks Story-Time is more important."

"Where *is* Pidgey O Dollars, by the way?"

"He's hiding under the blanket."

"Let me give him a kiss. And you, too. A big hug and a kiss." Sylvia felt the soft, combed cotton of Grace's rosebud pajamas and breathed in the sweet scent of soap and little girl. If only she could bottle it forever. "Sugar and spice and all things nice, that's what little girls are made of," she whispered. "Sleep tight, sweetheart."

Grace's eyelids fluttered. "Sing me a lullaby."

Sylvia sat on the edge of the bed and tucked the blankets tight around Grace's smooth, honey-brown neck. She pressed the war-torn veteran teddy into the pillow next to her, and began to sing:

"Row, row, row your boat
Gently down the stream . . .
Merrily, merrily, merrily, merrily,
Life is but a dream."

She crooned the same song four or five times over, then switched on the nightlight, a little Swiss chalet with snow on its roof, and tiny windows glowing golden—a comfort to ward off the gremlins. Her daughter had already fallen into a profound sleep.

Sylvia tiptoed out of the room and went downstairs.

Ruth was sitting at the kitchen table, pouring herself another glass of white wine. "Honey," she said, "little Gracie is just *divine*. I could eat her!"

"Isn't she? She changed my life."

"I heard her chatting with her dad on Skype earlier this evening. So *cute*! She sounded English when she was talking to him."

"I know. It's funny. I catch her all the time. English with him,

American with me, but with the local kids at school she blends in perfectly. She's quite a chameleon. Last summer, we had a Mexican au pair girl staying with us. Grace was actually speaking Spanish by the end of the summer. Incredible how fast they pick up stuff at that age."

"I was trilingual from the beginning," Ruth told her. "I think you make little compartments for each language when you start young. They've done psychological tests and say it doesn't confuse a child at all to know several languages."

"Always useful, that's for sure," Sylvia said. "She has a musical ear."

"Usually people who are good with languages and impersonations are great with music. Not me, though. I can't hold a tune. Unless I'm singing 'Happy Birthday Mr. President,' aka Marilyn Monroe. And I can do a mean Katharine Hepburn imitation."

Sylvia nudged her arm. "Go on then, show me."

Ruth proceeded to run a gamut of impersonations of Humphrey Bogart, Christopher Walken, Margaret Thatcher, Jack Nicholson, and Katharine Hepburn—all without hardly pausing for breath. Sylvia held her stomach she was laughing so hard.

"Stop," Sylvia said, her breath caught in her giggle, "be serious now; I don't want to wake Grace with all the noise I'm making."

Ruth went back to being Ruth and asked seriously, "So how are things going with hubby? When we Skyped the other day you sounded really down. Sweetie," Ruth said, putting her hand on Sylvia's shoulder and tilting her head to one side, "I'm so sorry he's not fulfilling your needs."

Sylvia looked at her friend. She had never thought of it that way before. She felt betrayed by Tommy and she'd been hurt by him, but having her needs "fulfilled," per se, sounded like some sort of therapist babble and was something that she had never even considered. Were people put on this earth to fulfill each other's needs, she wondered? She wasn't even aware of what her needs were. "He's a great dad," she replied in his defense.

Ruth took a sip of wine. "Yes, but what he did to you was so *wounding*, so belittling."

Sylvia had felt furious with her husband but for some reason her hackles rose like a defensive dog, "It's water under the bridge now. He's being really sweet. We've been having a rough time financially. I think it was his way of—"

"Of what?"

Sylvia shook her head. "Never mind."

"No, what do you think he was trying to prove?"

"I think he was asserting himself. I mean, I'm thirty-six, four years older than him. I was the one who pushed for Grace's adoption, and I seemed to have been the one to have held the reins in our marriage in many ways and . . . well . . . anyway, he got a real shock when I asked him to leave. I mean, he was only gone for a couple of weeks but I think he realized how much he had to lose. I think things will be much better from now on."

Ruth tilted her head again as if considering everything Sylvia had just said. "I mean Tommy is very cute and everything but—"

"How do you know he's cute?"

"Don't you remember? You e-mailed me that photo of you two together."

"Really? No, I don't remember that. But lately I've been a bit forgetful. Living here has turned my brain to mush. My life seems so mundane these days. So humdrum."

"No, it's just country living, that's all. People envy you, I bet."

"Well, we came here mostly for Grace's sake. Fresh air, low crime, a great place for a child to grow up."

"True. Anyway," said Ruth, "I guess I'm not one to give advice about other people's love lives. I've been engaged four times." She chuckled.

And Sylvia laughed too. She hadn't even *kissed* four guys—in a sexual way—let alone dated that many. "Four times?"

"Yeah, but none of my beaux were right. None of them marriage material in the end."

"*Four?*"

Ruth threw up her hands like an Italian throwing pizza dough. "I know—it's kinda crazy. But I think I learned a lot from each one of them. I got a lot out of each relationship, yet they were all very different from one another. I got in touch with one of them recently—I needed advice about shotguns for my novel—the Belgian guy, the rich one, you remember my mentioning him? He was a big game hunter so I thought I could pick his brains."

"A big game hunter?" Sylvia winced. "Oh Lord, what did he shoot?"

"Probably everything. He once shot a tiger. But it was in the '90's—a while ago."

"Oh my God. How horrific! No wonder you split with him."

"I left him because he was so possessive. And I ended it with the other three because they just couldn't meet my needs. We're still great friends, though, the Belgian and I."

Sylvia opened her mouth to say something but took a breath instead. How many tigers were even *left* in the world? She knew that some people paid a fortune bribing gamekeepers, and that many protected animals were being decimated for Chinese medicines, but she had never imagined she could know someone who *knew* someone who could do such a thing. The idea of anybody "educated" (and with money) shooting such a magnificent creature—an endangered species, to boot—was an enigma to her.

"So what happened to Jeff?" she asked Ruth, trying to wipe away the image of the murdered tiger. "I mean, it was just a few weeks ago that you and he broke up, wasn't it? Why did you finally end it?"

"He had an alcohol problem. He was a kind of manic-depressive. I mean, not clinically so, but I could read the writing on the wall."

Sylvia got up and walked over to the fridge and took out the lasagna she'd made earlier that day. "But you were planning to have his *baby*." Sylvia remembered the frozen eggs story. She popped the dish into the microwave.

Ruth laughed. "I know, I know. It took me a while to wise up to the fact it wasn't going to work out. And the vasectomy thing was making things really complicated."

"Didn't you know he'd had a vasectomy from the start?" Sylvia thought back to all the e-mails Ruth had written to her over the past year and a half about her boyfriend, Jeff, and the IVF saga, and the endless Skype calls they'd had. A veritable soap opera. Ruth had had seven eggs frozen but had put the transfers on hold until she sorted out her love life. She'd often begged Sylvia to join her at the clinic in Mexico, to have her eggs frozen, too. But Sylvia wasn't interested. She had done plenty of research before she'd adopted Grace. Even a healthy woman in her twenties had only a fifteen percent chance, but she, in her mid thirties wasn't going to put her body through the turmoil. Not to mention the expense. Besides, she had Grace, and the fact that Grace wasn't biologically hers made no difference at all to the bond they shared or the strength of their love. But for Ruth to be freezing her own eggs at the age of forty-six seemed extraordinary. There was a freak possibility of success, yet it would take a miracle for it to work. Especially as her boyfriend had had his tubes tied. Sylvia wondered if the doctor who had agreed to do it was just taking Ruth's money or was using her as some sort of medical breakthrough experiment.

Sylvia set some forks and napkins on the table. "Didn't you *know* that Jeff had had a vasectomy from the start of your relationship?"

"Yes I did, but I thought they had ways of reversing it." Ruth drained the wine in her glass and topped it up again. "More Chardonnay?"

Sylvia shook her head. "No thanks. Having a hangover when

you have a five-year-old just isn't an option."

"I shouldn't have more but, you know, it keeps my eating disorder in check."

"That's right, I completely forgot. You told me once about your eating disorder."

"I used to have a problem." Ruth's lips twitched. "But it's under control now."

"Not like *Bridget Jones* then?" Sylvia joked.

"No way! I hated that novel. So boring! Such bad writing! All that weighing out calories every day. I never do that."

"You didn't find the book funny?"

"So British that type of humor. I guess because you're married to a Brit you found it amusing. I didn't get it. I read your movie script, by the way, Sylvia. It's great. You've got to have the confidence to *finish* it! Did you read the new chapters I sent you of my novel?"

"I certainly did and I wrote down lots of suggestions. I think you need to decide exactly *whom* you're writing for. For whom you are writing? God I hate that whom and who stuff—I get so confused. What I'm trying to say is you need to decide exactly who your reader is."

Ruth took a swig of wine. "I told you. Housewives."

"Well in the first chapter you describe your hero taking a pee. In graphic detail. I think you can cut that out. Or at least save it till we know him better, till we've established the fact that he's a great guy."

"Oh. Ok. You don't like it, huh? It's just that one of my exes told me how he urinated, always trying to make the perfect arc and I thought it was really interesting."

"I don't know if your average woman would like that sort of thing. Hey, maybe I'm wrong. Take anything I say with a grain of salt. Maybe people would be fascinated. I mean look at all that erotica that's so popular right now—you never know. Oh yes, and another thing. Just a detail. You said something like, "there's a new iPhone that has a baby alarm on it," or something like that. It's not the phone *itself*, it's the app."

"I'm a bit behind on all that app stuff."

Sylvia grinned. "I'm so glad I'm not the only one around here who isn't a cyber-techie."

"Which reminds me, I wanted to talk to you about all that stuff. One of my ex-Harvard friends has told me that if I'm to be a successful writer I must have an online *presence*. That I have to have a Twitter account and a Facebook page."

"You. Are. Kidding? You don't *have* all that? I thought the entire world did nothing but Tweet and do Facebook all day long."

Ruth pulled a face. "No! I am completely illiterate. I know nothing. All I can do is send e-mails and Skype, only because my ex set it up for me. He also did something to hide my whereabouts on my computer so I could watch American TV when I was in Europe—otherwise they block you if they know you're not in the States. I wanted to watch ABC and things.'

"He hid your IP address?"

Ruth waved her arms again. "I have no idea what he did. Like I said, I'm *clueless* when it comes to all that. But will you help me do a Facebook page, sweetie? Set up a Twitter account?"

"Sure."

"Great. Agents want to see you have mass readership potential before they sign you. Sweetie, if I can show I have a big following on Facebook then I'm more likely to get an agent. I'm giving myself six months to get signed to one and, if I don't manage, I'm going to self-publish and sell through Amazon."

"You have it all worked out. Good for you, Ruth. My only goal right now is to get my script finished. Period."

"Oh, I'll be done very soon. Maybe even while I'm here. And thanks for the feedback, Sylvia honey—your points are always so useful. It's so great being friends with you, you're so direct. Also, I never seem to have women friends that are as attractive as I am. Women can get so jealous. You know, at college, they called me a 'man magnet' but not in a nice way. In a nasty, mocking way."

"But surely being a man magnet is good?" Sylvia joked. "Especially, if you're single. I was never a man-magnet. I was too tall and gangly as a teenager, and had train-tracks on my teeth."

Ruth went on, "Well, maybe you were an ugly duckling once, but now you're so pretty. You have a kind of poise in the way you carry yourself. I mean look at you, even when you just walk across the room to get something out of the icebox, you do it with a sort of *natural* elegance. Such grace. Spine straight, shoulders back. You're just as attractive as I am, maybe even more so. I know you'd never feel competitive with me in that way. How tall *are* you exactly? Aren't we about the same height?"

Sylvia answered, "I'm five nine. I was way taller than all my classmates but when I hit about sixteen I kind of stopped growing and other girls caught up with me."

"I'm . . . " Ruth considered . . . "quite a bit shorter, although I feel tall, you know? I've always felt tall. I'm five foot six."

Sylvia perused the face and body of this uber-confident woman. Ruth was attractive, yes. Slim. Ish. Could lose a few pounds. She was aware that she'd had a breast enlargement. Not because her breasts were big, but they were neat globes. Sylvia noticed them, for the first time, in fact, in their rock-hard, uniform spheres, nestled beneath Ruth's tight-fitting T-shirt. Ruth had a long nose, not big, but she had to admit little Gracie had had a point—there was something vaguely weasel-ish about her, in the nicest possible way; although Sylvia felt cruel to think it. Her eyes the color of poop? They were a sort of sludgy-green. But she had almost black hair; beautiful, flawless olive skin; perfect teeth, and Sylvia could see that her overall look might really attract a man. Ruth looked so much younger than her years, too, and Sylvia had no doubt that her flirting skills were honed sharp and that she could play the sex appeal card with aplomb. She'd obviously had plenty of practice with her four engagements.

"Anyway," Ruth said, "I'm not going to get involved with anybody right now. I need to concentrate on my *writing*. And when I make millions from my novel, I'm sure the perfect man will fall into my life just when I need him."

THE NEXT MORNING, after Sylvia had set her friend up with Twitter and Facebook accounts, Ruth gave Grace a big bag of gifts.

"Mommy, Mommy! Look!" her daughter shouted, skipping about. "A pair of *Wizard of Oz* shoes like Dorothy's with red sparklies!" She pulled more goodies out of the bag. "And chocolate!"

"Ruth, really, you shouldn't have—it's not her birthday or Christmas."

"And even more chocolate! And candy, too!" Grace squealed, her skinny brown arm buried deep in the bag.

"By the way, how did you know Grace's shoe size?" Sylvia asked. She glanced over at her daughter whose teeth were already stuck together in a green, chewy mess.

"I guessed. Look further into the bag, Grace baby, there's a red sparkly bag to match." Ruth turned to Sylvia. "I just couldn't resist. When I saw her cute little face when we Skyped the other day, I fell in love with her. She's a little dream." She swept her hand over her dark hair. "By the way, Sylvia, honey, do you have another shower I could use? Your plumbing is a little funky in my bathroom."

"Sure. Upstairs. First door on the right."

Ruth sashayed upstairs, her see-through negligee trailing behind her like mist. There was something very sexy about her and Sylvia felt relieved that Tommy wasn't around.

Grace strut about in her shoes, which were a tad too big, clicking her heels together saying, "There's no place like home. There's no place like home." Grace knew all about *The Wizard of Oz* because

Tommy was keen to educate his daughter with classic films. Some of them not suitable for a child her age, at all. *Men,* Sylvia mused— *they can be so clueless sometimes when it comes to child rearing.*

Sylvia gave Grace a kiss and held her close, but Grace, like a jiggling, excited puppy struggled free.

"Remember," Sylvia said, "to say a very big thank you to Ruth. Maybe you could draw her a lovely card."

"She's so nice to me. I really, *really* like her."

Sylvia felt a pang in her stomach which took her by surprise. Jealousy? Surely not.

5

Tommy

Tommy sat by the ocean in Malibu, watching the surfers, clad in wet suits like black seals waiting for the right wave. It was almost dark. He mulled over the day's events. He really hadn't meant anything to happen. He had just gotten off the plane when his cell phone rang. It was Marie—the Bel Ange, as Sylvia called her. Marie suggested they have lunch again—she'd seen from his Facebook post that he was in LA. Just to talk about her head-shots, she said. A little chitchat about music, acting—have a nice time out.

She was pushy, Tommy thought. A pretty girl used to getting men to do her favors.

Still, he found himself saying "yes."

He had no idea that Marie would be so flirtatious. So predatory. Her skin was silky and pearlish, smooth and taut. Her dark hair hung over her shining eyes like a wild mare's mane. She was wearing a short (oh so short!) black skirt and he could see a flash of knickers when she sat down. Wow, she looked young. So fresh. Innocent. So bloody . . .

Photogenic.

Just looking at her nipped-in waist and pert breasts, (so wantonly on display—visible through her tight little sweater), made him question himself. He felt old. Played.

But tempted.

It was as if she had some power over him and she could feel it. She played with it like a child bouncing a ball. Controlling where the ball went, how high.

He was the ball; a worn, leathery, old rugby ball.

Her French accent made her vulnerable, though—all the more enticing. Vulnerability and power mixed together, like a bomb waiting to explode. She had a slight lisp when she spoke. A little pussycat.

Ready to pounce on him.

Sylvia—a composer half-heartedly conducting an orchestra from an armchair, wanting him to play the right tune but with no direct input herself—flashed into his mind.

It was a warm day, and he and Marie sat in the restaurant's patio garden. Very LA. Relaxed. Cool. Smart, but not pretentious. She ordered a Margarita so he did the same, even though it was midday. She giggled and shuffled about in her chair. Her legs opened and closed as she crossed and uncrossed her legs—he saw that her kickers were white—a little twinkle of light flashed from them. Like a star. *That's right, the Americans call them panties.* He laughed, remembering a chant they used to have at primary school, playing Kiss-Chase with the girls, when he was a skinny little boy afraid of the opposite sex:

Up with skirts, down with knickers . . . Up with skirts, down with knickers . . . Up with skirts . . . .

"So what's your favorite kind of photography? Fashion?" Marie asked, her doll eyes wide, her lips parted.

He thought of Diane Arbus, one of his favorite photographers, how she earned an income from fashion photography, although her real love was finding the interior soul of a subject: portraits of dwarfs, giants and transvestites. She had broken a mold, opened doors, seen beauty in the distasteful. That was Tommy's goal, his passion.

This girl though, would probably have never heard of Diane Arbus.

He said, "Well what I really love is—"

"I hope you're going to take some amazing pictures of me," the girl interrupted.

"Well, I'm not sure if I have—"

"I need the pictures to get the attention of directors, you know? Look really sexy but also like I'm a serious actress." She licked her top lip slowly, flicking her tongue to catch a flake of salt, and then let her mouth caress the straw, gently sucking up more of her cocktail.

Tommy felt the fly on his jeans strain. He knew exactly what would happen next.

6

Sylvia

I t was four a.m. when the telephone rang, a couple of days later. The sound was swirled into the nightmare Sylvia was having; waiting for an ambulance, the red flashing sirens sounding louder and louder. She had to get Grace to the hospital—the house, which was not her house but one in a tropical forest, was on fire.

She woke with a start and grabbed the phone to stop the ringing. Sweat soaked her nightgown at the small of her back.

"Hello?" she answered in a groggy haze.

The voice was quiet. Sympathetic. Sylvia knew immediately something was wrong. It took her a while to understand who it was.

"Sylvie? It's me, Melinda. I have some terrible news," she said softly. "Sylvia, are you there?"

"Hi Melinda. Sorry, I was fast asleep."

"Of course you were. I'm so, so sorry, I have terrible news." She paused and sucked in a deep breath. "Wilber is in the hospital."

"Daddy? Oh my God . . . what happened?" She shot out of bed, knocking over a glass of water.

"He took an overdose sometime after midnight. Mom heard some groaning in the night and when she went into his bedroom, he looked marbled and blue. She called 911."

Sylvia swallowed hard. Her throat was thick and dry. "Thank God you and Aunt Marcy were there. Will he pull through?"

"The doctors say there's hope. They've pumped his stomach."

"Jesus. Is he conscious?" She staggered to the bathroom, ran the faucet and gulped down some water.

"Barely. He's in OR still. I'm so sorry, Sylvia. He seemed fine today."

She coughed, the water going down the wrong way. "Yes, he did. We spoke yesterday. He seemed just fine."

He'd told her he loved her. Was that his way of saying goodbye? He'd told her he missed her, he loved her; she should have understood. A cliché, it was true, but the writing really had been on the wall. She wanted to cry but no tears came because there was no time for tears. She had to get to him straight away. Something deep inside her had feared this moment, although she never imagined for a second he'd be capable of actually going through with it. Or had she? Had she known all along? Her dad had been lost without her mother. He'd been co-dependent, and since her mom's death he had hinted that his life was no longer worth living. Sylvia plunked herself down on the toilet seat and bowed her head, the receiver close to her ear.

"Mom feels responsible," Melinda told her gravely.

That made two of them. Sylvia knew, somehow, her aunt would feel that way but said, "Why?"

"She feels so guilty, she should have monitored him more closely, she should have taken them away from him, rationed them."

"The sleeping pills he'd been prescribed by Doctor Locke?"

"Yes."

Sylvia bit her lip so hard she could feel it smart. "She's not to blame. It's nobody's fault. It's not her fault. He could have done it at any time."

"He'd been stashing them. Saving them up. We couldn't know."

"Of course you couldn't." Sylvia should have been more on the ball herself, should have seen this coming. Was it a cry for attention? The fact he did it while her aunt and cousin were staying with him, made her wonder. He needed her, obviously. She'd get up, get dressed and go.

"So when can you get here?" Melinda asked in a quiet voice.

"As soon as I can. I'll go online now and book our tickets."

"You change planes in Chicago, right?"

"Or Minneapolis. And we have to change in Denver first. Two changes."

"What a bummer. Let me know your flight number and I'll pick you up in Saginaw."

"But you told me you had to get back to work tomorrow." She looked at her watch on the bathroom cabinet. "I mean, today."

Melinda cleared her throat. "I do. But Sylvia, this is an emergency. I'm not going anywhere right now. I want to at least wait until you get here."

"I'll call the second I have our flights booked. Tell Dad I love him and we're on our way."

"I will. I promise. Safe flight."

THERE WAS ONLY one seat available on the Denver to Chicago leg that morning. Nothing from Minneapolis. As if the entire world had decided to fly that day. If Sylvia could wait twenty-four hours there would be another seat for Grace on a later flight. But twenty-four hours was forever when her father was battling for his life. She remembered her mom, the guilt still wrapped about Sylvia like a blanket, thick with mildew—Sylvia hadn't been there for her at the end. She wouldn't make that mistake again.

She called Tommy—he wasn't picking up.

As if by osmosis, Ruth appeared as Sylvia was coming out of the bathroom. It was still dark—even the birds hadn't yet awoken.

"Honey—Sylvia, what's wrong? I heard something smash and it woke me. Oh my . . . your eyes are red, have you been crying?"

Sylvia related the dilemma. Her heart felt like a fragile piece of paper, fluttering in two separate directions, about to rip. Maybe she should just leave it—trying to get to Saginaw in record time was ridiculous. Grace took priority—she couldn't leave her behind. Grace had never been alone without either her or Tommy.

Ruth hugged her friend. Sylvia could smell sweet-scented cream on Ruth's face and her hard breasts—filmed in her thin, floaty negligee—pushed up against Sylvia's chest.

Her voice was soothing. "Sylvia . . . go to your father, he needs you. This is life or death—you'd never forgive yourself. I know, believe me. I looked after my mom in the last stages of breast cancer. It was grueling, but the best decision I ever made in my life. I wouldn't trade those last few weeks for anything in the world. Your dad will make it. I'm sure he will. But having you by his side will make all the difference."

"You're right, I—" The phone was ringing. Sylvia raced to pick it up. It would be Tommy calling back.

His voice was like balm to a wound. All her resentment melted away. She needed her husband more than ever.

"Baby," he said. "Are you okay? I figured there must be some kind of emergency, you calling at this hour."

Sylvia explained her quandary, her breath short, obligation strangling her like tenacious, wet ivy. Why did parents feel like children? Why the weight of responsibility? But that's the way it was.

"Well, Ruth is there, isn't she?" Tommy said. "I'll get on the first plane out of LA and come home. Gracie won't be alone. And then Gracie and I can both come to Saginaw if need be. Or not. Depending on your dad. We'll play it by ear. Get on that plane, anyhow."

"I've never left her alone before."

"Okay then, wait. But you said the next available seat wasn't for twenty-four hours."

"Yes," Sylvia said, her throat thick.

"In other words, tomorrow."

"But I can't—"

"One day. That's nothing! Ruth can drive you to the airport, then take Gracie to school—she'll have her usual routine. I'll be back shortly, and tomorrow, or the next day, she and I can both fly to Saginaw. I'll sort the tickets out. What's the big deal?"

"Okay. But what if you can't get a flight back home?"

"As long as some earthquake doesn't come ripping and roaring through LA, we should be fine."

"Okay. What about your new job?"

"We'll talk about that later. Your dad takes priority."

"I don't know. Maybe I should just wait until there's another seat for Grace."

Ruth, who was standing there, raised her eyebrows. She whispered, "It's not my business, of course, but by that time, Sylvia, honey, your dad could have passed away. He needs you. Sylvia, this is an emergency."

Sylvia had her father in her mind's eye; his stomach bloated from all the pills, his pallid face desperate. She said to Ruth, "I guess you're right."

"Are you listening to me, Sylvia, baby?" Tommy was still on the line. "I'll catch the next plane home."

"Wait one minute, Tommy." She turned to Ruth. "Are you okay looking after Gracie until Tommy gets back? It'll only be for the day—he's catching the first plane he can. I could ask one of Grace's school friend's moms, although it's a little short—"

"Don't be silly,"—Ruth jokingly rolled her eyes—"of course, I'll look after her; I'd be delighted."

SYLVIA HATED FLYING. She panicked every time. The liquid allowance, and all the fuss airplane traveling entailed these days, drove her nuts. In her rush, and with the added panic of dropping Grace off at school on time, she realized that she'd forgotten her passport, but luckily not her driver's license.

As Sylvia drove to Riverton Airport, Ruth beside her in the passenger seat, she reeled off a list of instructions, as Ruth scribbled it all down in a notebook. Sylvia's eyes were fixed on the road, almost without focusing, while Ruth then rambled on jollily about a boyfriend who had abandoned her on a backpacking trip on an Indonesian island (as things, he said, were "not going to work out").

"You know, Sylvia, I have something to say, that you may not think is important but . . . well . . . it's something that has marked my life."

Sylvia glanced at her friend. She had been so preoccupied by her father, she hadn't thought of much else. "Oh yes?"

"Just . . . I understand. I lost my mom to cancer and . . . well . . . you're doing the right thing going to see your dad."

Ruth is a good person, however quirky, Sylvia mused. They both knew what it was like to lose a mother to that insidious disease. She thought about the tragedy of her dad, and prayed he would make it through. She reflected on the vulnerability of her relationship with Tommy, and how she was about to leave the most important person in her life: Grace.

Trusting her to someone outside the family.

AS SOON AS SHE landed, Sylvia could feel disaster thick like syrup. She knew something was wrong. It was confirmed in Melinda's heavy, red-lidded eyes. Sylvia's dad, she told her in a whisper, had just died.

Melinda shielded her with her plump arms as Sylvia's lungs began to heave with disappointment. Why, oh why hadn't her father had more strength? She ached for him—why hadn't she been there sooner? Why hadn't she read the signs? She cried for her mother, too, for the deep love her parents shared during their forty-year marriage. If Heaven came through and wasn't just a myth, her dad would at least be reunited with the love of his life.

The drive from the airport felt surreal, as if everything was unraveling in slow motion—as if this were all happening to someone else. Melinda was babbling, words tumbling out of her mouth incoherently. She spoke several times about Aunt Marcy's upcoming mole removal operation—which was precautionary, she explained, because the mole was benign—and the guilt she felt about not being able to be there for her. The older parents got, the more like children they seemed. Just vulnerable beings without all the answers who needed looking after.

They drove along for several miles, each in their own world, each suffering from the wound of loss. The fact that Sylvia's father took his own life was a bludgeon to them both, not just Sylvia. It was Melinda who sat on her father's knee when they were girls, Melinda whom he taught to play golf, Melinda who used to chat to him about the stock exchange.

"I just can't believe dad didn't wait," Sylvia lamented, staring out of the car window, focusing on nothing, the blur of buildings flashing past her in a haze.

Melinda blinked away a deluge of tears. "I know, honey. Life can be so unfair sometimes."

There was a long silence and then Melinda said, "Sylvie, I made a promise to your dad recently—something you and I need to discuss."

"A promise?"

"We do need to talk about financial stuff—he worried about that—although now really isn't the time, so remind me later."

"Go on, then, spill it."

Melinda swerved, the car nicking the curb. "Later. We can discuss this later. Just don't let me forget, is all."

"Whatever it is I need to deal with, I might as well know right now."

"I'll call you tomorrow when you're feeling better," Melinda croaked.

They drove on in more silence, until Sylvia blurted out—in order to break the pain of death—"Just tell me what I have to sort out already, and I'll get it done."

Tears trickled down Melinda's round cheeks, her eyes on the road ahead, but she almost careened into the bumper of the car in front of her. "There's a shit load of paperwork to deal with. Bonds et cetera, a lot to sort through."

Sylvia blew her nose. Her head felt swollen as if she had the flu. She glugged down some water which she'd bought at the airport.

Melinda said, "The good news is that you've got that money in your joint account offshore."

Sylvia looked blank.

"The account you have together in Guatemala. You remember? You must be getting bank statements every month and be able to go online and manage your money."

"That's right, I forgot, we have a joint account." Sylvia remembered now. Her dad had been smart. He'd stashed his savings in an account with her name on it, too. Melinda was right; she still received bank statements once a month, but just shoved them in the filing cabinet, never even bothering to look—she had never considered the funds hers. And the last thing on her mind right now was this. She wished she hadn't asked Melinda to "spill it." Her father's money was tied with a dark ribbon of guilt about it.

Melinda continued, "Mom doesn't think he had any debts. But I don't envy you—it's going to take you a good few meetings with lawyers et cetera to deal with it all. Sadly, I have to get back to Chicago. Damn my job! I wish I could stay with you. I mean, of course I'll be there for the funeral . . . but . . . I'll drop you at home and then I have to get back to Chicago. You don't hate me, do you?"

"No, I don't hate you, silly," Sylvia said despondently, "you're like a sister to me. Better than a sister."

"By the way, Mom is going to identify,"—Melinda stopped mid-sentence and took a breath—"the body at the morgue so you don't have to. She's still at the hospital now."

"What would I do without you guys?" Sylvia's eyes pooled with tears again.

"You'll have to call Uncle Wilbur's lawyer for a meeting," Melinda rasped. "And his accountant. I've left a list of numbers for you. I mean, look on the bright side—that money's waiting for you. Available now. You and Tommy can finally pry yourselves out of your horseshoe world in Wyoming and start afresh. You have a choice again. I mean, hasn't that been the whole problem all along? No choice, because of money issues?"

The Money subject again. Even though Sylvia had unwittingly got the ball rolling, she wished Melinda would drop it. Had her dad really just gone and killed himself? Hoarding those pills, as he had done, and taking them all in one go, meant only one thing. But *why?*

"You are so vague, my love," Melinda went on. "Sometimes I don't think you're flesh and blood but some sort of ghost floating through life—a spirit that might start walking through doorways. How you manage, my beautiful Sylvie, to even pay a bill is an enigma to me. You are so disconnected with practical matters. Especially these days. You see, how clever your dad was? Thinking ahead. That way the money doesn't have to wait to pass through probate. It is legally yours. He was such a smart man."

Sylvia was silent. All this talk was making her insides flip and fold. She turned her eyes away from the cityscape—the empty crumbling buildings, the recession letting down a whole generation, and said listlessly, "But the account is in Guatemala."

Melinda tittered as if to say, *Money talk is easy. Feelings and relation-*

ships are the complicated truths to deal with. "So? Don't you see, Sylvie, hun? That way you can avoid paying death duties. Uncle Wilbur was pretty crafty. He must have chosen Guatemala because it wouldn't draw attention."

"Wouldn't draw attention? Who has a bank account in Guatemala?"

"Exactly. Who would even think to look there? Don't you see, Sylvie? It isn't considered an offshore tax haven like Switzerland or the Cayman Islands, yet it has all the advantages. They do not tax offshore-derived income and no capital gains tax on bank interest. No Tax Information Exchange Agreement with any country. You can get your hands on that money today if you want. It's yours. Your dad was always canny about money."

Sylvia sighed. "The duplicity of it all makes me a little nervous."

"Do you want to pay your debts off or not?"

"I guess. But it wasn't the first thing on my mind." *My father has just died, Melinda.*

But this was obviously her cousin's way of easing her own pain. Thinking practically so she didn't have to dwell on her own emotions. She'd always done that. Always been the listener, the one to focus on other people's problems, never her own.

She went on, "You can finally get the house in Wyoming finished, sell, and move back to Brooklyn, maybe. Perhaps you could even afford to buy a spacious apartment with a small backyard. Or somewhere near a park. You could even look into private schools."

A private school for Grace—that would be nice. As her mind wandered, Sylvia noticed a muscle-bound man in a wife-beater tank top, strutting along the street, with a pit bull wearing a studded collar. Poor dog was probably being used for dogfights in some disused warehouse, or car factory. She turned her attention back to Melinda, who seemed to be suffering from verbal diarrhea.

"I mean, Grace may not end up being a horse rider but she could do ballet, or even martial arts. Not bad for a girl to learn that sort of stuff, especially in the city. Or Sylvie, the other option is that you guys could come back to live in Saginaw, although come to think of it, I'm not sure that's something Tommy would welcome. I mean, I know the romance of the beautiful countryside wooed him in the first place, and a town like Saginaw in the middle of a recession probably wouldn't be much of a temptation. I guess you don't want to test your marriage."

"No."

"Speaking of which, are you and Tommy, you know . . .?"

"What do you mean?"

"Did you make up the other day, after you baked him that apple pie? You're not being all cool with him, are you?"

Sylvia shifted in her car seat. "Cool?"

"Detached. Unavailable. You need each other right now. With your dad gone, you need him now more than ever."

Sylvia stared out of the car window again, and focused her eyes on a woman pushing her baby's stroller ahead of her, across the road. She always marveled at how women could do that—use their children as a sort of buffer with oncoming traffic. The car fumes were nose level for a child. She had always carried Grace in a special sling until she was old enough to walk.

"Sylvia?"

"Sorry?"

Melinda shook her head and smiled. "Never mind, honey, I'm just being my bossy old self—ignore me."

7

Sylvia

Walking into the hallway of her childhood home without her parents, or at least one of them to greet her, was eerie.

Sylvia felt the pit of her stomach dip as she stood there in the hallway, her eyes moving about the still, quiet house; memories living in the walls, soaked in the furniture, the drapes, her mother's tennis trophies, the paintings that her grandmother had done. Like colorful friends supporting her through heartbreak and happiness, they'd seen her have her diapers changed and get ready for her first date. She looked up at the sweeping, wrought iron staircase and remembered coming down, one step at a time, as a princess, a witch, a fairy, dressing up with Melinda and their friends, her mom taking snapshots. The little Regency sofa, where she'd chatted for thousands of hours on the telephone, sat below, it too remembering, perhaps, the time she fell and landed on its arm, saving her life (or at least a hospital visit) from the hard, Spanish tiles below.

And Tibby, her Siamese cat, was his spirit here, too? Tibby, her best friend, who was one when she was one, eighteen when she was eighteen. It didn't seem right that he had died when he had, just as she was going to college, as if his heart could no longer bear the parting. He obviously knew; he could smell her treacherous suitcases, the betrayal of a girl grown up. Her eyes now wet with tears, Sylvia sobbed, her body heaving from all the memories. She sat on the cold terracotta floor and felt the weight of responsibility shroud her like a musty-smelling winter coat from the attic, demanding, *What are you going to do with us?* Armchairs, sofas, crystal, miniature wooden boxes, paintings—they all commanded her attention. Right here, right now. *Help us!* they cried. *We are all alone. We need your care. Remember . . . your parents are dead.*

Sylvia walked into the kitchen, opened the icebox door, and took out a Coke. Rows of pretty glasses, green with golden rims, twinkled in the glass-fronted cupboards. They too, wanted a promise. *Don't abandon us, we are part of you!* She looked inside a drawer for an Advil, or something to lift away the burden; her head pounding with regret, guilt, love, sadness. The drawer, packed with a hundred pill prescriptions, including perhaps, the ones that killed her father, laughed at her.

Where will you even start? You could put us all in a bag, dump us at the pharmacy (isn't that what you're meant to do with old fogies like us?) but we are a drop in the ocean, a speck of sand on a beach. What about the rest of the house—your mother's country club clothes, your father's suits, the silver, the candlesticks, your father's '68 Mustang in the garage, his diaries, golf clubs, photo albums, the letters, your essays from school, the boxes in the attic, the—

"Stop!" Sylvia cried out. "Please, leave me alone! It's all too much, all I want is to be home with Grace—"

"But this *is* your home," the paintings, the sofa-that-saved-her-life, the trophies and the '68 Presidential Blue Mustang all said at once. "You can't abandon us!"

"Hello? Hell-oh-oh? Sylvia?"

Sylvia's heart missed a beat. Someone had let themselves

through the front door, never locked, always open to friends—that was the way the neighborhood was.

"Hello Syl-via? Are you ho-home?"

It was the next-door neighbor, Mrs. Wicks, holding a large casserole dish. She looked just the same as she always had, squeezed into polyester pants, lemon-colored, paired with a tight blouse, her bra strap digging into the flesh in her back. She was one of those people who was always perky and kind, no matter the circumstance, no matter the weather. "I thought you might be hungry," she purred, "and Lord knows with everything you have to do around here, I know the last thing you have is time for cooking."

"Oh Mrs. Wicks, you're a saint! I was actually feeling ravenous and wondering where I could go to get a bite around here."

"Well isn't that lucky I arrived in the nick of time? Where are Tommy and Grace?"

"They'll be here in a couple of days. I'm just about to call Gracie, actually."

"When's the funeral, honey?"

Sylvia gasped. "The funeral? I don't know. I need to make a thousand phone calls. Speak to the funeral parlor. I guess I need to call everyone, too. Tell them Dad has died."

"Let them know he's passed away?" Mrs. Wicks corrected. "Good idea, though most of his friends already know. I can make some more calls if you like."

Passed away. It was a word everybody insisted upon using these days. Nobody dared say the word "died" or "dead." Some people didn't even add on the "away" part, just, "he passed," or "she passed." But her dad was dead and making him "pass" didn't make it any less painful.

"Mrs. Wicks you're an angel, thank you so much for your help," Sylvia said, taking the dish. "Umm, this smells delicious."

"Pop it in the microwave for a few minutes. You know you can call me Marg. I'll come back later, and remember, if you need me to do anything, anything at all, just say the word. Is Jacqueline coming today?"

"I think today's her day off."

"So she'll still continue to work here?"

Sylvia hadn't thought that far ahead. Jacqueline had been with them forever. Sylvia's forever, anyway. She loved that woman. She knew that she would probably be sitting at home, with swollen red eyes, devastated about the death of her boss, her working life now over. She should have retired long ago—she was too elderly to be pushing a vacuum cleaner about. But she didn't want to retire, she'd said so a hundred times. To Sylvia, Jacqueline had never been a maid—she had been her lifeblood. Sylvia could keep her on a while longer, of course, but not indefinitely—she wouldn't be able to afford it. But the idea of not having her in her life didn't bear thinking about.

"I guess that's something I'll need to discuss with her."

"Well," Marg said. "See you later, honey."

"Thanks a million. See you later, Marg."

The Coca Cola tasted good. It tasted of America, of everything Sylvia knew and trusted. This house had been her world. She, a nice Midwestern girl with her wholesome friends and a college degree from the University of Michigan, should have been content with her lot. But New York changed all that and she doubted she could ever return to Saginaw for good. Especially now. Poor Michigan. Once synonymous with growth and opportunity, now smashed hopes and run-down housing projects seemed to be the symbol to the outside world of this great state.

She loved this house, though. It was considered a historic property, built in 1930, Spanish in style, with a red tiled roof and balconied windows. Could she ever live here again? It was too raw to even consider that now, but she couldn't keep two homes going at once. The truth was, as Melinda had sensed, Sylvia would have liked to have moved back to Brooklyn. Get back her old life, or a semblance of it. They'd gone to Wyoming mainly for Grace's sake. Fresh air, plenty of space, low crime—a place where her daughter could ride a horse and go hiking and camping. The first time Sylvia set eyes on Wyoming—when she and Tommy drove across the country and stopped by Yellowstone—she thought it was the most beautiful place she'd ever seen. Sweeping blue skies, mountains, and rivers with gushing crystalline whitewater, beckoned them to return. And they did return with open hearts.

But it was challenging, she discovered, living in a state where international adoption was rare. Most people assumed Grace was of Native American heritage, but one little boy at kindergarten, a farmer's son, had called Grace a "wetback," something Sylvia assumed would never have occurred in a melting pot like New York City. Sylvia's parents denied it later (falling in love with their grandchild the moment they saw her smile), but they had originally been scathing about trans-racial adoption, trying to convince Sylvia to choose, "a child who has something in common with you, who won't raise questions"—e.g. a white-skinned baby. They argued that it wouldn't be in the "best interest" of the child, and that Sylvia and Tommy would not be able to prepare her to effectively deal with racism in later life.

Sylvia knew Tommy wasn't feeling fulfilled with life in Wyoming either, despite his love for fly fishing, which was one of the main reasons they chose the town of Crowheart—so close to Wind River Canyon. Sylvia had never pegged herself as a career girl but she guessed she was; not having a proper job didn't suit her. She missed communicating, being involved in several people's lives at once. The "creative freedom" dream came with long, tangled strings attached and it was time to make a change. Melinda was right—they had a choice now.

But how could she break up this house? It would be impossible. Sylvia wished she could airlift it to Brooklyn. Her mother's dresses hung like ladies who lunch, gossiping in her walk-in closet. How was she meant to take them to Goodwill? Or find a new home for her dad's faithful old golf clubs that sat like guardians by the backyard door? Having money in her bank account would be bittersweet. Parents die, she thought, they pass what's theirs onto their children; that's life, but her father's death shouldn't have happened the way it did. He had not "passed away," he had killed himself. It didn't seem right that she should be benefitting in any way, at all.

She thought of Tommy, how he had always worked hard for privileges. He hadn't grown up in a world of country clubs the way she had. He'd won a scholarship to Cambridge, one of the top universities in England, and his first Saturday job was when he was fifteen. He'd joined the Territorial Army, a part-time commitment. It helped with expenses and he learned how to parachute, one of his childhood dreams.

Although they spoke the same language, they were from two different worlds, in a way. Tommy had that sarcastic British wit that caught her off-guard sometimes. Clever, quick. He was precise and it showed in his hobbies, the fly fishing (which he said needed "the touch of a surgeon and the spirit of a Zen master"), and his interest in precision shooting. He didn't hunt, had never shot a living creature—as far as she knew—but he was attracted by long-range fire; something else he picked up in the Territorial Army. She'd observed how meticulous he was, the way he loved the ritual of setting up the shot, the millimeter accuracy, the importance of the rifle position. Sylvia presumed it wasn't far removed from photography, honing in on a target with a critical, razor-sharp eye. Some people thought Tommy a nerd, his obsession for detail, his endless chitchat about angles, lenses and exposure. But she loved that about him. It kept her on her toes and she was thankful for not having a baseball fan for a husband, but a man whose own expertise and appetite for knowledge drove his passions.

That's what made her so furious about that pouting Bel Ange

whom he'd obsessed over, as if she were one of his projects or targets. Sylvia wanted to shake Tommy and shout in his ear, "*She doesn't give a damn about you or how your mind works, she wants to feed off you, use you to gratify her ego. Look at me, Sylvia. I'm here, I'm real! I care!*"

She prayed that he would put all that behind him and love her, his *wife*, the way he had before. She remembered how soon after they'd met, he took her face in his hands as if she were a delicate porcelain plate worth hundreds of thousands of dollars. He had examined her, tracing his fingers across her nose—remarking on how pretty it was—her curvy lips, stroking the line of her pale eyebrows. "You're the most precious thing in the world," he told her. A ripple of pleasure shimmied through her core now, remembering her first orgasm with him. Her first orgasm with anyone. She thought she would explode. Physically. Mentally.

That was what she wanted: for them both to feel that all-consuming passion once more.

To have her husband back. Truly back. For their little family to be as strong as a diamond.

And shining just as bright.

8

Grace

Grace and Ruth crawled along in the car, waiting in line beside the burger drive-by window. For some reason it was a busy afternoon.

"My mom never lets me eat this stuff," Grace revealed, feeling jiggly inside.

"Well, I thought we'd have a special treat today," Ruth conspired in a whisper.

"Mommy says we must always eat free-range meat and eggs when we can. She says all that Intensive Farming is *bad.*"

"Does she now," Ruth said.

Grace nodded. "There's danger of E. coli poisoning because they feed cows grain when they should be eating grass. It's dangerous for human con . . .con . . .something . . . and it's so cruel the way they treat animals in those Factory Farms."

"Human consumption."

"Yeah," Grace agreed, her eyes wide and earnest. "A little girl once ate a take-out burger and died from E. coli poisoning."

"I buy free-range chicken because I can taste the difference," Ruth told her. "But the eggs? The pork? The beef? I can't taste the difference so I don't bother."

"But what about the *animals?*" Grace asked.

"I don't *care* about the animals," Ruth said quietly, "I care about my wallet!"

Grace knotted her brow. How could a wallet have more feelings than a live animal?

"You don't have to tell your mom," Ruth pointed out, putting Grace's thoughts into her mouth. "There are such things as secrets."

LATER, GRACE SAT on her bed surrounded by her teddy bears. It was tricky for her to decide who got to be where on the bed so she rotated them every day so they wouldn't get jealous of each other. Pidgey O Dollars always had the prime spot, though. She knew it wasn't fair but then she had been told that life wasn't always fair so she decided it was okay. Plus, Pidgey O Dollars had spent time in the hospital. She'd taken him to a friend's house once, and their Jack Russell attacked him. His face was "Mauled Beyond Recognition" her Mom had said and announced he needed Emergency Plastic Surgery. Poor Pidgey O Dollars. Grace hadn't understood why he had to have plastic put on his face when he was not a doll but a soft teddy bear, but her mom kept using that word. But in the end, no plastic was used. Her mom sewed on a whole new soft face, with a new nose and new, button eyes. The new face was whiter than the old one and the nose too pointy. The eyes were a glassy blue and not chocolate-brown like before. He had no legs and only one arm. It changed Pidgey's personality. Secretly, Grace didn't love him quite the same, which made her feel guilty so she decided to love him Double to make up for it. So she always gave him the best position on the bed.

After Grace had rearranged the teddies, she took Carrot, her pajama-case teddy, and pulled apart the Velcro on the invisible seam on his back. She took out her light summertime nighty and unrolled her dad's recording pen, hidden inside. Nobody knew. It was a secret she shared with her teddies. Her dad had forgotten all about this little machine because he used his iPhone to record instead.

Finders keepers, losers weepers.

She carefully took the clever pen—that looked just like a normal pen and even wrote like one too—out of the back. She was going to make stories, and a diary of her life. Her writing, she knew, wasn't grown-up enough yet. She could almost do joined-up writing but it wasn't perfect. Recording was better. It was fast and she could listen to it afterwards and laugh at her voice which sometimes sounded like Donald Duck.

She pressed down on the pocket clip and saw the tiny red light flash on. She whispered so Ruth couldn't hear her because this recording was private:

"Me and Mommy Skyped. She looked sad. But she wasn't wearing her Wolfy Face. It was more like the Ground Dog Face. Ground Dog is a sad dog that I made up. His belly is close to the floor and his tail goes between his legs and he has long sad ears. Mommy had Ground Dog Face but she was trying to hide it. She kept smiling but I know my mom, the kind of feelings inside her tummy, like if I get told off sometimes my tummy makes a little jump inside. Or if I see a dead animal by the road that's been run over by a car, I get that funny feeling like a piece of me is missing. Like I have a hole inside of me.

Today I did so many things that I've forgotten! Let me see. Auntie Ruth—she told me to call her Auntie Ruth but she said it's a secret as Mommy may not like it as it could hurt her feelings—took me to the drive-by! I had a burger and fries but then I felt sick after. I went to school and Auntie Ruth talked to Mrs. Pitt for half an hour and they laughed and laughed. I don't know what they were laughing about but they sure looked happy.

I love school. I did a painting of a pony. Mrs. Pitt showed us how to mix colors. She showed us how to mix red and white and it comes out pink! It was like magic. Red and blue goes purple! But then I mixed green and red and it came out brown. So in the end my pony was brown but Ruth said it was pretty anyway, and she put it on the fidget rator door with my painting of Mrs. Paws.

Oh YES! There is a beautiful, beautiful blackbird who has had babies and she made a nest in the barn. These babies are called chicks. Daddy once told me that in England men used to call women 'Birds' and that in America, men call women 'Chicks.' Daddy says it is Dee Rog Tree but I don't know what that means. Auntie Ruth told me that I mustn't touch the nest or my human smell will make the mommy bird fly away and then the babies would die. Let's hope that naughty Mrs. Paws won't find them. Auntie Ruth talked a lot about Mrs. Paws being dangerous and said that cats were bad. She said she had 'just the tonic' for Mrs. Paws but I don't know why she talked about tonic. Daddy drinks tonic water when he makes a gin and tonic. But I don't think Mrs. Paws would drink something so yukky.

Daddy Skyped me today. He's coming home very late in the middle of the night and we'll be going to Saginaw together to see Mommy soon.

Auntie Ruth did lots of writing today. She says she is going to make a million dollars with her book. When she came to school to pick me up, I saw that she was wearing a pin just like Mommy's. And a dress like Mommy's too. Isn't that funny? But she told me not to say anything, just in case. She said that for every secret I keep she would give me a dollar. So far I've made two dollars! In one day! I'll be rich and can buy myself the Computer Engineer Barbie Doll.

I don't usually have secrets from Mommy, only that time when

I wet my bed and then on purpose I spilt milk on the sheet so that she didn't know I had peed. Maybe she knew and that was her secret too but she never said. Anyway, Auntie Ruth says it's okay to have little secrets from Mom, that it shows I'm a grown-up and a big girl. I don't care about being a big girl but I do want to be a grown-up so I can invent something and buy my own pony.

When me and Mommy Skyped she took the laptop around Grandma and Grandpa's house so I could see. I wish Mommy could fly on a magic carpet and come and get me in the night so I could be with her at Grandma's. I have to go now, I hear Auntie Ruth calling me for dinner. We're having popcorn and she said we could watch *Chitty Chitty Bang Bang*. Yipeee!"

9

Sylvia

S ylvia sat cross-legged on the sofa-that-saved-her-life and picked up the old telephone. She dialed Tommy. She felt odd knowing that everything she touched or looked at was now hers. The dial telephone. The big old icebox that hummed away too loudly in the kitchen. The spiders that spun their webs in high corners that nobody could reach. All these belonged to her.

Tommy answered his cell. "Hello."

"Hi, honey, it's me."

"Sylvie, darling, hi, I'm on my way to the airport now. So glad you called. I have great news. Are you sitting down?"

"I'm sitting on my special sofa." *He called her Darling. And Sylvie. That felt good.*

"I've been offered the job."

"*The* job? What job? I thought it was just a two-week assignment. And that it was all about to go to the dogs because of you having to come home."

"No, it was a job interview. But I thought that you might think

71

it a bit excessive to go all the way out to LA for just an interview, so I didn't say."

Sylvia was mute. She didn't know how to react. Why couldn't he have just been straightforward with her? She conjured up possible images of the nubile Bel Ange doing a photo shoot with him, and a wave of mistrust shot through her, making her stomach churn.

"Sylvia? Are you still there?"

"Yeah, I'm still here."

"Are you cross with me?"

"No, of course not. How can I be mad at you for getting a job offer?"

"But if it hadn't worked out. If I *hadn't* been offered the job, then you'd be pissed off, wouldn't you." His voice had a downward inflection at the end of the sentence, no question mark, just a statement—disappointed with her. As usual, she'd said the wrong thing. Reacted in the wrong way.

"I would have wished you'd told me. I mean, I still wish you'd told me," she offered.

"But you might not have wanted me to go all the way to LA if it wasn't a sure thing."

"I wish you had more faith in me." She took in a sharp intake of breath, and exhaling said, "You always pre-empt what my reaction will be."

"Anyway, I'm glad you called as I've just heard back and I wanted to share the good news."

"It *is* good news. What is the job, exactly?" she asked brightly.

"In-house photographer on *Image Magazine*. It's well paid, too."

"Great, Tommy. Congratulations."

"How are you faring? Gracie told me you two Skyped."

"You Skyped her too?"

"Of course. God I love that little minx. She's just the best and I'm not just saying that because she's my daughter."

"Yes you are!" Sylvia joked. "*So* Daddy's Little Princess."

"Too right she's Daddy's Little Princess. I've bought her a mini electric guitar."

"An electric guitar? What gave you that idea?"

"She's got a really good ear, you know that. The way she picks up accents and languages. It must mean she's musical. You've heard her do all those different voices and songs for her teddies and dolls. Didn't you see that music school she set up for them?"

"But an *electric* guitar. Tommy. *Really*. You couldn't be happy with a regular, classical guitar?"

"It's *made* for her. A mini, pink, metallic guitar with flecks of gold sparkles, set beneath the paintwork. Designed for a child her size. And it's good quality, too. It even comes with a little amp."

Sylvia laughed. "Only in LA would they come up with such a thing. I bet you're planning to make another video of her and post it on YouTube again."

"Too right I am. We could get her ready for *America's Got Talent*," he teased. "But don't say a word—it's a surprise."

"Well you'll see her in the morning, right?"

"Yup, can't wait. How's it been going with Ruth? Gracie seems happy."

"Yeah, it sounds as if they've been having a ball."

"Seems very reliable."

"Absolutely. She's great with Grace. But I still wish I hadn't had to leave her behind. I miss her."

"You did what you had to do. Anyway, it sounds as if she hasn't even noticed we're gone. As long as this Ruth woman is genuinely being nice to her and isn't some sort of lesbian pedophile."

Thanks Tommy, for putting that sweet idea into my head. "So you're still both coming to the funeral? You think that's okay for a five-year-old?"

"If it's too weird, Grace can have a play-date instead. Have you set a day?"

"Saturday."

"Okay, good," Tommy said.

"And then what?"

"Well, the sooner I start at the magazine, the sooner I begin earning. So after the funeral, I'll head back to LA. I'll look for an apartment for us, just a two bedroom to start with, and then you and Gracie can come out the minute it's ready."

Sylvia would now be dealing with not two, but three homes. "So what do we do with Crowheart?"

"Darling, you told me you were done living there. You said you'd had it with the winters and stuff."

"Yes, but I didn't know it would be so sudden, and I'd always imagined we'd go back to New York."

"New York City is not the best place to bring up a child. You know that. What can be better than LA? Great weather, the sea—"

"The ocean, not the sea."

"Whatever. I'm British—we always say sea. We don't get to see oceans in Europe. Get the pun? We don't get to *sea* oceans in Europe."

"Very cute."

"Anyway, LA's an easy, fun place. There's loads to do for a child. And for you, too. I mean, hello? It's far better than New York for script writing. Can you imagine the kind of contacts you'll make there, Sylvia? If you ever wanted to go back to work as an agent—"

"Listen, I'd love to chat but I've got a million things to deal with, and I want to put in an early night and get some sleep. Got a meeting with the lawyer tomorrow. And guess what? I'm going to transfer $247,000 into our account, Tommy. I can do it online. If I can remember that goddamn password. We'll be able to pay off the credit cards, the mortgage, and get the last bits of plumbing and wiring finished. Finally we can sell! It feels so good, I can't tell you how *great* it feels. Apart from the fact, of course, that the source of the money does not exactly fill me with joy—I mean, I wish we hadn't come to it this way."

Silence. Sylvia heard no more than Tommy's measured breath. "Tommy?"

"You know I'll be earning pretty good money with my new job," he said quietly.

"Honey, I didn't mean to belittle your job in any way. That's great. It's so *great* you've got this, I'm really proud of you! Just . . . well . . . just my dad's money will take away the panic. Let's face it, the wolf has been clawing at our door for quite a while now."

"Look, I've got to go now. I'll call you later. I'm driving and I think I see a cop."

"What? You aren't driving and talking on your cell at the same time, are you? I told—"

But Tommy had hung up. Crap! Whatever she did, whatever she said, it always came out wrong. Damn Tommy's silly pride. The fact was, they had nearly two hundred and fifty thousand dollars.

Now they could start afresh.

SYLVIA'S MIND SWIRLED relentlessly as she lay in bed, staring at the ceiling. Thinking of her father. Of Grace. She had never once been parted from her daughter before, except when they went to England and Sylvia stayed with a friend in London for the night, instead of at Tommy's parents. The thrill when Grace learned a new fact, or the laughter when she said something funny like, Labradors being "Love Adores," or, "Puff Adders must be very clever snakes because they're good at math." Sylvia had waited her whole life for Grace—she was just a little being with a fragile heart. At least she knew Ruth would be treating her like gold. And Tommy would be home later tonight.

Sylvia's thoughts wandered back to Melinda. Poor Melinda. The great love of her life, a guy called Mike, had died in a car accident. Since then, Melinda had been unlucky. The boyfriends were a string of disasters, one after another. She opened up too soon and was then deceived by her own high expectations. She'd put on weight, too, and she'd given up dating altogether. The weight didn't obscure her prettiness though—her thick dark hair and twinkling blue eyes—but her self-confidence seemed shot. Sylvia believed that Melinda should just go ahead and adopt as a single mother. Tough, but still, she'd have a purpose in life, other than her career. Living alone was only letting her sink further into the cushion of her solitary ways. She wished for Melinda to feel her own heart burst with love for a child the way it did for her.

Sylvia's mind ping-ponged about.

Tomorrow would be jam-packed with things to do. She made a mental list:

* Visit to funeral parlor.
* Pick out songs and readings for Dad.
* Sign death certificate.
* Meetings with lawyer and accountant.
* Call old friends and set up a string of play-dates for Grace.
* Call catering company.
* Transfer money to pay mortgage off from Dad's and my Guatemalan joint account.

Transfer money . . . . Sylvia's mind ticked and turned, mental papers piling and jumbling in her head. That goddamn password! Unlike Tommy or Grace, she could never remember numbers or passwords. They drove her nuts! Some with capital letters, others with numbers or signs. As much as she hated the Big Brother spyware threatening to take over the world, she longed for the day when her thumbprint would do, and passwords would be history. They always had to be chopped and changed, and she lost track, forgetting them. They must all be written down in the filing cabinet under P. Or had she written them in her old address book? She'd need to get that transfer done soon. She could move the whole lot, and next week, when things would be calmer, she could concentrate on paying off their credit card debts. She'd do it after the funeral. That reminded her, would her driver's license be good enough ID to show for the death certificate? She'd left her passport at home. Also in the filing cabinet under P.

Sylvia forced herself to swap all these worrisome problems for images of Grace. She had her in her mind's eye, sleeping like an angel, her long lashes making shadows on her soft, caramel-colored skin, her little arms clutching her teddy. All that love in such a tiny body. It made Sylvia feel warm just thinking about her.

10

Tommy

Tommy had missed the fucking plane. Stopped by that zealous policeman on the freeway and ticketed for talking on his cell while driving. The cop was young, eager, took forever—wanting to see Tommy's license which, after a whole lot of fumbling about, Tommy found he'd put in the pocket of his suitcase in the trunk. All that "put your hands on the wheel where I can see them" shit. In England you got out of your car. It was the polite thing to do, and expected. But in the States, you were the criminal in every circumstance. They suspected everyone. Shit, men had been shot over cigarette lighters or biros being mistaken for a gun. Usually people were charmed by his British accent, but not tonight. This cop seemed to have had it in for him, and the whole ordeal took forever. A huge fine . . . questions . . . more questions.

He missed the gate by four fucking, lousy minutes.

The last thing he needed was for his wife to berate him for it, or to panic about him being late home for Grace when Sylvia already had enough to deal with after her father's death. She'd told him she wanted a good night's rest. There was no point calling her and waking her up. So he texted Ruth and let her know—luckily he'd gotten her number from Sylvia. He sat on an airport bench, getting his breath back after sprinting to try and make the plane in time.

His fingers hovered above his cell. Tommy suspected that Sylvia might still be awake, though, tossing in her sleep, feeling riddled with guilt for not having been to visit her dad sooner. Feeling guilty, for basically, not having been a mind reader. How the hell was she meant to have known that her dad was harboring suicidal thoughts, and worse, that he'd act on it?

Tommy knew all about that one. The Guilt Trip. He'd been on that roller coaster ride with his own father. Years and years of trying to wean his dad off the bottle, as if he were a baby letting go of the breast. And his mum: neurotic, hysterical, dependent, almost as if every time his father would try to get his shit together, she would unwittingly sabotage his recovery. She hated it when he got too involved with his AA meetings. Felt lonely, she said. Stigmatized, even. The odd one out. She liked the odd hot toddy herself, every now and then.

No, Tommy wouldn't call Sylvia. Let the poor thing sleep. His mind wandered back to his dysfunctional family. He and his sister weren't close, either. Nothing dramatic, they just had little in common. What a breath of fresh air it was to have escaped to the States. But the Guilt had followed him there. E-mails, sad Sunday phone calls, and cheap Christmas cards, recycled from the year before. "Come home," his mum begged every so often. But when he did go home all they did was watch TV, or go to the pub. Not even Gracie inspired them when she and Tommy visited. The opposite. She wasn't "flesh and blood," his parents whispered behind his back, and Tommy even heard them refer to his daughter as a "Paki."

"She's from India Dad, not Pakistan," Tommy told them at supper, when Gracie was tucked up in bed. TV dinner, not at the table. God forbid, that would be far too intimate. The TV had always been a reassuring third party. A buffer.

His father just turned up the remote and said, "One minute, son, I need to catch the football results."

Since then, Tommy had managed to avoid going back again. It was easy to play happy families with thousands of miles between them.

He remained on the bench, and started surfing on his cell for another flight. Because he lived in the middle of bloody No-wheresville, getting a connection to Riverton wasn't so simple. He had to change in Denver. The 6:15 am was fully booked. Damn, he'd have to wait until 10:40 and wouldn't arrive until 3:42 pm. He'd ask Ruth to pick him up.

He dreaded admitting to Sylvia why he'd missed the plane. One thing Tommy hated about marriage was the I-Told-You-So factor. It was as if it had become a competition to see who could score the most points. He was losing big-time. He'd be in the doghouse now. Fuck.

He got up and went to sort out his new plane ticket. Texted his friend, Gus, to tell him he didn't need to pick him up from the airport tonight after all, and Ruth to let her know his arrival time tomorrow. He booked himself into a motel—the closest one, which he could get to by shuttle.

"OH YEAH BABY, right there, that feels sooo good," Tommy murmured. The girl's hair swished back and forth over his cock; the soft tickling sensation was driving him wild. "Oh fuck," he groaned as she took him in her mouth. He could feel how huge he was, how thick, as she sucked hard, not managing all of him because of his size. He laced his fingers through her silky hair, gripping her head, scraping his fingers gently along her scalp. If she didn't stop soon, he'd come. Hard.

"Get on top of me," he ordered. "Ride me. I want to feel myself inside you."

The room was so dark he couldn't even make her out. Her body was beautiful; long limbs, graceful arms. Yes, she was full of grace, like a dancer. She had a ballerina's body. Breasts not too big, strong shoulders, a long neck. He gripped her pretty waist to guide her as she slid on top of him. He could feel his rock-hard erection stretch her open and she cried out—not in pain but with pure, girlish lust.

"Fuck me," he said. "Really fuck me. I want to feel you come."

She started her ride and it felt incredible, like ocean waves consuming him. Every time their bodies met—him deep, deep, inside her—she mewled, slapping her face on his, kissing him. Softly at first and then lashing at his tongue with hers, tangling, gasping, groaning each time she came down hard on him. She began to circle her hips, grinding herself into him. This woman could really fuck.

And how.

He raised his hips to meet hers and grabbed her ass, pulling her even closer towards him. Her hair flopped over his neck, his face, and she started moaning. He moved his large hands up and down her curvy butt, and felt beads of sweat gather on the small of her back. She was coming. She didn't even have to say a word. But he could tell.

He knew her every movement. Her every sign.

"Sylvie," he moaned into her mouth as he exploded into her. "I'm so in love with you. So in love."

Tommy awoke with a start. He felt as if he'd overslept, but only a few hours had passed. He double-checked the alarm was set on his cell—he had several more hours sleep time.

He was still hard, even though he'd just come in his sleep. His erotic dream, starring his very own wife, reminded him how deep their bond was. How much he still needed her. Desired her. Fantasized about her.

He wished things hadn't gotten so complicated.

His family, which had seemed so indestructible, was now as delicate as an eggshell. How had that happened?

He thought of Gracie. He couldn't wait to get home to her and see her face when he gave her that sparkly pink guitar.

11

Sylvia

It had been such a full-on day, and even though Sylvia wanted to sleep more than anything, she couldn't. She thought of Aunt Marcy. The hospital had told her to call back and she'd forgotten. Damn. Sylvia had offered to bring her to the house to look after her till Melinda arrived for the funeral, although her aunt was insistent that she could take good care of herself and wanted to go straight home. If she changed her mind, it would be a lot to take on all at once, but what was family for? Infallible Jacqueline would soon be by to help. Thank God.

Her first memory of Jacqueline's presence was when Sylvia was about three. Sylvia had stolen her dad's underpants from the washing basket, and secretly put them on. In those days, she wanted to be a boy. But then she peed her pants and the undergarments were saturated with yellow. Jacqueline didn't say a word. It was their secret. She took away the enormous soiled Y-Fronts and soaked them in soapy water. Then she took Sylvia to the bathtub, pretending that the child had muddy knees and it was easier to put her in the tub. The pee was humiliating enough, but being discovered in her father's giant underpants was doubly shameful to a small child, even a Tomboy like Sylvia, and Jacqueline sensed that. Never did she mention it to anybody. So loyal.

Grace had occasional little mishaps in bed but, just like Jacqueline, Sylvia never made a big deal out of it, or she pretended she didn't even notice.

The other indelible memory of Sylvia's was when Jacqueline took her to her church. Sylvia's parents' church was uneventful, with only white people looking sour and bored, but Jacqueline's was wild with song, full of Praise-The-Lord. One man, in a wheelchair, was rocking so hard he popped out. The force of it set him rolling about the floor, still singing, praising the Lord even harder. After that, Sylvia begged to *only* go to Jacqueline's Baptist church—it was so much more fun! But her mother told her to wait until she was older—then she could choose. But by the time she was older, Sylvia had lost interest in church of any kind.

She had been brought up with so much goodness around her. The neighbors, Aunt Marcy, Jacqueline. She knew she'd had a blessed life.

Earlier that evening, Mrs. Wicks had brought Sylvia another tasty meal in a casserole dish—wouldn't accept no for an answer—such kindness.

Sylvia rolled over in her bed for the umpteenth time but couldn't even close her eyes, let alone sleep. She decided to tackle her father's closet. She'd pick out the right suit for him and make a Goodwill pile and a Special pile. What she would do with the Special pile she had no idea, but at least it was a start. Tommy was not her father's size.

She got up and walked with trepidation into the spare bedroom, which her father had used as a dressing room. There were two Regency-style single beds and a chest of drawers to match. She opened the top drawer. It smelled of rose-scented paper liners, and

was full of lavender bags that her mother had once bought on a trip
to France.

The walk-in closet was stuffed with hand-made shoes, too
small, unfortunately, for Tommy's feet. The same could be said for
the tailored suits, which was a shame as some of them harked back
to the sixties and were pretty stylish. Sylvia stood on a stool and
rummaged through the shelf above. There were hats—even a top
hat that folded flat, which she remembered her father had said
belonged to *his* father. It was an opera hat, designed to sit on, so
when you went to the theatre, it didn't take up space. There were
shoeboxes, all clean, meticulously organized. Except for one that
nestled in the top right hand corner. Strange, thought Sylvia, it was
unlike Jacqueline to let dust gather. It was obvious that it hadn't
been touched for years. She reached over on tiptoe and grasped the
shoebox with both hands. At a closer glance, she saw that it was
sealed tight with duct tape. Why sealed? Could there be a pistol
inside? She didn't think so. Her father was not a pistol kind of man.

She sneezed from the musty attic smell of the box. It reminded
her that the attic would have to be next; it didn't even bear contem-
plating the amount of junk that must be up there. Maybe the luxury
of having $247,000 in her bank account, despite the guilt attached
to it, would stave off selling the house a while longer. The idea of
sorting through it was horrifying; the memories, the sheer volume
of stuff. In fact, she'd leave it all. No suit sorting into piles—the
whole thing would be too much of an ordeal right now.

She brought the box close to her chest and stepped down from
the stool. She took it to the bathroom and wiped off the layer of
dust with a damp cloth. She set it down in a corner.

But then she sat on the edge of the tub and took a breath, eyeing the box with suspicion. There was something ominous about it.
Pandora's Box? Was she even ready to look inside?

No, she wasn't.

She loved this bathroom. It was all white with a huge old tub in which you could stretch out so your tiptoes touched the end. The mosaic tiles were original. There was a laundry chute where you could shove your stinky socks and sports clothes at the end of a tiring school day and they would magically appear fresh and ironed forty-eight hours later. Sylvia hadn't realized how spoiled she'd been as a girl, how privileged. Because of the breakdown of the automotive industry there was a lot of unemployment now in Saginaw, even for people of her class.

She remembered the time she had made a new friend. Not from school, but from one of the streets behind, where the worn-down clapperboard houses were, and working class families lived. Her grandmother was staying with them for the summer. Sylvia must have known that her grandmother would be unhappy about her new friendship because she took her friend upstairs, like a secret, and they played in the bathroom. And Sylvia locked the door. Her grandmother lost her temper, banging her fists on the locked door, shouting, "Sylvia, get that poor-white-trash out of this house!" The girl heard. Sylvia was speechless, she'd never heard her grandmother, who was usually so kind, raise her voice like that or be so rude. The little child (how old were they, seven or eight?) slipped away and never dared play with Sylvia again.

It wasn't until she went to college that Sylvia had a mix of friends from different backgrounds and races. At school, the black kids and white kids tended to sit at separate tables for lunch, not because they didn't like each other or were racist, but because they felt more comfortable with classmates who were most like them, with whom they related to best. Kids would say things like "across the river," "the East Side," or "the First Ward," as if they were foreign countries. Sylvia discovered that these terms all meant the same thing: the poorer neighborhoods where most of Saginaw's racial or ethnic minority population lived, mostly African American. Things probably hadn't changed much. The river dividing the city into two geographical areas might as well have been the Berlin Wall.

She never understood this racial chasm, how her parents could adore Jacqueline so, but be struck with shock any time she suggested bringing home a friend "from a different world than ours, honey" (as her mother would politely put it). Once, Sylvia confronted her parents at the dinner table. "How about Jacqueline then, you love *her*?" she shouted. "*She's* black."

Her father cleared his throat and went quiet. Her mother smoothed her perfect hairdo and said, "Jacqueline is *different*."

Sylvia looked at the clandestine box again. Some force was preventing her from ripping it open. It was true what Melinda said about her—she could detach herself. Other people wouldn't be able to contain themselves the way she could. She'd always done that. Saved her candy in a jar while Melinda ate hers all in one go, and then begged Sylvia to share (which she always did). Sylvia prided herself on her composure; being able to stay cool when others lost themselves. She had lost herself with Tommy and it hurt. Snooping through his cell phone, surrendering herself—losing herself when he made love to her. The unopened box was her way of mastering that control, showing that she wouldn't crumple with her father's suicide.

She stood up, had a pee and washed her hands. She turned on the faucet and out poured steaming water. She wished their plumbing in Crowheart could be as reliable. She went downstairs, holding on to the banisters as she descended, because the house was still semi-dark. She went into the kitchen. She opened the fridge door and took out the Sara Lee chocolate cake she'd bought earlier that day, and poured herself a tall glass of milk. Why she felt she could eat Sara Lee only at her parents' house and nowhere else, she wasn't sure. A bit like having cream teas in England, or Piña Coladas in the Caribbean; they tasted better in their original environment. Sara Lee tasted of childhood. The Sara Lee chocolate cake had been beckoning her for hours.

She went back upstairs and soaked herself in the tub, her body fully stretched out, carefully eating the cake so as not to let any crumbs fall in the hot water, and glugging the cold milk to wash down the gooeyness of the icing. Something about prolonging the opening of the box made her feel strong, powerful. Some women had eating disorders and wielded their control by not eating. Like Ruth. But Sylvia had willpower when it came to small things.

She thought about Tommy. A tingle of fearful exhilaration crept along her backbone at the idea of moving to LA. She was aware of it being a false, ruthless place, full of phony promises given by people with perfect smiles and wrinkle-free expressions. But there was also an artistic community, a plethora of fascinating individuals if you dug deep enough: yoga classes, hiking, all year-round barbeques, art openings. It could be a fun place for Grace, too, if they found the right neighborhood to move to and a friendly school. It was a fresh start for their family. Crowheart had been a beautiful experience but living there for the rest of her life, however stunning the countryside, filled her with dread.

Tommy. She had in her mind's eye his hard body, his firm stomach, ripped by chopping wood all winter, the soft down of the hair on the small of his back, the way his jeans hung from his slim hips, and the curves of his biceps. His eyes could still penetrate; just a look could send a double flip through her. Still. After all these years.

She took the showerhead and turned on the faucet again. She opened her pale thighs wide and let the water spray between them. She raised her hips and rubbed the metal head gently between her legs. She felt her pulse throbbing in her groin like a heartbeat, the water coursing and surging; small vibrations trembling, pounding. She held her breath and pressed herself against the head of it a touch harder. She gasped. It felt so . . . . ah . . . the water was coming hard at her like thousands of tiny pin drops of beating rain. She imagined Tommy and her ex, Lance. But it was only Tommy who had ever made her come, and Tommy she desired. She turned the pressure of the water up and flexed her hips, holding the snaking shower hose in one hand and with the other, slipping her index finger inside herself. She had an image of Tommy's erection poised at her entrance and heard his groans when he would thrust himself inside her. Sometimes if she moaned a lot, he'd really fuck her hard and she loved that—loved being claimed by him. Dominated. That's when she really let go of herself.

She could feel her own slick moistness now, despite the bath water. She hooked her finger inside her soft flesh and pressed it high up against her G-spot. Her eyelids were half-closed and her lips parted as she felt the tension build up. It was coming deep from within. She took her hand away and concentrated the spray between her legs again and felt the heat rise through her in a thunderous bolt. Such relief and ecstasy both ripped through her at once. It was almost a surprise it was so intense, so satisfying. It reminded her how badly she wanted Tommy and how she wouldn't give up on him. She needed him. Doing this alone just wasn't the same. She wanted his body pressed against her. She needed him inside her.

She wouldn't push him away anymore.

She lay there recuperating from the carnal after-shocks; closed her eyes and tried to meditate. But the sealed box was calling her name. She stood up in the tub—the suddenness of her movement, and the Sara Lee sugar-rush, caused blood to stream to her head; white stars and water dropped from her body like little diamonds. She stepped out, dried herself off slowly with one of her mother's soft, floor-length towels, put on her mom's flowery silk robe, and picked up the box. The scented soap on her skin mingled with its dank, old, bookish odor.

Finally, she succumbed. She needed something sharp to open it with, so took it with her downstairs, grabbed a knife from the kitchen, floated to the dining room—her robe flowing behind her—and set it on the table.

She ran the blade along the lip of duct tape which was sealing the shoebox as tight as a wetsuit.

Inside was a pile of letters, some photographs and a couple of children's paintings. Sylvia, careful not to shuffle the order, flipped through. They were all of the same person: a little black boy. The little boy playing a toy drum. The boy smiling at the camera, sitting high in a tree. Younger now, holding an ice-cream cone. That one was black and white.

Sylvia spread the letters out one by one, in order, on the table. There were ten. No dates and no postmarks, just hand-delivered envelopes with letters inside. Ten letters exactly, and ten photographs. Two paintings on paper, of airplanes. The last photo showed a boy of about nine or ten years old, dressed up in a military uniform. He was cute, debonair, his skin not dark but a pale caramel, similar to Grace's coloring. Jacqueline's son? But Jacqueline didn't have a son, Sylvia was positive, only daughters. Her nephew?

Sylvia picked up the very last letter in the pile. Beside it was a Polaroid, faded, the colors muted like a watercolor. The picture was of a young black woman holding a baby. She was pretty, with large brown eyes and a wide smile. The baby was wearing a little red cap.

Dear Mister Wilbur,

Please forgive me for not telling you before. I was fritened. I was scared that someone mite take my baby way from me. So I didn't say nuthing not to you not to nobody. I herd that you got marreed to Miss Debra and I send you my congratulatons. I did not plan for things to work out this way. I was hoping that I could mannage myself. I sure would be gratefull if you could help me money wise. I have a job but I need money for the baby. I promisse I wont say nuthing to nobody not Miss Debra not nobody. But pleeze help me. His name is Leroy.

Loretta

Not say anything? *Oh my God!*

Sylvia picked up the last letter in the sequence, which had the photo of the little boy in the soldier uniform attached to it with a paperclip.

Dear Mr. Mason,

You can see from the photograph what a handsome and strong little man LeRoy has become. This photo was taken on his tenth birthday! I am very proud of him. One day, he wants to be a soldier. I hope knowing he's your son too, makes you just as proud as me.

God bless you and your family.
Loretta

Leroy—or LeRoy—belonged to her father? Her dad *fathered* a little boy? Impossible. She would have known! That wasn't his style at all. He was so conservative. But then this obviously happened before he married her mother. How did he and Loretta meet? Sylvia held the two letters side by side. Ten years must have passed (one photo for every year?) and each one had its distinctive style of writing, the first of an uneducated teenager, the final one as if the writer was a completely different person. Yet both from this woman called Loretta. How could she have never heard about this woman? She, Sylvia, was now thirty-six years old! *How*, in all those thirty-six years, had this been held as a secret from her?

Did her *mother* know? God forbid, she didn't think so. She would be rolling in her grave now. Her upstanding husband, father of an African American child? No, her mother wouldn't have borne that for a second, nor the ladies at the country club. *Where had this box been all this time?* Sylvia had never seen it before, yet as a girl she'd sneaked into her parents' closets on a regular basis, rooting around for Santa's Christmas gifts, catching any loose change from her dad's suit pockets. Could this box have spent its life in the attic? Or the garage? Her mother didn't like the garage—at least she never spent time there. Her father did have his little workshop going on. *How could someone keep a secret for her entire life—for thirty-six goddamn years?*

Sylvia scanned the letters, running her eyes along them, the white paper framed against the dark of the French-polished mahogany table. When did the writing style start to change? She noticed one which was typed: letter number seven with its photo. This photo was the one with Leroy in a tree.

```
Dear Mr. Mason,

College is great. Thank you from the bottom of
my heart for giving me this opportunity. I am
learning a lot but it is tough! When I come
out I will have the skills to get a very good
paid job.
    Leroy is doing good. His grades are pretty
okay  at  school  and  he  has  lots  of  nice
friends.
    I still have not had the heart to tell him
bout you cos I want him to be happy with what
he got. If he sees your fancy house and fancy
car he could feel bad about himself. He still
thinks his Daddy died in 'Nam an that's what I
tell his teachers at school. I think it best
to keep to that old story.
Loretta
```

A frisson of both excitement and worry shot through the back of Sylvia's neck, the pale hairs on her arms erect. She had a half-brother who maybe still lived somewhere in Saginaw, at the other side of the river, perhaps, who had been told that his father had died in the Vietnam War. He must be about thirty-eight or forty by now. Her parents had been married a few years before she was born. Did anybody else know? Did Jacqueline know this Loretta lady? Was Loretta even still alive? Why did the letter stop at number ten, and the photo too? Why wasn't Leroy (or LeRoy as it was spelled in the most recent letter) provided for in her father's will? Where was he now?

And how on earth—with no last name to go on—was she going to find him?

12

Grace

Grace was howling, her little body heaving with sobs. Mrs. Paws was dead. The cat lay near the barn, the same barn where the blackbird's nest was. Poor Mrs. Paws had dried blood and foam in her mouth. Her sharp little pussycat teeth stuck out as if she was crying out in pain, covered with frothy spit. She was all stiff; her pure white fur no longer as soft as snow but matted and cold. Splotched red.

"Mrs. Paws is dead," wailed Grace. "Miss ... is Paaw ... Haws—"

Ruth walked up to Grace and cradled her arms around her shaking little body. She stroked her dark hair. "There you are! I was looking for you. Up so early this morning?"

Grace continued to wail, her breath hitching, swallowing great balloons of air.

"Baby, it's okay. It's okay baby, Mrs. Paws has gone to a better place."

Grace didn't understand how any place could be better than

this. Mrs. Paws had the perfect pussycat life! She was free and everybody loved her! "There is no Better Place for Mrs. Paws," she wept. "She loved living here. She loved her life!"

"When animals pass they go to a *special* place," Ruth soothed.

"You mean Heaven?" They'd spoken about Heaven at school and her mom said that Grandpa had gone to Heaven.

"No. Only humans go to Heaven," Ruth replied quietly. "Animals go to a 'special' place. Anyway, now those blackbirds are safe from being killed by that cat. Don't you see that's better?"

Grace's skinny arms clung to Ruth, her hands clutching the material of the flowery dress that was just the same as her mom's. She gulped another mouthful of air and said, "Maybe Mrs. Paws didn't like the tonic water. You said you had just the tonic for her."

"No, baby," Ruth reasoned in a gentle voice, "I think a coyote killed Mrs. Paws in the night."

"We need to tell Mrs. Paws's mommy. She lives over the hill in the big white house."

"Okay, baby, I'll call her later."

"We can give Mrs. Paws a funeral." Her mom had explained about her grandpa's funeral.

"No, baby, animals don't have funerals."

"Why not?"

"Because a funeral is when you say goodbye to somebody who has passed away, like your grandfather."

Grace furrowed her brow. That Pass word again. Pass Away. Her mom had taught her how to pass the bread at dinner, or the salt. She said it was Good Manners. Like saying Please or Thank You. What did Pass Away mean?

"Has Mrs. Paws passed away?"

"Yes baby, Mrs. Paws has passed away."

"Then why don't we get to give her a funeral, to say goodbye?"

"Like I said, animals don't have funerals, baby. I'll just chuck it in the trash."

Grace's tiny body began to tremble again and tears gushed from her large eyes. "I want for us to give Mrs. Paws a funeral! I want to say goodbye!"

"Okay, okay, we'll give it a funeral," Ruth mumbled. "But we need to hurry." She drew Grace close to her and kissed her on the head.

GRACE HAD HER knees tucked up under her and she was sitting on her bed thinking about Heaven. She pressed the pocket clip on her magic pen to start recording:

"We buried Mrs. Paws. Auntie Ruth dug a little hole and I said a prayer. Not a real Jesus prayer but a song I made up. We put her under the big oak tree at the end of the garden. I cried a lot.

Auntie Ruth says she's going to buy me a swimsuit. Maybe a white one, with pink flowers. My favorite color! She says we'll be going swimming but Mommy didn't say anything about swimming.

Right now Auntie Ruth is downstairs and very busy. She has made lots of Skype calls on her laptop. She sounded very serious but she was not talking to Mom. She said she had business calls to make and asked me to play in my room. She spent a lot of time looking in Mommy's filing cabinet. She has everything out on the floor and was putting papers into piles. She told me that she was Orgon Izing as a special surprise for Mommy. Wait. Hold on, Auntie Ruth is calling me."

Grace clicked the pocket clip back up to stop recording.

"Grace? Grace, baby, who are you talking to?"

Grace heard the footsteps come into the room. She quickly shoved the pen under her bedclothes. The iPad—which she made

96

paintings with—was on the bed, open. She couldn't decide which she preferred. The iPad was more grown-up but the pen was so secret, she felt like a police detective when she used it.

Ruth entered the bedroom and glanced about. She had foam in her hair, piled high on her head like a lathered-up helmet. "Hi, baby. To whom were you talking?"

"My teddy bears," Grace lied.

"Okay. Cute. Who is your favorite bear?"

"Pidgey O Dollars," she lied again. She really wanted to say, "Blueby." She could wind Blueby up by a key on his heinie and he'd play the tune: "When Teddy Bears Have Their Picnics." He was her number one teddy since Pidgey's accident with the Jack Russell. But she owed it to Pidgey O Dollars to love him the most.

"Will you be taking Piggy O Dollars with you to Saginaw?"

She giggled as if Ruth had said the silliest thing in the world. "Not Piggy . . . *Pidgey.*"

"I thought it would be a good idea to get your packing done early. You know, so your dad doesn't have to worry. Do we need to pack Pidgey?"

"I guess."

"But I think we should leave Daddy's iPad home, don't you, baby? I saw you playing with it earlier."

"No. I need his iPad because I can do my drawings and paintings and I have 22 storybooks in my library."

Ruth narrowed her eyes. "But doesn't it have a Wi-Fi connection?"

"I don't know."

"Can you connect with the outside world?" asked Ruth. "Can you Skype or phone?"

"No, that part of it's broken. That's why Daddy got a new one and gave me this old one. I just use it for painting. Look, do you want to see?" Grace took the iPad from the bed, opened it up and showed her a painting of Mrs. Paws when she was still alive. "See?"

"I do not understand any of it, baby, but you're quite an artist I can tell."

"Yes, I am. I love painting. Mommy says it's not the same as real paint, but I like it."

Ruth pointed to the set of pictures in Grace's bedroom: twenty-six individual canvasses with an animal for each letter. "Who did the alphabet paintings on the wall?"

"My Mom. *A* for Aardvark is my favorite. But she cheated with *X*. She didn't know an animal beginning with *X* so she did an ox, making a big deal of the *X*. See, it says o*X*."

"Your mom's very talented. Did she paint them in oil?"

"Uh-huh, I guess so. Why is your head all foamy?"

"I thought I'd change the color of my hair."

"What color?"

"A kind of pale blond."

"Like Mommy's?"

"Yes, baby. Exactly like your mommy's."

13

Sylvia

Knowing that Tommy was going to be bringing Grace to Saginaw in a few days gave Sylvia a serene feeling of comfort. Being without her child made her feel the same way she did when she turned up to a party one time without a fancy dress costume. Everyone was dressed up except for her, and she felt lost.

As she brushed her teeth, she shifted her memory back to the stark, motherless days, the Before Grace days, after she and Tommy had decided to start a family but nothing happened. Making love to Tommy with a child as her goal hadn't done their sex life any favors; the desperation that ensued, the longing and the aching feeling that somehow, she had failed. Becoming pregnant became an obsession, and it took a long time to surrender herself to the fact that it just wasn't meant to be. The doctors offered no explanation. Technically, everything was in working order for both of them. Tommy's sperm-count was unusually high. *Yet everything happens for a reason.* Grace was a gift from God and Sylvia thanked Him (Her?)

every day that she hadn't gotten pregnant.

She heard her cell go and raced into the bedroom. It was Tommy.

She heard him suck in a long breath. Uh oh, something was wrong.

"Is everything alright? You're at home, right?"

"I missed the fucking plane."

He spent the next five minutes explaining that he'd be arriving late that afternoon, and going into details about the drama of his driving fine, and excusing himself. The shitty policeman and so on, how it was a terrible injustice, blah, blah, blah. As if she hadn't warned him a zillion times that he must never, ever speak on his cell while driving without his headset.

"I mean what if you'd had an accident and killed someone? Someone like Grace," Sylvia said, with toothpaste still in her mouth.

"You don't need to rub it in that I've been an idiot," Tommy replied with a groan. "I always use my Bluetooth headset but it was in my jacket pocket in the trunk. So yes, I fucked up."

"Ugh," Sylvia growled, and hung up. She didn't have time to argue. She called Ruth.

Ruth was jolly and unfazed. Her cheery voice a delight in the middle of their matrimonial strife.

"No problem at all," Ruth said happily when Sylvia double-checked that she could pick him up from the airport. "Tommy texted last night so I already knew he'd missed his plane."

"So did you take Gracie to school? What time is it anyway?"

"Just leaving now," Ruth said.

"Can you put her on the line?"

"Sure."

"Hi Mommy."

"Hi sweetie, are you having fun with Ruth?"

"Uh-huh."

"Daddy will be home later—you and Ruth are going to pick

him up from the airport after school. Then you'll be coming to Saginaw to see me in a couple of days' time. I'm so excited."

"Me too. Can I bring Pidgey and Blueby and Carrot to Saginaw?"

"Sure, sweetie. But maybe just choose two teddies. Three's too many."

"Okay. Mommy, Mrs. Paws—"

There was a shuffle and Ruth came on the line. "Sorry, Sylvia, I know Gracie wants to chat but we'd better get going; we're running really, *really* late for school. Everything okay?"

"Well, you know."

"Gracie misses you. I'll get her to Skype you tonight. Gotta go."

"Thanks, Ruth—we'll speak later. Bye."

THE MORNING SAW a clear blue sky, crisp, and the air light without any humidity. Sylvia got behind her the worst chore of the day. The funeral director was a kind man, full of ideas, so calm as if dead bodies were quite "by the by," nothing to be phased about at all. So seeing her father had been less of a shock than Sylvia imagined. The director could organize simply everything and she found herself nodding at whatever he suggested. What a relief.

She said she would find the perfect suit for her dad, and raid his library for the right poem. Wasn't Walt Whitman his favorite poet? She'd look and see who dominated the bookshelves.

It made her regret the times when her dad would chat at dinner and she, with her thoughts on school or cheerleading practice would cock an ear and say, "ah, ah, oh really Daddy, that's great." She longed now for just one snippet of their past conversations, more clues about who her father really was—other than her daddy and a husband to her mother. He'd spend hours reading, writing letters and pontificating about golf and Greek philosophers. It seemed dull to her at the time. Why hadn't she asked more questions, dug deep inside his soul?

Sylvia had a good hour before she needed to set off in the car again to see the accountant and the lawyer. She wasn't driving around in the Mustang, though. The Buick was far more reliable. She'd "been there, done that." The countless times she could recall sitting on the sidewalk waiting for a tow truck or her dad to come and rescue her while the old Mustang spouted steam, overheated, panting like an old dog who wanted nothing more than to just lie down and get her breath back. There she still was, the loyal thing, waiting in the garage with a dust cloth spread over her, perhaps hoping for a trip to the log cabin in Elk Lake where they spent their summer vacations when Sylvia was a girl. After the funeral, Sylvia could take Grace there and maybe, instead of flying back to Crowheart, they could drive cross-country. It was crazy, but the real truth was that Sylvia had never seen the Grand Canyon and she'd like to experience it for the first time with Grace—see that majestic place through the eyes of a child. Her child. Grace had a way of making everything brighter, bringing magic to the way a bird jerked its head or a tree's leaves shuffled in the wind. She noticed the tiniest details and had an opinion about everything.

Yes, it was important that Grace should see America's shining star. You couldn't call yourself a real citizen until you'd seen the wide belly of the whole country; the mundane, the magnificent, the vast fields of wheat, the great skies that yawned into an immense horizon, and the roads which glittered like arteries through the Giant that was this great nation. Sylvia loved America. It throbbed through her veins.

She and Tommy had driven via the northern route through Wisconsin and South Dakota before they arrived at Wyoming and discovered Crowheart. She remembered being transfixed by the Badlands. The earth looked like mini mountains, but was actually mounds of dried mud, ringed with striped rainbows of orange, red and gold. They drove through the Black Hills where they saw bears and the presidents' heads carved into the rock at Mount Rushmore. That was before Grace. Before Amazing Grace came into their lives. Sylvia shuddered with anticipation—she couldn't wait to hear her daughter's thoughts on the Grand Canyon, read her expressions, see the awe on her pretty little face.

14

Grace

A cool morning breeze wafted through the linen curtains. Bubbling with excitement, Grace jumped up and down on her bed, leaped off and skipped around her bedroom. Ruth was packing Pidgey O Dollars and Carrot into her Disney Princess backpack. She needed Carrot because she could hide her magic pen there, and Pidgey... well... poor, poor Pidgey—he only had one arm. He needed her. And as she could only choose two, Blueby would have to stay behind.

Ruth's blond hair made her look really different. So much prettier. She almost looked like her mother now! Well not really... her mom had a smaller nose and a softer face (when she wasn't wearing her Wolfy Face) and beautiful blue eyes with long, black eyelashes. Sometimes her mom gave her an Eskimo kiss with those lashes. Grace loved that. It tickled. Yup, her mom had to be the most beautiful lady in the whole wide world.

Ruth whispered, "Hi baby, are you sure you've chosen your two favorite teddies?"

"Uh-huh."

"Because I don't want you thinking later that you wished you'd chosen a different one. Make sure you don't leave someone special behind. Are we all ready, then?" Ruth zipped up Grace's Disney Princess backpack and lifted it from the bed. Then she closed the window shut.

"But we don't need to bring my backpack to school." Grace said.

"I thought we'd just put it in the car. So it's done, you know."

"But it's dark inside the backpack and my teddies might get scared."

Ruth stood with her hands on her hips. "Okay, I was hoping it would be a surprise, but I guess I need to let you know." She smoothed her bony hands over Grace's butterfly dress to pull out the wrinkles. Grace noticed that she had sticking out blue veins, like rivers on the back of her hands. "Today, as a special treat, no school," Ruth said with a huge smile.

"But I *like* school."

"While you were chatting to your teddies earlier, I had another talk with your mom. And I called your teachers at school so they know you aren't coming. I'm taking you to Saginaw today, instead! Isn't that exciting? We're getting on a plane!"

"What about Daddy? Is he coming too?"

"We're meeting your daddy at the airport and we're all traveling together."

"That's not what Mommy told me."

Ruth gripped Grace's hand and pulled her out of the bedroom. "Because plans have *changed*, sweetie. Wouldn't you rather see your mom than go to boring old school?"

Grace nodded. "Can I bring my red sparkly Dorothy shoes?"

Ruth stood still for a second, cocked her head and thought about this carefully. Then she answered, "No, baby, I wish you could, but I think they might draw a little too much attention."

"They can draw? Are they magic?"

"No, they can't, but if you want to see true magic I'm going to make something *super* magical happen. Just you wait and see."

RUTH STRAPPED GRACE into her car seat of the SUV, opened her door, adjusted her own seat and the rearview mirror, and started the engine.

The car drove off with a squeal and Grace looked out the window, watching Crowheart get smaller and smaller, and wondered if Mrs. Paws would be feeling cold underground, or if she had already arrived in Heaven.

"Oh, by the way, baby. Just one thing," Ruth said. "Just for the plane trip, I don't want you to call me Auntie Ruth anymore."

Grace shuffled her little body into a more comfortable position. "But you said! You said to call you Auntie."

"Yes, baby. But now, just for the plane trip, I want us to play a little game. I want you to pretend that you're my little girl. I want you to call me Mommy."

"But I have a mommy!" Grace's eyes welled up with tears.

"Of course you do, baby. But just for fun. Just for fun, you can call me Mommy."

"Why? I have my *own* mommy!"

Ruth looked into the rearview mirror and spoke to it. "You are sooo cute, do you know that? You're as cute as a *button*."

Grace thought of Pidgey O Dollars's new, blue, glassy eyes that were buttons, and of the buttons on her dresses. She didn't think buttons were so cute.

"Baby," Ruth continued, still staring in the mirror, "I want you to do this for me, it's important. I want you to call me Mommy for the plane trip."

"But *why?*"

"Because there are some really big, bad, Bogeymen out there.

They are dangerous. If they think I'm just your auntie they might not take me seriously enough and they could take you away. But if I'm your *mommy* then I can protect you."

"But I *have* a mommy." Grace thought Ruth's smile looked like the Joker in *Batman*. Her dad had let her watch *Batman* one time, although her mom said it was too grown-up for her. She got to see the scary Joker, anyway, before her mom changed the channel. His smile didn't move. Just like Auntie Ruth's now.

"Okay, baby, I have an idea. How about if you call me Mama? Not Mommy but *Mama*? That could work. Then you can have *two* mommies."

Grace crumpled her forehead. "I don't know."

"If you call me Mama then I can buy you a really pretty gift when we arrive. But you have to call me Mama for the whole plane trip. And also when we're at the hotel tonight. Can you do that for me?"

"What hotel?"

"We have to change planes twice, so you need to be a very good girl. We'll be spending the night in Chicago and then arriving in Saginaw the day after, and your mom's coming to pick us up at the airport."

"Where's Chick Ah Go? Do they have baby birds there?"

Ruth laughed. "It's a city, baby. Remember, if you behave really nicely and do as I say, I'll buy you a beautiful gift."

This sounded to Grace like an okay deal. "What gift will you get me?"

Ruth changed gear, taking the bend in the road a little faster. "Whatever you want, baby. Anything at all."

"The Computer Engineer Barbie Doll?"

"Sure."

"Okay."

"Good girl. You promise to call me Mama, then?"

"Okay.

15

Grace

There were no chicks in Chick Ah Go.

Nobody had warned Grace that they'd be speaking Spanish here. She could hardly understand a word—they were gabbling so fast, but she knew it was Spanish because they talked like her old Mexican Oh Pear. Even Auntie Ruth (oops, Mama) was speaking funny. Grace had slept most of the journey. They had to change planes. They had another long flight and were now at the next stop. When she woke up everything was very different from home, even the smell. It was hot.

Grace had been crying for her mom, and her dad. Ruth told her that he had gone to Saginaw instead, and that they would see him there. Plans kept changing every five minutes. Ruth said one thing, and then something else.

It just wasn't fair.

She held Pidgey O Dollars close to her heart and then pressed her cheek against the new part of his face, the clean, white, plastic surgery part. She thought about how much she loved him for real.

He understood everything. Maybe *he* knew what people were saying.

"Auntie . . . Mama, why are you speaking funny?"

"Because baby, the plane was sent to a different place."

"Where are we?"

"A different place, that's all."

"How come we're not in Chick Ah Go?'"

"Because. But be a good girl and don't ask any more questions. Mama needs to concentrate." Ruth was wheeling a carry-on, looking up at the television screens. Her eyes had changed color since that morning. Like magic. They were now blue. She looked weird.

Grace clutched her little pink backpack with wheels, trailing it behind her like a pink tail. Ruth told Grace they needed to move quickly, "as quick as deer," she explained. But she was wearing high heels and a big cowboy hat so she didn't move like a deer at all. Grace looked at other people who had bigger suitcases, with white tags stuck around the handles which said *MEX*. Were they all going to Saginaw, too?

"Come on baby, don't dawdle, we have to be snappy, we have another plane to catch."

Grace rolled her eyes. "But I'm tired. You said we were staying in a hotel in Chick—

"Please hush-up already about that! I told you we are going via a different route. Hold my hand, hurry up now, don't drag your feet."

The journey through the airport was endless, on and on it went like the inside of a snake. Turn left, turn right, straight on. Grace was hungry. She heard her tummy rumble. She wanted her mom. And her daddy.

"Look, this is taking forever, I'm going to carry you. Damn this goddamn princess backpack." Ruth hoisted Grace onto her right hip and battled with the two pieces of luggage with her left hand, elbow and knees.

Grace didn't understand why they had to hurry, only to wait in a long line five minutes later. A man in uniform took their passports. He looked at them carefully.

"That's Mommy! That's a picture of Mommy!" Grace shouted, pointing at one of the passports.

"That's right, baby. That's *me*." Ruth cackled. "That's Mommy."

Grace stamped her foot. "But that's *Mommy*!"

The man handed the passports back and said something Grace didn't understand. Then he smiled.

Ruth took her by her skinny, upper arm. It pinched. "Now look!" she whispered in a hiss, "remember what I told you about the Bogeymen? There are a lot, all dressed up in normal clothes but they are *everywhere*. *They are watching*. Even the walls have eyes. Now be a good girl and don't say a word."

Ruth was wearing her Joker Face again. She had on a huge smile but her voice was *mean*. Then Grace noticed that the people ahead of her in line started taking off their jackets. Were the Bogeymen making them take off their clothing? They were removing their belts and shoes, undressing in front of each other! They put keys and money and laptops into big plastic dishes. Did they have to give away their laptops and the keys to their houses to the Bogeymen? Would they find her secret pen hidden inside Carrot? Would they want to take it away from her? Tears filled her amber eyes and slid like raindrops down her cheeks. She watched and waited while the Bogeymen felt the people up and down all over their bodies with big, black-gloved hands. There were Bogey Women too, touching the ladies. She wondered if that part was going to tickle.

It didn't tickle.

But it sure was scary.

In the end, they didn't find her pen. They didn't even open her backpack. But now she had to look out for the walls that had invisible eyes.

Watching her.

Waiting silently.

16

Grace

Mama Ruth was wearing the high heels again. Grace watched her from her bed in the strange-smelling hotel that had ugly brown and yellow curtains. Ruth was putting on make-up, smacking her lips as she looked at herself in the mirror, her glassy blue eyes glinting back at her. That must have been the magic trick she'd talked about—changing the color of her eyes.

Grace wondered if they had arrived in Saginaw yet. Sometimes, if the family went out in the evening, her mom would carry her from the car directly to bed and she'd wake up the next morning, not knowing how she got there. But it was Mama Ruth who had carried her to bed, not her mommy. And she remembered that it wasn't even night time. They'd arrived in the afternoon and she took a nap straight away.

Now Mama Ruth was brushing her newly blond hair. She was looking at her mom's passport picture, smoothing her hair at the same time. Then she put on the big straw cowboy hat.

"Why do you have Mommy's passport?"

"Hi baby. Did you have a good siesta?"

Grace yawned. "Uh-huh. But it smells in here."

"I know, baby, it's a bit funky, but we're leaving straight away. We're just here so you could take a nap and I could get changed."

"Are we in Saginaw?"

"Not yet, baby. I *told* you we got delayed. We won't be there until tomorrow."

"But you promised."

"It's not my fault, Grace baby. There was a problem with the aircraft and so they sent us a long way round."

Grace hated the word "baby." She wasn't a baby, she was five and three-quarters. Well, almost. "Does Mommy know?"

"Of course she does. I spoke to her while you were asleep. She sends you a big hug. She's very busy right now. She knows we've been delayed."

"What's Dee Layed?"

"When things take a long time."

"I want to speak to Mommy. Let's call her."

"I told you, she's busy."

"My mom always has time to speak to me."

"She told me to send you a big hug but she really does *not* have time right now. Now let's get you dressed as we have to get to the bank before it closes. We need to hurry. Are you hungry?"

"Uh-huh." Grace thought about how they were always hurrying. But they still weren't in Saginaw yet. Hurry, hurry, hurry, but they were late anyway. Ruth strutted uneasily toward her.

"Why are your eyes blue now? Why are you wearing high heels?"

"Because I need to be a little taller. Now come on, Grace, let's get you dressed. We have to go."

"What time is it?"

"It's later than it needs to be. We *must* be at the bank soon."

"Why do you have my mom's passport?"

"Because, baby, she left it behind and asked me to bring it."

"So you get to use it?"

"That's right. Your mommy said I could use it."

"Is that why you changed the color of your hair and your eyes so you could look like her?"

"Too many questions, young lady. Come on. Up!" She grabbed the butterfly dress that was slung over a chair, yanked off the T-shirt that Grace had worn to bed, and pulled the dress roughly over her head.

Grace battled with the dress. "Ouch! That hurts."

"Hurry up, don't dawdle."

"I don't want to wear the same dress I wore on the plane!"

"Come on, don't argue. Quick! We haven't got all day."

"Can I bring Pidgey with me?"

"Okay, but let's get a move on."

THE BANK WAS BORING. Mama Ruth spent a long time signing papers and talking to a fat man with a moustache, her Joker smile fixed on her face. Then they counted out money. A lot, lot, lot of money. Once, Grace remembered, she had played a game called *Monopoly* with her parents and her Auntie Melinda. But the money at this bank was real. It was dollar money. Ruth had a bag around her waist and another around her neck. She stuffed the money inside the pouches and the rest in her purse. She shook hands with the man. The whole time she spoke Spanish. Grace kept hearing them say the words, *Gwat a Maala*. Gwat a Mala this, and Gwat a Mala that. Who *was* Gwat a Mala?

After the bank, they went to have lunch. But the food was funny, so Grace just chose a Bun Weylo, as Ruth called it. It was a bit like a doughnut but served with hot, cinnamon syrup. Ruth had a taco with avocado inside and melted cheese. Mama Ruth was eating with her hands. Auntie Melinda had told Grace it was not polite to eat with your hands but Ruth said it was okay and the way things were done in this country.

"So where are we?" Grace asked. "What country?" She had never been to a "country" before. Except for India, where she came from. Oh yes, and England once. But she couldn't remember that so well.

"In South America, baby." Mama Ruth was smiling and happy. Really happy, not just Joker Face happy. She took off the high heels and said, "Well, I won't be needing *these* anymore." Then she took off her cowboy hat. "Or this."

She put on some flip-flops.

Grace watched her open up her cell phone; take out a chip inside which she dropped to the ground. On purpose. Then Ruth rubbed her eyes, played around with them, popping up the eyelids so you could see the whites inside and the bloody pink bits like a scary ghost. And like magic, her eyes were back to their old poop color again! Then she waved her arms at the waiter, grinning. Like a crocodile, Grace thought. Ruth asked for something and five minutes later a bubbly drink appeared.

"Oh Gracie, I'm so, so happy! We're going to have a lot of fun from now on."

"Because you have lots of money?"

"Well yes, that's part of it."

"And what's the other part?"

"Because, baby, *you* are with me. And we're going to be a team!"

"Like in baseball?" Grace asked seriously.

"Something like that." Ruth flung her arms around Grace, picked her up and, placing her on her lap said, "You are the cutest, most adorable little girl in the world. And I am the luckiest Mama!"

"You're not my real mommy, though. And why aren't we in Saginaw? You said—"

"All in good time, baby."

"Can I taste your drink, then?"

"No, baby, it's for grown-ups. But when you're sixteen I'll let you try a glass." She finished her bubbly drink and smacked her lips the way she had earlier when she put the lipstick on. "Now, baby, we need to go and get one more thing before going back to the hotel."

"But you said we were *leaving* that smelly hotel!"

"We are, but I need to go to the store and buy some hair color, use the bathroom at the hotel to do my hair, change what you're wearing and then, guess what?"

Grace pouted. "But you just *changed* your hair!"

"I know, *mi amor*. But I think I should go back to my natural color. That way, you and I will look just alike. People will think I'm your real mommy."

Grace felt hot and prickly. Her long lashes sprang damp with tears. "But I *have* a real mommy."

"Oh baby." Ruth kissed her eyes and stroked her forehead. "Don't you see how great everything's going to be? You and me together like a little dark-haired team? We have the same colored eyes, almost the same kind of skin, especially if I get a tan. Which I'm planning to by the way. I thought you and I could go to the beach for a while. Would you like to wear your new pink swimsuit I bought you at the airport, and play on the beach?"

"What about Mommy?"

"I *told* you, she's very busy right now. She loves you very much but she has a lot to do."

"I want my daddy."

"Daddy's delayed. And busy too. We'll see him soon."

Grace looked down at her half-eaten buñuelo, the thick spicy syrup swimming on the plate. It wasn't fair. None of it was fair. Her throat felt all lumpy.

"Don't cry baby. Don't you see how much I love you? I have a big surprise."

Grace looked up. Maybe her dad wouldn't be so busy and he could come and fetch her.

Ruth's eyes opened wide. "We're going on a bus!"

Grace didn't see what was so great about going on a bus.

"A chicken bus! All brightly painted in different colors. And you'll see how the locals put their *animals* on the bus. Chickens, sometimes pigs, too. Isn't that exciting?"

"I guess so."

"You see, baby, we're free to go anywhere we like. Any country."

"By plane?" Grace wondered about Saginaw.

"No, baby. No more plane trips. Just buses from now on."

"Does the bus go to Saginaw?"

Ruth stared at her. She had her Joker Face on again.

17

Tommy

Tommy had been prowling about the airport for the best part of forty minutes. Ruth and Grace were nowhere to be seen. He'd called Ruth's cell several times already. No longer in working order? What the fuck? He called Grace's schoolteacher.

"Hi, Mrs. Pitt?"

"This is she," the teacher answered.

"It's Tommy Garland here, Grace's dad. I wondered what time Grace left school today? What time my wife's friend Ruth came to collect her?"

The teacher cleared her throat. "But Mrs. Garland called this morning and told us Grace had the flu, that she wouldn't be coming in today."

"No, there must be some mistake. My wife definitely told me that Ruth would be picking me up from the airport after Grace's school. Unless . . . what time did my wife call?"

"Around nine-thirty this morning."

"Oh, okay. Wish she'd told me. Thanks. Bye."

Not like Sylvia at all to not keep him up to date about Grace.

But that didn't explain why Ruth wasn't picking up her cell, nor why nobody was answering the landline at Crowheart. He called his wife.

"Hi, Tommy, I'm at the funeral parlor, so be quick," Sylvia said.

"Why didn't you tell me you called Grace's school to call in sick? I've been waiting here at the airport for ages. I would have just got Gus to pick me up."

Sylvie's voice pitched up an octave. "I never called her school. Called in sick? What's wrong? Is Gracie ill?"

"Nobody's answering at home, and Ruth's cell is out of order, no longer in service. I spoke to Mrs. Pitt. She said you called."

"*What?*" Sylvia shouted.

"Mrs. Pitt said you called. She clearly said 'Mrs. Garland.' "

"But this is crazy! I'm going to hang up and call Mrs. Pitt and hope she answers."

Tommy went outside to get some fresh air. A feeling of doom coiled in his gut. That bloody cop stopping him. He, Tommy, fucking up. He'd done a lot of that lately. He raised his eyes to the sky. An afternoon sun warmed his skin, and just a faint breeze rustled his blond hair. He looked into the distance, scanning the horizon. There were a few small planes in this regional airport and just a handful of cars . . .

Fucking Hell!

Their car! There it was. Parked next to a truck. He hadn't noticed it, forty minutes before, when he had stood outside the airport door. He raced up to it just to make sure he wasn't having visions.

Their car was sloppily parked. But Grace and Ruth were nowhere to be seen.

And that's when Tommy knew that this was just the beginning . . .

The beginning of a full-on nightmare.

18

Sylvia

S ylvia felt as if she were looking at an actor on stage, hearing and seeing somebody else, yet she, herself, was the player. There was no script, no words to learn by heart, it was improvisation all the way—the unexpected had twisted her world into tragedy. She had seen movies where this sort of thing happened, occasionally read a story in a newspaper, or seen it on the news, but to be living the nightmare herself, ensnared in her own body as it heaved and shook, speaking through lips that coiled into a tight screw, spitting out words, moaning and swallowing vowels, gasping for air as she sobbed uncontrollably, trying to assimilate the truth of what had happened to Grace. To her. To Tommy. To everyone who loved them.

But there was still hope and she clung to it like a rock climber on an overhang. *She would find Grace.* What seemed impossible *could* be possible. If she didn't believe that, why bother living? She had to muster faith from every cell in her body. Believe that Ruth would slip up with her crazy plan, or her daughter—even at her young age—would find help.

Somehow.

THE LAST FORTY-EIGHT hours had been lost in a void of phone calls and meetings with police and the FBI. Strangely enough, it was when the money was stolen that the authorities pledged their attention—when the penny dropped that Ruth was the criminal, and that Ruth, not Sylvia or Tommy, had kidnapped Grace. At one point, Sylvia was being cross-questioned. Good cop, bad cop. She couldn't believe it was happening—a suspect of her own misfortune. Was she certain, they asked, that she hadn't taken Grace *herself* to Guatemala? Caught the plane from Wyoming to Denver, changed planes for a flight to Mexico and then another to Guatemala, all in the same day? After all, a woman called Sylvia Garland had gone through passport security three times with her very own passport. She even had a signed parental consent form from Tommy, giving her permission to travel with her daughter alone. With parents divorcing and battling over child custody these days, and with kidnapping, foreign borders were getting strict.

Sylvia couldn't believe how conniving and thorough Ruth had been. She'd thought of *everything*. Forged signatures, called Grace's schoolteacher, imitating Sylvia's voice. How anyone like Ruth could operate was an enigma to her, but that Sylvia had trusted her so wholeheartedly? That was the worst of all.

Was Sylvia in no doubt, the authorities grilled, that the woman traveling with Grace Garland wasn't Sylvia, herself? Because using someone else's passport was a felony, major fraud, and with security as tight as it was, how could anybody pull that off? *Was she sure that she wasn't just a stressed-out parent having problems?* Problems with her husband who had left her to go to Los Angeles, because he was seeing someone else, perhaps? Maybe the fact that her husband had gone off, leaving Sylvia all alone with her daughter—a woman alone who couldn't cope anymore—had pushed her over the edge? Perhaps, they said, Sylvia felt a need to rid herself of her own child? Because who *was* Ruth Steel? She didn't exist. No Ruth Steel had gone to Yale, nor Harvard Law School. They checked records. Ruth Steel, they said, wasn't a real person. At least, not the same Ruth Steel that Sylvia described.

It was Ruth's Facebook page that finally convinced the authorities, and the e-mails she had sent Sylvia the year before. That was before they realized that the bank balance on Sylvia's joint account with her late father showed a credit of $5. Cleaned out in one fell swoop, like an eagle diving down on a field mouse. Two hundred and forty-seven thousand dollars swallowed in one single withdrawal, done the very same afternoon Ruth and Grace arrived in Guatemala.

Ruth's Facebook page was the only one Sylvia had ever come across where the list of friends couldn't be viewed. She hoped she might find a clue about who Ruth was, but not one single friend could be clicked on because *there was no list of friends in the first place!* She looked at the trickster's page again, tears streaming down her face. The page she helped Ruth set up earlier that week! There they all were: the lies of Ruth Steel: Yale, Harvard Business School.

And her updates—stopping the day she took Grace away.

They made Sylvia sick:

Ruth Steel

16 May

We're off to see the wizard, the wonderful wizard of Oz . . . (sadly without Dorothy's red shoes)

Like • Comment • Share

———————————

Ruth Steel

16 May

Oh Happy, happy, happy days!

Like • Comment • Share

_____

Ruth Steel

15 May

Finally realized my purpose in life

Like • Comment • Share

_____

Ruth Steel

15 May

Loving my role as Mom

Like • Comment • Share

_____

Ruth Steel

15 May

Falling in love with a child is beguiling but beautiful

Like • Comment • Share

_____

Ruth Steel

14 May

"Baking" mud pies with my little angel

Like • Comment • Share

_____

Ruth Steel

14 May

Grace is 42" of Heaven

Like • Comment • Share

———————————

Ruth Steel

13 May

Getting a ton of writing done

Like • Comment • Share

———————————

Ruth Steel

12 May

Just love being in the countryside

Like • Comment • Share

———————————

Sylvia conjured up images of saints and gurus who were said to radiate an aura of light around them. Sylvia's own aura was Guilt, dark like a mud-cloud, wrapped about her like a second skin. She could smell it. She could taste it. She wore Guilt to bed, breathed through it, feeling it tighten around her throat, letting her off for snatches of moments. Minutes, seconds, here or there. Beautiful flashes of Grace; laughing, playing on a swing, painting a picture, eating apple pie. And then Sylvia would wake again—back into the black void, the abyss—falling, falling, with nobody to catch her.

Tommy had stopped by their house in Crowheart before he hopped on a plane to Saginaw. Everything that mattered had been taken from the filing cabinet. Grace's adoption and medical papers, passwords, bank statements, birth certificates (both British and American). The lot.

On top of her skin-crawling guilt, Sylvia wore an invisible cloak that was embroidered all over, with the words, *STUPID FOOL.* How had she been such an idiot, so trusting of a virtual stranger? As if Grace were a chip to gamble with in a game of roulette. She did not know Ruth and never had. All those Skype calls and e-mails, and even hanging out together, told her nothing. If only she'd paid more attention to each conversation! How could a woman date a man who had shot a tiger? How could *she*, Sylvia, not have taken that clue as evidence as to the kind of person Ruth was?

She gleaned through the e-mails again, the only ones she had left—the ones she had never erased. For the sixth time that day, she reread for clues. Who *was* this woman?

Hi Sylvia,

Like a teenager at school waiting for my exam results and wondering if I've passed, I'm awaiting the results of my latest blood test at the clinic. I'm shaking with anticipation waiting to see if my three follicles are mature enough for collection. The Doctor is confident that collection will be later this afternoon but needs to double-check my hormone levels: LH, E2, and P4. So, I'm feeling extremely nervous as you can well imagine!

The risk lies in waiting until full maturity in case I ovulate spontaneously and then all those precious eggs could be lost. Help!!

Collection is really uncomfortable and I'll be pooped afterwards.

There are all sorts of characters here. As you can imagine, at forty-six, I am the oldest woman in our little coterie. Nobody can believe my age, they all think I look so much younger. There is a lovely lesbian couple, both with donors, and a Mexican socialite whose father owns half of Mexico and is very powerful! We have become great friends. We all take care of

each other when we can.

My relationship with Jeff is going through the wringer – he is threatening to break up with me because he found my morning pages and read stuff I'd written about his kids. Well, his children are, I have to be honest, not my cup of tea – to put it politely! He believed it was my diary . . . . why couldn't he see the difference? Morning pages are a stream of consciousness – how can I be held responsible for my first thoughts of the day?

He's extremely wounded and angry. Being quite cruel to me.

I've decided that I'll have my baby, with or without Jeff. I can get a donor. Maybe I'll even stay on in Mexico, after all, I speak fluent Spanish – it feels like home. Or maybe I can go to Brazil and bring up my baby there. I grew up there. Write, live an inexpensive existence. We'll see. I'm feeling very emotional, crying a lot, but that's to be expected with the drugs et cetera.

How are things with you? Still busy with your script?

I send you and Tommy a big hug. Let's Skype soon.

Xoxo, R

P.S If you were to describe me in one sentence what would you say?

Sylvia reread the clues. Fluent Spanish. Lived in Brazil, which meant she was also fluent in Portuguese.

Mexico, Brazil.

Would Ruth return to Mexico? Assume the police would imagine that she wouldn't be foolish enough to do so? She obviously had an influential contact there—the socialite with the rich father.

The FBI had already contacted the clinic in Guadalajara. But there was the problem of patient confidentiality. Another country outside US jurisdiction. It wasn't easy to force them to hand over information. They had never treated a Ruth Steel, they said. What were they meant to do? they protested. Hand over information for every single one of their patients? Finally, they did comply. They had a Ruth Vargas, forty-six years old, but even when they did forward her contact information, it didn't do much good. A bogus New York address and phone number. An e-mail address. The same e-mail address that Sylvia had, anyway. No match to a Ruth Vargas of her description in the USA. There was no information about her boyfriend, Jeff. None whatsoever. Her eggs were still there. Frozen. Waiting for a rainy day. But she hadn't contacted the clinic for six months.

Why would Ruth even bother? She had Grace now.

Sylvia read another e-mail sent two days after the first.

Hi Sylvia,

I told you, didn't I, that Jeff found my notebook and read a whole lot of my morning pages? He wants to split from me. Temporarily anyway. I believe his daughter is jealous of me – she's sixteen – and it's causing problems. But that's life, huh?

But I'm sad today – missing him. Like Dracula without his fangs. I'll be alright, though. I can already see that we've each given the other the most precious of gifts. He has given me the gift of motherhood – I would never have taken this step if it hadn't been for Jeff. And now I'm here in Mexico *actually* going through with it! Can you believe it, Sylvia? I'm going to be a mother! And I'm forever grateful to Jeff for this.

And I gave him the gift of sobriety – he would never have had the strength to get sober and stay straight if it hadn't been for me. We are both conscious of this and I'm sure he will truly acknowledge all the wonderful things about me in the future. Time is a great healer. So, if we're only meant to be in each other's lives for these reasons only it has been worth the agony, the heartache.

He never did give sperm – like I told you, the vasectomy would have brought a slew of complications. But I did keep my

hopes up about that. I really did.

Keep your fingers crossed for me! I'm waiting for my eggs to be collected today at 2pm. The doctor says my ovaries are responding to stimulation like the ovaries of a 24-year-old. I'm SO excited! I've been up since the crack of dawn; blood-work, ultrasound, and . . . praying!

Oh Sylvia, isn't life just amazing? Why don't you come and join me?

I send you a huge hug, R x

"Going to be a mother?" The confidence! Ruth wasn't even pregnant! Why, oh why, hadn't Sylvia seen the signs? She couldn't believe how dumb she'd been. Blind and trusting, the wool pulled tightly over her eyes. Ruth's fantasy, the against-all-odds risk-taking at any cost. The woman was convinced pregnancy was just going to pop into her life like a magic wand being waved! Using her own eggs at *forty-six* years old? Even for a twenty-five-year-old there was only a fifteen percent chance of success.

Kidnapping Grace was simply another route on her twisted journey for her prize:

The prize of motherhood.

Underneath was Sylvia's own reply to the "how would you describe me" question. Sylvia had written:

I would describe you, Ruth, as an international, multi-lingual, cultured hybrid whose residence is the world. A woman who is unpredictable, open for adventure and change yet organized in her diversity. A person who could mix with royalty or blue collar – someone who has inner confidence yet is vulnerable and with a sharp sense of humor and an appreciation for the absurd.

Sylvia had got her right on many counts but hadn't thought to add: *And a ruthless (Ruth, what a perfect name) callous, cold-blooded witch who will stop at nothing to achieve her objective.*

She clicked on another e-mail:

Hi Sylvia!

Things are back to normal with Jeff so I'm back on track as before. He promises to attend AA meetings and has agreed to go to therapy. I'm trying to find him a shrink. He's looking after himself taking a million vitamins and will be coming out next month for the sperm thing.

Guess what? I've had my 3rd collection and got 3 eggs. Total frozen: 7. Can you imagine how fantastic! My ovaries are the superstars of the clinic! It's painful, though. I am sore but it's worth it when I know what the pay-off will be . . . . a beautiful, hazel-eyed baby! Motherhood, here I come!

Next month will be the next step: fertilization, blastocyst culturing, and transfer into the womb. Then I'll know if I'm pregnant. Isn't that amazing?!

Then I can live somewhere warm. Key West? Brazil? And you can come for a long visit to escape the winter. I'll be pregnant, wolfing down ice cream and pickles, deliriously happy, and furiously editing my novel!

R xxx

P.S Just realized you may not know what blastocyst culturing means – it's a way of reducing multiple pregnancy rates. The way they used to do it was that embryos were transferred to the uterus on day 3 (called Day 3 transfer) after fertilization, and it is still not uncommon to transfer three or four embryos. But now, it is possible to *grow* embryos in the laboratory to the blastocyst stage of development which happens on day 5 after fertilization when the embryo has between 50 to 200 cells. Usually, the strongest, healthiest embryos make it to blastocyst stage as they have survived the biggest part, growth and division processes, and have a better chance of implanting once transferred.

Just think, my baby will be a little modern miracle!!

The last e-mail spelled another story:

Hi Sylvia,

It's been an emotional rollercoaster with Jeff. He pulled out of the sperm thing, wouldn't come out to see me, said it wasn't fair on his daughter. I guess that was just an excuse. We've decided to split; or as he says, "taking a break." But the truth is, he's a recovering addict and he does not have the emotional resources to be supportive of my needs. His ability to be a fulfilling partner is negligible. I am just not willing to forego the kind of support I need. I want a healthy, satisfying relationship! Don't we all?

I began to notice Jeff's shortcomings whenever the baby subject came up. And the truth is, when I examine the situation, I see the reality of what the dynamic has always been in our relationship. I am the giver. He is the taker. Plus, we have such different backgrounds. He is a blue-collar worker. Me? I come from a different class altogether. I speak three languages, I've read Dickens, I have a college degree. Even the books we read speak volumes. (Get the pun??!!)

So I am going to continue the IVF on my own and get a sperm donor. I am grieving like a child who has lost its mother at the fairground but I believe it is the right direction for me to take.

Take care of your relationship with Tommy. I have to say, you really have it all, don't you? Brains, talent, a sexy, gorgeous husband, a beautiful child. Lucky you. Nurture it.

When are you coming to join me? Come on, have an adventure – hurry up and get here!

Hugs R xxxxxxxxxx

Sylvia read and reread that telling line, "grieving like a child who has lost its mother at the fairground."

And," come on, have an adventure." Now that Ruth had abandoned the IVF project, was that what Grace was to her? "An adventure?"

How did Ruth imagine Grace *felt* losing her family? Had that crossed this woman's mind? A pair of sparkly Dorothy shoes wasn't enough to win a little girl's heart, however gullible. Grace must be beside herself with confusion. Desperate. What would Ruth have told her? "I've stolen you. I've kidnapped you." Hardly.

Sylvia couldn't even imagine what lies Ruth must have spun into her tapestry of deceipt.

She reread the most chilling paragraph of all: "Take care of your relationship with Tommy. I have to say, you really have it all, don't you? Brains, beauty, talent, a sexy, gorgeous husband, a beautiful child. Lucky you. Nurture it."

Jealousy? Sylvia wondered.

19

Tommy

Tommy was sitting in the Saginaw dining room, his eyes closed, head buried beneath his hands, his insides jelly. Grace, Grace, Grace. He could think of nothing else. She was his life. His heart. He stared at the wall, tears stinging his eyes. There were no words to describe how he and Sylvia felt. Grief didn't even begin to cover it. Horror?

He needed a plan so that their feelings could be supplanted by action.

They had to find Grace.

They *would* find Grace.

He let his gaze drift to the table. The Loretta letters were still spread out, his father-in-law's silver-plated golf trophies placed strategically on the sideboard, glittering in the background—a dead man's paradox.

A dark horse.

Wilbur Mason had lived a lie.

The sort of person, Tommy understood, who had been caught by circumstance, but had surrendered to his own fear and ego, letting it take over his life. He had perjured himself and those around him. His whole marriage to Sylvia's mother had been a lie.

Tommy did not—he was clear about that now—want to be that sort of man.

He did not want to be a liar.

But there was no chance he could talk to Sylvia about how things had panned out in LA. Not now. Not after what had happened with Grace. His wife was barely holding it together, and he was all she had. He didn't want to bring the subject up—just mentioning it could tip her scales.

He had to be strong for her.

For Grace.

Things could be worse, he told himself. At least Ruth wasn't a killer. She wasn't going to sexually abuse Grace and bury her in a ditch somewhere. At least, he sure as hell hoped not. No, she wanted Grace for herself, to fulfill her perverted, fantastical dreams of motherhood. All that frozen egg business proved it. It didn't work out, so she stole Grace. What a sicko.

Every now and then, Sylvia asked him if there had been some mistake, that perhaps Ruth and Grace had *both* been abducted. Tommy understood that his wife just couldn't fathom how a woman could do that to a child; to thieve a happy, well-adjusted little girl from her family to feed her own needs and ego. Perhaps, Sylvia reasoned, it was just a sort of holiday, and Ruth would bring Gracie home. His wife always did see the good in people. She was far too trusting. That's what had gotten them into this mess in the first place. Sylvia's trust. Tommy didn't blame her, though; it was her sweet nature. And he hadn't suspected Ruth at any point, either. In fact, he blamed himself for not being more on the ball. Then again, how could anybody imagine a person like Ruth could be that crafty? That wicked?

He'd scrutinized Ruth's e-mails and Facebook posts. She was a selfish bitch with an inflated opinion of herself; clever yes, but a nasty piece of work. Someone who would obviously stop at nothing. She'd committed fraud—a serious offense. She'd stolen money. There was no way she'd turn back now. This Ruth bitch was in it for the long term. And the only thing he could possibly do . . .

Was hunt her down.

20

Sylvia

Four days had passed since Grace's abduction. They'd done everything to find a trace of Ruth. The FBI was treating this as top priority, obviously. A detective named Agent Russo was in charge of their case. She'd told Sylvia that they could access Ruth's DNA with blood tests from the clinic. But what use would that be? The DNA of someone who didn't figure on any database? Ruth had given the clinic a false name and had even paid for the treatments in cash. There were no credit cards in the name of Ruth Vargas, at least not *that* Ruth Vargas. There were twenty-seven women called Ruth Vargas on Facebook alone, but the police could find none to match *the* Ruth Vargas. Ruth Steel. Same difference. She didn't exist. Her laptop had had its IP address hidden all along. Another "convenient" thing in her favor that made it impossible to trace any of her last movements, assuming she had even taken her laptop with her. She seemed too wily for that.

Sylvia went over it once more with Tommy, just to be sure.

"Explain this IP address thing again," she said.

Tommy's eyes were sharpened flints. "If she told you an ex of hers had tweaked her laptop, or bought a program to hide her address so she could watch American TV in Europe, then that must have been what happened. In order to get an American IP address you have to connect to a VPN server."

"What's VPN?"

"Virtual private network—it's far less complicated than it sounds. When you connect to a VPN server it will act as a middle-man between you and the website you want to connect to, and if the VPN server is located in the United States it will then look like you are there, too. There is even a provider called Hide My Ass Dot Com. Anyway, the woman's no fool. She will have dumped her laptop by now, with all your money she could buy as many laptops as she wants."

"*Our* daughter. *Our* money," Sylvia mumbled.

Tommy continued in a monotone, "We know her last stop was Guatemala—where she went after is anyone's guess. Two hundred and forty-seven thousand, seven hundred and twenty dollars, and eighteen cents. What cheek to use *your* passport, Sylvia."

"They said the signatures on all the paperwork were identical to the signature they had on file. 'A nice woman,' the bank said. 'She had her little girl with her,' they said."

"Evil bitch," Tommy murmured, his mouth twisted with disgust. "Ruth must have spent hours practicing your signature. And mine, too. Nice touch, that parental consent I supposedly signed."

They sat in silence, holding hands, Sylvia dissecting Ruth's last known movements. There had been no traces of a "Sylvia Garland and her daughter" boarding any more planes. Ruth was no dummy, obviously. She knew that by the time she'd cleaned out the account and hadn't turned up in Saginaw, the cops would be looking for her. But South America was her oyster. She spoke fluent Spanish and Portuguese. That part wasn't made up. That part of Ruth Steel was a razor-sharp truth. Sylvia had heard her chat on her cell one time, while they were Skyping. Ruth really could navigate her way around languages. Not to mention her gift for mimicking people. She could go anywhere by bus, by car. She had cash. Just one country in Latin America alone would be a maze in itself, but the *whole* mass of it? There was the Amazon. Where could Sylvia and Tommy even begin? Sylvia's greatest fear was that Grace, with her caramel-colored skin, would blend in with the locals. She could easily pass for a Brazilian or any Latin American child. And Ruth, trilingual as she was, could become invisible. Mother and child.

Sylvia observed Tommy as he navigated about his iPad, gathering ideas. She had never seen him so focused.

They'd made two videos and posted them on YouTube. Appeals to find Grace. They showed footage of her playing and talking to the camera—on a trip they made to Yellowstone one time—mixed with a compilation of photos and their own personal pleas to help them find their daughter. They'd already had 97,000 hits in two days. But they didn't posses one photo of Ruth to show anyone. Her Facebook page was the generic blue and white outline of a non-person. Her Skype account had disappeared. So had her e-mail account. Sylvia had not taken one photo of her in Wyoming. She had nothing. And the only thing the CCT cameras showed evidence of (at the airports and the bank in Guatemala), was a blonde woman in heels and a dress (Sylvia's dress), wearing a straw cowboy hat that hid her face. A blonde who could have been Sylvia herself.

Tommy also had the idea to put advertisements in all the papers, notably the *Herald Tribune* which ex-pats read. He put posts on Internet forums on the *Lonely Planet* and *Fodor's*—anywhere where backpackers and travelers might wander. He set up a Facebook and Twitter page with Grace's photo. A picture of her with Pidgey O Dollars. He sent out regular tweets, and although he'd had several replies, he and Sylvia were no closer to finding Grace's whereabouts.

THE MORNING LIGHT was warming the great hallway of Sylvia's childhood home. An orange glow shone on one of her grandmother's paintings, bringing the characters to life; naive stickmen in a swirl of abstract colors. Sylvia felt it was foolish, but she prayed to them anyway.

Tommy's backpack sat bulging on the terracotta floor, a pair of Territorial Army boots tied to a ring by their laces, and a lightweight sleeping bag, neatly rolled, was attached to its sides.

"It won't be too cumbersome, then?" Sylvia asked. She observed him standing in the hallway, his legs astride, his stance erect. He looked tough. She had seldom seen him this way. His jaw looked more angular, his sandy hair darker, his chest muscles more prominent. He'd been working out the last couple of days. He'd found some old 1960s weights in the garage and had been pumping iron in between organizing the Grace alerts. Everything about him looked resilient, determined. In the past, he'd shared stories about his Territorial Army days in Britain, but Sylvia had just assumed it was a way for him to help fund his university expenses, and that the part-time activity hadn't meant that much to him. She hadn't seen the tough side of him before. Now he looked like he'd stepped into another persona altogether.

He was on a mission.

"It won't be too bulky, then, too heavy?" she repeated.

"The rucksack? No, it's nothing. I've carried heavier."

She made a mental list of the essentials inside and wondered if he'd forgotten anything. Compass, micro-flashlight, mosquito net. He'd be taking his iPhone: it had God-knows-what fancy apps— compass included—but neither knew how much network would be available down there. Who knew where Ruth was headed? With all the newspapers and Internet noise the couple had made, she might be hiding out in a rainforest somewhere.

Sylvia slipped some baby wipes in one of the backpack pockets, handy, she thought, for a quick cleanup. She'd heard from friends and from Tommy about the hardships of traveling in third world countries but it was something she'd never dared do herself. She had read about the prehistoric-looking iguanas of the Galapagos Islands, the wonder of Machu Picchu with its Inca trails, and the UNESCO towns like Cuzco, boasting colonial churches and old world charm, yet she had never had the courage to pick up a backpack and go herself. She'd always supposed that she couldn't take the time off because of her job, but she knew, deep down inside, that the challenge of traveling on a budget was too much for her.

"Are you sure you don't want me to come with you?" she asked for the fifth time.

"Positive."

She chewed her lip. "I could help. I'll feel so useless here alone."

"Look, darling, we've already been through this. You need to stay behind in case the FBI gets any leads. Two of us stuck in a jungle somewhere getting eaten by mosquitoes with no way of being contacted, isn't going to help. Besides, you're not feeling strong enough for this sort of traveling—dirty tuk-tuks belching out two-stroke, stinking fumes in your face, or schlepping about on filthy chicken buses with sticky plastic seats, driven by devil-may-care Catholics with the Virgin Mary dangling from the rear-view mirror, overtaking on hairpin bends above precipices, hurtling along pot-holed roads at eighty miles an hour, beeping at stray dogs on the road" –he stopped for breath—"which they wouldn't hesitate to mow down by the way."

Sylvia's stomach dipped with a feeling of hopelessness. "I guess it's true what you say about being here for the FBI. But I want to be *with* you. Grace is my daughter too."

"And you also have the funeral in three days time," he said gently.

"I know. If Daddy hadn't killed himself, we wouldn't be in this mess." *Ouch, how did that come out?*

"Look," Tommy said, "give me a couple of weeks. If I don't have any luck then come out and join me if you like."

If you like. Not the most encouraging invitation. They stood in the hallway in silence. Tommy's lips parted as if he was about to say something important but then he stopped himself. He suddenly blurted, "You know we're not going to LA anymore, don't you? I mean, not now this second, but in general. The LA job is off."

"But after we've found Grace—"

"After we've found Grace, we're not going to live in LA."

Sylvia scrunched her brow. "But what about the job?"

"I've told them to look for someone else. Even if I find Grace tomorrow, I don't want the job."

"Oh."

Tommy looked as if he were trying to sell her an idea. "The whole reason I let go of IT was to pursue my dreams as a photographer. I mean, that's why we went to Wyoming, wasn't it? Because of the beauty, the awe-inspiring landscape, the strange characters you find there. I didn't give up my successful career to become a second-rate fashion photographer in LA."

"Oh," she said again. But Sylvia knew that he had a point. She secretly thought the same thing but didn't want to wound his pride. LA wasn't Milan, Paris, or New York; it was hardly the fashion capital of the world. Fashion had never been Tommy's thing, anyway.

"I don't give a fuck about fashion," Tommy continued. "I never have, I never will. I don't care what's going on in the vapid, vacuous head of some pretty girl, or what outfit she's wearing. I care about people's souls, what makes them tick. I care about beauty from within."

Sylvia pictured the Bel Ange, pouting and posing—an obsession he'd nursed for over a year. It was strange, she thought, how people perceive themselves. Tommy *did* care about external beauty, he did choose a book by its cover. Unless losing Grace had changed his whole outlook on life.

"What made you change your mind?" she said, trying not to sound cold.

"Let's just say I had an epiphany in LA. I had a close shave."

What close shave? she wondered. But said, "So when we find Grace, what's next then, if we don't go to LA?"

"We'll live here. In Saginaw."

"Are you serious?"

"Yes, why not? We could do that for a couple of years. It's not a good idea to sell when emotions are still raw. You've hardly got over your mother's death, and now your dad. And now Grace's kidnapping. A triple whammy. Oh, and finding out you have a half-brother, too, and that your father was living a lie for forty odd years. A quadruple whammy."

Sylvia flinched. "We don't know that for sure."

"Oh yes we do. You can bet your bottom dollar it was his big secret. If your mother had known about his love child, she would have divorced him. Trust me. Anyway, the last thing you need right now is the stress of moving somewhere new. And we both know that Crowheart is out of the question. Been there, done that."

"Michigan is in the worst crisis since the depression," Sylvia said. "And this is everything you hate! Suburbs, Midwest America—*'obese people slurping neon-pink milkshakes, hanging out in shopping malls'* – those were your very words."

"I know darling. I know. I felt that way before but it's different now—I was being judgmental. I've been bowled over by people's kindness here."

There was Before Grace, Sylvia thought. The Before the Adoption part of their life. And now there was another Before. The Before the *Abduction*.

"And what happens," she ventured, "if we *don't* find Grace?"

There, she said it, that hideous question that had been festering in the air like a virus. Her heartbeat raced, and blood pounded her ears. White heat pooled in her stomach. She thought she might actually faint.

Tommy shook his head. He wasn't having it. "That's not an option. Not acceptable. We *will* find her."

"But, honey, I hate to say it, but it *is* a reality." Sylvia bit her lip to stop her mouth from trembling.

"It's also a reality that France, sweet little picturesque France which makes wine and cheese, has a submarine that has six missiles—each one of them has a thousand times more power than Hiroshima, enough nuclear power alone to blow up the world twenty times. All that power contained in one single submarine! But we can't live that way, can we? Worrying about the what-ifs."

Sylvia knew she needed to change the subject. She'd spoken the wrong words. Negativity at a time like this was the last thing Tommy needed. "Do you want something to eat before I drive you to the airport?"

"No."

"Oh. Okay." She'd pushed him away again. Pushed him away with her pessimism. She thought of Gracie's name for her when she was this way: the Ground Dog way, her lips turned down, the sadness in her eyes giving her the "Ground Dog" nickname. All she yearned for was to be Grace's Mommykins again—the other nickname Grace gave her. If she were Mommykins, once more, she'd never let Ground Dog return.

Tommy took a step toward her and said in a softer tone, "I don't want anything to eat, but I do, darling, want to say goodbye. I want to lie with you for a while, Sylvia. I want to hold you." He took her by the hand and drew her close. His arms were muscly and warm, his hold tight. Even at five foot nine, Sylvia felt petite against his strong, solid frame. "Let's go upstairs," he suggested. "We don't have to leave for an hour yet."

Sylvia sat uneasily at the edge of the silk-backed bed and kicked off her shoes. She needed to do this. She needed, just for a snatch of time, to escape her dark, Graceless world. She needed to help Tommy too—give him strength. She inhaled the scent of him and rested her head against his shoulder. He smelled of sweet grass and sun-warmed skin. He unzipped her dress. His generous hands slipped around her waist and moved up the length of her body, then stroked her back. She shivered. His fingertips caressed her skin and she closed her eyelids—a twirl of colors swam beneath them: red, twinkling green. She could hear some birds tweeting outside the bedroom window, perched on the weeping willow tree and, as one flew past, the shadow darted across her colored vision, just a second, just a flash. Tommy continued to stroke her—his touch tender. Warm.

She remembered how much she loved this man. How she ached for him. How much she desired him physically.

He pushed the dress away from her shoulders and it fell in folds about her waist. He pressed his hand under her white cotton panties and cupped her crotch, lifting it a millimeter from the bed. She cried out. Taken aback, almost, by the tingling flurry between her legs. She had forgotten that could happen. She could feel herself moisten, and she wriggled out of her dress, letting it fall to the floor. His hands moved upwards toward her breasts, his touch soft, hardly there, letting a finger flicker on her nipple, quiet and restful. She turned herself around to face him, her legs straddled either side of his, the saddle of her thighs and bottom pressing against his groin. He was rock hard. Bigger than she remembered. Her stomach pooled with desire and she heard herself moan quietly. They kissed. He tasted of sun and apples. He tasted of Tommyness. She let her tongue explore his top lip, then his mouth, and felt the rough stubble of an unshaven face. He groaned and pulled her closer. She remembered how little they kissed these days, really kissed—deep, probing—and she remembered, too, how he craved that.

She could feel the steady throb between her legs, and edging herself up on her knees, still straddling him, she offered his mouth her nipple. He licked it. Softly. The end of his tongue flickered like a glinting light. She let out another little cry. Her need for him, like a volt, made her push him to the bed. His head thumped on the puffed linen pillows and hungrily she unbuttoned his shirt, grappled the belt, reaching for the buttons of his jeans, feeling the rock that was his desire, the pulse in her groin rhythmical and hot. She drank in his chiseled abs, the definition of his pectorals. She pulled off his pants, halfway. She kissed him on his muscular thighs, her head resting against his hips, her tongue and lips searching for his cock as she looked up at him, a monument of flesh and bone and blood and love. They needed each other. For the first time in years, they could really give to one another. They needed each other's strength, each other's weakness.

Being united was imperative right now.

"Come here, my angel, my light. I need you close to me." He grabbed her, pulling her up toward him from the waist, placing her on top of him. Her toes tingled, and she heard him hold his breath for a second as she let him slide into her, her hands guiding him in. It felt huge, unfamiliar, as if it were her first time. She caught her breath at the smarting pain. It lasted a second and then it was over, her wetness welcoming the man she loved, the fit perfect. She had forgotten how well they slotted together.

She had forgotten that.

She gyrated her hips in a tiny figure of eight, then opened her mouth so her breath could come faster. She shut her eyes again and moved down, closer, tighter, her lips pressing on his, her pale hair flopping about his concentrated face. Her body needed this.

"I love you, Sylvie. I love you." He kissed her harder and groaned. "So beautiful. So, so beautiful."

She said nothing but carried on with her rhythm, fearful to break its spell, her elbows planted either side of his shoulders, up and down, the skin of their torsos clapping, she mewling with each plunge, controlling the penetration, teasing him, the throbbing tip, now the whole, now just the tip. He felt incredible.

His patience could no longer bear her coquettish torment.

She could feel him grab her buttocks with his large hands. He spun her round, her on her back now, gently, careful not to let their groins part. He started pumping. Hard. Deep. Her man had taken command. The captain of his ship. His vessel. He started fucking her rhythmically. Dominating her. She splayed her legs open even wider.

She moaned at every thrust. She tilted her thighs higher and still with her eyes on him, grabbed a cushion beside her head and pushed it under her hips. They were closer now. Her fingers grabbed his ass, smooth and hard like a rounded boulder. She pulled herself back. Just a touch. Steady. Slow. She was in control again. She needed to change the pace. Slowly she pushed herself toward him and held the motion. Pulled him in tighter. Still. Together. One.

Then she drew herself away.

He let out a deep, guttural growl. "Jesus you're incredible."

Again, she pulled him, her nails like little weapons, clutching his buttocks. She could feel it now. Her racing pulse, the heat like an orange flare, the deep quiver inside her, taut as a boxing glove. The sensation, she knew, could rush like a falling cascade, or evaporate to an invisible mist. The timing was crucial. Her eyes were tight. Closed like a knot. The tunnel of both light and dark was rushing behind her head. She pulled him closer. She stopped. Her breath was fast, her heart pounding like a fighting fist.

He moaned. She could feel him expand inside her. Huge. Filling and pushing the edges of her walls. She lifted herself toward him. And stopped. She held her breath.

One. Two. Three. Four.

"I'm coming," he moaned into her mouth, lashing his tongue around hers. His hardness inside her throbbed like a raw red heart.

She arched her back a little higher and pulled him closer with her hands, clawed like eagle's talons. And then it came.

The unexpected.

The expected.

The moments of bliss that for a woman can never be guaranteed. The seconds where brain and soul meet flesh, and the brain goes blank. The second that can be snatched away and melt like an ice cream on a sweltering day to a helpless mess of nothing, or that can load you with a rush of blood, love, seed and Heaven—the bolt of thunderous orgasm. It came in her, under her, pulsing through her like a flooding river. Deep. Hard. Powerful. She could hear a woman scream and she realized it was her own lustful voice.

She had escaped. And now she had arrived.

"I love you too, Tommy," she gasped.

She lay there. Weak. Strong. Fulfilled. Beads of sweat gathered on her back, behind the creases of her knees that were still wrapped around him like a vice.

He kissed her again and pushed away some strands of hair from her hot face. "You are the light. You're my everything, Sylvie. I love you. I do."

Then she remembered what she had escaped from and her guilt surged back like a current pulling her under a dark ocean. "Please find Gracie for me," she whispered.

"I promise," he said.

21

Grace

Grace had not said a word all day. They were sitting on the beach in the roasty sun, both wearing hats. But not the big straw cowboy hat that Ruth had been going around with when they were on the plane and at the bank. That, she had sold. She had also sold her computer and all Grace's clothes. And her princess backpack on wheels. Ruth hadn't sold the secret recording pen because she still hadn't discovered it, tucked inside Carrot, wrapped in her nighty. Grace knew, though, that the pen was in danger. Perhaps Carrot was in danger, too. And Ruth had not bought her the Computer Engineer Barbie Doll like she promised.

"Please don't be sad, baby. Please talk to me. I told you—he must have been stolen." Ruth's voice was honey-sweet.

"But he was in your bag. You said he'd be *safe* there!" Grace's amber-green eyes were filled with burning tears. But she knew crying had gotten her nowhere so far, so she stayed quiet. Mama Ruth had promised her fun and happiness but Grace didn't see how she was meant to be happy with her ugly new Boy Haircut and without Pidgey O Dollars.

"I know I did, baby, but I told you—the Bogeymen must have taken Pudgy O Dollars away."

"*Pidgey* O Dollars, not Pudgy."

"Whatever," Ruth said.

"But I was the only one who loved him! And Mommy, she loved him too. But everyone else said he was ugly. Why did the Bogeymen want *him*? Why couldn't they take a *different* bear? A bear that belonged to another girl?"

"Because, baby," Ruth replied softly, "Bogeymen take everything they want, *whenever* they want. There is no rhyme or reason to what they do." She shook the black glittery sand off her towel and shuffled her body into a better tanning position. She had turned very brown. Brown like treacle in a treacle tart, Grace thought.

"Baby?" Ruth went on, looking at the surfers in the distance waiting for the next big wave. "There is something very serious I need to tell you. And I'm so sorry that you don't have Pidgey O Dollars to comfort you, but look, I have a surprise!" She stopped, turned her head away from the surfers and pulled a teddy out of her beach bag. It was bright yellow with big black shiny eyes that were plastic, and it had a pointy mouth. Grace thought it looked like one of those bears at a fairground that you win by throwing beanbags. She didn't want to hurt the bear's feelings but she thought it was Hideous. She wondered if bears like this had souls. She guessed so. Maybe they needed to be loved first to get the soul ticking. But she didn't think she could love this poor, ugly bear. Her mom only picked out hand-made bears for her. Some of them came all the way from Germany, or Hamleys in London, or FAO Schwartz in New York City. This bear looked like it came from a factory. Like the Factory Farming her mom told her about that was BAD. This yellow bear had been Factory Farmed. It was obvious.

"Look baby, isn't he cute?" Ruth whispered. "Or maybe it's a she. What do you want to name this bear?" Ruth was whispering because she had told Grace that in public, they must talk Very Quietly until Grace learned to speak Spanish, and then they could talk loudly again. Mama Ruth's voice was strange when she spoke Spanish. It was like a song, up and down, and she spoke through her nose a lot. She gave Grace Spanish lessons every morning and then again before bed. She read her books in Spanish, and at the hotel they watched Walt Disney films, only in Spanish. They sounded terrible. The voice of John Smith from *Pocahontas* called himself John Ey-smith. Luckily, Grace already knew the stories so she could understand everything. But all she heard was Spanish, Spanish, *Spanish*. Mama Ruth had told her not to speak to anyone who spoke English because some of them were agents for the Bogeymen.

"Does this yellow bear have a soul?" Grace asked.

Ruth snorted with laughter. "Of course not, silly. Teddy bears don't have souls."

"They do too! Pidgey O Dollars has a soul and Blueby and Carrot. All my teddies have souls!"

Ruth rearranged her legs. "Well that's nonsense. Only humans have souls."

Grace shouted, "That's not true! Animals have souls too. Dogs have souls. Dog is God spelled backwards!"

"Now you're being a naughty girl. What would God say if He heard you say things like that? Huh? That's blasphemous."

Mama Ruth had used that word before. Blast Famous. And it was always when she spoke about God. Her God was not like her dad's God who lived in the flowers. No, not at all. Mama Ruth's God was mean and spiteful.

Grace watched Mama Ruth play with the little gold cross around her neck. That's right, she almost forgot—she wasn't allowed to say that word, "Ruth," ever again, or even think it in her head.

"Mama *Ruth*," Grace mumbled, and then louder, "Ruth, Ruth. RUTH!"

"Babeeeey? What did I tell you? I explained that my name was now Rocío. It means dew in Spanish. Like the dew on morning grass. It's prettier than my old name. I don't want to hear that other R-word ever again. It's history. So is your old G-name. Something in the past. Do you understand? I am Rocío. And *your* new name is Adela. Like we agreed."

Grace dug her tiny nails into the glittery sand. "But I don't *want* to be Adela."

"But baby, you chose that name yourself. You picked that name from *The Little Mermaid*, you thought it was pretty."

"I want Pidgey O Dollars back!"

"But he's *gone*, baby. There's nothing we can do about it now." Mama Ruth sat up on her towel. "Come here, I need to tell you something." She took Grace by the hand and placed her between her slippery knees—she smelled like sweet cake covered in syrup sauce. "You know that I told you that the plane was delayed and we couldn't get to Saginaw?" She said "Saginaw" so quietly that Grace could hardly hear. "Well, there has been some terrible news. Just terrible. But maybe you aren't ready to hear it. I'm sorry, baby. Maybe I should break it to you next week when you're feeling happier."

Grace had been getting used to this. Yes, no. Up, down. Mama Ruth would say one thing, and then do something else. Sometimes she would promise they'd have tourist food for dinner but then they'd end up eating tamales or *papusas* instead. Or she'd promise they could see *Beauty and The Beast* in American but then say they had to see it in Spanish. Or she'd change her mind at the last second about the hotel they would be staying at, or catch a different bus than the one she'd promised.

"Baby?"

"*What?*"

"Are you ready for the bad news?"

"I *guess* so." Pidgey O Dollars had been stolen by the Bogey-men. She didn't have the Computer Engineer Barbie Doll because they didn't sell them here. The plane that was going to take them to Saginaw to see her mom and dad had broken down. She was forced to wear new clothes that didn't even look nice—she looked like a boy. Hideous Yellow Teddy Bear. Ugly Boy Haircut. Nothing could be worse than it already was.

Mama Ruth held her close. Her body was pressing oil and sticky scratchy black sand all over her swimsuit. But Grace didn't care; she hated this new swimsuit anyway. Let it get yukky, she thought. *I don't care!*

"Baby, I'm so sorry. I really am." Ruth had wet, sad eyes when she said it. "Your mommy? Your mommy has passed away." She paused and kissed Grace on her forehead and squeezed her even tighter. "But the good news is that *I* can be your mommy now."

22

Sylvia

Sylvia stood at the back of the church, the only white woman there. But nobody stared at her, nobody begrudged her presence—quite the reverse: on her way in several people had said, "welcome to our church" and smiled. One lady, dressed in a flamboyant red hat, asked her where she had been all these years.

Why, Sylvia wondered, didn't everyone go to places of worship like this? This was what praise was all about. She actually felt close to God.

She reflected on the hours she had wasted as a girl, bored out of her mind at her own dull church, miming along to the same old organ songs, listening to the clergyman drone on with tight lips, no smile, about the duty they all had to be good Christians. Her mind was always on something else: school, lists, plans, cheerleading. It was different here; she was actually praying with her heart— beseeching God for Grace's safe return. She felt so much hope in this church. The entire congregation was singing—the gospel music made people sway and dance—she felt as if she were at a rock concert. Sweeps of color flashed about the room. Women in purple and fuchsia pink, their hats like flying saucers or tropical birds, blocking dashes of bright yellow or orange—blocking the other worshippers in the front row. The colors sashayed, shimmied and jived. Pitch-perfect notes, like waves, danced through the room, reaching corners and resting for a second on the crimson carpet, before lifting up again like sweet bells jingling in the air.

The pastor had a sense of humor. Sylvia fixed her gaze on his warm smile and clicked her eyes shut and open, like a camera. She wanted to take a snapshot of his smile and save it in her album of memories, keep it in her mind's eye for the tough times ahead. She watched him in motion. Little freckles dotted his dark skin, and his robe swung like a slow pendulum when he turned in different directions to speak to his flock. When he got excited, the fabric of his garment swished like the tail of a great cat. He was talking about releasing control, having the guts to let the Lord do the hard work for you, that no matter how hard you try to control your life, it had a way of sneaking up behind you. "And *astonishing* you." He said that God could be like your "personal assistant," your "right hand man," but "the great thing is you don't even have to pay him! He does all that work for *free*! A *thank you* might be nice, though," he cried, "just a friendly thank you once in a while goes a long way with the Lord God Almighty."

Jacqueline stood by Sylvia, in her white suit and hat. Still. Plaintive. She was older than Sylvia remembered. She wore her hair swept up in a loose bun, revealing her fine bone structure, her straight, graceful nose. Like the pastor's, it was also peppered with freckles. Sylvia had always thought Jacqueline so beautiful. She originated from the West Indies, from Trinidad, and had come to Michigan when she was six years old. She had one daughter and four grandchildren, all now at college. Sylvia watched her out of the side of her left eye. She wondered if Jacqueline was mulling over her father's funeral the day before, and asking herself, *what next?*

Was she sad, or accepting? Or both? She had acted like a psychologist to Sylvia's mother all those years. Never judging, always there, listening, nodding her head, and every now and then throwing in a gentle suggestion, her quiet voice wise, sagacious. Sally, Sylvia's mother, would say, "Huh, Jacqueline, I hadn't thought of it that way—very interesting," or, "Really? You think so? You really think that's a good plan?" She would ask Jacqueline what outfit she should wear. What flowers would go well for the party she'd be giving that weekend. Where she should hang a particular painting or place a vase. Sally even wanted Jacqueline's opinion on Sylvia's choice of college.

After the service was over, Sylvia rode home with her. She'd left the Buick behind on purpose. The two hadn't had a chance to talk at the funeral, especially with everyone gathering around Sylvia like butterflies on a spring flower, to commiserate about Grace. Although she didn't feel like a spring flower at all, but like a half-eaten fruit going bad, because guilt and remorse were nibbling at her.

It felt to her as if everyone was almost grateful to not have to mention her father or the overdose. It had all been glossed over and passed off as "accidental" but perhaps they had an inkling? They all concentrated on Grace's disappearance instead. Everyone was doing their bit: chain e-mails, Facebook posts, telephone calls, flyers. Middle America was kind. These were wholesome, caring people who had a sense of community and loyalty. Sylvia never thought she'd even imagine it, but the idea of coming home to Saginaw was a welcoming relief. It was where her heart lay. She was glad, now, that Tommy had wiped LA off the table.

Jacqueline adjusted her seatbelt and checked the rear-view mirror. She seemed too fragile for this vast dinosaur of a car, the same old Oldsmobile she'd had for nearly thirty years. "So what did you think of our new pastor?"

Sylvia's lips twitched a smile. "I thought he was wonderful, a real live spark."

"He's that alright. Some of the old folks think he's a little too crazy with his ideas."

"Are there always more women than men at your church?"

"You noticed that too, huh? The congregations of African American churches are predominantly women yet the pastors of our churches are nearly all male! Why do you think that is? Why aren't black women serving as spiritual leaders? That is something I sure as sugar would like to know. I don't know what other female churchgoers make of that, but I do wonder. Church, I guess, is more important to us than to the men. It must be, or why wouldn't more of them show up?"

"I guess the Catholics," Sylvia added, "must be really cheesed off. I mean, women don't figure *at all* as their leaders."

"Uh-huh." Jacqueline was concentrating on maneuvering the huge steering wheel, which she sat sunken behind like a tiny child— her almond eyes fixed on the labyrinth of the parking lot from which she was trying to exit. "It's clear as daylight that we need more women clergy and for women to be in positions of pastoral leadership. We are in the twenty-first century! But I don't even know if women themselves have pondered much on this gender inequality in the church. They're too busy worrying about what dress to put on!"

Sylvia nibbled her lower lip. Only half an ear was taking in what Jacqueline was saying. She was thinking about Grace twenty-four hours a day. But also chugging away in her motor-mind was the mystery of her half-brother, LeRoy. Did Jacqueline know about the box of letters? She assumed that she must have been aware that it was in the closet. Maybe she even put it there herself. But its contents? Should she say something or just let it rest? She could trust her, she was sure. Jacqueline had never, in thirty-six years, breached her confidence or that of her parents. But did she really need to burden her with this can of worms—the disillusionment of who her father was? Or rather, what he'd done?

"Did you trust Daddy?" Sylvia asked suddenly.

Jacqueline looked over at Sylvia with a quizzical look as if she'd said something ridiculous. "Yes siree, I trusted that old fool with all my heart. He never let me down. Not once."

But he let down your side, Sylvia thought. Not owning up to having an African American child was cowardice.

"Was he honest with Mom?"

Jacqueline squinted. "Now honey, what is that supposed to mean?"

"Did he always tell her the truth?"

"Does *anybody* always tell the truth?"

"Sometimes things unsaid are as good as lies," Sylvia ventured, also thinking of Tommy and the Bel Ange. She watched Jacqueline's face for a reaction. But she stared ahead, peeping through the steering wheel of her colossal ship of a car.

"You been snooping around in the closet?"

Sylvia felt her face burn like a fried tomato. It was her house! Everything in it was hers, including the box. But she still felt like a naughty child.

"You been reading them letters?"

"Yes. I read all ten of them. And I looked at all the photos too. Of LeRoy. *Leroy*."

"You said it right first time. LeRoy. I wondered how long it would take you to discover that box. Actually, I kind of hoped you'd find it—get this all out in the open, finally."

Sylvia felt a ball of air gather in her stomach. So Jacqueline knew *all along? Thanks for letting me in on the secret!* "He's my half-brother, you know."

"You got that right."

Sylvia sat in cold silence. Furious with Jacqueline for the first time she could remember. So cavalier! As if half-brothers popped out of closets every day of the week! Secret half-brothers who seemed to vanish at the age of ten. "So where *is* LeRoy? How can I find him? Why didn't you *tell* me, Jacqueline? How long have you known about him?"

"Forever. I mean, since before LeRoy were born. Figured all those years something woudda snapped. That your mama woudda found out. But she never did. I wasn't gonna be the one to go telling on nobody, breaking up a happy family. No siree."

"I hate to say it, and I hope Mom rests in peace, but if she hadn't been such a *racist*—"

Jacqueline jolted her head around and stared at Sylvia for a long beat before she turned her attention back to the road. The car slowed to a snail's pace. In that look there was quiet rage. "You think only white people are racist? You know what they told me when I first came to Michigan? Not white people, but black folks. African Americans. They would ask me in all seriousness if people from Trinidad were savages, lived in trees and wore grass skirts. I remember being called a West Indian Monkey and a Coconut Ape! I was told to go back to the jungle where I came from and that my folks were stealing jobs from the *real* black people who needed them. They said we practiced voodoo and were evil. And then I heard the other side of the coin. From my own kind. That I should watch out for *African* Americans—that only wanted to live on welfare, that they were lazy and all of them criminals. You think my mama trusted them or they trusted us? Racism is everywhere, Sylvia honey. Ain't nobody gonna tell me white folks is the only racist people round here."

Sylvia sighed and slipped down into the bucket of the leather passenger seat. She had underestimated Jacqueline's fierce loyalty to her parents. "So where is he? Where is LeRoy now?"

Jacqueline shook her head sadly. "I'm so sorry, honey, but LeRoy had a fatal accident."

Sylvia felt her nose prickle, her eyes mist. "What happened?"

"Loretta had cancer and was having radiation treatment, paid for by your father. She was exhausted and in and out of the hospital. It was your dad's idea to send LeRoy off to summer camp. Fun for him, he thought, and a break for Loretta. At least, that's what Loretta told me. LeRoy went to one of the lakes to a swanky, expensive camp, I can't remember the name. The only trouble was, he made friends with a group of bullyboys. You know, troublemaker, show-off types? The boys sneaked off to swim one evening and LeRoy didn't come back. The boys said he'd swum off onto that platform float thing—you know, the thing with oil drums, used for sunbathing? They found his body the next morning, washed up on shore."

"Oh my God. Where had the camp leader been all that time? How did they let something like that *happen?*"

"Things were different back then. In those days, children ran around more freely—there were less rules back then."

"True," Sylvia said despondently. "What a *tragedy!* You think those boys did it, then?"

"Maybe they were horsing around. Only the Lord knows what happened—a mystery, never to be solved."

"*What?* They didn't do an autopsy? What are you saying?"

"I'm saying that his mama, my friend Loretta, passed away thirty odd years ago, very soon after the tragedy, so I never did get to ask her details. At the time, she was so destroyed by his death, plus the fact she was weak and dying from cancer, that she didn't want to discuss it with no one. Maybe those boys were innocent, maybe they weren't, but we'll never know for sure." Jacqueline swerved the Oldsmobile hard to the right, catching the sidewalk and bumping back down again. She didn't seem to notice.

"Didn't Daddy do anything? Didn't he sue the summer camp for negligence?"

"I surely don't know the details. Maybe he did, maybe he didn't. I never thought it my place to ask."

"Nobody told Mom about LeRoy? Even after he died?" Sylvia glared at Jacqueline, accusation dancing in her eyes.

"Sylvia, honey. I'm sorry. But what was I meant to do? Get a big wooden spoon and stir up trouble? Your mama was happy. She had no idea that LeRoy existed. It was not my place to go round stirring up no trouble. If your Daddy wanted to tell me bout LeRoy, he woudda. But he never did, not even after your mama died. So I kept my pretty little mouth shut."

Sylvia tried to process all this information. Her dad must have been riddled with guilt. His own son dying because of his bright idea to send him off to summer camp. And she, too, had left Grace with Ruth, neither of them imagining, in their wildest imagination, what ills could befall their child. Her father's suicide was making more sense every day. Guilt. Remorse. The feeling of culpability. Knowing that your choice had fatal consequences.

One split-second decision could ruin your life and the life of the person you made that decision for. Grace. LeRoy . . .

Both victims of one, fatal choice.

Sylvia propped her head in her hands, her elbows on her knees, and began to sob quietly.

Jacqueline took one hand off the steering wheel and laid her elegant fingers on Sylvia's head. She stroked her hair softly. "I know, honey, I know. It's a very, very sad story. And I can imagine what's going through your mind right now about Gracie. But as God is my witness, I have a very strong feeling that you *will* find her. You have to have faith, honey. You have to keep strong. For Grace's sake."

23

Grace

Grace was hiding in the bathroom. When she last saw Mama Ruth, Ruth was sipping a cocktail by the bar, watching the sunset. Grace pretended she was tired and wanted to go to bed early. Ruth was talking to a man in Spanish. Of course. She didn't speak to anybody in English anymore. She'd been flirting with this same man for a few days already. His name was Lucho. He was one of the surfers. Ruth was even spending nights with him. Grace didn't mind him too much because he bought her candy and took her swimming. He was okay, she decided. Ruth thought he was the Bees Knees. She laughed a lot when she was with him and Grace had seen them kiss. Not a smoochy kiss, but still.

Grace had enough time. "Mama Rocío" was busy. Unless she came up to the bathroom to be sick. She often did that. She'd stuff her face, especially with ice cream and sweet things, and then she'd vomit afterwards. Grace didn't understand why she did that, but one thing she knew for certain—it was Mama Ruth's Big Secret.

She unrolled the recording pen from her nightgown. The battery was almost dead. She'd have to find a secret place to charge it—she knew about charging batteries; her dad had taught her. She'd need to charge it with Lucho's computer. She'd do it tomorrow when he was surfing.

She pressed down on the pocket clip to record:

"I have to whisper. Because if Mama Ruth, oops, Mama *Rocío* hears me, I know she'll take this pen away from me.

Today she gave me another haircut. Even shorter. Boy, do I look like a boy! That sounds funny, 'boy do I look like a boy.' But it's true. Every time I look in the mirror, I get a big surprise. I miss my mom and dad. Mommy passed away. Ruth told me. She said that Mom was in a car accident and died instantly which means she died straight away and felt no pain. I cried and cried for a week without stopping. She—Ruth, I mean—wants me to call her Mommy but it feels funny. She says that Daddy might come out and see us and that Daddy will grow to love her more than he loved Mommy. I don't think so.

Yesterday, she was speaking on the phone to a doctor. She was talking in Spanish. But then she also spoke English. I can understand quite a bit but I can't say much. I can say *perro* which means dog and *osito de peluche* which means teddy bear, but it doesn't sound as cute. She says she's going to Rio de-something-or-other but it's a secret. I heard her talking in English to someone else and she was talking about plastic surgery. About her nose. The same thing that Mommy did with Pidgey O Dollars! I miss him. I hope the Bogeymen decided they didn't like him anymore and gave him to a nice little girl. That's what Ruth says could happen. She says there are children in Rio who live on the streets in boxes and in garbage. She says that one day she might get me a baby brother from the garbage and wash him and then

I can have a brother all for myself.

She says that soon Daddy and her will be together. She thinks Daddy is very cute. But right now she likes Lucho the surfer boy. He comes from Colombia. He said that when he was a little boy they had guns at school and it was very dangerous. Mama Rocío says that if she goes to Rio de what's-it-called, Lucho can look after me here in El Salvador and he'll buy me lots of candy and I can do anything I want. I can stay up late.

I'm still not used to my new name. I guess Adela is okay. I keep forgetting things. Yesterday I forgot how to say, 'brush my teeth' in English and I said *limpiarme los dientes* instead. Nobody speaks English here. Mama Rocío never speaks English to me anymore. Only sometimes, if we're alone. She says it's time for me to go to school but only if I promise not to tell anybody my secrets. She said if I talk about my old Mommy, the Bogeymen will take her out of Heaven and take her down to Hell where there's fire and where the Devil lives, so I mustn't ever talk about her to *anybody*.

I wonder if I go to school there will be guns, like at Lucho's school. Mama Rocío says I'm Catholic now—she gave me a gold cross to prove it. She says in a few years I'll get to wear a long white dress and take Communion and then I'll be like a princess. Wait! I can hear her. I hear footsteps—"

Grace was in the bathroom. She could hear Ruth tiptoe into the bedroom. She was calling. "Adela, mi amor? Are you there?"

Grace hid the pen under a towel and scuttled over to the toilet. She pulled the chain.

"Adel-La? What are you Doo-Wing?' Her voice sang like the Child Catcher in *Chitty Chitty Bang Bang*. Ruth entered the bathroom, stared at Grace for a second, and then her eyes swept about the room. Grace could feel her heart go *boom*. It felt hot and poundy—

her tummy was doing somersaults. Her little hands were sweaty and as sticky as lollipops.

"Adela? What are you doing in here?"

"Nothing."

Ruth came close. Her breath smelled of cocktails. "Well you must be doing *something*."

"Nah-ah."

"Are you *lying* to me? You know what that cross around your neck stands for, don't you?"

"Uh-huh."

"It means you're a good little Catholic girl who always tells Mommy the truth."

Grace stood still. But she let her gaze wander for a second to the towel. But then quickly looked at the floor.

Ruth turned her head. "Have you done something with that towel?"

"Nah ah."

"Because if you are lying to me you know what will happen, don't you?"

Grace remained silent.

"I will take Carrot and your other bear to Rio with me and give them to the poor street children."

Grace could feel a trickle of wee-wee running down her thigh. She looked down at the floor and saw a tiny puddle of yellow that had appeared like magic—a splash of lemonade.

"Oh nooo! Not again! Adela, what is *wrong* with you! Stop already with this piddling business. I'm getting so *tired* of changing your sheets in the middle of *every single goddamn night*! I thought you wanted to be a big girl, not a little baby! Do you want me to put you in diapers? Do you want to wear big, ugly, padded diapers like a *baby*? Because if you don't stop already with these uncontrollable waterworks, that is *exactly* what I am going to have to do. Act like a baby and I'll treat you like a baby, little Missy!" Ruth raced toward her, scooped her up and plunked her on the toilet. Grace's skinny little bottom sank down the hole in a big U. It felt like a giant bucket and she was scared she might plop to the bottom. She concentrated but no wee-wee would come. What had been inside her body was already on the floor.

"You're like some pissing machine! It's so gross. You have to learn to be a grown-up, okay?" Ruth was frantically mopping up the puddle with a big wet cloth.

Grace wriggled about on the huge seat and tried to get comfortable. It was pinching her. She hoped Ruth wouldn't touch the towel where the pen was hidden—then she'd *really* be in trouble. She'd change the subject. "Why are you going away?"

"Because I have a little problem with my nose, baby. I have a deviated septum and can't breathe properly." She was now rinsing out the smelly cloth under a hot tap and mumbling, "Gross, gross, gross. I am so not cut out for this parent *shit!*"

"Are you going to have plastic surgery like Pidgey O Dollars?"

"*What?* Where did you hear that?"

"I dunno."

"Have you been spying on me? Have you been listening to my private telephone conversations? Have you been *eavesdropping?*"

Another trickle of wee-wee came out, luckily straight into the toilet this time. "No."

"I think you *have*, young lady. I think you've been listening to my private conversations! And you know what happens to naughty, spying, eavesdropping girls, don't you?"

"The Bogeymen?" Grace whispered.

"That's *right!*" Mama Ruth cried, washing her hands with soap for the third time. "The Bogeymen come and take little girls like that away in the night when it's dark. Snatch them from their beds when they're fast asleep. And they take them and throw them on big, stinking piles of garbage onto the streets of Rio where there's no food. No nothing!"

"But then you can come and find me? Can't you? If the Bogey-men take me to Rio and you're going to Rio too, you can come and look for me."

Ruth suddenly changed from Dragon Face to Cheshire Cat Face. "You know what, baby? You are funny. So *so* cute! You are so *adorable* I could eat you. Now wipe your tush, then wash your hands—"

"Are you going to wash my hands for me?" Grace remembered how good it felt when her Real Mom washed her hands.

"No, you're big enough to wash your own hands. Hurry up now and we'll go downstairs for dinner. Guess what, baby?"

"What?"

"Tonight you can eat as much ice cream as you like."

THEY WERE SITTING at the table, eating dinner on the beach. The floor was a bed of sand. There were candles and it was now dark. The sand wasn't hot beneath Grace's feet the way it had been earlier that day. It was cool. Lucho was with them. He was wolfing down a tamale saying, "*Está bonissimo. Bonissimo!*"

Grace knew that the wee-wee puddle had made Ruth forget about what was hidden under the towel. The cocktails she had guzzled had also made her forget—Ruth was a bit woozy, her eyes glazed. But Grace was aware that she might remember any moment. She needed to go back upstairs and hide the secret pen in a new place, before it was too late. But if she left the table, Ruth would get suspicious and the Dragon could return.

Grace watched Lucho eating. He was as hungry as a lion. Ruth would, as usual, pay for his dinner. She always paid for everything. Grace had never seen him with money. He wore red swim shorts that came above his knees, and he surfed all the time. How could he carry money when it would get lost in the waves? His chest was always bare, bald. Not like her dad's that had a few soft hairs like a cuddly bear. No, Lucho was smooth. Smooth as a boiled sweet. The hair on his head, though, was shaggy and black, and he had big brown eyes. Like Bambi's. He had long, long eyelashes but when he came out of the water, all wet, he looked like a black Portuguese water dog. He shook like one too. She'd seen those dogs on YouTube. Droplets of water like lots of glittering diamonds and goldy-black sand like golden nuggets, would fly from Lucho's body. Her Real Mom had told her that when dogs shook themselves they moved hundreds of miles an hour. So maybe Lucho was more doggy after all. Not like a deer, except for his eyes. He laughed a lot and Grace liked it when he was around because it meant that SHE was in a good mood. He was twenty-four. Grace knew because she asked him. Her Real Mom told her it was rude to ask women their age or older men, but it was okay to ask boys how old they were. Grace figured that Lucho was still a boy because he played video games with her and giggled a lot. So she'd asked him his age.

One day, she thought, she would marry Lucho.

But that was her secret.

She didn't want to tell HER because she might get jealous.

Grace was also eating a tamale because if Lucho liked them, then she knew they must be good. She decided that she would always order whatever he ordered.

Mama Ruth was eating a hamburger. She had her mouth full and said in Spanish, "Adela wet herself again. She's like a leaking hot water bottle. I don't know what to do."

Lucho winked at Grace and said, "What's that pretty blouse you're wearing? You look like a little princess tonight."

Ruth looked at him and knotted her brow. "Did you hear what I said?"

"What you said, Rocío, has no place at the dinner table," he replied smoothly. "I was admiring Adela's lovely blouse. As I was saying, Adela, you look like such a pretty princess tonight."

Grace blushed and jiggled about in her chair.

Ruth glared at her. "Stop swinging your legs, baby."

"Bathroom Mommy," Grace said in Spanish. She couldn't say the whole sentence yet. She knew she wasn't allowed to say one single word of English in front of Lucho. She wasn't even allowed to speak Spanglish. She didn't dare. Just in case. Just in case her Real Mom was sent to Hell to live with The Devil.

Ruth rolled her eyes. "Go, GO! Hurry to the bathroom, I don't want to be cleaning up any more stinky mess."

Grace jumped off her chair. She ran from the beach into the guesthouse and up to her room. She now had a bedroom of her own because Ruth shared a room with Lucho.

Grace dashed into the bathroom and took the secret pen from under the towel.

She ran to the bed and pulled apart the Velcro on Carrot's back, took out the nighty and quickly rolled it around the pen. She pushed it all neatly back inside, pressed his back together again and, just to be sure, popped him under the bedclothes.

24

Sylvia

Sylvia lay stretched out on the wall-to-wall carpet of the living room floor, giving her back a break from the soft mattress of the guest room. She was staring at the ceiling, transfixed by a fly meshed in a spider's web. The spider was busy with her legs, spinning and rotating the helpless fly in a threaded whirl. On a normal day, Sylvia would have been glad to see one less fly buzzing around the house, but now she felt sorry for the creature. Only a spider, she thought, can make a fly helpless.

She hadn't heard from Tommy for three days. He'd been gone for nine. She knew she shouldn't be worried; he'd warned her that he could be out of reach at times but she, like the fly, felt helpless. On two occasions, she'd been a click away from booking herself onto a flight to join him, but she wasn't even sure where he was, which country he was in. Was he still in Guatemala? Had he crossed the border to El Salvador or Belize? Besides, she was still waiting for her new passport to come through. She'd paid for the expedited service and was expecting it any day now. And Agent Russo had pulled some strings to hurry things up.

The FBI had sent alerts out to all the border crossings for Ruth and Grace but Sylvia had been online—getting a fake passport would be easy for Ruth. Right there on the Internet were websites offering false documents. For less than a thousand dollars you could have a brand new passport and pay by Western Union, Moneygram or a bank transfer. The passport could be ready in less than a week, sent to you, courtesy of UPS or Fedex. Simple! Sylvia was amazed such companies existed. There they were, blatantly online, breaking the law. If businesses could disappear into thin air (surely the police must be trying to stop them?) then a woman and child traveling incognito was, by comparison, a piece of cake.

South America was notoriously corrupt. If Ruth and Grace were moving about on chicken buses or taking private cars, they'd just blend in with the locals who had simple IDs, easy to forge. *Who knows*, thought Sylvia, *Ruth could have been smart and just double-backed into Mexico.* Sylvia recalled Ruth's Mexican socialite friend with the influential father—the one she talked about in one of her e-mails—who would be able to organize papers for her. Ruth could have cooked up any sob story lie to get what she wanted.

Ruth was a confidence-trickster, what they called a "grifter." She could be anywhere. Latin America was vast. It was like when people talked about "going to Europe" as if it were a postage stamp they could add to their collection. Central and South America were huge landmasses, replete with mountains, inhospitable terrain, rainforests, and the Amazon which was the biggest river in the world. Ruth had backpacked in Asia; she wouldn't be intimidated by such a place, especially being fluent in the languages there. She was intrepid and could have gone in any direction. She might be hidden in a tree house in the jungle somewhere, or equally as likely, sipping cocktails in someone's grand apartment in Mexico City, hooking up with high-ranking politicians and luring them with her "man-magnet" charms. Grace could be *anywhere*. If Sylvia hopped on a plane now, where would she even begin? Especially, when she wasn't even sure where Tommy was at this point.

Up until a few days ago, Sylvia had been following his every move, online and by phone, suggesting ideas, gleaning any clue she could from Ruth's e-mails which she read over and over. His first stop trailing Ruth had been the IVF clinic in Mexico. He'd hoped he could find someone who'd been close to her, had a photo of her or something. Nothing. The doctors hardly even remembered what she looked like, they told him. Tommy reminded Sylvia that he had never even caught a glimpse of Ruth, not even when she and Sylvia Skyped on all those occasions. Neither had they crossed paths at the airport. Sylvia had described her a hundred times to him.

The more Sylvia thought about it, the more she realized she needed to get out there too. The funeral was over, what was she still doing in Saginaw? She kept looking at the phone and checking her e-mails for Tommy's update. The last time they spoke, he was still in Guatemala. She assumed he must be in a jungle somewhere by now, or he would have called.

Sylvia wondered what the IVF clinic was like. The whole baby factory idea made her feel queasy. There were enough children seeking "forever families." Why battle to create more children on purpose when all the odds were against you? The lesbian couple that Ruth had mentioned in one of her e-mails, for instance. Why didn't they want to adopt instead? People's egos? she asked herself. Or their biological need to reproduce? Tommy had tracked the couple down via the clinic. He managed to wheedle a phone number out of the secretary at the front desk. Apparently, one of the women was a barrister (an attorney) in Leeds, England. But when Tommy called, the woman said she hadn't heard from Ruth for months. The only contact she had was the same old e-mail, the same defunct New York phone number. "What about the Mexican socialite?" he'd asked. The woman didn't seem to know what he was talking about. And when Tommy grilled the clinic about her, they laughed. "This is Mexico, we have hundreds of Mexican socialites passing through our doors," they told him.

Sylvia had so many secret fears. Grace's adoption papers stolen by Ruth—she could have those forged and put into her own name—whatever her latest fake name was. Sylvia and Tommy had no proof that Grace was even their child. A DNA test? What good would that do when neither of them were her biological parents? What if they didn't find her for ten years? By which time, Grace could have forgotten them.

Agent Russo had kept in touch, but there had been no leads.

Nothing of any significance from any of the website forums had come up, just hundreds of messages of "condolences" and good wishes. Almost, it seemed to Sylvia, as if people had already given up because there was no hope for Grace at all.

Tommy's next stop had been the bank in Guatemala. He even took the same flight Ruth and Grace had been on, in hopes that one of the airline staff would have remembered a five-year-old girl with a woman wearing a straw cowboy hat. But nobody could help. The bank in Guatemala remembered Ruth very well, though. They let Tommy see all the CCT footage, but the police had been right. He relayed to Sylvia that Ruth's face was always in shadow, her head tilted down. She was aware of the cameras, it seemed. All you could make out was a blond sweep of hair and her flowery dress. Sylvia remembered that dress. It was the dress she wore on one of her first dates with Tommy. They'd had a picnic together in Central Park. She now felt violated. Knowing Ruth was flouncing about in her special memory. But that was nothing compared to how her stomach turned when she imagined Ruth with her own child. The words that came to her were: Disgusted. Abused. Desecrated.

She thought back to the conversations they'd had over the last few years. To think she had given this woman little pieces of her heart so freely, her intimate thoughts and feelings. It made her feel like she'd been raped.

For the past few days, her fury toward Ruth, the Perpetrator, had become more jagged, and the guilt toward herself had softened. How could she have known that psychopaths like Ruth existed? She was aware that it was an illness, but imagined that only murderers, serial killers, drug barons—people who had stridently broken the law many times over—could be that way. She knew that there were axe murderers out there, she knew that, and she had explained to Grace how she mustn't speak to strangers, never get tempted by someone to see a puppy or a kitten, or get into an unfamiliar car. But how could she have been prepared for Ruth?

Sylvia sat on the sofa-that-saved-her-life with her laptop beside her and looked up "psychopath" on Wikipedia. It said: **Psychopathy is a mental disorder** *characterized primarily by a lack of empathy and remorse, shallow emotions, egocentricity, and deceptiveness.*

Ruth. To a terrifying T. Cold as a blade. A steel blade.

Ruth Steel. How fitting.

What was it that made Ruth different from other human beings? We, Sylvia thought, can feel sympathy, empathy, sadness, or fear because we can step into other people's shoes and imagine how it would be for them. We can *feel* in an abstract way. We can see seconds ahead of ourselves into the future and avoid hurting others, simply by basing our emotions on our own experiences from our past. We have been hurt so we are personally involved, and we learn not to repeat others' mistakes, or our own. We can predict how others could react because we are able to see ourselves in them. We can identify, Sylvia concluded. We can identify with others.

Something Ruth was incapable of doing. *That* was what made her a psychopath.

A psychopath without a sense of humor—Ruth couldn't even appreciate *Bridget Jones*.

Was Ruth an opportunist? Had she made her crime up as she went along? Had she thought, *Ooh, passport, money, child, what a great opportunity?*

171

Or had she planned it all from the start?

Sylvia needed someone to talk to. All these thoughts spinning in her brain were giving her a migraine. She picked up the old dial telephone and called Jacqueline. Who wiser than she?

Jacqueline picked up after the second ring. "Let me just turn down the TV, Sylvia honey." She came back on the line and said, "I know, you need to let it all out or you'll go crazy, right?"

"What is it, Jacqueline, that marks someone as a psychopath? That makes them different from a normal person? I mean, not Charles Bronson, or some murderer, but people who appear normal?"

"Sylvia, you know, I've been mulling over the same darn thing. What kind of person would do what this woman has done? And fool you so? I guess individuals who appear to others to have genuine sentiments, and often function in the real world as average human beings. Ruth seemed warm and caring, right?"

"Well yes. She did. Or I wouldn't have made friends with her in the first place."

"You know, honey, I think you were feeding Ruth's ego, her appetite; reading her novel, giving her critiques—acting as a sounding board for her life dramas. She needed you in some way. She was using you but you were too kind to see it that way."

"I guess you have a point."

Jacqueline continued, "You know them big cats you see on the Discovery Channel? They'll fine tune all kinds of crafty functions in order to stalk their prey, cut 'em out of the herd, hone in and exhaust their kill, just like this lady Ruth has done. Like a predator. Am I not right? She's like a hunter, hiding behind all kinds of elaborate camouflage to get what she wants."

Jacqueline was right. Ruth had a predatory hunger. Everything she craved was useful to her in some way; *to have her needs met.* If her needs weren't met, she simply moved on. A Ruthless Predator. But a clever one. Ruth-Less.

Jacqueline went on, "Like a big greedy cat, working on instinct, not on common values. She has no moral code."

To have her needs fulfilled, Sylvia thought. Those were Ruth's words. Lies mixed with snippets of truth and "vulnerability," blended together in a careful cocktail to gain whatever she set out to subjugate, to manipulate. Whatever, whomever, she marked out to become her prey.

"How come you're so wise, Jacqueline?"

She laughed. "I've been around the block a few times."

Sylvia snapped her laptop shut. "Well thanks. Just talking to you has made me feel a lot better."

"Any time honey. If you need to call in the middle of the night, you just holler—I'll be here. My phone is by my bed. Bye honey. You get some rest now, you hear?"

But Sylvia didn't feel better. She thought about the satisfied spider she'd been staring at earlier, feeling as if Grace were the unsuspecting fly, and she curled herself into a fetal position. She gulped great mounds of air in between her yowling sobs as she thought of poor little Gracie. Was her daughter aware, she wondered, of who this monster was?

She knew that if Tommy did find Ruth . . .

He'd be capable of killing her.

And although Sylvia hated to admit it, she'd be cheering him on.

25

Grace

Grace was sitting cross-legged beneath a mango tree, facing the beach. The sun was turning as orange as the mangos, and Lucho was still surfing. Nobody was around. She was quite alone.

She pressed down the pocket clip on her recording pen:

"SHE's been gone five days. Hooray! Now Lucho's in charge. I heard her give him instructions about how to look after me, what I'm allowed or not allowed, and my bedtime. She went over the rules twenty times. She gave him money and promised extra if he did a good job. She said we'll all meet up again in three weeks, when she's better from her operation.

I'm still not sure what a Devious Septum is, but she explained she'd need a vacation afterwards because her nose'll be sore, and she also told me that she could do with 'a break from being Mommy.' My Real Mom never took a break but I guess Ruth doesn't like being a mommy so much. Lucho's doing a perfect job anyway. I don't need HER. Things are fun now! Except I still feel sad about my Real Mom, about the car accident. Ruth said I'll never see her again cos she's died forever and she'll never *ever* be coming back. So I might as well stop praying, she said, as I'm wasting my words and my tears."

Grace pressed the pocket clip up to stop the recording. Her nose felt all burny again, just thinking about her mom. She imagined that her bright yellow bear Hideous was Blueby, and mimed winding up the key on his bottom, listening to his imaginary tune. She sang in a croaky, teary voice, "And that's the day that teddybears have their pic . . .nic."

She daydreamed about Heaven a lot. About how her mom was getting on there. And Mrs. Paws. She knew what Ruth had said—about animals not being allowed in Heaven—wasn't true. She knew this because her Real Mom had told her that *all* animals went to Heaven. Guaranteed. No exceptions. She explained that some humans, if they'd been *really* bad, would have to wait their turn and come back to Earth for a second, or even a third go around, until they learned to be kind. But animals always had a place waiting for them, no matter what. Mrs. Paws would be there with her and they'd be able to cuddle.

She wanted to ask Lucho what he thought of Heaven but it was too complicated to talk about in Spanish. Grace also got the feeling that Lucho felt as if he was already living in Heaven with his surfboard, anyway, so it was useless to discuss Heaven with him.

Grace took a big breath and pressed the clip again. She wanted to tell her story, so when she saw her dad, he could hear all about it:

"Five days ago, all three of us—me Ruth and Lucho—left El Salvador and came to a new country by different buses, and then a fishing boat. The buses took two days! We changed buses A LOT! And boy, was it a bumpy ride! And dusty. Our faces got real dirty. SHE was not happy at all, but she kept saying that we had no choice, that we had to take the *camioneta*. The journey was really long and, once, we slept on the bus overnight. But that was okay because I got to rest my head on Lucho's shoulder. He always made sure I was comfortable and he called me *Cariño*. He's so kind to me. He let me listen to his iPod, and when the bus stopped we went outside, and sometimes he guarded me and held his sarong around me while I did a pee behind a bush. He bought me little bunches of bananas from children selling really funny fruit.

I saw bright green parrots and naughty monkeys with black arms and faces, the color of toffees. They were running about free on the roads. They came down from the trees and tried to steal the bananas from people's carts! Little boys were chasing after them, shouting and waving their fists like they wanted to punch them. But there was no way—the monkeys were too fast! I didn't know about wild monkeys, I'd only seen them at the zoo and on TV—so cool to see them running free.

After we got off the last bus we got a taxi to a beach where we waited to find someone with a boat. But it started pouring with rain—crazy, crazy rain, so we hung out there for a whole day until the water was calm enough to leave. SHE was in such a bad mood. The Dragon Mood. Finally, a fisherman with just a few teeth said he'd take us in his little boat. It took a while to get it into the water. He put two small logs under the boat so it was resting on top of the logs like wheels. Then Lucho and him rolled the boat out. They had to stop a lot and kick the logs in the right place so it rolled out nicely. Otherwise, Lucho said, the boat was too heavy. It was small, and in the water it rocked about in the waves and we got really wet and cold. It was night and I was shivering and my teeth were clattering like a scary ghost, but I felt safe because Lucho held me in his arms and said, '*Tranquila Cariño.*' So it was okay.

The fisherman with two teeth dropped us off in a mangrove. I could count his teeth because Mama Ruth paid him lots and lots of money and he smiled. So funny! His whole mouth opened and I could see inside, right up to the top of his mouth. Oh yes, and I saw a seagull sitting on a turtle! The turtle was floating and the seagull was just hanging out using him like a raft!"

Grace stopped the magic pen recording and looked around.

The sky was now getting dark pink and was streaked with purple. There was the moon, too, not full the way it had been the week before, but like someone had taken a great bite out of it. Grace thought she could see the eyes and lips of the Man in the Moon but she wasn't sure. She'd have to check with Lucho.

She stood up and looked toward the ocean. She wondered when he'd be finished with his surfing. Usually Lucho surfed just mornings, but sometimes the swell was high later in the day, too. She didn't like being alone, but he told her she wasn't allowed to go in the big waves. And never when he was surfing. He warned her it was too dangerous for little girls. Besides, she nearly got bitten by a jellyfish and was too scared to go in alone. Sometimes she watched him. He stood on his board with his knees bent a little and went under the big curly wave and under the big, foamy, bubble of white. Each time, she wondered if the wave would eat him up but then he appeared again smiling. She wanted to be a surfer, too. When she grew up.

She remembered when they arrived, after the toothless fisherman had dropped them off five days ago, the bright moon glowed like a shiny quarter in the sky. She had never seen mangrove trees. They were half in the water, half on land, and they had roots like great eagles' claws. Lucho explained that the trees in a mangrove ate and drank more and more water every day and, bit by bit, turned the water into land with their big claw roots that fed on a mixture of sweet and salty water. Monster trees that guzzled the water! Grace was sure she saw the legs of one tree move right in front of her nose like the trees in *The Wizard of Oz.*

They all spent that night in a hut with a straw roof. Wild birds swooped about, high in the sky, and Grace could hear animals making noises in the black night. Spooky. Way better than Disney-land. Then, the next morning, very early, they all got into a taxi and drove. After about an hour, Ruth dropped them off, and she went on alone in the taxi. She was heading for the airport to go to Rio to have her Devious Septum operated on.

Now, Grace thought, *I have Lucho all to myself.*

She still couldn't pronounce the name of the new country where they had arrived by fishing boat. Like the British word for panties: Knickers.

Knickers and water.

Knicker Agua.

Her dad, she remembered, once told her a joke that went like this:

> *Knock knock.*
> *Who's there?*
> *Nicolas*
> *Nicolas who?*
> *Knickerless girls shouldn't climb trees!*

She missed her dad. She missed him a lot. Maybe he would come and join them. Ruth said she was "working on it."

Because of her dad being English, Grace knew all about knickers and thought the word knickers was much funnier than panties. It made her giggle. And now they were in a place called KNICKER AGUA. It was beautiful, too, even if it did have a silly name.

After Ruth dropped them off and carried on to the airport,

Grace and Lucho got another car to the beach. And that was where she was now. It was called The Boom because of the great surf. The sand wasn't black like in El Salvador. The sand here was goldenish. The waves were enormous, and she had never seen Lucho with such a big grin. SHE wouldn't let him bring his surfboard on the journey. She said it would *draw* too much attention. But how could a surfboard draw? SHE forced him to sell it in El Salvador but promised to buy him a new one when they arrived in Knicker Agua.

So the day they arrived at The Boom, Lucho bought a board from another surfer. He said the new one was lighter and better than the last. He was *contentisimo*, he said.

And Grace was *contentisima* because she could do anything she wanted now.

Every morning she woke up and felt her mattress. It was dry! No pee-pee. She wished she could show HER the clean, dry bed to prove that she wasn't a baby. She and Lucho had been at The Boom for five whole days and nights. She had counted the days. And every single morning Grace felt the bed after she woke up, just to be sure, and it was as dry as a freshly laundered towel. Five nights of dry bed. Not even a trickle!

They lived in a secret little cabin deep in the woods, just next to the beach. Lucho was renting it from another surfer for eight dollars a day. Grace thought it was the most perfect house in the world. Well, not as perfect as Crowheart or her Granddaddy's house in Saginaw where she spent last Christmas, but almost as good. It had three single beds, wooden, like the beds in *Goldilocks and the Three Bears*. There were three chairs and a table, too.

Outside in the garden was a solar shower hanging from a tree behind a screened area, a few steps down from the porch. It looked over to a wild garden dripping with banana, avocado and mango trees. The toilet was a wooden seat around a hole that dropped a long way down. Grace wondered what happened to her poop and she soon found out. A hairy hog lived nearby and would come to their garden for visits. He'd wait patiently down below and get excited when he heard anybody approaching the toilet. If she just did a wee-wee, he grunted crossly. Lucho joked and said that her poop was like caviar to the pig. She didn't know what caviar was but it was obviously delicious.

At least the hog thought so.

Every day before sunset, Lucho surfed, and Grace listened to music and played games on his iPod. Lucho knew about the secret pen. He never said a word about it to Ruth, and luckily, Ruth had never looked inside Carrot.

Every night so far, Grace and Lucho ate next door with the caretaker of the cabin. She cooked for them. Her name was Angela. Grace thought she had cheeks like rosy red apples, the kind Snow White was offered by the Evil Stepmother. Except Angela was very kind.

Then, after dinner, Lucho would tuck Grace up in bed and tell her a story. Not a story from a book but an invented, Lucho story. Some were funny and some were scary, but if he told her a scary one, he would give her a big hug and wait until she fell asleep.

She didn't understand every word because, of course, his stories were only Spanish, but she didn't care. She loved Story-Time. Not as much as her Real Mom's Story-Time, but almost.

Grace wondered if Ruth was going to come and see them in three weeks. She'd said she needed a break from being a mommy. Maybe Ruth was leaving her with Lucho forever, and she wouldn't come back from Rio. If that was true, she wouldn't have any mom at all.

She'd have to wait, she thought, until she got to Heaven. Her Real Mom would sing to her:

"Row, row, row your boat
Gently down the stream . . .
Merrily, merrily, merrily, merrily,
Life is but a dream."

26

Sylvia

"**I**'m in Rio."

"What?" Sylvia pressed the phone closer to her ear. Just hearing Tommy's voice made her heart flutter—a hummingbird above a flower.

"I'm in Rio," Tommy repeated. "I'm so sorry I couldn't call or e-mail earlier, darling." His voice sounded tired, and distant.

Sylvia's voice was shaky. "I've been beside myself with worry. What *happened?*"

"I got really sick. Food poisoning, or dodgy water. I ended up in some filthy little dive in San Pedro Sula in Honduras. I was literally too weak to talk, to see a doctor. Nobody spoke English there. I tried to get someone to get a message to you, but my Spanish is pretty unintelligible, they couldn't understand what the hell I was saying."

Sylvia felt sick just hearing about it. The thought of losing Tommy *and* Grace was terrifying. "That's it. I'm coming out. I'm booking a flight for tomorrow. My new passport has arrived so I'm

181

good to go. At least I speak schoolgirl Spanish. At least *I* know what Ruth looks like." Sylvia thought this could happen, Tommy practically dying and she sitting there helpless, with no way of even knowing. Or Tommy ending up being munched by a crocodile in the Amazon somewhere.

"NO! Don't be silly. Stay where you are." His voice was urgent.

"But Tommy, this is *insane*! What if you get ill again? What am I supposed to do in Saginaw all alone, being so useless?"

"You're not being useless, you've been amazing with all these forums and stuff, speaking with the FBI, helping them with the photofit of Ruth, getting it all out there on the web. What if a lead came in and we were both incommunicado here? It's good you're home, Sylvia darling. Let me handle things down here. You've done all you can do already. I know it's hard, but just to give your mind a few minutes rest from all this. Try and relax a little."

"What is *wrong* with you? You think that's even possible with Grace gone? Why don't you want me *with* you? We used to be a team! What is *with* all this Indiana Jones macho crap, you trying to do everything on your own?"

She could hear him sigh. "Because darling, I just don't see the point. I'm thinking of what's best for you. For Grace."

"No you are *not*. You think I'll be a burden, that's what! Just because I've never backpacked before and you think I'm some prissy princess who can't handle traveling on a chicken bus. Well thank you so much! How do you think I feel? I swear to God when you act like this we may as well be *divorced*." Sylvia sucked in a lungful of air. *Oh no, that came out wrong.* She didn't mean it. But she couldn't take it back now—the words were already out there, the gale that was in her mouth had let loose. She said that awful D word. "What were you doing in Honduras?" she asked, praying he might not have taken on board what she just said.

"I got a tip-off from the *Lonely Planet* forum. Somebody thought they saw them."

"How come I missed that? I've been reading all the posts."

"I got a text message on my cell."

"And?"

"Well, I tracked them down, the mother and child. Only problem was . . . it wasn't Grace. It was this woman whose ex-boyfriend was Peruvian and she was white. From San Diego."

Sylvia sighed. "Well, I guess that's good that people are at least on the alert. So disappointing, though. I'm glad I didn't have to go through that emotional roller coaster the last few days—thinking I'd found Grace and then running up against empty. Maybe next time we'll get lucky. So now what?"

"Exactly, Sylvia, that's my *point*. It *is* an emotional roller coaster. Maybe yes, maybe no. I don't want to put you through all that. Please stay home."

"Stop locking me *out* Tommy!"

"I'm not locking you out. I'm trying to protect you. How d'you think I feel with all this pressure about Grace, *plus* if I had to worry about you getting sick and stuff, on top of it all? The one comfort I have is knowing that you're safe at home in America." Sylvia could hear him groan with exasperation. As if he were the only one to be feeling that way. "Look," he continued, "I got another tip. From someone anonymous, posted on the *Lonely Planet* forum. They said they'd seen a white woman with olive skin, brown hair, about five-foot-six with a dark girl, five or six years old who looks just like Grace. Identical, the message read. They're here in Rio, apparently. I even have the name of the hotel where they were last seen."

"Where?"

"The Copacabana."

"Rio would make total sense. Ruth told me that she grew up in Brazil; speaks Portuguese like a native Brazilian." Sylvia could just see Ruth swanning about in the Copacabana Palace, one of the flashiest hotels in the world, with *her* inheritance money paying for it all. "Okay, great, Tommy. This is *so* hopeful. I'll meet you tomorrow or as soon as I can get there. I'll get packed right now. What do I need, a lightweight backpack? How big? Should I bring a mosquito net in case we end up in a jungle somewhere?"

"Darling, let me check it out first. It could be another wild goose chase. Listen, my battery's about to run out. I'll call you later, okay? I'm on my way to the hotel now."

The line went dead. Sylvia held the old dial telephone receiver in her hands. Not even the weight of it could steady her trembling hand which was quivering in uncontrollable spasms. She put the receiver on its cradle and tucked her knees up to her chest, holding her arms around herself to stop herself shaking. The sofa-that-saved-her-life felt comforting, at least, but could not calm the bubbling rage she felt coursing through her body. How dare Tommy try and control her like this!

She made up her mind. That was it. She was going online now to buy her ticket and tomorrow morning, as early as she could, she'd get a backpack. Or maybe even buy one at the airport, itself. She'd catch the first available plane.

She'd show her husband what she was made of.

Damn right she would.

27

Tommy

T ommy walked along the paved sidewalk of possibly the most famous beachfront promenade in the world, its black and white wave motif beneath him in a dizzying geometric pattern. As if by design, a matching soccer ball—also black and white—and kicked up by a barefooted boy, rolled in front of him. Tommy sent it spinning back into the air. As he turned with his back to the ocean, he saw the grand facade of Rio's Copacabana Palace rising before him like a massive wedding cake, sparkling between the water and the green hills behind.

In every direction there were joggers, street vendors, cyclists, body-builders, and people playing a game that looked like a cross between soccer and volleyball. There were surfers, swimmers and body-beautifuls in bikinis as thin as dental floss.

Tommy stopped at a stall and bought a fresh T-shirt which he changed into on the spot, but he still felt dirty, like a smelly old hippy with his stained rucksack and smutty, unshaven face. He crossed over the road to the hotel and made his way to the en-trance. He wished he had the budget for a hotel like this but at a minimum of $820 a night, he was out of his backpacking league. Anyway, staying here would eat at his conscience—he'd been harrowed by guilt since his arrival in Rio, just knowing that he was one of the lucky ones.

He wiped his sweaty brow with the back of his hand and took in the cool white of the Mediterranean-style edifice, set off by a cloudless cobalt-blue sky. Not far away there would be children in ghettos who sniffed glue, joined together in gangs to survive. Then they'd start to work for traffickers selling cocaine, anything to be able to feed themselves. Twelve-year-old girls would be already working as prostitutes, abusing themselves with self-inflicted abortions because the hospitals wouldn't take them. Such a vicious circle. He'd heard that these children were periodically rounded up by police and shot. As if they were vermin. The idea that that could be Grace, or any child, shot shivers along his spine.

What a surreal place. What a paradox. The uber-rich and the snot-poor, only blocks away from each other. This was the land of *The Girl from Ipenema,* the birth of the tanga, the butt implant. Once, Sylvia had read him an article from one of her fashion magazines which said that Rio had more plastic surgeons per head than anywhere in the world. This was the land of the impossibly glamorous.

Tommy did not belong here.

He entered the lobby with trepidation. Polished marble. Grand. He hadn't imagined that Grace and Ruth would be in a place like this. So conspicuous and packed with tourists, maybe some of them even reading his Internet posts. Perhaps Ruth, being so obvious, was clever? An odd slant to things but possible to get away with. Or had Ruth simply been tempted by a splash of luxury? With all the money she now had, she could stay wherever she liked. Tommy couldn't afford to book a room—he'd just have to hang around until they showed up.

He pictured seeing Grace again and prayed that it would really happen. Running up to him and jumping into his arms. He could swing her around and then carry her on his shoulders. He knew she loved that, feeling like a giant, watching the world from a great height. He remembered how excited she'd got in London at the Changing of the Guard at Buckingham Palace. She was on his shoulders, yelling at the Guards, who had stone-dead expressions on their faces, dressed in their special fur hats. She was bellowing at them through the black iron gates to try and make them smile. When he and Grace got back to where their car was parked, to their horror it had been towed away. Things had got tough since Tommy had last lived in London—double yellow lines, even red ones, everywhere. When they came across a policeman, Grace said in her assertive voice: "If you want a car, then don't steal ours. You should buy your own!" She always was precocious, learned to talk and walk way ahead of other children her age. He suspected Grace had forgotten about that trip. Too young to remember. Time was different for a child.

The ten days she'd been gone now would seem like twenty years to her.

And for the first time in forever Tommy prayed to whoever was listening: God, Ganesh, Hanuman, Allah—the whole damn lot of them.

"Please bring my little girl back to me," he begged under his breath. "*Please.*"

28

Sylvia

S ylvia bought her ticket online. It wasn't perfect; she'd have to change twice, first in Chicago and then again in São Paulo. The trip was going to take her twenty hours. She hadn't even let Tommy know. She'd wait until she was just about to board the plane, that way he couldn't try to dissuade her.

Her words, those Divorce Words, ricocheted in her mind like a spiteful echo. Their lovemaking, just before he left, had her inside out, upside down. Thoughts had crossed her mind like, *What's the point of us carrying on if we can't find Grace?* But then he seduced her into falling in love with him again. She felt vulnerable, exposed like a window to dashing rain. She should have felt protected but she didn't. Afterwards, after she dropped him at the airport and he had gone from sight, she felt weak. She wasn't sure what he wanted. Was it real? Did he *really* love her? She couldn't believe she was the light in his life—as he'd whispered to her after they'd both come—when she, she thought, had been so dark. Like a cavernous hole. Or was *she* the only one who sensed her darkness inside? She wondered how many other wives felt like this. That mistrust. The aching insecurity. The doubt that shoved its nose into their marriage like a pushy busybody on a mission to stir up trouble. His making love to her had just made her suspect him more, like an adulterer buying his wife flowers while he planned a weekend away with his secretary.

She was in love with Tommy again and it hurt.

She tried to picture how he was getting on and wondered if this time it really would turn out to be Ruth and Grace. Why would someone post an *anonymous* message on the bulletin board forum of the *Lonely Planet?* Surely someone would be proud to help out a desperate couple? An "anonymous" message could be tracked by the forum managers themselves. This one had been traced to Rio, itself, to an Internet café, but some people had multiple e-mail addresses—not much of a clue, and the person posting had never used the forum before.

Sylvia wished she'd gotten herself down there sooner. Perhaps things would have gone more smoothly. Tommy had obviously been battling with Spanish. Now he'd have to contend with Portuguese.

She went into the living room and looked in the travel section of her father's little library. Her parents had been all over Europe, taken six months for their honeymoon—the dreamy honeymoon that had given birth to albums full of photos. Meanwhile, unbeknownst to her father, LeRoy had already been born, poignantly not part of her father's book of life memories.

Sylvia browsed through the selection of books. There were quaint travel guides, dog-eared, loved, smiling out from the bookshelf, remembering the good times they had along the French Riviera, Rome, Barcelona, and the island of Majorca. Sylvia turned the pages of a Spanish phrase book. Latin American was a bit different from Castilian. She remembered from classes at school that in Spain they said *coche* for car but in South America they said *carro*. As for Portuguese, it seemed her parents hadn't needed it. Still, she could brush up on her Spanish—just in case they ended up in neighboring countries.

She sat down cross-legged on the carpeted floor and laughed at herself. Why always the floor? She used to do her homework here, books spread out, her body contorted into yoga-like positions that were easy enough for a nimble twelve-year-old, while she wrote essays and did her math. It used to drive her mother crazy that she would never sit at a desk. Here she was again, about to do a little Spanish revision. She'd got an A once—perhaps it would come back to her. It was such an expressive language and a subject she'd always hoped to re-visit, but she'd never happened to have the time. Or the will.

But now she had the will alright.

And *how*.

SYLVIA COULD HARDLY SLEEP. The excitement and nerves were too much to bear. She wanted to take a sleeping pill but ever since her father's overdose, she'd fought against the temptation. Could she call Melinda so late? Her cousin was like a sister, but sisters could also be mean. Melinda worked. She had a real job. She was some important analyst in computers, databases. *Why is it that the people closest to us get the least attention*, Sylvia wondered? She felt ashamed that she didn't even know what Melinda did, *exactly*, for a living. She'd inquired several times. Melinda had explained, but if someone had asked Sylvia to describe Melinda's job in detail, she found herself lost. Shameful.

Melinda had been great, calling every day for updates. She felt mortified that she hadn't suspected Ruth's motives. She had unwittingly aided the "psycho ball to get rolling" as she described the situation. But how could Melinda have known that Sylvia's "nice friend" would be a psycho in the first place? Was Sylvia that bad a judge of character? *Obviously, yes, she was.*

As she lay in her parents' bed, Sylvia pressed the buttons on the telephone.

Melinda's yawny voice answered, "So you didn't take a pill?" Sylvia hadn't even said hello, Melinda knew obviously, that only one person could be calling her at three a.m.

"No. I've been," Sylvia said, "resisting. I want to be alert. Awake. It's my daughter at stake. I don't want to be comatose on a sofa somewhere, sleeping."

"Comatose on the sofas in your parent's house? Sorry, *your* house now. Not likely. So uncomfortable."

Sylvia smiled but didn't laugh. "I'm going to Rio tomorrow. I've booked my flight."

There was silence.

"But Tommy's taking care of stuff down there, isn't he?" Melinda asked.

"What is *wrong* with everyone? What makes everyone think that a man can take better care of this situation than a wooo-man?"

"Honey, d'you even *know* where Grace is?"

"We have a lead."

"Great! Where? What?"

"Someone posted an anonymous tip on the *Lonely Planet* forum. They've been seen in Rio. But whether it's Ruth and Grace, we have yet to find out. We've already had one false alarm."

"What about the FBI and the police? Haven't they come up with anything?"

"Maybe I should say that Grace is carrying an Al-Qaeda bomb strapped to her body—maybe then they'd perk up. So far, all they've been is, "understanding." I mean, maybe they're really working on it behind closed doors, who knows, but nothing's come up yet."

"Does Tommy know you're coming?"

It annoyed Sylvia that Melinda knew her so well. "No," she admitted.

"I figured. So I guess I'll have to pack. What do I need? A suitcase? A backpack? Are we going hippy-style or medium-comfort style?"

"*We* are not going any style. You have a serious job, Melinda."

"My serious job, my dear, is my family. Fuck my day job—I get the feeling I'm about to be let go anyway—everyone's walking on eggshells at work, eyeing each other up, wondering who'll be the next to be fired, so it's only a matter of time. Jobs are jobs, and family? Well family is for life. And if the FBI are too pussy to hunt this bitch down, and Tommy's too . . . whatever. You need assistance. Obviously."

"I can't let you get into this."

"Oh Pl-eeaze, do you know how guilty I feel for not having had the feelers out about Ruth? You've always been gullible, Sylvia, when it comes to friends—always so trusting of everybody—I should have second guessed this."

"Thanks, Melinda—that makes me feel *even* better."

"Sorry, sweetie, I didn't mean it like that. Of course you couldn't have known some nut-job was going to steal your daughter, but you do need help. Okay, I'm booking my flight *as we speak*. What's your flight number? I assume you'll be changing in Chicago? I'll meet you there."

29

Tommy

The staff at the Copacabana was helpful but Tommy realized that he should be working directly with the police and needed a translator. He had hoped that, by some miracle, he'd see Grace by the swimming pool or around the lobby, and that would be that—they'd be reunited and it would be over. He showed everyone his daughter's photo but nobody, not even the kitchen staff, had seen her. Nor anyone like her.

Tommy's Portuguese was even worse than his Spanish—zero. He could hardly understand a word. Another bloody fiasco. Grace obviously wasn't here. Could someone have been playing a practical joke, posting false information on the *LP* forum? He did think the anonymous side of it strange. If so, that person was beyond sick.

Another blow for Sylvia. He reflected on their telephone conversation earlier. He'd tried to stay calm, unemotional, but the way she lashed out words about divorce sliced through him like a shallow, but poignant, razor-sharp paper cut. It was totally unexpected. *Where* had it come from? He thought their moment together—making love the way they had—was a magical connection that he feared they'd lost over the past year. For him, it was like bright sunlight slipping through lugubrious clouds after a British winter. Yet there she was, flaying him with divorce words only a week later. She was still punishing him, he decided.

His mind wandered back to his last dinner in LA with Marie, the "Bel Ange" as Sylvia called her. He felt pleased with himself for having overcome temptation. There she was, this beautiful young thing, licking her lips, flashing off her knickers, enticing him with come-hither eyes, and although he desired her physically (or his dick did), he did nothing. He knew she wanted to use him for his photography, get a load of free pictures and, even though he could have used her too (isn't that the unsaid contract in LA?), he paid for the meal and left. In the end, the whole idea had been a turn-off. He remembered he had a wife who had been loyal to him, who loved him. She was the mother of his child and that counted for everything. He didn't even kiss Marie. His big sin? Taking a pretty girl out to lunch and harboring secret desires that he never even played upon. And, as uneasy as he felt about it now, Sylvia didn't even know. So why was she punching him with the threat of divorce? He'd been planning to come clean, tell her about their meeting, and reassure her that his prepubescent mid-life crisis was over, but then they heard about Grace. Just bringing up the subject of seeing Marie again could, quite rightly, ignite a fire.

She was an enigma, his wife. They'd been married seven years and yet he felt he still didn't know her. He wondered if he had ever truly reached her. Grace had. Grace had a place deep in her soul, but did he? Would she ever let him in? Thinking about that lovemaking session made his heart swell with love. And desire. He loved fucking Sylvia and wished they were constantly doing it. But she'd iced him out, bit by bit, and they'd drifted apart. He had to win her back. All of her. Every last inch of her. Her mind, her soul, her body. He wanted IN.

"Excuse me. Sorry to interrupt your daydream, but I overheard your conversation with the manager earlier, and I wondered if you needed some help?"

Tommy, startled, turned around. A woman was studying him, searching his face with an air of quizzical pity. She had a strong accent when she spoke English, Brazilian maybe? Auburn-red hair, olive skin. "I heard you were having trouble," she went on, "that you have a missing daughter and you need some help translating."

"Yes. Do you *know* something? Do you know where she is?" Tommy's voice was thick with desperation. He could hear waves of it roll and tremble from his mouth.

"I'm afraid not," the woman said. "But I can help you with translation. I'm Brazilian but my English isn't bad."

He swallowed. *Help at last.* "Your English sounds perfect."

"Perfect? I wish. But I have worked for the UN in the past. Amongst other things."

"How much is your daily rate?"

She shook her head. "Oh, no. I wouldn't want to charge you a fee. Your daughter is *missing*. I want to help. You look so lost, so lonely." She looked up at him almost seductively. Was it his imagination? Maybe it was. Maybe none of these women desired him—it was all in his fantastical, mid-life crisis head.

"Come on." She linked her arm into his. His dirty backpack, resting at his feet, acted as a buffer between them. "Please," she offered. "I really want to help a man in distress. You have that expression in English, don't you?"

"Usually it's a damsel in distress," he replied.

She laughed. She had a friendly smile that flashed white even teeth, like an American smile. Around the bridge of her nose there was a faint purple bruise. Bumped into a lamppost, had she, or involved in an abusive relationship? He saw her notice his stare.

She touched her retroussé nose and told him, "A horse whinnied up at me the other day and bashed me right here. Nothing broken, but still a little tender."

"Oh no, that must have been a shock. Horses can be scary when spooked."

She was still smiling. "Oh, it was just an accident. Now if it had been a *cat* that would have been another story."

Tommy furrowed his brows. "A cat?"

"Cats scare the crap out of me. Their nasty vicious claws and sharp, pointy teeth. Just something that happened to me when I was a child, you know."

"Your English—it's impeccable. How does a Brazilian know a word like whinny?" *Good. She can really be useful,* he decided.

"I had an American fiancé once. Come on, let's go by the pool. The meal's on me. I bet you could use some sustenance after your long journey."

"How do you know I've had a long journey?" Tommy asked.

"Just guessing. Your backpack kind of gives you away."

They walked out to the terrace by the pool. Tommy had been hanging about the hotel all day, and it was now past sunset, the dark closing in. The terrace and pool were lit up, the water shimmering and twinkling, catching reflections on ladies' jeweled earrings and gold-sparkled arms. The guests here were loaded, obviously.

Rio—*Beauty and the Beast.*

"I'm sorry," he said. "I completely forgot to introduce myself. I'm Tommy. Tommy Garland."

"Like Judy?"

"Sorry?"

She grinned. "Judy Garland. Bet you've heard that before."

"No, never," he said deadpan. "Sorry, I'm just very tired, that's all, not very on the ball."

"Yes, I've noticed."

Cheeky, he thought. Flirtatious and over-intimate like she'd known him for years. Not that he was adverse to an attractive woman chatting him up. Especially if she was going to help him find Grace. "Sorry, and your name is—?"

"Oh, how silly of me." She held her gaze for a moment, and looking directly in his eyes said, "I'm Ana. But I won't tell you my last name as you won't be able to pronounce it!"

"Nice to meet you, Ana." Tommy picked up a menu from a table and glanced at it. He raised his eyebrows when he saw the prices. "About buying me a meal? Really, no. I wouldn't feel comfortable. Since you've offered to help me out, let me treat you. But I have to admit it can't be here at this hotel, it's a bit beyond my budget, I'm afraid. I don't have too long, either. I really want to get going about Grace as soon as possible. Is a quick snack okay with you?"

"No problem. I know a place nearby. As I happen to be staying here on business, I don't mind the exorbitant prices at this hotel because *they're* footing the bill." She laughed and laid her hand on his shoulder.

"Your English really is word perfect."

"I went to the International School. Here, in Rio."

Tommy narrowed his eyes. "I thought you said you had an American fiancé."

"That too."

There was an awkward silence.

"We can leave your backpack in my room—"

He cut in, "Oh no, really, that would make me feel awkward."

"Then we'll leave it behind the front desk. They won't mind."

Tommy looked down at his dirty sneakers. "Normally, I don't think they'd be so welcoming in a place like this. But I have to say, I think every single member of staff knows my life history, all my woes, and they've been extremely kind to me, considering I look like a dirty old hippy."

"Not so old. Let me take a guess. Thirty-two?"

He frowned. She was getting personal again. "What are you, a white witch or something?"

"Something like that." Ana threw her head back and laughed

again, her smile enormously wide, fixed for a snapshot. "I know a nice little place where they serve local food, cheap but delicious. We can come up with some sort of plan for Grace."

"How d'you know my daughter's called Grace?"

"I heard you talking, telling the manager her name."

"Ah, I see."

THE RESTAURANT WAS simple; little wooden tables and straw chairs with a seashell theme as a backdrop. Ana seemed keen to order for them both. Tommy hadn't realized how hungry he was. It was the first proper meal he was about to have since his illness and he hoped he wouldn't throw up.

Ana widened her eyes. "Okay, the best thing to do is to share as there are so many delicious things to try. Have you ever eaten Brazilian food before?"

"Once, years ago in London, but I can hardly remember—just that I liked it."

Ana stroked her nose. "You'll love it, trust me. It's like a mix of all the different cultures we have here—Indian, African—you know, a lot of slaves were brought here by the Portuguese—a lot of coconut milk and palm oil is used."

Tommy felt himself uneasy. Palm oil, coconut—was he ready for such rich cuisine? He'd been expecting something more down-to-earth—he didn't want to take up the whole evening with some elaborate dinner—every minute was a click on the clock, every second a moment further away from finding Grace.

"Maybe I should just have something light. I was pretty sick recently."

"Oh you'll love everything," she assured him in her thick, Brazilian accent. "We can start with *Acarajé* which is a popular street food snack here, especially at the beach. The main ingredients are black-eyed peas seasoned with ground dried shrimp and onions—"

she licked her lips, "which are shaped into balls and deep fried, then split and filled with a spicy shrimp and caramelized onion filling. Sounds good, huh? I love them. Then I thought we could get some octopus and some *Xinxim de galinha*, which is chicken, flavored with garlic, salt, and lemon, or maybe some *Carangueijada*, which is whole cooked crab."

"Sounds way too much for just two." *Damn his English manners*—he should be nipping this fiasco in the bud right now. Instead he was being polite. Tick-tock. He wanted Ana to help him, not waste time with an elaborate dinner!

She laid her fingers on his hand. "We can always get a doggy bag which I can put in my mini-bar fridge. We can eat the rest tomorrow."

Tomorrow? Tommy hadn't yet thought ahead to tomorrow. So far, the topic of Grace hadn't even come up. This was crazy. He needed help and soon. But he didn't want to be rude to Ana; she was his ticket to getting something done around here. He'd ask her to accompany him to the police station, the second they'd eaten.

A waitress approached their table and Ana ordered the spread she had described. She turned to Tommy and said in an excited voice, with her hands clapped together, "I love to eat. Oh, and I've ordered us *Caipirinhas,* too. I adore that heady mix of limejuice and *cachaça*. The sugar kind of takes the edge off the lime and makes throwing these drinks back just a *little* too easy." She chuckled. "I'm so pleased we met, Tommy. I really am." She rested her hand on his again and her fingers slowly fondled his wedding band. "You're married?"

"Why do you sound surprised?" he said edgily. "I have a five-year-old daughter, after all."

"Of course. How silly of me. What's she like, your wife?"

The question took him by surprise. But Ana *was* South American—their culture was more open, he supposed.

"She's great," he replied with a frown. *Like a beautiful ice princess.*

199

Hard to get close to, but when you do you see that she can melt and is just the sweetest, most trusting woman ever. "But not in the best of spirits right now, obviously."

"So things are a little tough between you?"

Jesus! What was she like, this woman? "Our daughter's missing, Ana. We're just under a lot of strain—beside ourselves with worry about Grace."

"Is she intelligent, your wife? Serious? Funny?"

Why all this interest in my wife? "Yes, very intelligent. She reads a lot."

Tommy thought of how Sylvia loved poetry, how she was deep, philosophical, and sensitive. But with a quirky sense of humor, too. That he had to work though, to keep her spark lit, that sometimes he thought he wasn't interesting enough for her. She'd be reading *Anna Karenina*, or something, and he'd be looking at books about fly fishing or photography.

He blurted out, "The closest I get to reading literature is a Tom Clancy novel." As he spoke, he mentally kicked himself. Why the fuck was he giving any personal information away? It was none of this woman's bloody business. But he went on, "How about you then? Married?" Again, that ingrained be-polite-at-all-times British bullshit. But she was his ticket to get stuff done—she could help, so he didn't want to be curt or rude. His foot tapped the floor impatiently. *Hurry up! Let's go to the fucking police station and find Grace.*

Ana looked down. "No, I'm not married. I'm single."

"What about the American fiancé?"

"Oh, we split up a little while ago. It just wasn't working. I guess he wasn't able to fulfill my needs, you know?"

Tommy felt ill at ease—his nerves had him revealing things about his private life with a total stranger. This dinner was a time waster—she'd offered to help and he needed to pin her down.

"About Grace, Ana. We need to go straight to the police station after dinner so you can translate for me."

Ana threw her arms up. "Oh, you don't want to go there! Have you any idea how corrupt they are here? They're really not going to give a damn about a missing child when they already have tens of thousands of their own on the streets of Rio to deal with. That's not counting the rest of the continent—there are homeless children living on landfill dumps everywhere."

Tommy could feel a lump in his throat. "That sounds very cynical, Ana. And Grace isn't *homeless*. She was *kidnapped* by a very sick person. Her parents are desperate for her. She *has* a home. I'm sure the police will be as helpful as they can."

"I'm sure whoever took her had a reason."

His brow furrowed into a hard knot. "Hitler had a reason. All nutters have a 'reason' in their own sick minds."

"You think this woman was sick?"

"*Is* sick. Yes. Very sick. Psychotic even."

Ana smiled faintly and stroked her nose again. "Perhaps she regrets what she's done."

"If so, she would have brought our daughter back to us by now."

"Maybe she can't."

"Can't or *won't?*" he retorted.

"Same difference. Maybe she realizes she doesn't even *want* Grace anymore."

"I doubt that very much. This woman is forty-six and can't have children. She stole Grace because she was obviously desperate to be a mother. The woman went to all that trouble to steal her in the first place. Besides, Grace is an angel. So easy to fall in love with. She's the sweetest, smartest girl in the world. Anyone would topple head over heels for her. And I'm not just saying that because I'm her father. She's special. Unique."

"You never know. She might decide that being a parent isn't what she thought it would be."

All the food arrived at the table at the same time. Ana's eyes lit up, her wide grin planted on her face like a poster for a toothpaste commercial. She started to serve out the dishes on both plates. Tommy noticed she'd been smoothing her fingers across the fine bridge of her nose all evening.

"Does it hurt?"

"What?"

"Your bruise. That bash from the horse. Is it sore?"

"Oh, that. No, not really."

"Look, Ana, I don't mean to sound pushy, and you've been very kind to offer your help but I really *do* want to see the police. I got a tip and I need to get Grace's picture out there ASAP. I could really use your help."

"Do you have a photo of the woman?"

"No, that's the whole trouble. She seems invisible."

"I guess she must be super-smart."

"Something will make her slip up," Tommy said bitterly.

"You think so?"

He took a bite of one of the shrimp ball things. It was good but he really didn't feel like eating. There was something about this woman that was really irking him. She seemed strangely detached for someone who had seemed so keen to help earlier.

"You don't have kids, then?" he asked, with an accusing shift of his eyes.

She looked up at the ceiling for a second and when her eyes rested back on him, he saw they were filled with quiet tears.

"Sorry, have I touched a nerve?" he said, feeling awkward.

"I did have a child," she answered softly. "Grace's age. Her name was Adela."

Oh dear, I've put my foot in it. "And what happened?"

"She went missing one day. Just vanished. And I never found her again."

Tommy clawed his fingers through his messy hair. "Oh my God. I'm *so sorry*. So then you're in the same boat as us? You *understand* and that's why you want to help—you identify with the kind of pain we're going through."

A tear slid down Ana's cheek. "You see my point about the law here? They don't give a damn. Trying to find a missing child in Brazil is like searching for a needle in a haystack."

Tommy's insides churned. "I'm not just dealing with Brazil. I'm dealing with the whole of Latin America. Grace could be anywhere."

"Have you tried Central America?"

"I was just in Honduras. Why?"

Ana shrugged her shoulders. "I don't know. Just a hunch. You might try somewhere like Nicaragua. The rainforest there is second only to the Amazon in size. With miles and miles of deserted beaches. It would be a clever place to hide a child."

"But I got a tip that she was seen here. They were *here*."

Ana took a long sip of her cocktail, and then said, "Well perhaps that tip was full of baloney. Perhaps that person was pulling your leg, have you thought of that?"

"Yes, we had. The tip was anonymous which was a bit off-kilter." Jesus, he needed to get out of this restaurant. But the poor woman looked so forlorn. So that's why she offered help—she wanted sympathy from someone who'd understand.

"I'd try Central America."

Tommy couldn't stop chewing his lower lip. "When I think of Nicaragua all that comes to mind is extreme poverty. You really think she would have taken Grace *there*?"

"Well I think you might want to investigate places like that. Do you have any idea what this woman looks like?"

"My wife does, of course. But all *I've* seen is the police photofit. You must have seen it too—it's all over the web. On TV. My daughter said she looks like a weasel with eyes the color of poo. Funny that—you should always trust your first instinct about a person. We should have heeded more attention. Sadly, Grace changed her mind when that bitch bought her a pair of bloody shoes."

"Eyes the color of Pooh Bear?"

"No. Eyes the color of shit."

Ana gazed downwards, a pained look on her face. Then she touched his hand. She downed the rest of her Caipirinha and said, "I'm sure you'll find your daughter. I'm sure she's just fine as we speak. Probably devouring an ice cream somewhere."

"Something makes me doubt that very much, I'm afraid, but nice of you to be so upbeat about it. So how do you cope never having found your daughter again? How do you get *through* each day?"

Ana touched the gold cross around her neck. "Faith."

"You know what gets me most about this woman? The mendacity of it all," he said in a low rumble. He felt like his insides would split. "The filthy lies, the tricks, the schemes. The pain she's putting everyone through makes me want to literally *kill* her."

"But you said you don't even know what she looks like."

"One day I'll find her. And when I do? Well, that bitch had better watch out, that's all."

"Tommy, you were right. We ordered too much. I don't feel so well myself. Can I ask you one little favor? As one lost desperate parent to another?"

"Sure."

"I could really use a hug right now." Ana got up from her seat and moved over to his side. She sat on his knee as if she were riding sidesaddle. He thought she was wiggling about to get comfortable but he felt her pressing the muscles of her butt into his groin. She flicked her auburn hair close against his neck. She wriggled some more on his lap—he could feel the tension of her gyrating buttocks. Then she put an arm around his shoulder. She rested her lips against his ear and placed her other hand beneath her ass, cupping his crotch firmly, palming it with her whole hand. "You are *so* hot, you know that? So goddamn handsome! I would just love to straddle you—I bet you've got a really huge cock. I'm wet right now just thinking about it." She put her tongue inside his ear and licked it slowly. "I could so fuck you all night and suck your huge dick, lick it up and down, up and down, put that huge, thick cock in my mouth and then ride you all night the way you *deserve.*"

Tommy's conscience was doing one thing, his dick was doing another. How could he undo millions of years of male DNA? He simply couldn't help it.

He felt himself getting hard.

30

Sylvia

Sylvia's nerves about her trip to Rio de Janeiro had her teetering on the edge. Excitement, mixed with terror, and sprinkled with hope, surged through her fragile veins. Tommy, oblivious to her plans, still didn't know she was on her way, and Melinda had insisted on coming to Rio with her. Good, she needed the support. They *would* find Grace. The thought of the contrary was too painful to contemplate and, as Tommy had said, "unacceptable."

For too long now, she had been reacting, instead of acting. Things, from now on, were damn well going to change.

Finally, Sylvia succumbed and took just one half of a Valium to get her through the night. She had thought that by reading poetry she could bring on sleep, but was suddenly horrified by her choice: Sylvia Plath. Why had she chosen her, of all people? Her namesake? A wave of sadness enveloped her when she envisioned the great poet's suicide, wondering how she could have put herself through such a gruesome death; sticking her head in a gas oven with her two little children in the next room. Sylvia had the sensation that she was now re-living her father's own desperation, the anxiety that must have plagued his mind. He took his own life! How could somebody actually go through with it? Would Sylvia take *her* own life if they never found Grace? She could never imagine doing such a thing but perhaps she would. It would take a lot of guts to pull it off. Were people who committed suicide brave, or cowards? Who was she to judge others? Desperation had a way of stamping on Hope. Hope . . . she mustn't give up. Ever. She had to remain resilient. Strong. They *would* find Grace.

In a haze of sleep, she could hear noises. Was someone vacuuming downstairs? She got up and threw on her mother's silky bathrobe and stood at the top of the sweeping staircase. It was already daylight. Someone was vacuuming, all right.

"Jacqueline?" Sylvia glided down the stairs, her mother's robe trailing behind her like a wedding train.

Jacqueline was in the living room, standing on a chair, pointing and poking the long tube of the vacuum at the ceiling. She screamed. "Oh my Lord, Sylvia! You scared the living daylights out of me. What are you doing up when you need all the rest you can get?"

"Are you killing spiders?"

Jacqueline turned off the noisy machine. It was the same old sky-blue one from the 1970s. Still working, still faithful. Jacqueline, Sylvia knew, refused to allow a new one in the house.

"Not the spiders themselves, honey, just their mangled old webs."

"You're meant to be retired, Jacqueline. What are you doing standing on chairs?" Sylvia knew that the pension plan her father had set up for her was all in place and that the money had been sent that week. She'd checked with his lawyer.

"I know. But you think I can relax during the day knowing creepy crawlies are taking over this house with their webs and the kitchen ain't been cleaned and—"

"That is *not* your problem. It's mine, for being untidy. You should be playing with your grandchildren, not clambering about on furniture here."

Jacqueline stepped down from the chair. She had on her special work outfit. Faded, red velvet slippers, shiny flesh-colored panty-hose, and a pinafore over her dress. She always wore her hair up, too. "I had a feeling you was up to no good, planning trips and plotting and scheming."

"I'm going to Brazil. Today. To find Gracie. I was going to call and let you know."

"Oh my Lord. I knew it! I just knew it! You have news?"

"Maybe. We'll see. Don't get too excited. Nothing's sure. If we get good news you'll be the first to know about it."

The old marble clock on the mantelpiece said ten fifteen. She still hadn't finished packing and had some important calls to make. She realized she didn't have that much time to get ready for her trip. Her plane was leaving at three.

She raced upstairs to pack. Never mind taking a silly back-pack—who was she kidding? She'd use a small suitcase with wheels. But then she did find a faded old backpack she'd once used for summer camp, at the back of the guestroom closet. Her parents seldom threw stuff out.

As she slung her clothing into the backpack, Sylvia felt ap-peased, knowing that she was about to take action to find Grace. She asked herself if LeRoy would have aided her—used his military skills—had he ended up being a soldier. She imagined the what-ifs and fantasies of what could have been. Sylvia had been spoiled as an only-child, never had to share her toys, was never passed hand-me-downs. Her parents had both helped her with her homework. LeRoy was raised by a single mother in a poor neighborhood. Jacqueline never mentioned a stepfather, nor did Loretta speak about another man in the letters. Had it been tough for LeRoy?

Sylvia supposed so. She knew that being white and privileged was an alien world to so many. Would LeRoy have resented her had he lived? What if she'd met him and disliked him? Or perhaps he'd been the sweetest kid ever. Maybe he would have disliked *her*. Thought her snotty. Or they could have ended up being best friends. Who were his ancestors?

She wondered what Loretta's and LeRoy's roots had been. She supposed they'd suffered the racial segregation left over from the discriminatory housing policies. The problem was still rife. Saginaw's river sliced the neighborhoods in two.

Sylvia went back into the living room, her mouth poised in an O, ready for more conversation. Yes, she had a lot of questions.

"I don't want to retire," Jacqueline grumbled. She had turned her attention to dusting. "There's still life in me yet and this old house has been like my sanctuary. I find peace here. Even when your mama was hollering about this or about that, I still found my little corner of peace in this house."

"Nobody's forcing you to retire, Jacqueline. Tommy and I have been thinking about staying in Saginaw, at least for a while. Put Grace in school here. When we find her."

"You will. Just keep praying—keep believing."

"I do."

Jacqueline stopped what she was doing and turned her head and gazed at Sylvia. Her almond-shaped eyes sparkled with hope. "You mean you ain't going back to that mean and cold Crowheart house of yours?"

Sylvia felt as if she had betrayed Crowheart in some way, with all her complaining. "Oh, it's not *all* mean. It's beautiful in summer. And the winters in Michigan are just as severe as they are there. The cold is drier there. Here it's damp and it creeps into your bones."

"Maybe Sylvia, honey, but at least this old furnace is still working like a dream. You got friends here. People that care."

"Very true. And we're ready for a change, that's for sure."

Sylvia picked a small Spanish phrase book from the bookshelf and leaned against the fireplace, flicking through its thin pages. "Jacqueline, where did Loretta come from?"

"Why here, in Saginaw."

"But where were her parents from?"

"Saginaw too, I think."

"So LeRoy's family went back a long way, then?"

"I don't rightly know for absolute sure, but I think that family goes back a few generations. Saginaw through and through."

Sylvia knew just a little about black history in Saginaw. She'd learned at school that some of the earliest African Americans settlers were the first freed slaves from the North and Canada. Many of them found work in the lumber business, and then later, to join the automobile industry in nearby Pontiac and Flint. General Motors was booming then. Perhaps that was when Loretta's parents arrived. Although many were poorly educated, there was a strong middle class of entrepreneurs and professionals, even artists and doctors. Some blacks became extremely wealthy.

"What did they do for a living?" Sylvia asked.

Jacqueline swiped the feather duster over small crystal chandelier. "Well, Loretta was a secretary. Her father was . . . what was he now? I think he was a manager at one of them automobile plants. Her mother was a homemaker."

Sylvia cleared her throat and said, "Now there's something important I'd like to know."

"Let me guess. You wanna know how your daddy and Loretta got involved in the first place?"

Sylvia nodded. Jacqueline knew her so well. It seemed she could read her mind.

"Loretta was mighty pretty in her day."

"Yes, I saw that from her photo."

Jacqueline got down from her stool. "She was your father's family maid."

"But I thought *Hyacinth* was. For forty years!"

"And Loretta was Hyacinth's niece. She came to help one summer. And that's when it happened."

"When she got pregnant?"

"When they fell in love."

"So my dad wasn't just taking advantage of her, then?"

"Nuh-uh. He was crazy about her. She was a few years older than him and he thought she was the most beautiful woman he'd ever set eyes on."

"How do you know all this?" Sylvia asked.

"Loretta told me the story."

"And then she got pregnant?"

"Nobody knew. But your grandparents did get wind of what was happening, that your daddy was fool crazy for Loretta, so they arranged for her to leave. Gave her double pay just to get her outta the house. But she kept that baby a secret. Kept her stomach hidden the whole time. She once told me she planned to give the baby up for adoption, but when he was born she couldn't go through with it. She was mighty proud. Didn't wanna ask for no help, no money."

"Yes, I gathered. From her first letter to him."

"By the time she gave birth, your daddy was already engaged to your mama. Lordy, Lordy, *that* was a quick marriage because he'd made your mama pregnant, too."

"*What?*"

"When your parents got married, your mama was with child."

"But not with me?"

"No, not with you. She lost the first baby. Miscarried after a few months. But they were good 'n married by the time he found out about LeRoy."

Sylvia stood there, open mouthed. "I had no idea he was . . . like that."

"He was mighty handsome in his day. A little bit of a ladies' man, I guess."

"Well did he *love* my mother?"

"Yes, siree. You know he did."

"Well I knew how dependent he was on her. But dependency isn't always about love." She pictured Tommy. Was he dependent on her? Was *their* union about love? "So then what happened to Loretta?"

Jacqueline finally sat down. "You got the gist of it from them letters, didn't you?"

Sylvia took her position on the floor. "You read them too?"

"I may be able to keep a secret, Sylvia, honey, but if you think I was able to contain my curiosity and not look into that box, I'm sorry, but your expectations of me are too elevated. I'm made of flesh also. I had to know what I was dealing with, but I kept that box good and hidden all those years in the garage so your mama wouldn't find it. It was me who put it in his closet for you to find after he passed."

Sylvia shuddered. LeRoy didn't have a clue who his real father was. He had a phantom in his mind, the soldier who died in Vietnam, a hero, perhaps. A man who had joined the forces for idealistic reasons. Maybe LeRoy had also wanted to join the military as a way of getting close to him: the father that never existed.

The theme tune to Jacqueline's soap rang loudly through the living room. "My show's just started so it's eleven. Sylvia, honey, you better get a move on or you'll miss your plane."

Excitement and hope suffused Sylvia's bloodstream. She was on her way to find Grace!

31

Grace

Grace was feeling lonely. She sat on the beach with Hideous Teddy, counting the seventh wave. Once, her dad had told her how the biggest wave often came every seven times. Seven was her lucky number. Maybe because her birthday was the seventh. The 7th of September. She knew she was five and three-quarters. Well, *almost* five and three-quarters.

She was bored. She played the Great Bird Ziz with Hideous Teddy but he didn't find it funny—there was no expression in his big, black, plastic eyes. She didn't find it funny, either. It wasn't the same playing the Great Bird Ziz without her dad. He could make it swoop down from a great height and bite her bottom, or suddenly flip up into the sky again, snapping its beak (her dad's long scary fingers and thumb), and then eat a big chunk right out of her thigh! Or her foot. Or even her big toe. The Great Bird Ziz liked juicy toes. But Hideous Teddy just sat there, dumb, not laughing at all, sand all over his shiny yellow fur. She brought him to the beach so he would lose his Factory Farmed look. *Poor* Hideous Teddy, she'd even taken him swimming. He tried surfing, too.

Even though Hideous was ugly, she loved him. It wasn't his fault. She'd love him double to make up for it. And he was only Hideous because she liked the word. He wasn't really hideous—how could he be when he was her true friend? *Unlike some people* with names beginning with *L.*

Lucho wouldn't let her go in the water when he was *busy*. Busy = surfing. All he did was *surf, surf, surf!* The whole day long. Even when it was pouring with rain! When he wasn't surfing, he was sleeping. And there was no way to wake him in a million years once his head hit the pillow.

She had nobody to play with. There were no other children nearby. Just surfers. Some of them were American and they had a funny language that even she couldn't understand, like "dude" and "bitchin" and "bogus." She heard one of them say "touries with mouries," and found out they were talking about tourists doing body surfing and getting in the way of the *real* surfers.

She knew that Lucho thought she was getting in the way, too. He spent all his time with a French girl now. Grace heard him talk to her about going down to Peru to "catch some waves." Where was Peru? Grace had caught waves with Lucho. At night. They went swimming by the moon, and the ocean lit up with little green sparkles like emeralds and diamonds. When you splashed they landed on your shoulders and hair like jewels as if someone had waved a magic wand. Every time a wave whooshed over them, the sparkles flew in the air like butterflies with lights on their wings. It was the prettiest thing she had ever, ever seen. Like sea fairies. Lucho said it was the microscopic creatures that the whales lived on that lit up only at night. He said they were called *Fósforo* and *Plancton*, and were lit up by the moon.

But now Lucho only played with the French Girl. They were speaking bad English to each other because the French Girl couldn't speak Spanish. She wondered what Mama Ruth would think of Lucho kissing another woman. The French Girl . . . her name was Elodie. Hell O.D. She was pretty but she didn't smile much.

She smoked cigarettes instead.

Grace got up from her position under the stripy shade of her favorite palm tree. She had eaten two mangoes, and a fruit that looked like a potato but had her favorite color pink inside, and three quarters of a papaya, slurping the juice that had dribbled all over her body. She loved papaya. Almost as much as pineapples which were sweeter here than back home. Now she was sticky, like a toffee apple that had been licked all over, and she had sand stuck to her. She felt all rough like a cat's tongue.

She buried the fruit skins under the sand. She knew that was not Littering because, her Real Mom promised her, it was natural. It was okay to throw Natural things away if you were in the country-side and you could hide it in bushes. The sand, she decided, was as good as a bush. Candy wrappers, though, were not allowed. She hadn't had any candy at all in Knicker Agua. Mama Ruth told her they made chocolate here from cocoa beans but she hadn't seen any chocolate at all. Not one single bar.

Grace decided to have a shower to wash off the sticky sand. She knew how to work it and had learned that it was best to get there before it got dark because the water heated up from the sun all day and would still be hot. It was solar-powered. But first, she thought, she would go and tell her secret pen about her day. Mama Ruth had told her how she was going to make a million on the book she was writing, and Grace thought that she could also make a million on her *own* book. If she had a million she could get her mom's DNA and make her come back to life like they did with the dinosaurs in *Jurassic Park*. That was another movie her dad let her watch before her mom told him it was too grown-up for her. But Grace *was* grown-up. Kind of.

If she wanted to make a million dollars selling her book,

though, she'd have to think of a story first. And she'd have to do it soon. Then she could buy her own surfboard. And her own plane to fly to go and see her dad in Saginaw, or wherever he was.

Grace skipped along the hot sand, feeling it between her toes, hopping fast so her feet didn't burn. She saw a big black iguana look at her sideways with his big bulging eyes His floppity neck was held up by strong arms—not legs but arms—like a knight in armor from a storybook. She asked herself how old he was. The oldest animal she had ever seen. More than five and three-quarters, for sure.

She rushed to the cabin but remembered that her secret pen was being recharged at Angela's. What would Angela be cooking tonight? Silly question. Red beans and rice. *Gallo Pinto.* But with what? *Quesillo* with avocado? *Cajeta de Coco?* Angela liked cooking as much as Lucho liked surfing.

She ran over to Angela's house. Angela had electricity. Although, Grace still preferred her and Lucho's Three Bear's Cabin. She didn't think it was fair that Hell O.D. was obviously trying to be one of *The Three Bears.* Why should she get to sleep in the cabin? How could *she* be a Bear when she smoked so many smelly cigarettes? Or worse, maybe she thought she was Goldilocks herself! Goldilocks with dark brown hair.

Grace stood in the doorway, feeling angry about Elodie, but soon forgot when she smelled something sweet wafting from a big orange bowl. Angela was cooking a dessert.

Angela looked up. "Hola mi corazón. ¿Dónde está Lucho?" Angela was always asking where Lucho was. Grace wondered why Angela bothered, when she knew the answer.

"Con el surf."

Grace slipped into the little house. There was a painting on the wall of green hills and a waterfall. Very different from the palm trees and beach here. There was a big table in the middle of the room, with chairs, and an old ripped-up sofa in the corner with its stuffing coming out. Sometimes Grace would take an afternoon siesta on it.

"¿Y tu mamá. Todavía en Rio?" Angela asked, still stirring her cake mixture.

"Sí."

Angela raised her eyebrows with disapproval. "¿Y la francesa?"

Grace knew what Angela was thinking, Angela didn't like Elodie, either.

"¿Cuando vuelve tu mamá?" she pressed.

Grace wished she knew the answer. Maybe Mama Ruth would never come back. "No sé."

Angela continued stirring the mixture with a huge wooden spoon. "Cuántos años tenés? Seis?"

She was pleased that Angela thought she was already six. Well, it wasn't *really* a lie to say yes. She was *almost* six. "Sí."

"Vos debés estar en la escuela no acá solita en la playa."

"Sí," Grace agreed. Angela was right. She *should* be at school and she *was* bored with being all alone on the beach. And now that Hell O.D was taking up all of Lucho's time . . .

She'd seen the children on the yellow school bus, the girls in their white socks and blouses, their navy blue skirts. She could be like them. She could do math and make friends.

"¿Dónde esta la escuela?" she asked Angela, her eyes burning with curiosity.

"Hay una pequeñita en El Viejo y una mas grande en Chinandega."

"Chin Anne Dega," Grace repeated to herself. School, she decided, was a brilliant idea. Her Real Mom would be so proud of her in a Knicker Agua Uniform.

Tomorrow she would go to Chin Anne Dega for her first day of school. She could catch the bus. She knew where she could find coins to pay the fare.

Maybe *then* Lucho would miss her.

GRACE SAT ON her chair at the restaurant table, swinging her legs. In the end, Lucho decided they would go out instead of eating at Angela's. The sun had just set and the sky was a dark purple, streaked with orange. They were all speaking English but Grace hardly understood a word because all the expressions they were using were strange. Everybody was eating barbequed fresh fish and drinking cold beers. There was Lucho, Elodie, an Australian, and two Americans. All men, except for Hell O.D and her. Grace didn't speak because she didn't know what to say. They were all yelling at once and she wondered if anyone understood each other at all, because nobody was answering anyone's questions.

The Australian said to the table, "Have you been to the Island yet? La Isla? It's just a short boat ride away. The Island has two breaks that have high performance waves on all tides. The waves are maybe a little less peaky and hollow than The Boom but it's a rippable, sectiony wave that works from about chest high to double-overhead and sometimes offers barrel sections—"

"Yeah, man, but," replied the really skinny American with tattoos—who looked to Grace like a stretched-out, painted Totem pole—"you can't compare La Isla to The Boom, dude. I mean we have world-class beach break tubes here, and an excellent left point. There are nearly always three to four decent peaks up and down the beach, plus—"

"Shame it usually blows out by ten every morning," Lucho said.

Bore. *Ring*, Grace thought. Would this conversation ever end? She wished she had some children her age to play with, instead of listening to this surfy talk.

Then the other American, the one with super-blond hair said, "Yeah, but hey, aren't you glad you have time for an afternoon siesta? I'm kinda surfed out by noon, dude."

Elodie flicked her lionish hair. "Has anyone been to San Cristobal, zee volcano?"

Grace was pleased that everyone ignored her question. *She* had seen the volcano from a distance on the taxi journey to the beach when they first arrived, but she didn't say so because she doubted anyone would hear her. Besides, she was still too scared to speak English because of the whole Heaven problem with her mom— Lucho might tell Mama Ruth. That volcano, she remembered, was amazing. Great puffs of blue-black smoke rose from the center, billowing up like a fire that hadn't caught alight. It was the largest volcano in the country. *That* was something to show her dad when he arrived. Mama Ruth said she was "working on it." What did that mean? She knew he'd love it here and could spend all day with his camera, photographing animals. They could go walking together by the streams and watch for the crocodiles in the dark green mangroves. The crocs were clever and it was really hard to see them because they were the same color as the estuary and they hardly moved.

Once, with Lucho, when they went kayaking (it seemed donkey's years ago now), Grace saw a big round eye looking straight at her. It blinked slowly and she was sure the croc was saying, "Come, come in for a swim and I'll eat you for my dinner." Lucho told her that the crocs lived alone and each one was master of his own bit of mangrove. That mangrove the local people called "La Cuna"— cradle in Spanish. *La Cuna,* because so many different species were growing up there. That outing they went on was before Lucho met Hell O.D. She'd ruined it all, and Grace wished he'd never set eyes on her. Elodie said she was "bored of seeing animals" and wanted to go somewhere else! How could anyone be bored of that? That's why Grace called her Hell O.D. Apart from the fact that that was the way her name sounded, Elodie was too blind to see how beautiful everything was.

Grace decided that Knicker Agua must have been the first place on the Planet that God created when he was busy with his seven days. It *had* to be because no other place had so much life. There were sea turtles, iguanas, millions of fish—even jumping ones—

butterflies, crazy-colored crabs, millions of creepy crawlies, and every insect you could imagine. And, of course, dogs, pigs, chickens, and other more usual creatures that she'd seen in America. She hadn't come across raccoons, coyotes, and bald-eagles here, like in Crowheart, but she was sure they must be around somewhere.

Grace watched Elodie out of the corner of her eye. Her enemy chewed one last mouthful of the barbequed dorado, scraped her plate noisily, then lit up another cigarette. She flicked her hair again and rested her pretty head on Lucho's shoulder.

Lucho had his arm around her. "Has anyone surfed Hemorrhoids?" he asked.

"Yeah, me, man," said the tall skinny one, grinning and opening another beer. "I was pretty stoked the first time. It's like a heavy, hollow, and totally unforgiving wave, dude, breaking on shallow and urchin infested reef. But if you know what you're doing you can airdrop the takeoff and get like barreled for several seconds there."

But the blond didn't look so happy about it. His white eyebrows scrunched together in a big bow tie. "You can get seriously hurt surfing that wave. It can be mean, man."

"The only trouble is," the tall one said, "that Hemmi's only got one peak, a small take-off zone and can get too crowded."

Grace yawned. Bore. Ring.

The blond one shook his head. "I don't know, man, it's not just the crowds. I only caught *one* wave. I broke a board, cut my face with my fin getting rolled, and had multiple hold-downs. Way better here, dude, it's got a really hollow, consistent wave. When it's working and if The Boom is breaking clean and you know how to drop in and hold your line it's *so* sweet. I mean, it's an all-out, thumping A frame that is sure to get you pitted—"

"What got me hooked originally," the Australian added, "when I came here, was surfing those awesome empty barrels, yeah, and watching pelicans swoop down in trains and glide off the lip with stiff afternoon off-shores—"

"Cool," Elodie said, trying to join in the conversation.

The word pelican caught Grace's attention. She'd seen herons too. There were so many birds here. All different colors: scarlet-red, yellow, green—there were parrots, too. She loved watching the pelicans fly in groups with their long beaks. They didn't look like regular birds, but prehistoric. Maybe there would be pelicans in Chin Anne Dega, too.

While the others continued with their Surfy Language, she imagined tomorrow—how school was going to be. She'd need some extra money to buy herself the blue and white uniform. She thought she might know exactly where to find it. It wouldn't be stealing exactly—spending money on school was better than wasting it on cigarettes.

With all her excitement, Grace knew it would be hard to sleep tonight.

THE FOLLOWING MORNING, Grace woke up at the sound of the cockerel who lived somewhere up the beach. She had never seen him, but every day, before dawn, he would call out.

She could hear the waves lapping and slapping the beach. The sound was so lovely that she wanted to slumber back to sleep but she knew there wasn't enough time for that. She had to leave before Lucho came back from surfing, or he wouldn't allow her to go.

She sat up in bed, yawned like a lion cub and rubbed her eyes. They had pushed the two single beds together, Lucho and Elodie. Elodie was still fast asleep. Lucho was still surfing—morning was best at The Boom. Grace looked at her enemy. Elodie wasn't so terrible, she decided. Elodie did smile at her once at dinner last night when she took her photo and asked her what her favorite color was. Grace told her it was pink but now she wasn't sure. She'd seen a parrot, bright, bright turquoise and yellow. The colors together were sooo beautiful. It wasn't the same as paints or crayons. The feathers were turquoise but if you looked closely there were other blues and greens, like tiny dots all joined together that made up the whole big color. She wondered if these birds knew how pretty they were.

Anyway, from now on, her favorite color was not pink anymore, but turquoise.

She slipped out of bed without making a sound and tiptoed to one of the chairs, where her shirt was hanging over the back. She pulled it over her head. She put on her shorts. Then she snuck over—her feet soft on the concrete floor—and ruffled through Elodie's bag, without making any noise. She took out some coins, as many as she could find, and put them in her shorts pocket. Still on tiptoes, Grace took Hideous Bear from her bed and tucked Carrot up under the sheet. She owed Hideous Bear an adventure and some extra attention—he would come with her to school. But Carrot needed to get a little extra sleep and, anyway, he'd be with Lucho and Elodie so he wouldn't get lonely.

Finally, Grace slipped her feet into her flip-flops, and with quiet, giant paces, left the room.

Outside, it was already warm but not yet hot. She looked at the ocean and saw the stripy yellow colors of sunrise streaking the sky to a clear blue. Not being able to hold it in much longer, she ran to the toilet to do a pee. Her ears were pricked but she couldn't hear the pig. He was a late riser. Lucky, she thought, or his angry grunts might wake Hell O.D.

In the open-air bathroom, Grace washed her hands with soap, the way her mom had shown her, making a creamy lather and rinsing them with lots of water. Once her Granny told her that if you didn't wash your hands, tiny worms that you couldn't see would wiggle all over you and find their way into your mouth. Then they would set up home in your stomach like it was a hotel! Yuk! So she knew that washing hands was a good thing to do, especially before you ate so you didn't get nasty worms living in your tummy. Grace brushed her teeth, rinsed, and spat.

High above her, the tall palm trees were swaying very gently in the breeze. The sky was even bluer than the ocean, and scurrying about on the sand, taking up their positions in the early morning sun, she could see the lizards. And her favorite turtle, big and slow, who had a shell the shape of a huge heart (whose name was Olive Ridley) was there in his usual place, hiding under the shrubs. Today he looked up at her with his sweet round eyes like glass balls and said, "Have a good day at school, Grace." At least, that's what she liked to imagine. Truthfully, she couldn't see him so well, but still, she knew he must be there somewhere.

Lucho had explained to her how important the turtles were, that the females came at least a couple of times a year in huge numbers, sometimes thousands at a time, to lay their eggs on the beach—the same beach where they were born. Always at night. It had a name, he said: the *arribada*. The female turtle would dig a hole in the sand with her fins and lay about a hundred eggs. But, Lucho warned, the local people had to be taught to not only *not* eat the eggs, but to not eat the turtles themselves! The locals had been doing it for centuries and it was hard to change old habits, he told her. Grace's special turtle wasn't the only Olive Ridley. In fact, they were all called Olive Ridley, because that was the name of the breed.

There were other breeds too, all in danger, all on the menu for dinner. And those baby turtles, even if they were lucky enough to survive in the egg and hatch, had a dangerous journey. From the moment they split open the eggshell, they had to get across the beach and into the ocean. Would they make it? Snakes, big birds, and pigs could get them. Yes, even the greedy pig who liked Grace's poop might like a tasty little baby turtle. Poor Olive Ridley and his family. Grace thought more about the DNA solution, and how she wanted to be a scientist when she grew up. Not only was she going to bring her Mom back, but Olive Ridley and all his Olive Ridley family. That is, if they didn't make it in the future.

She kept walking. Bits of stick kept poking her feet and she realized, too late, that her flip-flops had not been the best choice of footwear. And when she looked down at her shirt, white with yellow stripes (one that Mama Ruth had bought her after she got rid of all her real clothes), she saw trails of ketchup from last night's dinner had run all the way down the front. It looked like blood. And there were patches of dirt on her shorts, too, from sitting on the ground. Uh oh! Her mom would have called her a "Ragamuffin," a "Scallywag" or a "Street Urchin" looking so dirty. Those were her nicknames when she got all messy.

Too late now to turn back. Elodie might wake up and find her money missing and call Lucho. Then she'd *never* get to school. Grace wondered how she would pay Elodie back for the money or if Elodie would even notice it was missing. Grace could paint her a picture as a trade, or brush her hair—she'd find a way. She did that with her mom sometimes. She had set up a hair salon and her mom was her most important client. And her dolls too. Perhaps Elodie could be a client then she'd have money for the bus every day to get to school.

Grace kept on walking. She passed a farm with chickens and goats. There was a billy goat with big amber eyes, jumping up onto a rusty old tin drum, and jumping back down again, wagging his scraggy little tail. He was showing off to her, shaking his curvy horns and waggling his pointy white beard! The chickens were scrabbling about in the dirt, looking for things to nibble. Grace skipped on.

The sun was getting higher, brighter, the sand turning into pure dirt beneath her flip-flops, and crusted between her toes. She passed giant bamboos and lemon trees . . . so pretty. She held Hideous Bear against a lemon to compare the yellow. Hideous Bear was orangeier but he had definitely lost his Factory Farmed look. In fact, he looked as if he'd been to war. He'd lost an eye—where and when she couldn't be sure. It had happened overnight, one minute he had two huge shiny eyes, and the next he was half blind. She held him tight, his squidgy tummy pressing against her skinny brown arms, his pointy nose nestling against her birdy neck. Her heart missed a beat as she remembered Pidgey O Dollars and she gulped back a tear. But Hideous loved her with all his heart and soul, and "Yes, Ruth," she said out loud, "he does have a soul. Tiene alma!" she cried in Spanish.

In her head and in her dreams, Spanish and English mixed like a big flowery bouquet. It depended on what she was thinking about, what she was trying to describe. Ruth explained in her lessons that there were two ways of saying "to be" in Spanish. One way was forever and the other was just for a moment. If someone was pretty, Ruth told Grace, it was forever and she needed to use the verb *ser* but if they were hungry it wasn't forever and she needed to use the verb *estar*. At the time, Grace questioned this. What about a pretty girl who turns into an ugly old lady, or a hungry baby who never gets a chance to eat and dies of starvation? But after listening to people talk, it started to make sense. In English, when someone died, it meant forever and ever and there was nothing you could do about it. But in Spanish, it was only for a while and that *did* make sense. *Mi mamá está muerta.* It wasn't forever. Grace liked that notion, that her mother was only dead temporarily.

While all these thoughts were swirling about in her head, she saw a group of women standing together in a knot by the side of the road. They had baskets and colored plastic shopping bags, woven in patterns. One of them carried an upside down chicken by its feet, as she chatted to her friend, forgetting about the animal while she gossiped away. Every once in a while, it would pathetically flap a wing but it was useless. This was what happened, Grace supposed, to non-factory-farmed animals. It was more personal. She'd seen pigs, too, in giant wicker baskets being carried on the back of mopeds. Perhaps, she decided, it was best never eat *any* animal ever again.

A small bus pulled up next to the talking ladies and they all piled in, still babbling. Grace scurried up to the step, wondering where the big yellow school bus was and where all the girls were in their uniforms of blue skirts and white blouses. She heard the words Chinandega, all said together quickly in a row, and she climbed up the steps, following the women. They gave their coins, and as Grace was searching in her pocket for a *córdoba*, the bus driver drove off in a jerk. He didn't ask her to pay her fare as he thought the chicken woman was her mother. As if her Real Mom would hold a chicken upside down!

Grace thought about Ruth. Ruth would *never* be her mother. Only her *mom* was her mom and that was *that*. In fact, when Ruth got back, she wasn't going to call her "Mama Ruth" or "Mama Rocío" or "Mommy". *Any More*. She would call her just plain "Ruth." And if she didn't like it, well too bad!

Grace sat at the back of the bus, squeezed in between big sacks of something extremely bulgy and a mother carrying a baby. The baby was coughing and had a runny nose, his eyes streaming with tears. But not tears of unhappiness, tears of a sick child. Nobody really noticed Grace, except one woman who smiled at her. Everybody else was busy talking about what they were going to buy at the market. Grace looked at the baby-woman and asked, "Chin Anne Dega?"

"Sí, sí," she replied, wiping her boy's wet nose with her skirt.

Grace looked out of the window and watched trees and fields go by. She saw huts with rough straw roofs and washing laid out on spiky plants. There were bony oxen pulling wooden carts, plowing fields. She could see their knobby ribs shining through their pale skin and pointed hips, like big triangles, jutting through. They looked tired in the hot sun. Every time somebody held up a hand or waved at the bus, it would stop. And every time the driver saw something in his way, or even at the side of the road, he would beep his horn, long and hard. Poor people bicycling along were getting

beeped at—even little children her size, pedaling on bicycles too big
for them. Grace wondered how they managed to stay on their bikes
with the shock of the bus noise. She remembered her bicycle back
home, pink with bells and pom-poms. She hadn't seen children's
bikes here, and certainly not pink ones.

Her tummy was rumbling and gurgling, she already felt hungry.
When she got to the town she'd buy a doughnut or something
sweet. She wondered if Lucho would be asking why she wasn't at
breakfast. She pulled some coins out of her pocket to see how
much she had. She knew all about cents and dollars, her dad had
shown her and she knew how much each coin was worth when she
bought candy. But this money was different. There was a shiny one,
50 centavos and another that said 1 córdoba. She remembered her
dad giving her an old-fashioned British penny, a silver sixpence and
a thrupenny bit. He collected coins. The penny was big and looked
important but the smaller coins, the silver sixpence and the thrupenny bit, were worth more. She looked again at her Knicker Agua
coins and decided they must be the same—the bigger the coin, the
less it was worth—just like the penny. She had to be careful to keep
that 50 safe because it was a 50. And the córdoba was only 1.

32

Sylvia

S ylvia and Melinda had finally made it to Rio after a major
delay in São Paulo. They dragged themselves from the plane,
exhausted, heaving their small but tightly packed backpacks
onto their respective shoulders. As they stepped out of the Arrival
doors to catch a taxi, Sylvia felt a warm breeze blow the hair away
from her face. She switched on her old cell phone and waited for it
to light up. She listened to her voice-mail. Nothing from Tommy.
Why? She'd need to check her e-mail later, just on the off chance.
But there *was* a message from Agent Russo. She was the FBI agent
who had been in contact with Sylvia from the beginning, in charge
of her case. This time, the woman's voice was urgent. Good timing,
she'd only missed the call by ten minutes.

"What's up?" Melinda asked, steering them into the taxi line.

Sylvia's heart was pounding in her stomach. At least that's the
way it felt. "That was a message from the FBI. She's been tracked
down."

"Grace?"

"No, Ruth. But alone."

Melinda raised her eyebrows. "No sign of Grace?"

Sylvia shook her head.

"Holy crap," Melinda said. "Any news from Tommy?"

"No text and nothing on my voice-mail."

"And in your inbox?"

Sylvia held out her ten-year-old Nokia. "You see this? It's not even in color. It's not a Smartphone, I can't get e-mails on it."

"Sylveee! What are you thinking? With Grace missing, what the fuck are you doing with that old thing? You can't even see your *e-mails*? I don't know how I'd *live* without my iPhone!"

"I know, I know. I just haven't got round to buying one, you know? I happen to have had the first generation iPhone but it fell in the bathtub and then I didn't even need a cell *at all* in Wyoming, so I didn't bother buying a new one, just got the faithful old Nokia back out. I don't even use it, except to have in the car for emergencies. I've practically forgotten how an iPhone even works." Sylvia closed her eyes and took in a deep breath. She wasn't sure if she should feel elated or sick. Ruth had been found, but still no sign of her daughter. She pressed the agent's number.

"Where is she?" whispered Melinda.

"One second. Hello? Agent Russo? Hi, it's Sylvia Garland."

The voice on the other end of the line was professional but warm. "Hi, Mrs. Garland—excuse me, I know you said for me to call you Sylvia. I've been expecting your call."

"I'm sorry, I didn't pick straight up. I was on a flight."

"Do you want the good news first or the bad?"

Blood pounded through Sylvia's ears. "Please tell me that Grace is okay."

"I wish I could. The truth is we still don't have a clue where your daughter is. I'm so sorry."

"Oh my God!"

"Don't panic. The police are on their way right now to arrest

Ruth. We've located her. She still hasn't checked out of her hotel."

"Where is she?"

"In Rio de Janeiro at the Copacabana. She was seen, not with Grace, but with your husband."

"Yes, he had a tip she might be there. He went to find her and Grace." Why, Sylvia wondered, hadn't Tommy *called* her if he'd tracked Ruth down? Or at least sent a text. She'd messaged him from São Paulo, but no reply.

The agent added, "I'm really sorry to break this to you—it was quite a shock to us, but Ruth and your husband were seen together last night having a cozy dinner."

"Having dinner? But Tommy doesn't even know her. He's not even sure what she looks like, except from the photofit."

The agent said, "Well, I feel badly telling you this, but, whether he knew her previously or didn't know her at all, it doesn't look good. They were in an intimate embrace. They were seen with their heads, and I quote, 'locked together.'"

The world seemed to stand still in that moment. "Seen by whom?" Sylvia croaked out, her mouth trying to gather enough spittle to get the words out.

"The waiter at the restaurant. And the barman."

"Together?"

"Very *much* together."

The coffee she'd drunk on the plane, the roll she'd eaten—all rose in Sylvia's throat. She swallowed it back. She could feel short, panicked breaths tugging at her lungs as she fumbled for her half bottle of mineral water. She glugged it down in great gulps. Surely there had been a mistake? Yet . . . maybe not. That's why Tommy hadn't called—why he didn't want her to come to South America in the first place . . . because he was off to meet Ruth at the Copacabana, not to track her down, but to elope with her! That's why Ruth had the parental consent form which Sylvia had assumed Ruth forged. Not forged, she realized now, but signed by Tommy! A vision of what had happened flashed through her mind—Tommy had planned it all. Somehow, somewhere, he knew Ruth. They'd been lovers all along. He was sick of his marriage—he didn't love her anymore. He'd plotted the whole thing, planned it alongside Ruth—Grace's kidnapping, the money—he'd told Ruth to look in the filing cabinet for bank details. Perfect. Set the whole thing up to make it look like a crime when *he was in on it from the beginning!* Meet Ruth alone, then both of them would collect Grace from her hiding place and live together happily ever after on a remote beach somewhere, or in a tree house in the jungle. Tommy could hang out and take photos while Ruth wrote her novel, both living on *her* inheritance money. Sylvia's mind contorted itself into this *film noir*—maybe it was farfetched. But maybe, just maybe, this was exactly what had happened.

"Mrs. Garland? Sylvia, are you still there?"

Sylvia blinked her eyes. "Yes, I'm still here. Go on."

Melinda laid her hand gently on Sylvia's shoulder. "Honey, you look so pale. What's she saying? Are you okay?"

"Ssh, wait" –Sylvia waved her hand at her cousin—"I can't hear—as you were saying Agent Russo . . ."

The agent carried on talking while the nest of vipers writhed and twisted in Sylvia's incredulous brain. *Heads locked together?* If that was really true, Tommy was guiltier than Sin itself.

"Like I said," Agent Russo continued, "the police are on their way over now. It remains to be seen if Ruth is hiding your daughter."

"How did you locate Ruth?"

"Blood work. She checked in a week ago to a plastic surgery clinic to have a procedure. Rhinoplasty."

"A nose job?"

"Correct. Her blood work matched samples of DNA taken from the IVF clinic in Guadalajara."

"Good job FBI! I'm impressed. I was terrified that all this time you'd forgotten about Grace because no progress seemed to have been made."

"No, ma'am, we *were* making progress but didn't want to get your hopes up until we had confirmation. We've been working around the clock on your case. I can assure you we have it as high priority. Kidnapping is a serious crime. Not to mention grand theft and larceny."

"What's Ruth's real name?"

"That's the crazy thing. We still don't know. She checked under a bogus name at the clinic, under the name of Rocío Guirnalda, and paid cash—but the DNA is a match to the very same Ruth Vargas from the IVF clinic in Guadalajara. Get this: Guirnalda means Garland in Spanish."

Each word that passed the agent's lips made the horror of the situation magnify. "Oh my God. She's trying to take *everything* from me. My daughter, my husband, my money, even my name!" The image of Ruth slavering all over Tommy with her pretty new nose, enticing him with her "man-magnet" powers of seduction while playing Mommy to Grace, was repulsive. "I guess she must have always wanted a nicer nose and used my money to do it with. What even gave you the idea to search the clinics?"

"We've seen instances of this before with fugitives. Nose jobs are common, we pre-empted that possibility. We had Rio ear-marked—it's famous for its world-class plastic surgeons. The photofit was working in our favor, obviously. She was frightened of being discovered and wanted to change her identity. If she's abandoned Grace, it's because of that—fear of getting caught. On her own, she has a lot better chance of slipping into oblivion, but with Grace's photo everywhere, the alerts on TV, and so many people on the lookout for her—"

"You think for sure she's *abandoned* Grace?"

"Nobody has seen your daughter. Ruth/Rocío checked into the hotel alone. We verified—no food has been taken up to the room.

It looks as if she came to Rio without her."

A snatch of fury grabbed Sylvia by the throat. "Why didn't you just have her arrested immediately, for Christ's sake?"

The agent's voice was cool. "Because we had not come into contact with her up until now. Plain-clothed detectives will be waiting to arrest her the second she returns to the hotel—she stepped out a couple of hours ago. We only just had confirmation of the match and confirmation from the before and after photos the clinic did for the surgery. It only just all came through. It wasn't easy with doctor/client confidentiality in a foreign country but we were able to swing it. It was the clinic that furnished us with her hotel address. She was told to stick around for ten days or so—they took off her splint six days after surgery—yesterday afternoon. She must be using make-up to cover the bruising around her eyes and cheeks.

"Anyway, we've retraced her steps over the last forty-eight hours, interviewed everybody who has come in contact with her, hence the waiter at the restaurant, last night, revealing your husband's . . .er . . . presence."

"How can you be sure it was Tommy?"

"We have photos. We have your YouTube video clip. All the witnesses are one hundred percent sure it's him."

The agent's words were a stake through Sylvia's heart. "What was he doing having *dinner* with her? I still just can't get my head around it all—how could anybody *do* what she's done?"

"Whatever her reasons, she's obviously one sick puppy."

"Puppy is far too cute a word to describe her," Sylvia sneered.

"Anyway, don't lose hope—she can lead us to Grace. Keep your phone on. I'll be getting back to you as soon as they've arrested her. We'll see what excuse your husband comes up with. It had better be good or he'll be arrested on suspicion—an accessory to kidnapping and larceny."

"But he must have had a reason . . . anyway, I'm on my way

to—" The line cut out. Damn, her battered old phone needed recharging; the battery never lasted long enough. She hadn't even gotten a chance to tell Agent Russo she had arrived in Brazil, let alone Rio.

They were finally at the front of the line. Melinda bundled them both into a waiting taxi and, speaking to the driver, she said, "El hotel Copacabana, por favor, señor."

"Por favor, rapido, *rapidisimo*," Sylvia begged the driver, realizing she, like Melinda, was speaking the wrong language. There was no time to lose. She wanted to see the expression on Tommy's face when the police turned up.

And find out what the hell was going on.

33

Grace

The bus stop at Chin Anne Dega was huge. Motorbikes, three-wheely things carrying passengers, and people on bicycles were everywhere—wheels whirling in the dust. Grace spotted a wooden stall with posters stuck all over it and a Coca Cola sign. She asked the man behind the counter for a Coke, some peanuts and some small red bananas. Within minutes, a swarm of half naked children surrounded her, demanding food, begging for Coca Colas. She gave them her 1 córdoba pieces—poor things, they looked starving. They had no mother with them, no father, and were wild with matted hair and dirty faces.

"I like your shirt," one little girl said, her eyes big, her shy smile friendly. She was barefoot and wearing a Britney Spears T-shirt that came to her knees. "And your teddy-bear, I like that too. The colors match."

Grace looked down at her stained yellow and white shirt. She felt like a princess compared to the ragamuffins around her. She held Hideous tightly against her heart.

"What's your name?" the little girl asked. "My name's María."

She wanted to say Grace but it sounded funny in Spanish. "Adela," she answered. "I want to go to school."

The children giggled as if she'd said something ridiculous.

But Grace insisted, "Where's the school?"

"I can show you the school," said a boy in trousers way too big for him. They were held up around the waist with a piece of string. Grace thought he looked like Charlie Chaplin—her dad's favorite actor. "Come with us," he invited. He sipped his Coca Cola (that Grace had paid for) through a straw, making bubbles and slurping noises. She noticed the children had all kept the change from their 1 córdoba coins. Some of them hadn't bought any drink at all, they'd just pocketed her money. She'd get more tomorrow. "This is delicious!" he yelled, "the best drink in the world!" All the children laughed.

"Where do you come from?" another girl asked, who was taller than the others. She must have been about eight years old.

"America."

They now all howled with amusement, the slurping boy rolled on the ground in hysterics.

"It's true," Grace shouted. "I'm American!"

"You sound funny, different from us. Did you come on the bus from El Viejo?"

"I came from The Boom," she said seriously.

They all laughed again, fascinated by every word she uttered.

"Where's your mother?" one asked.

"She's dead," Grace replied, making patterns with her flip-flops in the sandy dirt.

"Me too, both my parents are dead," mumbled a boy holding an old butter knife.

"I never had any parents," another said.

"Let's go back," María said. "Come with us!"

Grace hesitated. "But I want to go to school."

"Come, I can show you the school afterwards," the Charlie Chaplin boy said.

María slipped her hand into Grace's and pulled her into their tight group. "Come on, let's go back."

"Where to?" Grace asked.

"To my uncle's house. Everybody can meet you. Come on!"

They ran through streets, dodging sleeping dogs lying in "beds" they'd made for themselves—small piles of leafy rubbish—and the children zigzagged around noisy motorbikes, and skinny horses pulling carts of vegetables and great sacks of bananas. Grace got a whiff of coffee and trash and wee-wee and fresh flowers, all mixed in a medley of smells. There were striped umbrellas shielding market stall people from the hot sun above, with pretty bags and fabrics in pink, yellow and parrot-green, hanging down in curtains of color—more colors than *Joseph and his Multi-colored Dream Coat!* Mama Ruth had told her all about Joseph and his coat of many colors in their "Sunday school" classes.

Grace saw great chunks of bleeding meat drooping with buzzing flies, and pyramids of fruits piled in baskets. There was a baby being washed by her older sister with dirty water from a blue plastic bucket, and another girl, only seven or eight, was carrying a toddler on her hip. There were pots and baskets spread out on the street which Grace tried not to trip over, and giant sacks of overflowing grain. Little plastic bags wrapped in triangles with bright, bubblegum-pink powder inside caught her eye—um, tasty. Grace wanted to stop but the children raced ahead. She trailed after them as quickly as she could, scared of losing her new friends.

She cantered on, keeping Charlie Chaplin in her sight.

They finally arrived at a garbage dump. Just like the one Ruth described when she threatened to give Carrot and Hideous away. They must be in Rio, Grace realized. Maybe Ruth would come and find her right there. "Why are we here?" she asked María.

"We live just over there. Come on, Adela!"

Grace found herself, not at the school she had imagined with smart uniforms and piles of books and crayons, but in the middle of this smelly trash heap. Around the edge she saw small shelters made out of wavy bits of metal in the shape of waffle irons. Children were walking about in their bare feet with nothing on but underwear, each carrying a stick with a hook. She watched them as they stalked the dump, picking up anything interesting they could find with the hooked stick. Not just children, but grown-ups, too, were searching through the trash. But mostly children, many of them about her age. As they walked ahead, away from the big mound of garbage, she saw something that caught her eye. "Who lives there?" she asked, pointing to a bigger cardboard house in the far distance.

"That's the church," María said. "Sometimes the priest comes to visit and says prayers with us. He's Italian. Sometimes he gives us food."

"And what are the other things, back where we came from?" Grace asked, turning round and pointing.

"Those are our houses. That one we passed earlier, with the hairless dog outside, is mine. We can go there if you like."

They walked back toward the big piles.

"Why is everybody looking through the trash?"

"To sell, silly. We all need to make money."

"It smells of poop here," Grace said, holding her thumb and finger on her nose.

María didn't understand. "Of what?"

"Ka-ka."

The little girl giggled. "Come and meet my family."

But Grace stood still, her stare fixed on a little boy covered in black soot, standing by a smoky fire. "What's he doing?"

"He's burning old electrical wires to get the plastic off the copper."

Grace didn't understand. "What?"

"The metal, silly. He needs to burn off all the plastic. The copper's worth a lot of money. He can sell it and give the money to his mom."

"What's that little girl over there doing? The one in the red skirt?"

"She's looking for food. The truck was here just an hour ago. There's fresh stuff for the picking."

Grace noticed a cow eating a piece of cardboard, and a dog doing a pee just near where the little girl was looking for something to eat. Grace held Hideous close to her chest and ran over to María. "Where's the school?"

"I don't go to school. Come on, Adela, let's go and play baseball with the boys."

They ran around a corner of burning trash. Behind it was a group of boys hitting a ball with naily sticks. The ball landed by Grace's feet and she saw it was made of plastic bags with string wrapped around it tight, making it perfectly round. At home she had lots of real balls. Bouncy balls, tennis balls, beach balls. Even dogs had balls back home. And dogs had food and beds and toys. In America. But here, not only did the dogs have nothing, but the children had nothing.

Nothing at all.

34

Tommy

Tommy walked out of the Internet café. Sylvia still hadn't replied to his e-mails. And neither was she picking up the phone. Usually, she was always home first thing in the morning, and there was only a two-hour time difference between Saginaw and Rio. No point calling her cell as she hardly ever used it.

He just couldn't understand when, exactly, his iPhone had been stolen. Before or after the dinner with Ana?

He turned around and walked back to the Internet café—he should call Sylvia's cell after all, just in case. Like an idiot, he'd left his iPad in Saginaw. He thought he wouldn't need it since he had his phone—wanted to travel light—one less thing to worry about getting stolen. Ironic that. Not having his iPhone now made him feel handicapped. Yet people used to manage without cell phones. Once upon a time.

The dinner. His mind rewound to sixteen hours earlier. He wished the whole fiasco had never happened. He never did get Ana's help with translation. She was a real weirdo, that Ana. Never before had he had to literally manhandle a woman—to pry her off him. Like a leech. He knew how humiliated she must have felt; only someone so desperate would expose themselves that way. Yes, he got a hard-on. But who wouldn't? An attractive woman fondling his private parts, talking dirty in his ear? He was only bloody human. He was a full-blooded male! Men's dicks did their own thing— everybody knew that. It had happened to him before, once, with an innocent aromatherapy massage at the gym—it didn't take much to get it all excited. The whole scene had been embarrassing and shameful, having to push Ana off him that way and say, "Steady on, I'm a married man." He could feel the poor woman's anger, her hurt when she replied, "I was only trying to be nice, just needed a little loving . . . sorree." She picked up her handbag and walked out of the restaurant, and that was that. All that food still spread out on the table. What a strange scenario. What were the odds of someone else also having had a missing child the same age? Maybe that was why she was so needy and pushy.

He retraced his actions . . . Ana's actions, the way she felt him up, smoothing her wandering hands all over his thighs, his ass . . . his . . . back bloody pockets of his jeans!

Jesus! He pounded the heel of his hand on his forehead. Duh! *That crazy bitch stole my fucking phone!*

35

Sylvia

The first thing Sylvia did at the Copacabana Palace was plug in her cell to recharge. Melinda went to scout the hotel, to see if she could locate the Brazilian police the FBI had been in contact with, assuming they'd be plain-clothed—she wasn't sure how easy it would be to find them. Sylvia, hugging a corner near her recharging phone, was just about to ring Agent Russo, when a call came in. She didn't recognize the long number.

"Thank God, I've finally reached you." It was Tommy.

Because her phone was plugged in to a socket, Sylvia couldn't retreat to a more private spot. "What do you mean, 'finally'?" she hissed.

"Didn't you get my e-mails?"

"You know I can't check my e-mails from this old Nokia."

"Yes, but your computer—"

"Why would I have brought my heavy computer with me when I'm trying to travel light?" she snapped.

"*What?* Where are you?"

"What do you mean, where am I. I *told* you, I texted you this morning from São Paulo. I'm in Rio. Anyway, you know what Tommy?" She looked about her and lowered her voice. "I don't want anything to do with you right now. You make me want to *vomit!*"

"*What?*"

"So glad you enjoyed your little tête-à-tête with Psycho Woman last night. The second the FBI find you, they'll arrest you on suspicion of . . . larceny . . . and aiding and abetting a criminal . . . conspiracy . . . on kidnapping charges and grand theft and . . . and you know what, *asshole*, don't expect me to bail you out!"

"Sylvia, *what is going on?* I *told* you about the dinner in an e-mail! And yes, Ana was pretty weird, and no, she didn't help in the end with translation. I had no idea you were coming. When did—"

"'Heads locked together,' Agent Russo said. Was she *good*, Tommy? Was it worth it?"

"*What?*"

Sylvia's heart jumped. "Wait a minute, who did you say? What was her name?"

"The woman I had dinner with? Ana."

"Stop fucking with me Tommy! Tell me the goddam truth, for once."

"Calm down Sylvia, don't get your knickers in a twist. I *am* telling the truth. Let's take one thing at a time—let's just start from the beginning, shall—"

"Which beginning? When you snuck around for two years, sending love messages to a girl almost young enough to be my daughter, or when you and Ruth first met? Are you trying to send me to an asylum? Drive me insane with your deceit and lies? Steal Grace away from me? Hatching some sick plot?"

"*What?* Jesus, this is crazy! Darling, what's got into you? Met Ruth? I've *never* met the woman in my life, for God's sake! You know that."

"So canoodling with her over dinner doesn't count? You were *seen*, Tommy so don't you *dare*," she spat between gritted teeth, "lie to me."

"I had dinner with that woman I told you about in the e-mail. Ana. And she stole my iPhone, by the way. She was meant to help me with translation, go with me to the police station—she said she also has a missing child—and yes, she tried to seduce me last night but I shook her off—"

"Did you like her pretty nose, courtesy of *my* money? Was she as gorgeous as the Bel Ange? Because guess what, Tommy, you were slobbering all over Ruth *herself*, and her nice new nose job. But I guess you already know that. Maybe you and she have a little thing going on. *Who knows, you're such a good liar, how would I know what the hell is happening here?* I can't even speak to you right now because just thinking about what you did makes me want to *throw up*! Explain your liaison with Ruth Steel, aka Ruth Vargas, aka Rocío Guirnalda, aka Psycho Woman to the FBI and the Brazilian police, because you and I are *done*! Find yourself a divorce lawyer, and a criminal lawyer while you're at it, because it's *over*." She pressed "end" on her phone and exhaled with fury. She wanted so badly to believe everything he said.

But somehow, she just couldn't.

Her face raw, the Mars-red rage bubbling—unleashing itself on her husband—made her feel powerful for just a beat, but a gaping hole, an emptiness, filled her insides just a second later, and searing tears flooded her tired eyes. She was alone, without Grace, without a husband. She looked up, the thin wire of her phone holding her close to the wall. People were staring. She'd tried to keep her voice low but her hissing and growling had drawn even more attention. Her phone rang again. The same number. She ignored it and called Agent Russo instead.

"I've been trying to call you," the detective said.

"I was on the line with my husband. He says the woman he had dinner with told him she was called Ana, and he had no idea it was Ruth."

"And you believe him?"

"I don't know what I believe any more."

"Sylvia, the police were let into Ruth's room at the Copacabana."

"I'm here myself. I didn't get a chance to tell you. I'm in Rio, Agent Russo. Here at the Copacabana. But I didn't know whom to look for. My cousin is trying to find them right now. Are they plain-clothed?"

Agent Russo let out a heavy sigh. "If I'd known you were going there I would have told you not to. You could have put our plan at risk. Not to mention yourself. Anyway, as it is . . ." She paused, took a breath and said, "I'm sorry, I have bad news. Ruth has left. Her room was completely cleaned out. When she stepped out a few hours ago, Reception said she left with just her purse, no luggage. She even chatted with one of them saying she was off for a bite to eat. We all expected her to return, because she never checked out, never paid her bill. We think she may have flung her stuff from her window and collected it later. Whatever, however she did it— empty, gone, not a trace. Maybe she got wind that we'd tracked her down. Who knows?"

Sylvia felt a tornado of suspicion spiral through her veins. That text to Tommy she sent, telling him that she'd arrived in São Paulo . . . could he have passed that information on to Ruth? Yet . . . that's right . . . he said she'd stolen his phone. So Ruth would have read all his messages!

"Agent Russo?" Sylvia said. "Tommy told me the woman last night stole his iPhone. And as we know, that woman was Ruth. So she would have known I was on my way to Rio, and coming to find her and Grace at the Copacabana. I think I might have mentioned you, too, in my text—in my messages to Tommy—I can't remember. I can check."

"She stole the phone during their dinner?"

"So he says. He swears he's innocent, that he pushed her away, and that she tried to seduce him."

"Where is he now?"

"I didn't ask. I guess in a hotel or an Internet café somewhere. He made a Skype call, I think, because it was one of those long numbers. I slammed the phone down on him, figuratively speaking—it's hard to slam down a cell phone." She tried to smile at her limp joke but her mouth twisted and pursed into despair.

"We need him for questioning," the agent urged.

"Maybe he'll call back."

"Sylvia. I'm sorry we didn't catch her in time. I feel terrible. But don't lose heart. We have her photo now from the plastic surgeon, the "after" shot—it's on every database all over the world. She can't exactly go and have another nose job—we'll nail her sooner or later and when we do, she can lead us to Grace."

36

Tommy

Sylvia had been rambling on about divorce—this time Tommy knew she meant it. She never swore, she'd never insulted him that way. Ever. He could feel that he was like poison to her—she was repulsed. He could understand why. He'd been soiled by Ruth, but he'd let it happen—just for a second, but still. Ruth got to touch him, feel his body, bite his ear. She was able to speak that filth and he listened—it even turned him on. Turned his dick on, anyway. Only for ten or twenty seconds, but in that time she'd violated him. He felt disgustedly ashamed of himself. He'd even smelt her perfume.

She'd stolen their daughter.

She'd desecrated their life.

Filched, spoiled, destroyed—everything he loved.

They taught him in the Territorial Army how to kill. From a distance. Impersonally. Coldly. With no mercy. He'd done some training to be a sniper. He'd been a pretty good marksman in his day.

It was about time, he decided, to use his skills.

To hunt that bitch down, once and for all.
Force her to reveal Grace's whereabouts.
And then fucking well give her what she deserved.

37

Sylvia

The concierge had been gawping at her pointedly, whispering to his colleagues. Sylvia glowered back. *Yes,* her glare told him, *I know how embarrassing it is for your pristine, shiny palace to be spoilt by a screeching vagrant visitor, but what would you do, Mr. Manager, if your husband was hanging out—nay, probably having sex with—the woman who kidnapped your child?*

Sylvia smiled sarcastically at him, plucked her phone from its socket, and marched defiantly toward the Ladies' Room. She'd freshen up and get out of here as soon as she found Melinda. Agent Russo had texted her the number of the FBI contact in Rio and they'd go over and see him. They'd work out a plan. As for Tommy, he could fix his own problems—if he got slung in a Brazilian jail for conspiracy—too damn bad.

The dark-suited manager, in a fast clip, made his way toward her.

"Alright, alright, I'm leaving," she muttered, gathering her purse, standing tall and turning her back on him. "Don't worry, I'm outta here."

"Miss? Madam?" he called after her. "Please. Wait!"

Sylvia picked up her backpack and looked over his head to see if she could spot Melinda amidst the sea of potted palm trees, the tromp l'Oeil, and the glossy, cream-colored walls.

"Mrs. Garland? Sylvia Garland?" the manager insisted.

Sylvia turned around, her astonished face pale. "Yes, I'm Sylvia Garland," she said, embarrassed.

"Ah, good. I'm glad I've caught you. I have a package for you. Please come with me."

"Are you sure? I'm not even a guest here."

"Somebody who stayed here left it for you. I would like to say she was a 'client' but unfortunately she disappeared without paying her rather large bill. Her credit card was phony. I believe she is wanted by the police."

Hairs bristled on Sylvia's bare arms and goose bumps as small as needle pricks sent a shiver through her body. What was in that package? Anthrax? Dog feces? A bomb?

"Please come with me," the man beckoned with an air of professional smoothness. He led her to the front desk and pulled out a manila envelope with her name scrawled across in big letters.

Sylvia hesitated as the man handed her the envelope. "Please," she said, "would you mind opening it for me?"

"It would be my pleasure."

"Are you sure? You don't feel nervous about its contents, knowing a criminal left this for me?"

He laughed. "We've had many criminals here over the years. Ronnie Biggs used to come by often for a drink.

Sylvia wasn't in the mood to chat. She fixed her gaze on the envelope.

The concierge went on, "You must have heard of Ronnie Biggs? The Great Train Robbery man? The British villain who escaped England and lived in Rio for years? He even did a record with the Sex Pistols. Recorded it right here, in Brazil. That was before there was an extradition treaty with Great Britain, so they couldn't touch him. And we've had some other non law-abiding characters staying here. Usually, they pay their bills, though."

Sylvia smiled and watched his fingers while he opened the envelope with a sharp silver knife. She winced . . . *what would be inside?* "But you've had a few *glamorous* famous guests too, haven't you?" she said to be polite.

"Oh yes. So many—from all corners of the globe."

She kept her eye on the envelope. Why it was taking him so long, she couldn't understand. "Who was your favorite?"

"I was honored to meet Princess Diana once. My father worked here before me—he declared that Rita Hayworth was the most beautiful woman he'd ever seen. May I say you have a Rita Hayworth air about you, Mrs. Garland. Tall, poised."

She wished he'd stop chitchatting and *flirting,* and open the goddam envelope already, but she smiled to be gracious. "Thank you, I'm so flattered. I love Rita Hayworth. Gilda is one of my favorite movies." *Hurry up, goddamn it!*

"Ah yes, I know that film. The love-hate relationship between the two protagonists is alarming but fascinating. They are so in love yet they torture each other."

Sylvia looked down at the polished marble floor. It was as if the concierge *knew* about her and Tommy.

The man must have noticed her uneasiness because he maneuvered the subject back to the package. "What have we here? It feels like a cell phone." He peered inside the envelope and pulled something out. "I was right. An iPhone."

Sylvia instinctively stepped back. "What if it triggers a bomb?"

"You're serious, aren't you, my dear? Did you know this woman, this Rocío Guirnalda?"

Sylvia let out a long sigh. She had been unaware she'd been holding her breath. "Yes. And no. Tell me, what kind of identification did she show you, if any?"

"Her passport."

"A real passport?"

"The police already scanned it. Yes, it was real." He chuckled to himself—"a real fake, I suppose. Nothing surprises me anymore. It had *us* fooled, anyway."

"Was the photo with the new nose or the old one?"

"I can show you a copy, if you wish." He spoke to one of his colleagues in Portuguese and then handed Sylvia the phone. She held it gingerly in the palm of her hand. If she pressed it too hard, she feared the whole building would blow up.

"Isn't that what suicide bombers use? Cell phones? She turned it over, her touch soft, cautious. She let out a little yelp.

"Is anything wrong?" the man asked.

She re-read the engraving she knew so well: *For Daddy on his birthday – we love you, Grace xxx (and Mommy too).* "This phone?" Sylvia said. "It belongs to my husband."

Footsteps behind Sylvia made her heart skip a beat. "*There* you are! I've been looking for you everywhere." It was Melinda, rushing up like an unexpected exclamation mark. "You got me worried! I couldn't find the police anywhere. I've been all around the hotel, the pool area, the gym, everywhere. What have you got there?"

"Tommy's cell phone. Ruth stole it from him last night and then returned it to me in this envelope. Crazy, huh? This gentleman was kind enough to open the package for me. I was too scared to do it myself—thought there could be a nasty surprise inside."

Melinda gasped, "Oh my God! This woman is beyond insane." She looked at the concierge and held out her right hand, "Excuse me, how do you do?" Melinda said, shaking his hand. "By the way, should we even be touching it? What about her fingerprints?"

Sylvia rolled her eyes at her own stupidity. "That's a very good point."

"The FBI already have her prints," the concierge revealed.

"Oh yes? From her room?"

"Her room was swept clean. But her prints were on a broken piece of glass in the waste-paper basket. I overheard them say something to that effect."

"Strange, Agent Russo didn't mention that."

"Perhaps," the concierge replied, "because they are trying to be discreet. Who knows? Maybe she isn't working alone. There have been child prostitution rings, et cetera."

Sylvia felt herself blanche. *Child prostitution rings? Jesus, is that what Ruth is? A goddamn child trafficker?* She leaned against the desk to support herself. Her knees felt like Jell-O.

Melinda bit her lip and said, "Wasn't there something in the envelope apart from the phone? A message or a note?"

"I don't think so. Let's have another look." The concierge reached his hand inside the envelope and, fumbling about, pulled out a piece of hotel letter-headed paper that had gotten lodged behind the flap. "You're right. Here's a hand-written note. Lucky you said something." He handed it to Sylvia. But Sylvia felt too weak to read it. She passed it on to Melinda who read the scrawled writing out loud.

Dear Sylvia,

Tommy's iPhone enclosed. You'll find Grace in a cabin at a beach known by surfers as the 'Boom' but next to Playa Aserradores, nearest towns Chinandega and El Viejo in Nicaragua. She's being looked after by a very nice guy called Lucho.

Good luck with your script, sorry things have been a bit jumbled. Rx

P.S Did enjoy my time with Tommy – shame it didn't work out. He's pretty cool.

P.P.S Hats off to you for being such a great mom – not easy.

Sylvia could feel her knees quivering under her as she crumpled to the floor.

38

Grace

It was dark and Grace was lost in an ocean of garbage. Her flip-flops had broken and now she was barefoot. Her friend María had disappeared and Grace didn't know where to search. She felt for money in her pocket. She had one 50 centavo piece remaining. There were horrible smells of burning and her throat was sore from the stinky-gray smoke. She couldn't stop coughing and she now felt cold.

Nobody had taken her to find the school. The other children said she needed to buy a uniform, that nobody could go to school without one, and she didn't have enough money. Maybe, they said, she could talk to the priest and see what he could do to help. But she hadn't seen a priest. They laughed at her and said she should have stayed in El Viejo where she came from with her silly accent—that she was stupid to have gotten on the bus. That if she was better than them and had all the things she said she had then she wouldn't have come to the dump in the first place. They said she'd have to work the way they worked. That she'd have to scavenge and sell things. But she didn't see what anybody would want to buy. There were old rubber tires, plastic bags, broken glass, spiky metal, and bloody needles doctors gave injections with. Why would anybody want to buy these things?

They giggled at her when she told them she was American, and said Americans were rich and didn't have dirty clothes covered in blood like hers, and ugly brown skin like hers. That they were white and clean and they washed their hair every day with hot water and ate in restaurants. Not in a trillion years, they said, was she American. When she told them she ate French-fries with ketchup and fresh fish at the beach for dinner just the night before, they laughed even harder.

She was hungry. And tired. She wanted her mom. She squeezed Hideous to her heart as tears soaked into his dirty yellow fur. A little boy had tried to take him from her earlier that day but she screamed and screeched until he ran away. Now everyone had left her alone. They hated her. Where was María? The grown-ups didn't care. They didn't have time. Grace tried to leave the dump but it went on and on and on. Forever. She couldn't find a way out. The sky was dark and smelly and mean. Even the dogs ran away from her. Her only friend was Hideous. She was going to change his name. She decided to call him Amarillo.

She loved him even more than she loved Pidgey O Dollars.

Suddenly, she heard a pitter-patter. She looked up and saw the faint outline of María coming toward her in the purple, smoky air.

"Silly girl, why did you run away from me?" María demanded, smiling.

"I didn't."

"Come on. Let's go get some supper. You're hungry, aren't you?" She grabbed Grace's hand and pulled her away from an upside down broken bucket that was her seat. "Hurry up! Or all the tourists will have finished."

"Where are we going?"

"To get food! Follow me."

María ran ahead, as fast as the wind. Her bare feet were like hooves of a goat because she didn't feel the broken glass or the stones. She jumped over boxes and plastic, and leapt in the air like a running deer. Grace tried to keep up.

"Wait! María, wait!"

They arrived at María's little house, a wobbly shack with a wobbly tin roof. She pushed aside a curtain which was their front door. "Where's your bowl, Adela?"

Grace peeped inside from behind the curtain. "I don't have one."

"You didn't find one in the dump today?"

She shook her head. She didn't know she was meant to look for a bowl.

"Never mind. I can lend you one." The little girl wiped her hands and nose with her T-shirt and looked about the room. The floor was dirt. There was a funny-looking bed in the corner, with a stripy blanket, and a poster of a man playing baseball on the wall above it. There was a plastic vase on a table, with plastic flowers in it. Finally, María found a bowl under a pile of old newspapers.

"Where are your parents?" Grace asked.

"My mother works nights," María replied. "I don't know where my dad is. I haven't seen him for a long time. My brother's on the streets somewhere. Maybe we'll see him later. Quick, let's go. Here, take yours." She shoved a tin bowl into Grace's hand. "Never mind about a spoon. I can't find one now, we'll eat with our hands. If we're lucky. If the tourists are generous tonight. And if the restaurant doesn't shoo us away. Come on, let's hurry before the boys get there first."

They ran off again. This time Grace kept a tight hold on her friend, clinging with her little nails to the loose fabric of María's T-shirt. She wasn't going to let her out of her sight, ever again.

They stood outside the restaurant where there was a group of

American girls sitting around a table, eating. It smelled delicious. Fried rice, chicken with mango. Grace peeped over the barrier that separated them from the terrace outside, where the girls were eating. María didn't say a word. She just held out her bowl and smiled. Grace listened to the conversation. One of the girls was speaking. She looked about seventeen.

"I'm like so grossed out with this place. Have you seen the dump? It's sooo bad. It like, totally stinks. I'm so glad we can give something back."

Another older girl added, "I didn't get to have a shower today. I feel all scratchy and verminy. I can't even imagine how they feel. I mean, I'm surprised by how many kids don't really know how to wash their hands, and then when we did the actual hand-washing part today, how incredibly—and I mean incredibly—dirty their hands were. Not only were their hands dirty, with black under their nails, but there were like bugs swarming all over most of the children's faces, their eyes and hair. It's like the gnats just *live* on these children."

The seventeen-year old said, "I mean it's so *disgusting*, the dump is like practically *on top* of the sewerage system."

"What 'system'? It's all, like . . . open."

"I know. So gross. We need to get them clean water wells. So much more money is needed. I'm so glad my mom made me come here to be a part of this organization. I mean, you have to see it to believe it. I'm so proud to serve Jesus in this way." She looked over and caught María's eye.

María smiled and held out her bowl. "Por favor."

"You see? Every night they're here," the teenager said.

Just then a group of shirtless little boys appeared. Grace saw they were making signs with open mouths, their fingers gathered together, miming "feed me!" The older girl said, "They're here because people keep *giving* to them. I bet some of them have already eaten. She shouted at the boys. "No! Go away! FUERA!"

"Don't be so mean. You can't eat all that. I'm going to give them some of mine. "Aquí."

The boys scrambled over each other to reach the food, elbowing each other out of the way. "Quickly," one boy whispered, "before the manager comes!" They shoved their hands onto the tourists' plates, grabbing at rice and chicken bones. María ran over with her bowl and presented it at the table. She didn't want to miss out.

"We can't feed everybody!" one girl whined. "Look, wait in turns, you guys! We'll ask the waiter for some extra bananas."

María kept smiling patiently, still holding her bowl in front of her. Grace came forward and did the same. "I'm hungry," she said quietly.

"Oh my Gosh! This little girl speaks English." The seventeen-year-old emptied the leftovers of her rice into Grace's bowl. "Where do you live? Dónde vives? Everybody? Check out her *eyes!* Oh my God, this little girl has the most beautiful eyes I've ever seen! They're like, *golden.* Dónde vives?"

Grace wanted to tell her that she lived in Wyoming, but she couldn't remember the words in English; her tongue felt thick in her mouth. She wanted to explain that she was American but she knew they wouldn't believe her—they would laugh just the way her friends had laughed. Instead she held up her teddy and said, "Se llama Amarillo."

"This little girl is *so cute.* What's your name, sweetie?"

Grace? Adela? She didn't know what to say. "Grace," she whispered.

"Do you live at the dump?" the teenager asked.

"She leeve with me," María replied in English, barging forward. "At my ouse." She took Grace by the hand and dragged her away, the other hand holding her bowl, now full with rice. María smiled again at the Americans. "We see you tomorrow? No give food to boy. You give to us," she pleaded. "We more ungary than boy. We good, boy bad."

The boys started to jeer and yell. One screeched, "Boy unga-ree!"

"Come back tomorrow," the teenager said to Grace and María. "And have dinner *with* us. Okay? We invite you to dinner. You can eat anything you want. Understand?"

María smiled again and pulled Grace away. Grace's eyes lingered longingly.

"And . . ." the American shouted after them, "I'll buy you both a pair of shoes."

Tomorrow, Grace decided, at dinner, she'd tell the girls who she really was.

39

Sylvia

"Here we are again," Melinda said, managing a half-smile. She glanced up at the departure board in the São Paulo Airport.

"Delayed," Sylvia mumbled, as she stared at the flashing letters for their flight to Panama. She lifted her eyes to the ceiling in exasperation.

"I hope we don't miss our connection to Managua," Melinda said.

Sylvia felt the hollow in her chest. Each second that ticked by was a moment further away from being reunited with Grace in Nicaragua. Those seconds were crucial. Her eyes scanned the airport continually. Every woman she saw made her wonder if she could be Ruth in disguise. Every pair of sunglasses, every hat, made her get up from her seat and walk over to scrutinize the person.

"I was so hopeful," Sylvia murmured. "I really believed we were just going to swan into the Copacabana and find Grace right there. Dumb, I guess."

"So, still no word from Agent Russo?"

Sylvia shook her head.

Melinda was nibbling her nails. "Nothing at all from her police contacts in Chinandega? Or from the attaché in Panama? Did you check your messages?"

"Three times already."

"So no news at all?" Melinda insisted.

Sylvia sighed and stretched her arms. "Just what she told me. That the head honcho's away on vacation and he's the one—trust our luck—who's fluent in English. But Agent Russo promised they're on the case. They have my number—I gave them yours, too. They know we're going by our own steam to Nicaragua. The local police there should be on their way to this Boom beach place, to Playa Aserradores, to find Grace. Hopefully, they'll have found her by the time we arrive. If not, they're going to send over their agent from Panama."

Melinda rolled her eyes. "The FBI doesn't *have* anyone in Nicaragua?"

"No, they don't have an attaché there."

"Damn them for not having just flown us straight there in a helicopter—this journey is going to take so goddamn long."

Sylvia asked herself if she had made the right decision. "Well last night when we spoke, they were kind of offering us a ride in that oh-so-vague, Latin way, without giving us specifics—not even how long it was going to take to get organized, so I thought we'd better just get going. Not wait around. Tommy said empty promises seem to be part and parcel of the culture here."

"No, I think you're right—we had to get on with it," Melinda answered.

"I mean, maybe they would have pulled something out of the bag. Perhaps if they'd had an attaché in Nicaragua things might be a lot more straightforward. It's not all seamless like in the movies—that's for sure."

Melinda narrowed her eyes with suspicion. "Hey, you don't think this is some wild goose chase, do you? A little game to get us all flying up to Nicaragua—Ruth's sick little joke?"

"It's all we've got."

"You think it's true?"

"For some reason, don't ask me why, but I think for once she's telling the truth," Sylvia said.

"But surely this Lucho guy has a cell phone? Why didn't Ruth give us a contact number to call? Maybe this really *is* her idea of a joke. I mean why *didn't* she give us this Lucho's number? Or a phone number of the place Grace is at?"

Sylvia bit her lower lip. "It sounds out of the way—maybe they don't have a network there. Not even landlines."

"They do. I told you, already. It *is* remote but like I said last night, there are a couple of small surfer lodgings nearby, and a restaurant. That beach where Grace is, like Ruth mentioned in her note, is popular with surfers from all over the world. That guy Lucho could well be a surfer. I told you last night, Sylvia, don't you remember? I called them *all.*"

Sylvia's eyes stared ahead of her, fixing on the maze of people milling about the airport like worker bees. "That's right. You said. Sorry, Melinda, it seems you have to repeat everything to me a thousand times."

"Nobody has seen Grace, anyway, and nobody had heard of Lucho, but I did leave my number," Melinda said. "I Google Earthed that area. There's a bunch of massive beaches, winding estuaries full of mangroves—there's a nature reserve called Estero Real, not far."

"Maybe Ruth didn't want to scare this Lucho guy off," Sylvia reasoned. "If she warned him we were coming, he'd know something was up and he might abandon Grace. She probably convinced him she was Grace's mother or auntie, or something. I mean, most people are not okay with kidnapping, however laid back they might be. But my guess is he doesn't even know a thing or he would have reported it to someone, or contacted the police. Surely? Maybe he's even expecting Ruth to return, who knows. Let's just pray to God he's not some pedophile or something."

"I don't think so, Sylvia, honey. I know it sounds like a grand sweeping statement, but Latin men are usually great with kids. They make good au pairs, apparently. If he's a surfer dude, he's probably fine. But what confuses me is how come Grace hasn't *said* anything. I mean, if she'd told someone, that *someone* would have informed the police. I can't imagine that Grace would let Ruth get away with pretending she was her mom, or even her aunt. Grace is smart and gutsy. And she worships you—I can't envisage her being okay with that."

Sylvia shifted her eyes back to Melinda. "Maybe Ruth's just telling a half truth, telling people she's a friend of mine and looking after her while I'm in the hospital or something. Or perhaps she threatened Grace in some way. What a witch! You know what gets me most? I know I sound like a broken record with this . . . but that *note* keeps going round and round in my head. The way she was so nonchalant, so . . . so . . . by the by. Oh, 'shame it didn't work out with Tommy . . . he's cool and, sorry things were a bit jumbled.' Jumbled? What a psycho! As if she had nothing to do with it—no part to play—let alone the fact that she is *responsible* for ruining everybody's lives!"

Melinda took Sylvia's hand in hers and squeezed it gently. "I know, honey. But at least she *did* write that note. Assuming it's not bullshit. We have to give her credit for that, as insane as she obviously is. So you really think it was Ruth who posted that anonymous message on the *Lonely Planet*? As a kind of trap?"

"It would make sense."

"Why? So she could try and seduce Tommy? But she didn't know that Tommy would be traveling alone, did she?"

"You know what I think? As you say, Melinda, she has some

level of conscience—that's why she wrote the note. I think she may have planned to tell us where Grace was when she posted the anonymous message. Then she found Tommy alone, thought he was cute and made a move on him."

Melinda let out a half-laugh. "You know what? You are such a ridiculously nice person, Sylvia! Here's this psycho who tries to take your whole life away from you, and you give her *the benefit of the doubt?*" .

Sylvia raised her eyebrows. "You believe she planned it all ahead of time?"

"Well thinking about it again, yes, I do. *'Shame it didn't work out with Tommy.'* What does that tell you, Sylvia? Sounds to me like she had some fucked-up fantasy of her and Tommy running off into the sunset. And Grace too, as one big happy family. And when she realized—at that crazy seduction dinner—that he wasn't interested, despite all the effort she had gone to with her expensive new nose, she became pissed off and bailed completely. Gave up, in a sense, and revealed Grace's whereabouts. We *hope* she revealed her whereabouts, anyway. What makes her *really* nuts is that she believed it was all a possibility. Then she stole the iPhone, realized you were on your way, based on the messages she found from you to Tommy, and knew that the FBI was in contact with you."

Sylvia looked down at the floor. "I don't know how much was planned. I think she kind of made it all up as she went along, including the kidnappping and the theft. I've come to the conclusion that she's an opportunist. The nose job was maybe a mixture of trying to be invisible, plus something she always wanted to do. I remember her complaining about how long her nose was, that it was too 'strong a nose.' "

Melinda sniggered. "Wanted to get rid of the weasel look."

"Yeah, 'weasel' describes Ruth perfectly, with her keen beady eyes. I should have listened to Grace. Before she got seduced by the Dorothy shoes, and candy. First impressions are always right."

"Don't hit me for saying this, but Ruth *is* kind of fascinating. I mean, what makes a person like that *tick*?"

Sylvia thought about it for a beat. "Money. Power. Control. If she can't get it on her own merit, she steals it. Like her fake credentials from Harvard and Yale."

"The ironic thing is she's smart enough to have done all that. Shame her focus was all skewwhiff," Melinda replied.

"At least the Brazilian police are really on her trail after her little stint at the Copacabana. It seemed to have really bugged them that she didn't pay that bill. Kidnapping—a crime of passion for a motherless woman, but not paying a bill? Ooh, that's really naughty. Anyway, they have her photo, matched with her DNA and fingerprints. It'll be so much harder for her, now, even if she has an armful of fake passports."

Melinda laid her hand on Sylvia's arm. "So what about Tommy? What are you going to do about him? Are you going to tell him where we're going?"

"That's a point. I need to check my e-mails. In all this time since we've been in Brazil, I still haven't even looked. He said he left me several. Melinda, can I borrow . . .Oh yes, I almost forgot, I don't need your cell, I have Tommy's iPhone."

"I am *so* buying you an iPhone of your own. I can't believe how negligent you've been going around with that ten year-old dinosaur. What happened to the go-getter New Yorker who looked after movie stars, who cut deals and oversaw big contracts? You used to be so *with* it, Sylvia. Sorry, I'm being judging."

"Yes, you are. Some of us feel that there's life outside of work."

"Hello? I've left my goddamn job! What does that tell you?"

"I know, and I really appreciate what you're doing for me. For Grace."

Melinda stood up and stretched her arms above her neck. "I wouldn't have it any other way. Hey, Sylvia, how much time do we have before our next flight?"

"Another two hours."

"Okay, you stay here. Don't move. I'll be right back."

"I won't budge from this seat. But only if you promise to bring me a coffee and something good to eat. I'm starving. Nothing spicy or weird, just something wholesome and American. I'm feeling kind of homesick."

"Already? We just got here." Melinda laughed. "You think *this* is funky? Honey, we've only seen five star so far."

"That hotel last night was pretty grotty, you have to admit."

"Wait till we get to Chinandega where it's *really* basic—they're still suffering from the aftermath of Hurricane Mitch."

"But wasn't that *ages* ago?" Sylvia asked.

"1998, I think. It left, like, three million homeless and thousands dead, mostly in the north and northwest, and they've never recovered since. The flooding was really intense. I remember all about it because I once gave to a charity set up there—I can't recall its name—something to do with Jesus or Christ. There's a big network of Christian aid agencies still working there. A lot of those poor Nicaraguans are living off the landfills just to survive. Something incredible, like sixty-five percent of the workforce is unemployed. Or more. After Haiti, I think Nicaragua's the poorest nation on earth. Very few kids get to go to school, the illiteracy rate is really high, especially for women and girls. Poor things get earthquakes, hurricanes, volcanoes—the works. Some of them live on dumpsites."

Sylvia heaved a sigh. "Horrific, isn't it? I saw a documentary about a dump like that in India. I didn't realize they had the same problem in Nicaragua too. Poor children."

"I know. It's just so criminal the way half the world lives in such extreme poverty. And we think nothing of spending four or five dollars on a single coffee—money that would feed a whole family. Okay, enough of my doom and gloom. When you're done with your e-mails you can surf online about the area of Chinandega, the beach part that's away from the city. Like I said, I Google Earthed it to get an idea of where we'd be going. You can even see the swell of the waves and lots of green. There's also a whole chain of active volcanoes not far. It's pure forest and farmland there. That part looks really beautiful."

Sylvia stared ahead, not focusing, just letting the airport blend into a fuzzy blur. She rested her head on her hands, spreading them out like claws across her scalp. "You know, Melinda, the more I think about it the more I think you're right. If there were all these foreigners by the beach, why didn't Grace *confide* in someone? I mean, she's a brave little thing, it doesn't make sense." Tears flooded back again. Tears of hope. It was intermittent, the emotions rolling up and down—the fear, the hope, the currents of excitement that Grace was alive and okay.

Melinda put her arm around her. "Look, she's going to be fine. She's been on a horrible journey but has pulled through. We have to have faith. Like you say, she's brave. Grace is a fighter. Just stay calm. It'll be okay, I promise. Look, I'm going to find us something to eat. Being hungry doesn't help morale. I'll be right back."

Sylvia pulled out Tommy's iPhone from her purse. Another thing polluted by Ruth. This lovely phone that Grace had given him for his birthday—that they'd had engraved—touched and handled by that bitch—her grabby, thieving hands all over it. Ruth was no fool, though. She would have obviously wiped it over for finger-prints—but still, she'd been using it as one of her tools. Sylvia scrolled through the messages. Two old ones from Agent Russo. Four from Tommy, sent to her computer, which of course she hadn't seen. She looked at the latest and went backwards. The most recent read:

Darling,

Agent Russo wants me to go to the police for question-ing. She's not accusing me of anything but I'm reading

between the lines – maybe I'm being paranoid but . . . if I don't watch my back I could get slung in a Brazilian jail. I think they suspect I'm linked to Ruth in some way and stole your money. I really don't think that would help anyone if I'm arrested, least of all Grace.

I know you're furious with me. And I know you've gone to find Grace in Nicaragua. I heard about the note from Ruth and that she gave back my iPhone. I'll keep in touch by e-mail . . . I'm sure the FBI, police whatever, will be joining you there, or maybe they've even got there already. Anyway, for that reason I'm not going to come in case they pounce on me – then I won't be any use to anyone. Plus, I know you don't want to see my face right now. I have a better plan, just in case this is all a hoax – I'm going to find Ruth. I don't know how or where but I'm working on it. If Grace isn't in Nicaragua and Psycho Woman, as you so rightly call her, is taking the piss, then the only way to find Grace is through her, anyway. I know you're angry with me, and I don't blame you, I was really thick to not be more on the ball . . . but please, I beg of you, keep in touch and let me know the second you find Grace.

You are my light,
Tommykins

Sylvia scrolled down to the one sent earlier:

My darling,

My heart is heaving with pain. I feel sick about what happened, guilty as if I betrayed you and Grace. I feel that way. But I swear nothing happened. Nothing. For some reason, she set out to destroy us. Please don't let her win. Please don't let her take you away from me. I don't know where you are. I'm at the Copacabana looking for you. I'm desperate.

I love you more than you could ever imagine.

You are my Queen.

Tommy

P.S I've just remembered something important. Ruth, aka Ana, kept saying we should look in Central America for Grace, namely Nicaragua. I'm trying to rack my brains about the conversation that night but the gist of it was that she (disguised in the conversation as "the woman who took Grace") was fed up with playing mommy and couldn't handle it. And that maybe Grace was fine and eating an ice cream somewhere . . . seemed an odd thing to say at the time. If I remember any more clues I'll text/e-mail. Will be buying a new phone ASAP.

All my love xxx

Darling,

I'm sitting in an Internet café. My mobile's been stolen. It was stolen by that woman Ana who I had dinner with last night. Why? Why did she steal my mobile? She seemed well dressed, affluent, didn't look like she needed money. I mean, she was paying for a room at the Copacabana! What a fucking weirdo. I have no idea what her agenda was – she said she wanted to help me find Grace and then she got all personal on me and ended up not doing anything at all except making off with my phone. Fucking fruitcake! I've tried phoning you but you don't pick up at home. I'll try your mobile now . . . where ARE you??

Txxx

Sylvia darling,

Met a woman called Ana who says she can help me with translation and we can go to the police. Off to have a bite to eat. You're not picking up . . . where are you??? Will call again later.

Luv you. Tx

Sent from my iPhone

A wave of relief passed through Sylvia. Tommy had been telling the truth all along. He'd told her about the dinner with Ruth and he really did believe she was called Ana, and was just trying to help. Sylvia could have easily made the same mistake. After all, Ruth had dyed her hair auburn red and had a neat, pretty nose—so different from the photofit image Tommy had of her. It wasn't his fault. He was on the lookout for Ruth *plus* Grace—how could he have possibly known Ruth would be wandering around on her own, posing as a local from Rio with a fake, very convincing (no doubt) Brazilian accent?

Sylvia closed her eyes and sucked in a deep breath. She'd read so many self-help books over the years, thought them all fascinating, and then popped them back on the bookshelf and forgot most of the wisdom. Easier said than done to be sweet, spiritual, and continually forgiving. Random tidbits now resurfaced in her mind.

She enveloped herself in a ball of virtual pink light, and let it radiate around her body. She brought Tommy and Grace into her aura and imagined them all together, hugging and smiling. Melinda was there, Jacqueline, and her aunt. Even Mrs. Wicks from next door, and LeRoy, all smiling at them in their triangle of happiness and light. "Please make it well again, please bring me Grace and Tommy, bring my family back to me—they're all I have," she pleaded to whatever Higher Power was listening.

She knew she was meant to send a healing pink ray of light to Ruth, too, but she just couldn't bring herself to go that far. Sylvia was no saint.

Because secretly, she wanted Ruth dead.

40

Tommy

Tommy tried to imagine himself in Ruth's shoes. Like a game of chess, he needed to envisage the gamut of possibilities open to his opponent and pre-empt her next move. What would she do now? What does she want? Where would she go? He made a mental list:

a.) She has an inflated ego which could be her downfall.
b.) Wants her novel to be published at all costs.
c.) Needs to head to a country where there's no extradition treaty with Brazil or America.

He mulled over his last supposition. It was true, she'd be hard-pressed to get on a plane—the airports would be on red alert. Yet he also suspected that she felt invincible, uncatchable. Her ego was as tough as oilskin. Maybe she'd been breaking the law her whole life and it was second nature, and she was unable to tell the truth. Unable to not steal, to not lie.

He remembered Sylvia telling him that Ruth had traveled extensively, backpacked through Asia. Thailand housed some pretty unsavory characters, Vietnam too. Hadn't Gary Glitter been arrested on charges of pedophilia? Even there, they were clamping down on criminals. Cambodia? Laos? Burma? Ah yes, Burma, now called Myanmar. That would be a clever place to hide. Even though Aung San Suu Kyi had taken public office, after years of Burma being a police state and of not giving a damn of what other countries thought, they wouldn't waste their time ingratiating themselves with the FBI or any other foreign law enforcement body. They wouldn't have the resources or the time—they had other issues to attend to. Tommy could just see Ruth journeying up the Irrawaddy River, fancying herself as George Orwell, or hiding out in a jungle somewhere, maybe lording it over some pretty Asian boy. Bribing policeman, buying herself merit, the way corrupt officials did, to reach Nirvana faster. Tommy remembered reading about that, how Burmese Buddhists bought caged doves and set them free (even though they'd end up flying straight back to the cage they knew)— the officials totting up their spiritual bank account. He could just envisage Ruth doing that. Perhaps setting herself up in a tree house, simple and rustic, like the cabin Tommy imagined on the beach in Nicaragua. Remote but pleasant. A nice peaceful life for a writer— he almost envied her.

That guy Lucho, the surfer she mentioned in the note Agent Russo had told him about—Tommy bet he was a sort of toy-boy for her—someone for Ruth to dispose of when she got bored.

Tommy felt ashamed, just loathed to admit it, but there was an attractiveness about Ruth—vulnerability mixed with a sort of integral strength. No way did she look her age, either. The type of woman he would have easily jumped into bed with before he got married. Ugh, it made him queasy just thinking about that dinner with her. The proximity. She was right there! Why hadn't he seen the signs? She was telling him her *whole story* and he was too dense to pick up on it.

He needed to know more about her. He got out the new iPhone

he purchased that morning and sent a message to Sylvia:

> Darling,
>
> Tell me everything about the book Ruth was writing. Plot, characters etc. Was she working on anything else? Favorite places she's visited?
>
> xxxT

Sylvia replied not long after. The bleep made his heart race. They were communicating, at least, though it was clear that she was still enraged with him. Or disappointed. "Disappointed" was somehow even worse.

> **Tommy,**
>
> **Ruth is aiming for an epic saga type of novel. She was managing 6,000 words a day. That's a lot. So I can't imagine it being particularly literary. I only read the first few chapters. She wants to write a doorstop book which is not fashionable right now – it'll be hard to find a publisher. Normally, they want around 90,000 words for first time novelists. She's aiming for 2 – 3 times that. Her title was *The Jewel*. It was a sort of thriller cum love story about a man who finds his grandfather's diaries and it flashes back to his love story set against the 1957 revolution in French Cameroon (I think it was around then) when several women fought for freedom. The female protagonist, Ruth decided, should be played by Thandie Newton (don't you love the arrogance – she's already cast the movie).**
>
> **And then there was the modern day romance between an Indiana Jones character and a young Catherine Deneuve type. I wish now I'd paid more attention. She was also planning a non-fiction book based on her expe-**

rience with the IVF miracle that was about to happen –
she said she had publishers interested. Then there was
yet another project which she seemed to have abandoned, a chick-lit novel called *Sex Addict Anon* - its title
speaks for itself! (Get the double-entendre, get her bril-
liance? Anon, as in "bye, see you around" (like in
Shakespeare plays) and anon (as in "anonymous").

She said that she was going to give herself six months
to find an agent and if she didn't have any luck she'd self-
publish. She told me she had a list of agents she was going to target once finished . . . how I wish I'd gotten that
list when I had the chance. Who could have known?

What were you thinking, Tommy? To approach every
New York and London literary agent and ask them to
rummage in their slush piles for her manuscript? Funny,
the same thing crossed my mind. I did mention that to
Agent Russo but I don't know if she's following that lead.
What else? She's bulimic, has an eating disorder. Was engaged 4 times. As you know, speaks 3 languages, each
one like it was her mother tongue.

Good luck.

Keep in touch,
Sylvia

No kisses, no love, just, *Keep in touch, Sylvia.* He wondered if he
would ever be able to win her trust again. He wanted her back. All
of her. Losing his wife was not an option for him.

Sylvia had not been an easy woman to catch. He wooed her for
months in an old-fashioned manner: dinners galore, trips to the
movies, cards, books of poems. At first, he thought her arrogant,
standoffish; her peerless demeanor made him feel as if he didn't
stand a chance. She'd had, as far as he knew, only one boyfriend.
Later, he found out that she had a fragile heart, and her haughtiness

was her way of protecting herself. Tommy didn't consider himself ambitious but he was focused when something was important. The scholarship for university, and later, Sylvia. The moment he met her, he made up his mind that she would be his wife. He became obsessed—winning her became his mission.

He asked himself how much of his quest at that time was about love, and how much was about achieving a goal. Like a hunter catching his prey. He had been determined to win his prize. He became obsessed with claiming her, fucking her, making her his. And he finally won. When they married, he felt like his mission was accomplished, forgetting that a marriage was work—a garden that needed to be watered and nurtured. He could sense her drifting away now, like snowflakes in a cool breeze. The idea of losing her completely made him feel as if he had a hole in his solar plexus.

During their marriage he'd never stopped to wonder how much he loved her because she was always there. But her aloofness was now punishing. It wasn't his ego that craved her, but his soul. Perhaps it was all too late. What he'd been *playing* at, sending all those childish, ridiculous messages to that young Marie, the "Bel Ange" –he now had no idea. It seemed like a mystery what had been going on in his head. He felt pathetic, ashamed. He had a beautiful family and he'd really bungled things.

Going off to LA was a bad plan anyway, chasing a half-baked idea, selling his dreams short. If only he hadn't gone, none of this would have happened. And now, with Grace kidnapped and all this Ruth horror, mixed with his stupidity, everything had become even more poisoned. If they got Grace back, he had a chance to mend things with his wife. If not, why would Sylvia even bother with him? Then, he would have lost everything in the world that mattered to him.

Ruth. Rocío. Ana. He felt so humiliated. Dishonored. Disgraced. After reading Sylvia's e-mail, he needed to add another point to her list:

d.) Possible sex addict—will want a man with her as soon as she
    can get one.

The stakes were higher than ever. He *had* to find Ruth. How he
was going to trap the monster, he still wasn't sure.

But once he did? He knew exactly what he'd do with her.

41

Grace

Hardly had Grace woken up, when she smelled fumes and heard voices outside María's little shack. The two little girls had curled up together on the bed the night before, alone, and fallen into a thick sleep. Grace had no idea what time it was but it was already light—the night had been eaten up, as if a great gobbling monster had come and munched up the dark. This place looked better in the dark. She heard rain outside. The curtain was blowing softly in the breeze, a smelly breeze that let in stinky whiffs of rotten cabbages and burning plastic. She knew that burning plastic smell because once, in Wyoming, a farmer had been burning paper potato bags lined with plastic, throwing them in with wood on a big bonfire, and her mom told her that even a little bit of burning plastic was dangerous to breathe. But it was everywhere here.

She opened her eyes wide and looked about the makeshift home. María was still asleep. Her mother was not there, nor her brother. Grace wondered how old María was. She'd asked her but

María wasn't sure. "About seven," she guessed. But Grace thought she was younger because she wasn't as tall as the seven-year-olds back home. She had a wide face with almost black eyes, and was darker than she was. And very pretty. María didn't even know when her birthday was! Grace couldn't imagine how that was possible.

She squeezed her teddy close and gave him a morning kiss. Today, she was determined to find the school. So what if she didn't have a uniform? She needed to talk to a teacher. Maybe the teacher would know where The Boom was. Lucho might be worried about her. Not Hell O.D though. She was probably happy. And what about her dad? Where was he? Ruth said she was *working on it*. But now, not even Ruth knew where she was. Where would they have breakfast? The tourist girls had invited them to dinner but Grace was hungry now, and dinner was a long time to wait.

Outside, a motor was stopping and starting and she could hear boys shouting and laughing. She peeped outside the curtain and saw they had a piece of oily old machinery like a bit of the inside of a car. They pulled what looked like a string, stood back and waited for the engine to come alive. Whenever it did, they cheered and squealed. The rain was making puddles in the dirt. She looked down at her filthy, bloody feet.

María woke with a start. "What's that clatter?" she asked sleepily, rubbing her eyes.

"The boys."

"Why are boys always so noisy?"

"I want to go to school today," Grace said in a strong voice.

"Forget school, we don't have time."

"I want to go to school!" Grace shouted. Before she knew it, her face was red, her eyes gushing determined tears. "I want my Mommy. I want to go to school," she wailed stamping her bare feet.

"You said your mom was dead."

"She's alive!" Grace bellowed. "She's in Heaven and she's alive!"

"We can find the priest, then," María suggested. "He runs the school. He can talk to you about your mom."

"In the cardboard church?" Grace asked hopefully.

"Yes. He comes most days. He's Italian. People give him money and he has a school and sometimes you can get hot meals there."

"Why don't *you* go to school, then?"

María shrugged her shoulders. "I have to work, to give money to my mom."

"Where is she?"

"I don't know," María answered. "Sometimes she forgets to come home."

Grace opened the curtain. The rain had stopped. She put one foot out of the shack and felt mud oozing and squidging between her toes.

"Where are you going?" María asked.

"To find the priest."

"Wait for me, silly! I'll show you where."

THE CARDBOARD CHURCH was much bigger than Grace had imagined. In her mind's eye, she'd pictured a doll's house church, with the priest outside it, wearing a white and gold flowing robe like the Pope. She'd seen the Pope on TV. He wore a golden cross like hers, but his was a hundred times bigger and more important.

The cardboard church wasn't like a doll's house at all. It was way larger than a garden shed, and it was made of white and brown cardboard, like a patchwork. It was pretty, she decided. Some bits had red writing on it with names of things—of bananas or shops—but mostly the cardboard was pale brown, made in layers like fish scales, but square. Around the church, there was patchy grass, and instead of doors to the church, there were white curtains. Not like María's curtains—these ones were clean as if they'd just been hung up to dry. She could even smell them; they smelled of soap and sunshine. In the garden part, there was a big, black, tractor tire surrounding a deep hole. Inside, it looked like a well for water, with a metal bucket attached to a chain. There was a rusty bicycle leaning against folds of turquoise plastic tarp, clipped up against one of the walls. Half of the church had a wavy tin roof, while the other half was cardboard like the walls, with plastic on top to protect it from the rain.

The girls tiptoed up to the entrance.

"Shush," María said, "there's someone inside."

Grace remembered Ruth reminding her, over and over, that she was Catholic now. That she must be a good girl and that, one day, when she was twelve, she could have her First Communion and wear a dress like a princess. Grace twiddled the cross around her neck and mumbled . . . "six, seven, eight" . . . how many years until she turned twelve? "Nine, ten—"

"You're rich," María said, eyeing up her cross. "You have gold. You could sell that."

"But that would be Blast Famous." The Blast Famous part came out in English. Grace didn't know how to translate that word into Spanish.

"You're funny," her friend said with a giggle. "You say silly things sometimes."

A booming voice from inside rattled the cardboard walls. Grace wondered if the building would topple over. "Hello? Who's out there?" A big fat woman opened a curtain and stood with her legs like tree trunks, planted firmly on the scrubby lawn.

The girls looked up. Grace noticed she was extra tall. She saw folds of fat making mountains and valleys, trapped behind a tight, white bra underneath the lady's tight, white blouse. She had pale, foreign skin and although she spoke Spanish, she had a strange accent like karate chops.

"We came to see the priest," María ventured.

"I want to go to school," Grace added.

"Padre Marco isn't here at the moment,'" Extra Tall said. The girls looked at each other. Grace felt her body go heavy and she held Hideous Amarillo close. "But," said Extra Tall, "why don't you come in and wait?"

The girls followed her inside. The church was huge, with a pointed ceiling and wooden beams holding everything together. Inside was a table and a few painted chairs. There was a calendar on the wall, bottles of mineral water, and even an iron. There was electricity, too, with wires plugged directly into sockets in the cardboard. Grace wondered if the cow she had seen the day before had been eating a piece of the church, if one of the bits of walls had flown off in a wind, and if that cow was Blast Famous because she was eating cardboard church pieces.

"Would you little girls like a drink and a cookie?" Extra Tall asked.

"Yes please," they both shouted at once. Well, Grace didn't hear the "please" bit from María, just the "yes" but the woman was happy with them because she was smiling. Grace was thirsty, her throat dry like a crispy autumn leaf.

Extra Tall poured out two cups of orange drink. Grace could smell the sweetness, even from where she was sitting. The woman put four cookies on a plate. Grace looked at María and saw her eyes widen, her pink tongue lick her lips like a little dog. "Here we go," the woman said, and gave them each their drink and let them take their cookies. "So you want to go to Padre Marco's school, do you?" she asked Grace.

"Yes."

"You know you have to work hard and come every day. The uniforms are expensive and we can't go round giving uniforms away to little girls who aren't serious, who don't come to school every day. Do you understand?" Grace nodded. "How old are you?" the big lady asked.

Because Grace was sitting down, she had to push her head all the way back and hold her neck high into the air to see the lady's face. Her mom taught her that you must always look at someone when they are talking to you, especially grown-ups. "Five and three-quarters," she answered softly.

"Usually we don't accept children under six years old."

"Maybe I *am* six, I can't remember."

"I'm seven," María piped up, her mouth full of cookie.

"And you want to go to school, too?"

"If Adela goes, I go," she said.

The lady turned her gaze to Grace. "Is your name Adela?"

Grace wasn't sure. She nodded and took a bite out of her cookie, and squeezed Hideous against her chest.

"And what is your name?"

"María."

Just then, a man, short and fat, breathed into the church. Grace could hear him wheezing like her friend back home who had asthma, except this man's wheezing was a hundred times louder. He was almost bald, except for a thin sweep of hair that was combed across his shiny round head, which reached just to the shoulders of Extra Tall.

"Padre Marco, I have two new, potential students," she said.

"Excellent," he wheezed, sucking in the air. "Excellent." He had an accent, too, but different from the lady's. It sounded like a song. But he didn't look like the Pope, at all. He had regular man's clothes, not a flowing robe. But he did wear a white collar around his neck. The rest of him was black. Not his skin. His skin was pale, with a face the color of an almost ripe strawberry. But his arms were milky white.

"I gave them some cookies and a drink."

"But that's not enough!" he exclaimed, coughing now. The wheeze had got all excited. "They need a hot meal! Would you like a proper lunch, girls?"

Grace thought María's eyes would pop right out of her head.

María turned to her and whispered, "Those horrid boys said we had to be careful of him but I think he's nice."

"But you have to promise you'll attend school every day," the priest said slowly. "And be good girls. Huh?"

Grace managed to say, "What about our uniforms?"

"All in good time. All in good time." And he added, "Can you rustle up some *gallo pinto*, Helga? Something tasty? Meanwhile, I have some books to show you, girls." He brought out some pretty books with big, colored illustrations. Grace turned a page—Jesus feeding the five thousand with two little fish and five loaves of bread. *Where was Jesus now?* she wondered. He was never around when you needed him.

"Helga," the priest continued, "I think it would be a good idea to bathe these little girls, huh? Scrub their scalps clean, get out all the nastiness, the creepy crawlies, especially the older one with long hair. "Hey girls, would you like to be bathed with hot, soapy water?"

They nodded.

"In fact, give them their bath now. They can eat afterwards. I need them cleansed."

"Come on little ones," Extra Tall Helga said. She took them each by the hand and led them outside, behind the church. There was a big, enormous witches' cauldron bubbling away on a small bonfire. Grace pulled back. Was this woman going to throw her into the pot and mix her up with slugs and snails and puppy dog's tails? "What's wrong," the woman asked in a cross Dragon Voice. "Don't you want to be *clean*? Padre Marco doesn't like dirty children. If you want your uniform, Adela, you have to be bathed first. Now, sit on these stools and wait, like good little girls."

Extra Tall Helga placed them each on a very low, plastic stool. Grace's one was red, María's blue. They watched her, their eyes following her every movement. She went back into the church and when she returned, she had two big plastic buckets. Then she walked around the side and they could hear her drawing water from the well, the chain clanking, the water splashing. Then she came round to the witches' cauldron, and with a big soup ladle scooped out boiling water, adding it to the well water in the buckets. When she was done, she put her hand inside each one to test. "Das ist gut," she mumbled to herself. She rolled up the sleeves of her white blouse which had patches of sweat, like maps of the world, under the arms. She took out a small metal container from her pocket and opened it up. There was a bar of soap inside.

"Now girls, take off your clothes."

They both obeyed. Grace pulled off her mucky shirt and climbed out of her shorts which were stiff with dirt. María stood up and stepped out of her skirt. She pulled her T-shirt, way too big for her, over her head. She was not wearing any underpants. Grace sat there, still in her white cotton panties.

"Off with those," Extra Tall Helga barked. Grace took them off. The woman snatched them and turned them over in her giant hands. "These are new," she said, surprised. She grabbed Hideous Amarillo out of Grace's grip, and before Grace knew it, the woman had plunged him and all their clothing into the bubbling, boiling cauldron.

Grace started to howl. She could feel Hideous burning as if it were her own body. "He's dying!" she screamed, running over to save him. But before she could do anything, Extra-Tall-Helga-Dragon had Grace's windmill arms caught in a tight vice as the little child thrashed about, trying to jiggle and slip beneath her torturer. "He's boiling alive!"

"Hold still!" the woman shouted, "or I'll have to slap you! I will take the teddy bear out but you have to promise to remain still, or we could all have a very nasty accident indeed!"

"What is going on here?" It was Padre Marco, shuffling around from the side of the church.

"This little girl is impossible! She's screaming because I am trying to sterilize her teddy bear. It must be riddled with germs, crawling alive with eggs and lice and filth."

"Let me take the child," he snorted. "And you get the toy out of the boiling water."

While the priest held Grace, Dragon Helga took a giant wooden spoon, stirred the pot a second time, and scooped out Hideous Amarillo. He landed with a plop on the grass, his furry body steaming like a Chinese dumpling. He really did look yellow again. But soaking.

"Is he still alive?" Grace asked, her curiosity breaking her tears mid-flow.

"Quite alive, and hopefully, the creatures nesting inside it quite dead," the Dragon said.

The Padre let go of his grip and Grace raced over to the teddy and picked him up.

"Careful, it's still hot," the woman warned. "It could scald you. Now, leave it on the grass to dry and we can wash you girls. Hurry up or the buckets of water will get cold."

"It's alright," the priest said. "I can take over now. Have a break. Have a cup of coffee. I can do the girls."

"With pleasure, Padre. Be careful of that one," she said, pointing to Grace. "She's a cat. She scratched me with her sharp little nails. I'll be trimming those dangerous little weapons later, I can tell you."

Padre Marco took one of the buckets and knelt beside María on her stool. "It won't hurt," he assured in his singsong accent, "I'll be gentle. We just need to clean the dirty bits." Grace watched him as he lathered up a big sponge with soap. He carefully rubbed it on María's back, making it frothy and bubbly and white. "See?" he said, "I'm not going to bite." He frothed the sponge around her neck, her chest, and her arms. Slowly. Softly. "Now I'm going to pour some warm water over your head. Close your eyes." María closed her eyes tight and giggled when the warm water gushed over her skinny body. The priest took a bottle and spilled out a glob on his fat sausage fingers. It was shampoo. He massaged his hands into María's head, whipping it up like cream on a cake.

"This is lovely," María said to Grace. "It's all warm and clean and smells yummy."

Grace relaxed on her stool. She felt her itchy head and thought it would be nice to have her hair washed too. She loved it when her mom washed her hair. But then Ruth cut it all off and now she hardly had any hair at all. She'd seen her face in a mirror and knew she looked like a boy.

María was giggling now. "That tickles," she tittered. "That feels funny down there."

"But we have to wash in between. In those secret places," the priest panted. "We have to make it all clean and smell like roses. Now I'm going to rinse your lovely long hair with clean water. Hold still and shut your eyes again."

Grace waited for her turn. It didn't seem so bad. María was enjoying it.

"You see how pretty you are now?" he said. "Like one of Christ's little angels."

Grace wanted to be one of Christ's Little Angels, too. María was getting all the attention. But then, like a tornado, Extra Tall came by and surprised the priest with her heavy footsteps. Padre Marco stood up in a jolt, knocking the bucket over which splashed all over his pants.

"How are we getting on here, Padre?"

"All finished now," he said. Grace noticed his face had burst into an even redder Strawberry Red than before, and drops of sweat were dripping from his forehead. He quickly knelt down again, grabbing the now empty bucket and holding it against him as if he was trying to hide the zipper on his pants.

"I'll finish this, Padre. I'm sure little Adela has calmed down by now, haven't you?"

Grace managed a smile and watched as the woman stomped over in her white wooden clogs, the big, soapy sponge in her giant hands.

"Little girls?" the Padre said. "Do you have a home? Because if you don't, you can stay tonight for dinner. We can set you up in a crib. Do you have anywhere to go?"

"Not really," María lied. She was standing by Grace now, naked, dripping wet, as the Father wrapped her in a clean white towel. She skipped next to Grace and whispered in a hiss, "We can have a yummy dinner here."

"But what about the tourist girls? The American girls?"

"Never mind about them, we're staying here tonight."

"But we promised—"

"No, we didn't."

"They said they'd buy us shoes, they—"

"I can buy you shoes," the Padre interrupted. "For good little Catholic girls like you," he said, looking at Grace's cross, "the least I can do is buy you shoes. And then tomorrow we'll organize your school uniforms."

"See?" María said. "Told you it was better here."

"Can we start school tomorrow?" Grace asked.

The Padre raked his eyes over her little frame. "Yes, Adela, you can both start school tomorrow. But before that, I'll want to see you tucked up in bed nice and early so you can get a good night's rest. I'll be coming in personally to read you both a bedtime story."

María giggled and asked, "What will the story be about?"

He paused and thought about it for a minute and then said, "A story about Jesus, of course."

42

Sylvia

This time it wasn't Agent Russo that called Sylvia, but the FBI attaché in Panama. Sylvia and Melinda had caught a taxi from the unappealing capital of Managua and finally, after getting out of the entrails and endless suburbs of the city, they were heading north toward Chinandega. It was now five pm. The attaché had bad news. Grace had been reported missing by this young man, Lucho Reynes, the day before. The Chinandega police had swept the area by the beach. There was no sign of her having drowned, and there was a lot of morning activity there—somebody would have spotted her, they said.

But Grace had not been seen for thirty-six hours, since before dawn the day before. The man in question—this Lucho Reynes, a twenty-four-year-old Columbian surfer—was being held for questioning. He was a suspect, obviously, the local police assured the attaché. Just because it was he who had reported Grace missing didn't make him innocent, didn't let him off the hook. Casebook, they told him. Often the most helpful person at the scene of the crime turns out to be the perpetrator. Sylvia listened as carefully as she could to everything the attaché said but her heart was hammering in her ears, her breath short. It was happening again. Every time there seemed to be hope on the horizon, some outer force dragged them backwards through the dirt again.

"What's wrong now?" Melinda asked with a look of fear in her eyes.

Sylvia's body felt numb as if something had sucked out the nerves in her hands and limbs. She sunk into the corner of the taxi and looked out the window as they sailed past colorful buses belching out black fumes, dodging chickens and dogs, forcing bicycles to go wobbling into the verges of the road. In the distance, she could see a smoking cone-shaped volcano, the white clouds steadily climbing from its crater. It looked as if it could explode any minute.

"Just as I thought we were finally getting somewhere," Sylvia murmured.

Melinda held her cousin's trembling fingers in her hand. "What did they say? Grace isn't *there*?"

"She *was* there. Quite happily, it seems. Hanging out with this surfer guy, Lucho, and his French girlfriend—living in the cabin by the beach where Ruth left her. This Lucho has sworn to the police that he has nothing to do with her disappearance. Apparently, he was even in tears. Said Grace's *mother* left her with him and said she was going to return in a couple of weeks. Left him some money, the cabin paid for in advance. He met Ruth in El Salvador; she was acting as a kind of cougar cum sugar-mommy, it seems. She was going under the name of Rocío and he thought Grace's name was Adela. Can you imagine? Poor Grace not only has had to deal with getting kidnapped, but has had her name changed and been given a whole new identity, a new mother."

Melinda's eyes welled with tears. "Oh my God. That is so fucked up!"

"Tell me about it. I just feel sick. That's bad enough, but *disappeared?*"

Melinda wiped her face and her voice took on a fake cheery tone. "I'm sure Grace is okay. Somewhere. Maybe she's even looking for you, poor thing." Then she added, "If Ruth was passing herself off as her mother, where does Grace think *you* are?"

"I don't know."

"Why didn't Grace say something to this Lucho, tell him her story?"

"I don't *know*," Sylvia shouted to herself as much as to her cousin. "I'm sorry, I don't mean to snap. I'm . . . just . . . I really can't imagine, Melinda. Your guess is as good as mine."

"We need to see Lucho. We need to talk to him," Melinda said, more softly, "Where is he?"

"The police have detained him. He's at the station in a town called El Viejo, only a few miles from Chinandega. I'm not saying he's innocent but it just seems to me that if his plan was to do something nasty to Grace he could have done it ages ago."

"We just don't know till we see him. I want to look into his eyes. You can always tell a person by their eyes."

"Well that makes me and Tommy really dumb then, doesn't it? Both of us were hoodwinked, on different occasions, by Ruth."

Melinda flinched and said, "I'm sorry, putting my foot—"

"No, you're right," Sylvia went on, "you *can* tell who someone is by their eyes—if you're smart enough. We weren't, and look where it got us."

Melinda began to surf on her iPhone. "We'd better tell the driver, then, that we need to go to El Viejo, to the *Policía Nacional* and not straight to the beach."

Sylvia wiped the back of her hand across her face. She realized she'd been drinking her tears that were trickling into her mouth. Sometimes, she was unaware she'd even been crying. She was squandering her energy, she needed to focus.

"Look, I'm just thinking. Both of us going together is a waste of our resources—it would be frittering away precious time. Melinda, is your Spanish still pretty good?"

"Not too bad. I used to have to talk to the Madrid lot at work quite a bit. It's not great, but I can still recite bits of Pablo Neruda."

"I don't think poetry is going to get you very far with the police here."

"Sylveee, I was just kidding. We have to keep ourselves going with a *little* sense of humor or we'll just cave in."

"I'm sorry. I just don't find *anything* funny right now. Look, why don't you go to the police and I'll go straight on to the beach? See if you can persuade the police to let you talk to Lucho, and I'll find the cabin and anyone nearby who knows something. I want to get there before sunset—it's always early in the tropics—I don't want to be flailing about in the dark."

Melinda put on her glasses and typed on her phone. "Okay, let me see. Sunset in Nicaragua . . . Managua . . . in June, six pm. Managua's only a little further south, *mas o menos el mismo*, don't you think?"

"Tell the driver we need another car. If he could drop me off with a taxi friend of his somewhere. You go to El Viejo and I'll go to the beach—we'll meet later, depending on who has more info and where we need to be."

Sylvia looked down at her thumb and saw she'd ripped the cuticles with her teeth—she had blood on her dress. "And would you send Tommy a message?" she asked her cousin. "He needs to know what's going on."

SYLVIA WAS GLAD to get out of the car. Several times she'd closed her eyes—the possibility of a head-on collision with a truck, swerving to avoid some poor pedestrian or a split in the road, was terrifying. The passing scenery was like going back in time. She observed cream-colored oxen pulling carts with wooden wheels, buses that looked, for the most part, like old American school buses from the 1960s, aluminum with long noses, but top-heavy with baskets, bundles, and great sacks, accompanied by passengers clinging onto the roof rack. She feared they might topple over with the weight. Sometimes a child waved and cheered at her; she heard the word "*rubia*" –the obvious tourist, as she was, in her clean dress (despite the blood marks), leaning out of the window, letting her blond hair blow in the warm wind. There had been a dash of intense rain, too, and potholes had filled up in a matter of minutes, turning into ponds of brown mud-water, soaking poor bicyclists quivering by; the goose-bumps on their arms almost visible as they swerved the flooded, scarred road.

They'd hit the beginning of the rainy season. Sylvia was begging to whoever was listening, that Grace was dry. Alive. Safe. And that somebody could offer a clue as to her whereabouts.

By a stroke of luck, the new driver was familiar with The Boom and dropped Sylvia halfway down a dirt track, which apparently led to the cabin, which he also knew about. This was the countryside— the locals must know each other, she surmised. The driver was acquainted with the American surfer who owned the cabin, said they sometimes shared a beer together. He informed Sylvia that a woman lived next door, local to these parts—he couldn't remember her name—but that she looked after the cabin when nobody was there.

Sylvia walked along the muddy path, the earth gurgling beneath her, squelching and sucking—a sound like several children simulta- neously slurping sodas through straws. The sun was preparing itself for bed, casting golden dapples through the high coconut palms. She passed a hut, its thick straw roof toppled and cockeyed from the rain. A few chickens were pecking about in the fenced-in yard and she observed a small boy staring at her, barefoot, shirtless, holding a bleating kid in his arms as if it were a baby. She approached the gate, set her backpack down and took out a photo of Grace from her wallet. The child retreated.

"Hola," she offered tentatively. "Estoy buscando mi hija." She could hear the clumsiness of her accent. The inquisitive boy continued to watch her. She pulled some candy from her pocket and a biro. She'd heard how children were feverish for pens. The little boy stood stock-still. "Venga," Sylvia beckoned, "para tí." Then she remembered she needed to use South American Spanish, not Castilian Spanish. "Para *vos*."

The boy, still clutching the animal, came forward. She handed him the pen and he inspected it like an artifact. She wondered if he even had any paper at his simple farm—probably not. She showed him the photo of Grace and said, "Conoces esta niña?" He shook his head and looked at the candy, which she handed over. He smiled coyly and ran back to his shack, giggling.

Sylvia picked up her backpack, heaved it over her shoulder and strode on toward the beach. She could hear the lapping ocean and tasted its saltiness on her tongue. The air smelled brackish, of seaweed and damp earth. A vermillion sun was peeping through the trees, rendering reflections orange, and the muddy path shone like a mirror; her moving shadow elongated, the legs stretched out like a runway model, striding like an Amazon. She had reached the great sweep of beach, wide, empty. She wondered where all the surfers were. The sun was a fiery ball sinking lower behind the ocean, setting off twinkling crystals on its shimmering waters. There was no sign of wild breaks as Sylvia had imagined, no twenty-foot high rolls. All was quiet except for the sound of birds and the rhythmical slapping of waves. Had she already passed the cabin without noticing? She'd tried to follow the driver's directions but realized her faltering Spanish had let her down. He'd had to let her off sooner, because of the mud. Left, right? Retrace her steps?

Just as she was turning to go back, she saw a figure in the distance. She stepped away from the wet of the sand, watching her footsteps get swallowed. She walked south—closer to the vegetation and the palm-fringe of the beach—in the direction of the form: a black outline silhouetted against the coral of the sky. As she got closer, she saw it was a woman, slight in build with long brown hair—a tourist not a local, by the way she was dressed. The girl was bending down, maybe collecting shells, Sylvia couldn't see.

Sylvia ran toward her. "Hello! Hola? Habla inglés?"' The woman didn't notice. Sylvia shouted louder, "Do you speak English?"

The girl, for she couldn't have been more than nineteen or so, looked up, surprised. She'd been gazing at a multi-colored crab scrabbling across the sand. It was so bright it looked as if a child had painted it with neon pens.

"Habla inglés?"

"Sí," the young woman answered. "I speak English."

"Thank God," Sylvia panted, out of breath from her sprint and the weight of her pack. She detected that the young woman had a European accent, possibly French. "I'm sorry, I didn't mean to startle you. Are you staying near here?"

"Just over there. But all the guesthouses are in the other direction," she said, pointing to the distance.

"I'm not looking for a guesthouse—I'm looking for my five-year-old daughter."

"Adela?"

"Yes! You *know* her? But she's not called Adela, her name is Grace. She was kidnapped."

"Lucho is innocent!" the girl yelled. "Why doesn't the police believe us?"

Sylvia exhaled with relief. Finally, someone who knew something. "I'm her mother. Are you Lucho's girlfriend?"

"*Rocío* is her mother. This is crazy. What the hell she thought she was doing, though, leaving Adela alone—"

Sylvia looked the girl hard in the eye. "No. Rocío was the woman who stole her from me," she said slowly, annunciating the words. Where could she even begin? The whole story was so complicated. "Look, Rocío was *not* her real mother. *I'm* Grace's mother."

The girl smiled ironically. "Yeah, right. Adela was dark, like a Nicaraguan. You're very blond. Rocío also has coffee-colored skin. And they spoke Spanish together."

Sylvia shifted her weight and sighed. She was already exhausted; the backpack, the explanations. "Look, can we go somewhere and talk? I'll tell you everything. Are you living in the cabin? Are you Lucho's girlfriend?"

The girl raked her eyes over Sylvia suspiciously. "Lucho's not here. He's with the police."

Sylvia ignored her frosty attitude. She noticed how stunning the girl was, really beautiful, but being lost in this sea of deception, the girl had a little snarl playing on her lips. "I know. Boy, am I glad to have found you. My name is Sylvia." She held out her hand.

"I'm Elodie." She didn't shake Sylvia's hand but tentatively offered both cheeks instead. Of course, she was European, thought Sylvia; that's the way they did things.

Sylvia said, "Look, the sooner I know all the details, the better for Lucho. The FBI are on the case, I can—"

"American FBI?" Elodie's face reddened with alarm.

"Yes, I'm American. Grace . . . Adela, is American."

"Now I *know* you're not Adela's mom! Adela only speaks Spanish. I've never heard her speak English. Not once."

Sylvia stood there stunned. Things were beginning to make sense. She put her hand into her dress pocket and pulled out her wallet. She flipped out the picture of Grace and handed it to Elodie. The young woman inspected it, squinted her eyes and then capped her hands around the photo as if to shield the edges. "Adela has short hair. Like a boy. She looks so different here. I don't know." Doubt was etched across her face, crumpling her smooth, flawless brow.

"Please can we walk to your cabin?"

"Okay, come on then," Elodie conceded, finally letting a smile creep into a welcome.

Dusk was falling fast. Sylvia remembered that near the Equator, after the sun went down, night was already nigh, unlike the slow, meandering sunsets back home. She was used to lingering summer evenings when twilight danced between dusk and dark for almost two hours. But now it was nearly black. She followed the girl. She was a beauty, with a heart-shaped face, her skin unblemished, a few freckles scattered across her nose, but she donned a small pout on her lips like a spoiled child who had always gotten her way. When she at last cracked a smile, she had a real sweetness about her. Like a delicate doll.

"Give me half the weight," Elodie offered, pulling away the backpack from Sylvia's shoulders. "We can take half and half." Her accent was adorable; the *H* silent—'alf and 'alf.

Sylvia smiled. "Thank you."

They reached a clearing surrounded by banana, avocado and mango trees and a small garden full of flowers that looked like gladioli but weren't. Almost hidden, was a wooden cabin, no bigger than a large garage. A rope hammock hung from between two trees, and a cement porch provided shelter for a couple of chairs and a table.

"There's no electricity here," Elodie said apologetically. "The simple life. But we have a solar shower. Big luxury." She laughed. She opened the door which wasn't locked, and she and Sylvia placed the backpack on the floor. There were a couple of single beds pushed together and another at the end of the room. No kitchen, just a sink and a few tables. Sylvia imagined Grace living here and how it must have seemed a great adventure for a little child. Minus the Ruth part.

She heard something crunching outside and a snorting sort of grunt. Her heart leap–she'd heard how Nicaragua was full of exotic animals, even jaguars.

"Just the resident pig," the girl explained, "no problem, it's friendly." She lit a candle, an incense stick, and then two mosquito coils. "You better put on a shirt. *Les mustiques* love it after the rain. They attack after the sun goes down." She lit a cigarette and inhaled deeply as if to calm herself.

Sylvia took a light cotton shirt from her backpack and put it on. Then rubbed some citronella on her legs.

"That smells good," Elodie said.

Sylvia massaged her knees with the oil. "Want some? All natural, no pesticides. Are you here alone now?"

"Today I'm alone. They came and took Lucho away yesterday afternoon."

"So what happened exactly? When did Grace go missing?"

"Adela?"

Sylvia wanted to scream, "No *Grace!*" But said, "Look. Just so you understand, my daughter Grace, her name is *Grace*, is Indian. From Kashmir, in India. My husband and I adopted her. That's why she doesn't look like me. This woman, Rocío, who also calls herself Ruth, stole her. Kidnapped her. She's wanted by the FBI for kidnapping and for stealing a lot of money. I know it sounds farfetched and totally nuts and like some sort of Hollywood movie, but I swear it's true."

Elodie capped her hands over her mouth. "*O mon Dieu!* That sounds crazy. Crazy!"

Sylvia put her hand on her heart. "I swear, on my daughter's life, it's the truth. Now, when was it, *exactly*, that Grace disappeared?"

"I was sleeping. Lucho, went surfing early, like five o'clock. The big waves are always very early. When he came back, he woke me up. Adela . . . Grace . . . had already gone."

"What was she wearing?"

Elodie walked across the room and took out a digital camera

from her handbag. She pressed a button on the camera, going through the pictures. "Please sit down. I'll show you Adela." She handed Sylvia the camera.

Sylvia looked through the images—there were three of them. She pored over every detail. Grace having dinner. Grace playing on the beach. Eating fruit. She looked happy, thank God, but like a different person. It was strange how a haircut could change a face. It was cropped short like a boy's buzz cut; her neck, without any wisps of hair about it, made her look like a scrawny bird. If it hadn't been for her long eyelashes and her beautiful amber eyes, she could have been mistaken for the opposite sex. She was either in just bikini bottoms or wearing shorts. No skirts. No dresses. And clothes Sylvia didn't recognize. She was very tanned, her skin darker than she'd ever seen. She could have passed for a local child, especially with the gold cross hanging around her neck. Most of the population was Catholic in Nicaragua—El Salvador too, she presumed. Grace had been converted into an inconspicuous local child. Ruth had been clever. No wonder no traveler had noticed them. Seeing Ruth's latest photo, the passport photo, she too, was tanned. They could have easily been mother and daughter.

"I think she was wearing a shirt and shorts like in the photo, the same clothes as she had on at dinner the night before."

"You had dinner? Where?"

"At the restaurant by the beach."

"Who was there?"

"Just us and some surfers."

"Was anyone paying particular attention to Grace?"

"No, she was very quiet. She didn't say a thing."

"No man was, like . . . flirting with her or something?"

"No! She's a little girl! No, of course not!"

"Where did Lucho meet Rocío?" she asked, already knowing the answer. The Panama attaché had told her.

"El Salvador. On the beach, I don't know the name. Lucho already wanted to come here for the surf."

"Was Lucho Ruth's lover?"

Elodie winced. "She wanted to be. She tried, but Lucho said he didn't sleep with her. I believe him. She was much older than him."

Sylvia tried not to roll her eyes. *Men. Always in denial. Always telling fibs.* "What was Lucho doing hanging out with Ruth, then?"

"His money got stolen. He had nothing. She helped him."

"Whose idea was the cabin?"

Elodie took another drag on her cigarette. "He'd heard about it from other surfers. The Boom is famous. So they came across the *frontière* by boat."

"The border? They crossed the border by boat?"

"Yeah. Oh yeah, Adela left this." Elodie walked over to the bed—the one that was on its own, and rolled back the sheet. Carrot was lying cozily in bed. "You see, I don't think she wanted to run away. She took her other teddy with her."

"Pidgey O Dollars?"

"The yellow one."

"Pidgey is white. Well, kind of. Half and half. Have the police seen these photos of my daughter?"

"No way! They could steal my camera! Worse, they think Lucho killed her or something. I need your help. He's the sweetest guy, ever. He would never hurt a child. He loves Adela. He loves her!" The girl broke down in tears, her slim shoulders heaving with grief. "He is innocent. The jails here full of Sandinista and Contra scum! The police are violent. Please help me. I don't want my mother to know where I am, but . . ." she trailed off.

"Let's make a deal, okay? I *will* help you. And you must help *me.* The sooner we find Grace, the sooner Lucho will be proved innocent. Okay?"

Elodie gulped air between sobs, the cigarette still alight in her hand. "Okay," she sniffled.

Sylvia suddenly felt maternal. "You really shouldn't smoke, you know, Elodie. Your beautiful skin will get ravaged."

"Yeah, Lucho tells me the same thing. He hates it when I smoke."

"Well stop, then. For him. Surprise him."

"Yeah, I guess I could do that. Hey, I almost forgot something that could be important. Adel . . . Grace's funny pen is next door with Angela, the caretaker."

"Pen?"

"Yes. Grace's pen that records voices."

"Oh my God, she brought that with her? I forgot all about that thing. I gave that to Tommy years ago and Grace had her eye on it. She's such a little magpie. I didn't know it still worked."

"Yeah. Lucho says it was a secret from Rocío."

"Why is it next door?"

"To charge. Angela has electricity. Also, we keep all valuables there. She keeps things safe. Passports, money. Computer. Lucho didn't give the police his ID—he said he lost it. The police are crazy here, you know?"

Sylvia's stomach flipped with hope. "Well what are we waiting for? Take me next door."

ANGELA WAS IN her late fifties, Sylvia guessed. An affable woman, with round, jolly cheeks, although with Elodie she was less friendly, but then Elodie, she soon realized, could hardly speak a word of Spanish. The French girl was brave to have come all this way at such a young age to a country so alien to her and launch into a relationship with someone she could hardly communicate with. Perhaps it didn't matter. Young love. Long gone were the days when she and Tommy discussed world politics, movies, books. They always talked about Grace, or about the house, or bills. Their communication was different, but perhaps just as basic as Elodie's and Lucho's. But at least the young couple would be having passionate sex on a regular basis.

Angela was in her kitchen, cooking. In her rudimentary Spanish Sylvia explained her saga and asked the woman if she had Grace's recording pen. Without even asking, Angela set down two plates full of a steaming rice and bean dish, and insisted that she and Elodie have a meal. Sylvia was grateful, her stomach had been rumbling all afternoon from eating nothing but snacks and picking at bland airplane food.

"Ah, ha!" the woman cried in Spanish, after Sylvia had revealed Ruth's crimes. "I *knew* there was something fishy about that woman, Rocío. It wasn't normal to leave a five-year-old alone like that." Angela bustled out of the room and came back with the special pen.

Sylvia could feel herself flush. She, too, had left Grace with a stranger. If she hadn't gone to Saginaw without her, none of this horror would have happened. "Please, tell me anything you can remember that may give us a—" she paused, trying to remember the Spanish word for clue. "*Pista*," she said. "Any clue you can think of. When was it you last saw Grace?" She heaped some rice onto her fork.

"The day before she disappeared, she came over to talk. Poor little thing was alone. Lucho surfing, and . . . well . . . this girl . . . you see what Elodie is like," she said, waving her hand dismissively at her—"what can you expect from teenagers? I told them I didn't have the time to look after Adela, myself. I warned them something could happen." She glowered at Elodie while simultaneously pouring her some juice.

Sylvia knew that in Angela's culture a woman should feel responsible for a child. Any child, whether it was hers or not. Poor Elodie was obviously in the doghouse. Her fault, more than Lucho's, that Grace had not been sufficiently supervised. Yet, how could the poor things know that Grace would sneak out on them like that?

"You don't think there was an accident in the water?" Sylvia asked, wincing, not only at her pidgin Spanish but the appalling possibility of what she was saying. She couldn't remember the word for "drowned."

"No. She never went swimming alone. Never did I see her swimming without Lucho. She knows better than that."

"Is it possible a man was around? Somebody giving her sweet things?" She thought of the little boy she'd given the pen and candy to earlier.

"It's very safe around here. Did you know that Nicaragua has maybe the lowest crime rate in the whole of Latin America? We are no longer a dangerous country," Angela barked, "that's why tourists are returning. The war ended in 1990, you know. The *possibility* is there, of course, but I don't think she got taken by a man. Or anybody, for that matter."

"What do you and Grace usually talk about?" Sylvia asked, twirling the recording pen in her fingers and swallowing a mouthful of food.

"Adela doesn't speak much."

"Grace."

"Pretty name. Like I said, she didn't say much, just sat at the table and drank some juice while I was cooking."

"And did *you* say something?"

"Just asked her if her mother was coming back soon. Rocío, I mean. Not her mother, as I understand now, but a crazy woman— just *knew* something was strange about her. I told your daughter she shouldn't be alone, that it would be better for her to be at school with other children, not all alone."

A light flickered in Sylvia's head. She knew how much Grace adored school. "And what did she say?"

"Nothing. That's when she got up and left. Didn't see her again."

Sylvia squinted her eyes, trying to imagine the scenario. "But she had dinner with the others and went to bed that night. Elodie

303

has a photo of her. So you didn't talk about other children, or about schools or some—"

"Wait a minute! Yes, yes we did. She asked me where the schools were. I remember now. Oh Lord. Oh no, what did I do?"

"And what did you tell her exactly?"

"Well, there's a little place here but it often doesn't function in the rainy season. It only has a straw roof, gets flooded all the time. I think I said the nearest big school was in Chinandega or El Viejo."

"Angela, you're so kind, thank you so much!"

"I haven't been kind, I've been a fool! I put the wrong idea into that little girl's head. Yes, I bet you, she got it into her head to take herself off to school. Oh Lord, oh *Lord*!"

Sylvia finished her juice and got up. "Can I leave my backpack here? I'm going to Chinandega." She took out her cell phone.

"I'm afraid there's no network here. You need to get further out toward the road."

"Sorry? Say that more slowly, I didn't understand."

Angela spoke more slowly. "No cell phone *network*. You need to get closer toward the road."

"Ah, okay. Anyway, I'll return later. Thanks so much."

"Where are you going?" Elodie asked in a panic, her mouth full.

"To Chinandega. Quick, get your bag and come with me—we'll need your camera with those photos of Grace."

Elodie ran back to grab her things while Sylvia waited. Sylvia fixed her stare on the huge moon, perfectly round and stippled. It was rising slowly from the horizon. Sylvia thought of Grace, always keen to pick out the Man in the Moon in any form, shape, or size; a profile, the man doing a dance, a blotchy face, but how Tommy, with his personality, saw the moon in a different way. She remembered him once telling her that the same side of the moon always faces the Earth. Something she'd never considered before. And that a billion years ago, the moon was much closer to the Earth, and a day was only eighteen hours, not twenty-four. The tides were stronger, too, on account of the moon being closer, then. The moon tonight was huge and low. The Man's face was a laughing demon. Why, she wondered, did the Earth get a capital letter and the moon not?

Elodie ran toward her, her bag strapped over her shoulder. They walked in silence, the tall palms swaying in the gentlest breeze. No rain, thank God. Elodie had a small flashlight and shone it ahead. Sylvia could hear creatures rustling through leaves and undergrowth. Birds, snakes, scorpions, crocodiles, panthers . . . every type of animal sprang up in her imagination. The shock of Tommy's iPhone buzzing in her dress pocket nearly sent it flying to the ground as she fumbled in a panic, fishing it out. "Hello?" She could hear movement on the other line and voices mumbling in Spanish. "Ho-la-a?" she yelled into her cell.

"Sylvia? Are you there?"

"Melinda?"

"Finally. I've been calling for ages. Kept getting your voicemail. Listen, I'm still here at the police station. This Lucho guy has basically had the shit walloped out of him."

"Oh no, that's what Elodie feared. Did you get to speak to him?"

"Elodie? His girlfriend? You're with her?"

"Yes. I found her on the beach. I've been to the cabin and seen Angela, the caretaker of the cabin."

"Good work! Look, Lucho is not in great shape."

"What did he say?"

"Okay, let me remember every point. Firstly, he has no idea where Grace could have gone. Let's see . . . He came by boat with Ruth and Grace from El Salvador. He never saw Ruth's passport. Ruth told him Grace was her daughter and she had business in Rio and she'd be back in a couple of weeks. Left him money and paid for the cabin in advance. But then she called from Rio and said she was delayed."

"When?"

"Like three, four days ago. Post nose job, but before she hooked up with Tommy."

"Please don't use that phrase, 'hooked-up,' " Sylvia snapped.

"Sorry. No. Hang on! The first time she called him was about a week ago. Said she'd be delayed. Then called again to confirm. Confirm about being delayed."

"So that must have been when he moved Elodie into the cabin."

"Yes. Listen, Lucho is beside himself and it's not an act. If it is, he deserves an Oscar. He's frantic about Grace and has no idea what could have happened. He feels responsible—"

"Listen, I'm on my way. I think I know where Grace—"

"Sylvia, listen. He thought of something that could be important and I can't believe what he said. Listen carefully to what I am about to say. *Recording pen,* Angelina's cabin next door. I can't talk," and she lowered her voice to a whisper, "they are watching me. Talk to Angela."

"Yeah, as I said, I already have. I've just been with her—she gave us dinner. I know, I was stunned. I have the pen in my possession. I hope it works, who knows what information there could be? Grace was often playing with it—she must have taken it from Tommy's desk. Anyway, we're on our way to Chinandega. Seems like Grace could have been looking for a school. Elodie has photos of her, thank God. We can get those blown up tomorrow and put on every street corner, offering a reward. Just out of interest, Melinda, why didn't Lucho give up the pen as evidence to the police?"

"What do you think? He's a regular guy from Columbia, no frills, no money. What has happened to him is probably no surprise as far as he's concerned. He doesn't exactly have a lot of trust with the law. Or with anybody."

"But didn't he hear the whole saga of what happened from the

FBI, that Grace had been *kidnapped*?"

"It didn't appear so. Just knew he was in a shitload of trouble."

"What's he like?" Sylvia asked, striding through the leafy, muddy grove, following Elodie's flashlight, heading . . . she wasn't even sure where.

"Drop dead gorgeous, even with his black eye. But I swear that's not clouding my judgment. You know what I said about eyes? His are like classic puppy dog eyes."

Sylvia couldn't help but smile at Melinda's last sentence. *Classic puppy dog eyes.*

"Listen, I have to go, the *jefe* is back. I'll call in a bit. Bye."

Sylvia looked at her watch. Ten past seven.

"I have a number for a driver," Elodie announced. "We'll call and he can pick us up at the end of the road. Ten minute walk. And then?" she asked, "where are we going?"

Sylvia almost tripped over a log in the dark but caught her balance. "To find the school. I doubt anyone will be there at this time of night but we could find a lead."

43

Grace

The girls were lying side by side in a shaky bed, in a shack connected to the church. Extra Tall had dressed them in clean, white nightgowns. María was trembling with excitement. She'd been talking about the hot shower non-stop, and kept running her fingers through her clean, soft hair.

"I smell so yummy!" she squealed. "I'm so clean! I've never been in hot water like that. I wish I could be clean like this every single *day*. Look! Feel these sheets." She breathed in the white cotton and giggled. "And look at this pretty blanket. Shush, the priest is coming," she whispered to Grace who hadn't said a word.

Grace wondered what time it was. It was already dark. They'd had a big dinner of beans and rice, with mangoes for dessert, and even some chocolates. María told her she'd never had chocolate before. Grace could hear the wheezing of the priest long before she saw him come into the room. There was something Goblinish about him. She could smell that he'd sprayed himself with perfume. This time he was wearing a robe, a sort of white sheet, loose and flowing. But he still didn't look like the Pope. He was smiling. His teeth were yellow like a rat. Like Samuel Whiskers in the Beatrix Potter tale.

"Hello girls," the priest whispered. "I've come to read you your bedtime story. Sorry I'm late, I had some business to take care of." He took a stool from the corner of the room and moved close to the bed. He sat down and rearranged his dress. Grace thought his lungs might burst with Wheeze.

"What business?" María asked.

"Aren't *you* curious? If you must know, I promised a rosary, a *rosario*, to an old lady."

"Rosario is a girl's name."

"Yes, María, and it's also a way of saying the Lord's Prayer and your Hail Marys. Bead by bead. Important for you, because you're named after our gracious Lady herself. Shall we start the session off with a little prayer then? A little Hail Mary?" Padre Marco started to mumble quietly and María joined in. Grace hummed and moved her lips so she looked Catholic but covered her mouth with Hideous so they couldn't tell she didn't know the words.

"*Dios te salve, María. Llena eres de gracia . . .*" The Padre continued to mutter the prayer and ended with *Amen.* "Now, doesn't that make you feel better? Purged of sin? Huh?"

"You said you'd tell us a story," María shouted excitedly.

"Shush, not so loud. This is our secret bedtime moment, huh? I *will* tell you a story."

"That's not true! You don't have a book with you."

"You're right, María. You're a very observant little girl. I don't have a book with me. I thought we could play a game, instead."

"I love games," María whispered.

"Me too," he wheezed. "Especially secret games. But you must promise not to tell anybody. Not Miss Helga, not your parents, not a soul."

"I promise."

"And you, Adela? Do you promise too?"

She nodded her head and hugged Hideous.

"Because if you tell, we can never play again. And if you don't tell, I can give you chocolate—"

"Yummy!"

"Quietly now, María. Nice and quiet like a baby mouse. Don't say a word."

Grace wondered why the game was so secret. She had never played a secret game before. She wriggled nervously under the sheet.

"And I can also give you some coins. But only if you keep everything hush-hush. Do you know the story of Pinocchio?"

Grace nodded.

"And María, do you know the story?"

"Maybe," she said, playing with her hair.

"It was written by an Italian—"

"You're Italian!"

He smoothed his hand over his balding head. "Yes, María, I am. I thought we could play, and you two girls can pretend that *I* am Pinocchio."

Grace knitted her brow. "How?'

"Well, I'll show you. Now once upon a time, an old man called Geppetto decided to make a puppet from the branch of a tree. '*I shall call you Pinocchio*,' he said to the puppet, '*You shall be a little boy*.' First, he made a mouth and the puppet started to speak." The priest started to move his mouth like a fish. "Touch my mouth, girls. Go on, touch it."

Grace touched the priest's lips lightly with her finger. His lips were wet like squidgy, leaky, over-ripe plums, and she quickly took her finger away. He made fishy movements again. "Go on, María." María put her fingers in the priest's rubbery mouth and he sucked them and licked them like they were a tasty lollipop. "Uum, he said, Pinocchio likes that. He'll give María some chocolate for doing that."

She giggled, "Pinocchio's silly!"

The priest's eyes were alight with fire. "Then Pinocchio started to dance and he earned money at a puppet show." The priest put his hand in his robe pocket and pulled out some córdoba coins and a dollar bill. "Adela just gets coins because she only touched Pinocchio's mouth. But María gets a whole *dollar* because she really played the game." He divided the money and gave it to the children, licking his lips at the same time. "But then," he went on, "Pinocchio forgot to go to school. He'd been given a school uniform and had lots of money spent on him, but he didn't turn up. Then what do you think happened?"

"He told a lie," Grace offered.

"That's right. He *lied* and said he *did* go to school. And then what happened?"

"His nose grew long." Grace looked at Padre Marco's nose. It was already very, very long. And big. How could it get any bigger?

"Now we are going to pretend," he said, standing up and lifting up his robe above his legs, "that Pinocchio's nose is right here." His chubby fingers pointed between his naked legs—no underpants, just bare. There were two, round, hairy things hanging like rotten, wizened, kiwi fruits with his Willy in between, which he fondled and played with. "Now imagine this is Pinocchio's nose."

"That's not a *nose!*"

"We're playing a *game*, María! Do you want money and chocolate or *not?*" His voice had turned Dragonish. Grace didn't want to play anymore, if he was going to be mean.

María touched his Willy and it sprang up like a creature with a heart and lungs and a brain all of its own.

"Aah, aah," the father cried out as if it hurt, "you see how Pinocchio's nose grows when he tells a lie? How come a lie can feel so *good?*" he groaned. "Would you like Pinocchio to lie again? Come on little Adela, make Pinocchio lie."

"No."

"María?"

María took the live animal in her hand and laughed. Then she slapped it so it waved left and then right. "It's gone all hard," she tittered.

"Hold Pinocchio's nose, María. Hard. I said, HOLD IT!"

She obeyed.

"Squeeze it, move your hand up and down, he ordered, gripping María's hand, putting it under his own. Grace noticed lilac-blue veins popping out of the "nose" like rivers. "See how he lies?" he puffed. "See how bad he is? He's a bad, bad, wicked boy!"

María wriggled her little hand away.

"In fact, he's so bad I need to take this bad boy in hand *myself*," he panted, grabbing the thing in his right fist and rubbing and pulling it up and down like it was a cow's udder until he was going faster and faster and faster like a runaway train. His hips were making dancy circles in the air, his robe was swinging from side to side, wagging like a dog's tail. Finally, he grunted, "Aah!" White water came out of the wee-wee hole and Grace smelled a raw potato, bleachy smell. Clorox and potatoes. The priest started to cry. He had tears in his eyes. Grace felt badly for him because he must have been in terrible pain. "Bad, bad Pinocchio," he whimpered, and then he quickly wiped the thing—which had suddenly turned all tiny and Flopsy Bunny—he wiped it with his robe. Then he let the dress drop to the floor, covering his fat thighs once more.

"I'm sorry girls, that Pinocchio was such a liar tonight. Such a big, bad *liar*! But you Angels have been so good. So good, that tomorrow I'm going to buy you candy."

"And our uniforms?" Grace asked in a very small voice.

"Oh yes. Absolutely. Nice, neat, clean uniforms for two, clean little girls. Now remember what I said, this is *our* secret." He started to move toward the curtain to leave.

"Will we play Pinocchio tomorrow night and earn more money?" María asked.

"Perhaps. Although I'd like to keep Pinocchio under control. But then again, it's true, he does need some eyes, doesn't he, girls? Maybe you could paint some eyes on either side of his big bad nose. That would be fun. That would make the nose get *really* enormous. Ooh yes, that would be great fun." He crept out of the shack, tiptoeing like he wanted to be a ballet dancer but making a lot of noise as he went. Then he peeped his head back in. Grace saw how shiny and round and red it was, even redder than the snaky Willy with just one eye and a Life of its Own. "Night, night, sleep tight, don't let the bedbugs bite," he said softly.

Grace wanted to wash her hands. She had touched his wet mouth with her finger. She would have to keep this a secret. She wasn't sure why, but she didn't want anybody to know about this ever, ever, ever—there was something stinky about it all. She wondered if her mom could see from Heaven, if she had seen the priest playing Pinocchio with them. She hoped that she was busy doing something else, playing with Mrs. Paws, perhaps.

Because she never, ever wanted her mom to find out.

44

Sylvia

Using Elodie's ear-buds and connecting the recording pen to Tommy's iPhone, Sylvia spent the taxi ride, and every minute after, listening to Grace's recordings. It broke her heart to know that her daughter had visions of her dead in Heaven, to be taken any minute in a black limousine down to Hell to burn and fry with the Devil if Grace said a word to anybody about who Ruth was, or if she tried to speak English. Poor Grace. That witch had filled her head with images of horror: a spiteful God, Bogey-men, trash dumps in Rio. She'd killed off Pidgey O Dollars—of course she had, he was in the photo they'd posted everywhere on the Internet: Grace smiling with her teddy. No wonder Grace hadn't told a soul—she was terrified. Wetting her bed proved it.

Sylvia listened over and over to each session, starting from before Mrs. Paws's poisoning and culminating with whole tracts of Spanish. Grace was no longer speaking her own language, except for more complicated words and phrases that had no translation, like blasphemous.

Ruth was even more malevolent than Sylvia had feared. Melinda was right—she'd had designs on Tommy all along. But she was all messed up, too. Traumatized by a five-year-old wetting the bed even though it was she, Ruth, who was provoking her to do so. Grace hadn't wet her bed for two whole years, previously. Poor little thing. What was Ruth's plan? Dump Grace and take up with Tommy in her new guise? Just leave Grace with Lucho, and hope for the best? Or, hope for the worst? Sylvia noticed how, not even once, had her daughter declared that she hated Ruth, not once had Grace yelled "I hate Ruth." Yet by God, was that woman hateable.

Sylvia and Elodie met up with Melinda. They were sitting at a restaurant in the town of Chinandega. Melinda had dumped her backpack at a guesthouse, and now all three were waiting for some dinner. Despite having eaten at Angela's, Sylvia still felt hungry, as if food could sop-up the ache of anxiety and pain. Earlier, she'd found a couple of schools, although they were obviously closed until tomorrow. She didn't know what more she could do that night—be patient, wait until light.

Elodie's camera had been pulled out several times, but most of the people to whom she'd shown the photos were more fascinated by the gadget itself than the images it portrayed. Nobody, so far, had seen the little girl in the photos.

"Boy, is she one sick bitch," Melinda spat out, having just re-listened to the poisoning of Mrs. Paws.

Sylvia took a long swig of water. "It just amazes me that this pen was with Grace the whole time. Tommy and I'd forgotten all about it."

Melinda asked, "What I don't understand is how Grace got it past Ruth? Where did she hide it and *when* did she do all those secret recordings?"

Elodie had been doing her best to follow the women's conversation. "She had it inside her teddy bear. I saw her once."

"You mean she hid it in her pajama-case teddy, Carrot?" Sylvia asked.

"Yeah."

Sylvia grinned. "Of course, what a clever place! So smart. She's hidden stuff inside him before. She's quite a magpie."

"What did you get me again?" Melinda asked, who had been in the bathroom while they ordered earlier.

"You said you wanted something simple, so I just asked for a *gallo pinto*."

"And that is?"

"Basically, red beans and fried rice with onions and peppers. That's how Angela made it, anyway."

"Perfect," Melinda said. "What are you getting?"

Sylvia took a glug of Coca Cola. It tasted delicious. "Me? I ordered a *nactamale*, whatever that is. Thought I was still hungry but I've lost my appetite." She looked at Elodie. "Your English is good, Elodie. So you and Grace *never* spoke in English?"

"I had no idea she could speak English. No idea, at all."

"All that Brimstone and Fire that Ruth threatened her with, I guess. Grace was just too scared, poor honey. Where did you learn your English, Elodie?"

"I went to work for my uncle in New York. Did a crash course, you know."

Sylvia shifted in her chair with embarrassment and tried to hide a quiet curl of her lips—"Hell O.D." as Grace called her in the recording. Elodie was sweet, though, once she warmed up. But Grace had obviously been jealous. Being little didn't exempt her from feelings of love, even with a man old enough to be her father.

Sylvia had been so preoccupied by the recording pen that she forgot to see if either Tommy or Agent Russo had replied to her latest message. She scrolled down her iPhone and saw:

Darling,

Ruth has supposedly been spotted. Three times. The

Lonely Planet forum again. **On the Inca Trail to Machu Picchu, if you can believe it. What she is doing amidst all those tourists is beyond me – she's really pushing her luck. Another trap of hers? I think it very well could be. Will keep you posted.**

Love Tommy

She quickly replied:

Tommy,

Watch out – she's used the forums before to her advantage – definitely think it's a trap. S x

Sylvia looked up from her cell phone and noticed a gaggle of young teenage girls approach the restaurant, chatting. American.

"Excuse me?" Sylvia began. "I'm looking for a little girl who looks like a local child and I'm showing everyone and his cousin her photo—would you all mind taking a look?"

One of the girls, with slightly rounded shoulders, long stringy hair, and perfect train-track trained teeth, sat down. It seemed incongruous, Sylvia thought—a band of teenage girls in a non-touristic town in Nicaragua.

"Sorry, I forgot to introduce myself. My name's Sylvia. This is Melinda . . . and where's Elodie? She's got the camera."

"Went to the bathroom," Melinda said.

"Hi, I'm Casey and this is Amy and Sonia. We're here with *Christ's Little Workers,* a charity."

"Good for you." Sylvia sucked in a breath and asked, "Have you visited any schools by any chance?"

"Yes, we did the rounds. Played baseball with the kids—they're crazy for baseball here, or as they say, *béisbol.* We read them stories, you know, stuff like that," the girl called Casey told them.

"Uh, oh, here they come!" her friend Sonia exclaimed, a cherubic blonde who looked as if she'd stepped out of rural Ireland a hundred years ago. "Brace, brace!"

A host of little boys, barefoot and wild, swarmed around their table like locusts on ripe wheat. For such a ravenous lot as they obviously were, they were effervescent and cheery, as if being hungry were incidental. "No girl here, you give to boy tonight, boy have good food," one shrieked through a wide and cheeky smile.

"Fuera, niños!" The restaurant manager, a portly man with a handlebar moustache, came storming from inside, booming and yelling into the small crowd, waving his arms and fending them off like a pack of hyenas feasting on *his*—the lion's—meat. These were his customers and he didn't want to lose their business. "Fuera!"

The boys ran off.

"We're used to this," Casey told Sylvia. "The children come every night. Even if we pick a different restaurant, they'll track us down all the same." She was smiling, though. Scary, thought Sylvia, how one can harden to extreme poverty so soon. "We give them our leftovers," the girl continued. "We did invite some little girls to come tonight as our guests, real guests—not scraps, but a proper meal—but they haven't shown. You say you're looking for your daughter?"

Sylvia sat erect, her eyes shining with hope. "Yes, she was kidnapped and then abandoned. Good, here comes Elodie. Elodie, show the girls the photos of Grace."

"Grace? Why does that ring a bell?" The three teenagers moved toward Elodie and crowded around the camera. "Oh my goodness, it's *her*. It's that little girl with the mesmerizing eyes! She's the one who should be coming tonight to have dinner here!"

Sylvia's insides made a loop. "You *saw* her?"

"Yes. Last night. She was with another girl. Another beggar girl."

"Are you sure it was her?"

"Yes, those eyes and that pixie-cut hair. It was her. Sorry to say this but she was, like, really poor. I mean skinny and dirty with no shoes and like, totally filthy."

Melinda looked as if she was having heart palpitations. "She's alive. Grace is alive!"

"That's right. I remember now. She said her name was Grace, but she was speaking Spanish. She's your *daughter?* She looks—"

"Like a local. I know," Sylvia said.

"Except for those eyes," the girl said, her gaze wide. "They were haunting—I've never seen anybody with such a soulful, sad look."

Soulful yes. Sad? Sylvia had never perceived her daughter that way. It made her wilt to contemplate her five-year-old as being unhappy. But she was, as Melinda pointed out, alive. Sylvia explained the adoption to her listeners. It was beginning to irk her. Never before had she had to expound on the subject of her motherhood so incessantly and convince people that Grace did, yes really did, belong to her.

"Did she tell you anything about herself?" Sylvia pressed, unaware that her jaw was clenched from tension, her molars clamped together like a vice. Fear, excitement, hope—all glimmered in her keen eyes like silver goblets waiting to be filled with fine wine.

"No, she was really shy."

"That's not like Grace. She's usually so confident."

The teenager said, "Not this little girl. She was quiet, very reserved. When she spoke, she whispered."

Sylvia clutched the girl's wrist. "What did she say?"

"Anyone remember what she said?" the girl asked her friends.

Everybody looked clueless.

Sonia spoke. "Actually, the other girl she was with said they lived together. She lived at her house. She was the one who did all the talking."

"Where?" Melinda asked.

Casey said, "A lot of them live near the dump. Be prepared though, it's real disgusting there."

Sylvia leaned over and grabbed the girl's other wrist. "What time did you see them here last night?"

"About eight o'clock. They should have arrived here by now."

Sylvia looked at her watch. "It's past that now. We'll wait a couple of hours—see if they show. Actually, no! Melinda, you and Elodie wait here in case she turns up. And I'll go to the dump."

"We can show you where," Sonia offered.

"Really no, finish your dinner, I—" Sylvia stopped herself midsentence. Why had she spent her whole life denying help? Feeling like she was strong enough to handle things, always alone? The tough one. The Amazonian woman. Somebody was offering her help and she should accept. "You know what? Thank you for your offer. I would be extremely grateful if you could show me the way. Thanks."

"You're welcome."

"What did this other child look like? The little girl she was with?" Sylvia asked.

"Kind of cute. Older. Maybe six or seven. A sort of wide, open face, darker skin. Wild and grubby looking. Outspoken. Kind of adorable."

"Okay you guys. Let's get going. Elodie, can I take your flashlight?"

Elodie stood up. "I'm coming too."

"No, you stay with Melinda," Sylvia said assertively. "Let's go, girls. Let's find Grace."

45

Tommy

Finally—it seemed like *finally* after forty-eight, long hours—Tommy had tracked down his target: Ruth.

Tommy was somewhat of a computer nerd, it was true, but it was his old coder friend at his last company—a loner who lived with his pet snake—who had nailed it. At least, Tommy was pretty convinced that the guy had zoned in on Ruth's whereabouts, tracked back to her IP address, from the three new messages that had been sent to the *Lonely Planet* forum. The messages came from different e-mail addresses, yet were pinned down to the same source by his friend. Ruth was obviously still in Rio. But Tommy would need to move fast—he wanted to get to her before the police did.

For personal reasons.

It was the first time he had been alone at nights, and it made him uneasy. His family, college, the army, friends, work—he had always been with someone, always with a group or a team. As each new moment marked itself off, he understood the vows he'd made to Sylvia as he had never done before. Marriage really was sacred.

He longed for her, aching with desire for even a crumb of what they had once shared. Quiet, distant, aloof, the more unkempt the better, he'd take her any which way she came—in jeans, woolly hats, ugg boots, no make-up—he didn't care—all the more tangible she'd be, all the more possible for her to accept his faults. To love him. He—who was nothing, really, when he thought about it. Just a passably attractive guy with a basic skill, a smattering of talent—a dime a dozen. He was a speck of sand without her and without Grace.

He'd been through the wringer in the last forty-eight hours. His stupidity about Ruth, finding out that Grace was not at the beach cabin, but had gone missing. Everything seemed so hopeless—like a gaping wound waiting for flies to ravage. Sylvia and Melinda had kept him up to date, and his wife's conversations with Agent Russo (Sylvia had assured the detective of Tommy's innocence and ignorance about who Ruth, aka Ana, was) had kept the FBI off his tail. Agent Russo was no longer beckoning him to come in for questioning, but letting him know what was going on. The FBI was making progress, she assured him. Tommy guessed it wouldn't be long before they'd swoop down on Ruth. But he'd get there before them. Ruth must have counted on them expecting her to jump ship and leave the country, so she'd do the opposite. Call their bluff. Clever.

The game of chess which, up until now, she'd been playing so well.

Tommy had hung around, too. After much contemplation and reflection on Ruth's character, something told him that she, far from getting out of Rio as soon as she could, would be lying low, biding her time before she made that Burma exodus. It would be easy to hide in such a huge metropolis like Rio. She'd be waiting for the fuss to die down, waiting for Grace's parents to reunite with their daughter at the beach cabin when, soon, it would all seem like a mishap, not a kidnap. She'd be downgraded from "most wanted" to just "priority."

But Ruth wouldn't have reckoned that poor little Grace would do her own thing in an effort to be heard. Tommy knew his daughter. She was independent but liked being the center of attention. Normal, he thought, she was an only child, and a bright one, too. Not so much spoilt, but treasured. She needed love, mental stimulation, and if she didn't get it, she'd hunt for it. It hadn't surprised him that she'd pottered off on her own. Grace was a curious teenager in a five-year-old's body. Sylvia had still not invited him to join her search in Chinandega. Too many cooks? Or she still couldn't bear to see his face?

Tommy's mind had been playing volley with malevolent plans, although, when he analyzed it, he didn't perceive it that way, except in glimpses. He saw it as pure justice. He wanted Ruth gone—no future threats, no lurking about his family, no possible schemes that could bring them down. He wanted her *out*. Neat. The job done and dusted. He was aware that some people might perceive that as crazy, psychotic even, but if they had been through what *he'd* been through, perhaps they'd understand.

He had organized himself a precision rifle which, in one hour, he'd collect from the seller. They'd made a deal. He'd rent the weapon, not buy it. After all, once he was done with the piece, the last thing he'd want to deal with was finding it a new home. His international arms license had expired long ago. And he could hardly try to explain his way through customs, even if the gun was US made—it wasn't the sort of thing you went about with on a Sunday afternoon. Plus, there would be no tracing from the FBI, or local police. The key was to be clandestine. It had been a long haul tracking the right weapon down because of the relatively new gun control laws in Rio—the ban on possession and sale of firearms— despite half the population illegally owning one. But with help from an old army buddy who had a contact here, Tommy found himself a nice Barrett M107 from a gang-leader in a *favela* on the edge of a shantytown, up in the hills. A place called Rocinha. Ironically, not far from where his snake-loving ex-colleague had located Ruth.

Tommy knew he'd be happy with his find. A sleek, Long Range Sniper Rifle .50 caliber with attached optics that would do nicely in all weather, day or night. Accurate at two thousand yards. Not bad to be able to hit your target at over a mile away. And possible, too, with the clear light of a full moon, as it was now.

There were drug gangs everywhere, all weaponed-up to the nines, controlling the cocaine trade. It was part of life in Rio and beginning, even after his short stay here, to feel normal—the eyes in the back of the head, the gut reaction, the sixth sense, all of which had been missing when he was duped by Ruth.

Melinda had rung him on his cell and recounted in detail Grace's recordings on the magic pen. The poisoning of the neighbor's cat, the threats Ruth had made about plunking Grace on a dump and giving away her teddies, the merciless scolding about wetting the bed. Ruth's malicious cruelty made his blood bubble over. She deserved a taste of her own toxic medicine.

He had spent nights fantasizing about what he'd do when he found her. At first, he thought he'd terrify her at gunpoint, to give up the whereabouts of the stolen money. He'd make her transfer it into Sylvia's account, there and then, online. All of it. Then he'd take her out onto the biggest, shittiest most repulsive landfill wasteland in Rio and dump her there like the piece of garbage she was. Humiliated. Penniless. Maybe he'd even make her remove her clothes and hand them over, so she could feel how demeaning it was to have everything stripped from you. Then he'd call the cops.

But then, as quickly as he weaved this fantasy, he unraveled it. It could backfire. The whole thing could turn dangerously pear-shaped. No, what he decided to do was impersonal. Well, personal at the root, but impersonal in the execution. This baby could fire at an exceedingly long range. He wouldn't have to get up close and personal, at all. Ruth wouldn't even know he was there. It would be like a mercy execution. Clean. Quick. He might even catch her mid-smile, opening her front door, popping out to look at the full moon. Nobody would know where it had come from, least of all Ruth herself. She'd be dead almost before he pulled the trigger.

And in Rio, in the land of shootings and daily murders, nobody would even notice. Let alone give a damn.

Perfect.

ROCINHA WAS LESS of a slum than Tommy had imagined. It was a bustling community of maybe two hundred thousand inhabitants, with shops, banks and businesses, mingled with houses of concrete and brick. It looked like a massive patchwork quilt of jerrybuilt edifices piled on top of each other in a higgledy piggledy jumble, set on a steep hill, edged with trees. Great swathes of electricity and telephone wires crisscrossed in front of houses like curtains of spaghetti. The streets, even at this time of night, throbbed like clogged arteries with putt-putting mopeds, bikes and *combi* buses. It took a while for him to locate his contact: a drug lord cum arms dealer. Tommy assumed the two professions must go hand in hand in a place like this.

Tommy had taken no risks. Earlier, he'd called the man from an Internet café and adopted a hammy Mexican accent. At the meeting, he decided, he would pull a bandana across the lower part of his face. Anybody could snap a picture with a Smartphone these days—he didn't want to be set up: sold a gun and have the very same dealer grass him to the police later. He thought of Grace. That little pen she had taken a fancy to, well, one like that had brought down the *News of the World*. Its covert recordings opening up a can of squirming, British, hacking worms—clever Grace to have even thought of slipping that pen into her teddy bear. Her instincts obviously told her it could be useful.

Tommy arrived at his destination. He climbed some concrete

steps, topped by a graffiti-torn house. Not quite the abode he expected for a honcho dealer. He could hear a dog barking inside. He stretched his hand through the wrought iron bars of a firmly locked gate, and knocked on the door behind. A woman with a face as charmless as a pair of nail-scissors immediately appeared, her hand clutching the studded collar of a friendly, but simultaneously terrifying-looking pit bull. That wag could turn mean, Tommy warned himself. He already felt scared. What was he doing? He wanted to turn back, tell her he'd got the wrong address, but she opened the door and said in English, "He's expecting you. Come in."

Tommy followed her into a sparsely decorated room. There was a poster of the Brazilian football team in their yellow and blue, taking up prize position on the living room wall. The room was simple, not at all how Tommy had envisaged. No shiny marble, no four-poster beds and gold taps. Al Pacino's *Scarface* was a long way from *this* home. The wife pressed a button and spoke through an intercom. A six-inch thick, metal door buzzed open. Tommy took a step back, paused and turned around. But the unsmiling face urged him inside, and he heard his own, gingered footsteps creep into the room. It housed nothing but a limp double bed, a chair and a table. Tommy's whole "incognito" guise fell apart even before it had started. His pathetic attempt at hiding his face was hopeless. He stood there, brazenly exposed, green as a virgin at a brothel.

A smile spread across the man's face. "Come, I've been expecting you. I have what you need."

What I *need?* thought Tommy. The word "need" sent a shiver down his spine. In the army, the idea of killing somebody had never entered his head. The technicality of it, of course, but not the cold reality. Surprisingly. Despite his training. As if being part of a legal killing force had nothing to do with death. He was just in the army as an exchange, his time for help with university fees. The target was always a thrill. Like his fly fishing or photography. But incongruously, he had never imagined the target to be a human being. Certainly not a woman. What was he *doing* here? Negotiating death? Exchanging his soul for retribution? Revenge? Warped justice? He wanted to walk out, but the intensity of the man's pockmarked face, the hills and valleys of his foreboding countenance, his summoning eyes, lured Tommy closer.

The guns were laid out on the bed the way a child might spread out his Action Man dolls.

"Here's what you asked for," the man said. "This one's a real beauty." He picked up the M107. His American English was accented but perfect—a consummate salesman, not tripping up once. "A clean, shoulder-fired, semi-automatic with a manageable recoil. Nice and easy. Good for absorbing force, moving inward beautifully toward the receiver against large springs with every shot."

Every shot? Tommy had been thinking of one clean shot to the head. But now, his knees buckled beneath him. He lowered himself onto the edge of the bed and sat there trembling. He was speechless. The man's dancing eyes shifted from Tommy's edgy face back to his array of toys, taking Tommy's proximity to the weapons as a sign of enthusiasm. Tommy's arms felt weightless, floating, his legs like jelly.

"This one—this piece is just splendid," the man went on with a grin, picking up another. "This 700 VTR will wipe out anything in its path. A Beautiful sharpshooter. A classic. Popular with police. Look at that clean line, look at that precision. Perfect marksmanship every time. Here, hold it, see how it feels."

"Remington?" Tommy croaked, his throat parched, his fingers twitching. He tentatively took up the weapon, its metal cold and sharp, its black lines panther-sleek. "It's not as heavy as it looks," he remarked.

The man grinned. "Just over three kilos without optics."

"What's that, like seven pounds?" Tommy asked, holding it up.

Just touching it eased his tension. "Not bad, pretty light."

"What do you think? A great tactical rifle, huh? See the profile of the barrel? Not a round profile like a *typical* rifle barrel, but triangulated. Look at that. Real high quality. Also has an integrated muzzlebrake. Check out the X-Mark Pro trigger."

Tommy let his fingers run along its smooth lines. "What happened to the *regular* Remington trigger? Didn't it have a wider ribbed shoe and a few more options for adjustability?"

"We can adjust the trigger, no problem. Should cut dead center—on target every time."

Tommy swallowed. "What about the SPS?"

"This one has replaced that model."

"What else can you show me?" Tommy felt himself easing into the situation. His nerve cells were relaxing, his breathing more steady. "I need it to be practical. Light. The longest range you have."

He was beginning to feel chillingly at home.

46

Sylvia

The stench of the dump was vile. Sylvia scanned the horizon of mounds, swathed in smoke, the burning refuse lingering in the atmosphere like the aftermath of a war-zone. Never in her life had she seen such degradation first-hand. Television could not capture the squalor, made all the more heartbreaking by the resilient smiles of the scavengers rootling through the garbage like pigs searching for truffles. Her own life flashed before her like a wedding album. Glamorous, shining: a flawless diamond ring. She had everything and always had. She thought back to the howling winds of Wyoming, her complaints, her spoiled griping about the winter months, and she blessed the fresh air, the chilly crispness of cleanliness there, never, probably *ever*, experienced here by these poor human beings.

A topless child in a red skirt flew upon her—a blustering sail in a stinking wind, and shouted, "Tourist! Money!" Sylvia felt like a giant walking dollar bill.

Sonia said sadly, "Thank God for even the smallest thing you own in your life because these people don't even have that."

Sylvia, her throat gathering in a swell, looked at the teenager and answered, "That is so well put. You took the words right out of my mouth." She thought of her closet stacked with clothes and shoes that she never even wore, ornaments dotted about on tables, and the plethora of treasures in Saginaw. This little girl didn't even have a T-shirt. Or shoes. She took out some coins and gave them to the child, silhouetted as she was in the stinking haze of beige-brown landscape. Giving coins was useless. These people needed a life to call their own. "I so understand why you're here in Nicaragua," she said to Sonia. "These people are desperate. Just *desperate*."

"But you see how they smile?" Amy pointed out. "Nicaragua has one of the lowest suicide rates in the world, apparently. Ironic, huh? Yet we, who have it all, are so unhappy, so *ungrateful*. Follow me, I'll take you to where most of the shacks are. It gets even worse, believe me."

They trampled through the well-worn paths that cut through the waste. A glimmer of the full moon shone on the needle of a used syringe, stacked high upon rotting cardboard. Emaciated dogs whimpered, their eyes caught in the moonlight like spooked specters. "These kids have no footwear," Sylvia mumbled to herself, "no real food." She remembered what Melinda had told her, that there were several aid agencies working here and now she saw why.

"Sonia, how many charities are there here in Chinandega?"

"A few. Us, *Christ's Little Helpers*, *Amigos for Christ* also. There's a Catholic priest, Padre Marco, or Marcos, Italian I think. He started a school here for the children of the dump. It's pretty basic but at least he gathers the kids together. Teaches them to have goals, to aim for getting real jobs instead of foraging about here. People say he's done a great job."

"Where is he?"

"Follow me. His place is way over there."

47

Grace

G race couldn't sleep. She was thinking about tomorrow. She wanted that cool uniform and she wanted to go to school, but not the Padre's school. Not if she had to live here in his little house and play *Pinocchio*. She had come by bus and she could leave by bus. After all, that was where she'd met María, at the station. María could show her how to get there. She'd go back to The Boom and back to Lucho. María could even come with her. Maybe Lucho could help her find her dad? Lucho had a cell phone. She closed her eyes tight and tried to remember the phone number in Saginaw. She'd dialed her grandparents so many times, or rather, her mom had. Her mom usually did the dialing and she the talking, but she had dialed herself, once or twice. Maybe she could remember? And what about her dad's e-mail address? She didn't know. Tommykins@something-hot-or-other. Ruth had threatened her not to say anything or her mom could go to Hell, but Ruth wasn't around, so how would she know if she told? Unless God was on Ruth's side, but the Padre thought God was on his side, too. Was

He? Was God on the Padre's side? Had God seen them playing Pinocchio? And if he had, would God think it was okay?

She shuffled her little body under the sheets, trying to get into a comfortable position. The bed was like rock. She looked at María, fast asleep, her mouth open, making funny sucking noises, her pink tongue peeping out like a puppy. She thought about her friend—María didn't seem to mind playing Pinocchio, she thought it was funny and was laughing as if the Padre's one-eyed Willy was the silliest thing in the world.

But Grace didn't find the game funny at all.

Just then, she froze. There were footsteps outside.

Followed by The Wheeze.

Padre Marco slipped through the curtain. "Little girls? Girls, are you awake?"

Grace lay as still as a stone and kept her eyes closed tight. Perhaps he'd go away. She could smell his sweet perfume, his breath hot and panty on her face, the loose sheet flopping over them. That meant he was wearing the robe, not pants—that he wanted to play Pinocchio again. Quick to lift up, with no underwear on. And quick to let down if someone came.

"Girls?" he sang, "I've bought some colored pens. To paint the eyes. And a flashlight so we can see what we're doing. You see, I'm going away tomorrow, on a little journey. Taking the bus down south for a few days. Very early tomorrow morning. Thought I'd say a quick goodnight before I go. Couldn't resist."

Grace could feel María moving, and then sitting up in bed. She kept her eyes fixed closed like they were glued together. She didn't want to see. María nudged her with her bony elbows. Grace lay still, her knees rolled up high against her chest.

"Adela, wake up, Padre Marco is here. We'll get chocolate and money. Ad—el-la. Wake up!" María's voice was loud in her ear like a squeaking piglet.

"Shush María," the Padre hissed, like the One Eyed Cobra he

was—"What did I tell you, huh? You must keep your voice down. Remember that you're a quiet little mouse."

Yes, thought Grace, a mouse to be eaten by the Big, Fat, Greedy Cobra.

"Now girls, I have some—" He stopped mid-sentence. "What's that? Do I detect voices?"

Grace heard footsteps outside, and people talking. Suddenly, she jumped out of the bed like a jack-in-the-box. The priest's flashlight was shining around the room and in her eyes. She ripped the sheet from her body and ran to the curtain to look out. Padre Marco pulled his robe down and dropped the pens in surprise. The voices got louder. She could hear English words—women were talking. Grace poked her head through the curtain, outside the hut. She saw the American teenager, the fat one from dinner last night. She saw her walking closer. She was with the others. She was with . . .

It was the ghost of her mom coming toward her through the blue smoke. She was smiling. But she was different. Not exactly the same as her real flesh and blood mom who was in Heaven. This ghost was like her twin. Almost. But not the same.

Grace came out of the hut and gazed at the phantom. She had hair the same as her mom's, and she remembered how Ruth had tried to make herself look like her. Impossible! Nobody was as beautiful as her mom. But this ghost? She was. She really was.

Grace stood there, her white nighty blowing in the breeze. The ghost had tears running down her cheeks. But they weren't sad tears because she was smiling at the same time. Her blond hair was soft. She was wearing a dress with pretty flowers. *Maybe I'm in Heaven. I died in my sleep and my mom has come to collect me.* Because the closer the "ghost" got, the more Grace was sure that it was her Real Mom.

"Gracie?" Her mom crouched down on her knees and stared at her as if she didn't believe it was possible. She flung her arms tightly around her skinny body and hugged her close.

"Mommy?" *Are you real? Am I in Heaven?*

Her mom whisked her up in her arms. Her hold was warm and she smelled delicious, like sun and roses and Mommykins. "Oh my darling. Oh my little girl. I've missed you with my heart and soul! Thank God you're alive. My love, my life!"

"Mommy," Grace whispered, and hugged her neck, her fingertips gripping the fur of Hideous, who was hanging by his ear. "Estamos muertas?"

"No, my darling, we are both very, very much alive."

"And Daddy?"

"We'll see Daddy very soon. He loves you so much. We've missed you *so* much."

Grace clasped her war-torn teddy, and a hot tear trickled down her cheek. She wasn't dead. Her mom hadn't been dead—or if she had been, it was only for a little while. *Estaba muerta.* She was just paying a visit to Heaven, and Grace knew she'd come back.

"My, my, who's this?" her mom asked, picking her teddy out of her little hands.

"Se llama Amarillo," Grace replied, and then nuzzled her head back into her mom's soft blond hair.

The priest came out of the shack, his forehead oozing with greasy sweat, his bald head shining pink. "What's going on? Hello, can I help?" Grace saw him out of the corner of her eye. He had the Dragon Look.

But Sylvia was smiling. "Padre Marco?" she said in Spanish.

"Yes, I am he," the man responded with suspicion. María popped her head out from behind the curtain and smiled shyly at the group of women.

"And you're Grace's little friend! The American girls told me about you," Sylvia said to María.

"Me llamo María," she answered, twiddling her hair with her fingers.

"María, what a pretty name."

"And you are?" the priest demanded, his face redder than a ripe tomato.

"My name is Sylvia Garland. I'm Grace's mother."

"Grace?"

"I'm Adela's mother."

The man chuckled. His Samuel Whiskers teeth looked pointed and yellow.

Sylvia shifted her eyes to the sky. "Any of you girls speak better Spanish than I do? Because this whole mother explanation thing is getting pretty tedious."

"Ella es mi madre," Grace piped up.

The priest said, "Now look here—"

"Es mi *Mamá*!" Grace shrieked at him, "y me voy con *ella*! Y María viene también!"

"You want María to come with us?" Sylvia asked her daughter.

Grace nodded. María stood there in her fresh white nighty. Then she walked over to Sylvia and held her hand.

48

Tommy

He'd take the Barrett, after all. The M107. It might not be as light as the Remington and not as tough as some of the others the man had shown him, but he knew the gun. He understood it. He didn't want a surprise performance from something he hadn't used before.

"Good choice," the dealer said with a smirk. "You can't go wrong with—"

"Excuse me, my cell," Tommy broke in, fumbling his fingers into his back pocket and taking out the vibrating iPhone. He'd kept it on. Melinda had called him earlier with news that Sylvia might be close to locating Grace. "Hello?" It was Sylvia. He knew by the pause, the way she said nothing for a beat.

"Hi, darling, any joy?" he asked.

"I've got her. I've found Grace! She's in my arms."

Tommy heaved out a sigh. His eyes misted up. "Thank Christ for that. Well done, you. Is she okay?"

"She's traumatized. Has hardly said a word and she's very skinny—cuts and bruises all over her, but nothing serious. But I'm going to try and find a doctor to look her over, just in case."

He felt as if his heart would burst right through his chest. "What a relief—the happiest day of my life, where was she?"

"Being looked after by the Catholic priest, next to his cardboard church on the outskirts of the dump. The methane gases alone at that place are enough to generate a recycling plant—I don't know why something can't be done, it's horrendous. This priest, Father Marco, is doing all he can to help the kids around here. Thank God he'd given Grace a bed and food. I don't know what we would have done if it weren't for him."

The dealer was eyeing Tommy up with impatience. Tommy could feel his hands shaking again. He laid the Barrett on the bed and said in a soft voice, "Listen, darling, can I call you back in five min—"

"Is there something more important than Grace on your mind, Tommy?" His wife's voice was a cleaver. "Where are you?"

"I just can't talk right now, I—"

"Are you with Ruth again?"

"Don't be ridiculous, of course—"

"I don't like the way—"

"I've got *diarrhea*," he blurted out in a panic. "I've got to go." He switched the phone off and shoved it back into his pocket.

The arms dealer burst out laughing—a gold glint flashed from a back molar. "The missus?"

"Yes," Tommy said. But it wasn't funny. The most important thing in his life had just happened and he was mixed up in a swirl of mendacity. Of his own making. He'd just had a wake-up call. His hand in the cookie jar. But it wasn't a cookie jar where his hand had wandered; it was a nest of scorpions. "Look, I'm sorry. I'm going to have to pass. I've changed my mind."

"So this has all been a waste of my time?" The dealer's hollow eyes were caverns of mistrust. And disgust. His rubbery smile turned to a sour sneer.

337

"No! Yes. I mean, I'll pay you, all the same, I just don't want—"

"I understand. I saw that look on your face earlier. The writing was on the wall. Listen man, there are two camps of men in this world. The pussy-whipped and the lions." He snatched the weapon out of Tommy's trembling hands and reached for a soft packet of cigarettes, lying on the table. He took one out with his teeth, the gold twinkling like a warning light. He spat off a loose flake of tobacco. Tommy flinched. The man still held the weapon in one hand. The door was bolted behind them. Tommy's heart was clobbering his ribs. "Get the fuck outta here, *pussy*. You can pay my wife before you leave. Go on. Out!"

TOMMY WAS BACK on the street, three hundred and fifty dollars down, sweat drenching his T-shirt and dripping from his brow. He remembered the scene from *Scarface*—the man sawn up by the chainsaw in the bath. The blood and guts splattering the walls, splashing and spraying the faces of his murderers. That could have been him if this man had turned. What had he been thinking?

He took out his cell, wedged himself behind a tree so as not to be seen, and dialed Sylvia. Pussy-whipped? He'd take pussy-whipped any day of the week over being a killer. Hearing that Grace was alive, wrapped in Sylvia's arms, made his bitterness vanish. He'd accused Ruth of having an inflated ego but it was he, Tommy, whose ego was like a peacock on a bad day. Terminating Ruth wasn't going to solve a thing, even though he was sure he would have gotten away with it scot-free. But he would have paid heavily with his conscience. That bitch wasn't even worth his time, and certainly not important enough to risk his family life. Grace and Sylvia would need him. Grace had been found. That was all that counted now.

He'd wasted time with his stupid vigilante plan, literally saved by the bell. Saved by Sylvia ringing when she did. A close call if ever there was one. He'd wasted the FBI a whole half day. At least. Why didn't he tell them where Ruth was, instead of trying to be the big avenger, taking stuff into his own hands? Still camouflaged by the tree, he dialed Agent Russo. He enlightened her to what his ex-colleague had discovered—Ruth's whereabouts.

The detective cut in, reeling off the rest of the address. "We were onto it already," she divulged. "The Rio police might even be there as we speak."

"Oh," Tommy replied awkwardly, wondering what would have happened if his bullet had gone through Ruth's head just at the moment the feds were turning up to arrest her. Or, perhaps the police would have arrived first, just as he was setting up the shot, and he would have been too late, anyway. He hung up, tail between his unsteady legs.

He still had the image of gangster's orange-peel face imprinted on his mind.

Pussy-whipped.

He dialed Sylvia and listened to the long ring. It picked up. But it was only her voicemail. He said, "I'm so sorry, my darling, my stomach was inside out. I'm over the moon about Grace—I'm so proud of you. Well done! Listen, I'm on my way to the airport now—well, I need to pick up my backpack from the hotel first— then I'll get on the first plane out of here to Nicaragua. Even if you don't want to see me, I'm coming. You can't keep me away. I won't take no for an answer! I love you. You and Grace are my life, you know that. Give Gracie a big hug—tell her Daddy is on his way. Call me."

He slipped out from behind the tree and ran as fast as he could. In zigzags. Just in case that crazy fucker with the glinting tooth was standing on the terrace of his house with an M107 pointed at his head.

49

Sylvia

No sooner had Sylvia finished listening to Tommy's message, when Agent Russo called with congratulations about Grace. The detective told her how Tommy had revealed his findings from his ex colleague, although the FBI, she said, was already one step ahead. She recapped the information; that the three postings on the *Lonely Planet* forum had come from different e-mails, yet all had the same IP source. Obviously, they suspected Ruth of being the one who sent them.

Sylvia remembered Tommy explaining that to her—IP: Internet protocol. How IP tracers can see where an e-mail or picture has travelled, and IP sniffers will detect all the IP around a certain place. Most people, he'd explained, have a floating IP address but the sniffer can find the root of it. Why, Sylvia wondered, hadn't Tommy *told* her when he called, that his old colleague had tracked Ruth down? The Brazilian police, the agent assured her, were on their way to the source address. But she warned Sylvia not to get her hopes up—nothing was conclusive. Ruth was a slippery fish.

With Grace now safe, Sylvia could see the world in a different light. She imagined Agent Russo, now, working long hours, giving all her energy to this case. Washington DC was a couple of hours ahead. Was the detective back at home, sipping a glass of wine, working overtime, or was she still in the office, in a lonely, dim-lit room? Had Sylvia even said "thank you?" She supposed she had because that's the way she'd been brought up, but had she *felt* that thank you? She dialed her number. "Agent Russo?"

"Yes?"

"You know with all this commotion and drama, I don't even know anything about you. I don't even know if you're married or if you have children. I've been so self-centered, I—"

"Your child was kidnapped then went missing. It's normal. And yes, I am married and I do have a child. A little girl called Madison. She's eight now. That's why I took your case. I empathized. As you can imagine."

"Thank you with all my heart."

"How is Grace?"

"I found a doctor. She was on her way to bed but she kindly agreed to give Grace an examination. Grace is okay, but in shock. Hardly speaking, and when she does, it's a medley of Spanish and Spanglish. She's physically fine, just a few cuts and bruises. Thank God for that priest and her friend María."

"Did you find María's parents?" Agent Russo asked.

"No, we went to her little shack by the dump but nobody was there. Can you get your attaché on to that? She told me her name is María Bianca Macias Mora. Have you got a pen to jot that down?"

"Got it."

"Really?"

"Don't need to hear a name twice," the agent said coolly.

"And also, we need to get Lucho Reynes out of that cell. It's late and I've just put Grace to bed. We've checked into a hotel here in Chinandega. So I really don't want to go down to the station right now—I need to stay with her, but I can't bear the thought of that poor guy in there another minute. I've asked Grace about him. She adores him. He didn't do anything wrong, I'm sure of it. Can you pull some strings to get him out of there ASAP?"

"I already have."

"Always ahead of it all, thanks."

"That's my job."

"You know, when I'm back in Saginaw and things have settled down, I'd like to come to Washington one day. Have lunch with you."

"That would be my pleasure."

"And Agent Russo? One more thing? You know Tommy had nothing to do with the money being stolen, don't you? That he wasn't involved in Ruth's shenanigans?"

"We know that."

"He's totally innocent. I mean, you believe that, don't you?"

"Put it this way. He hasn't committed a crime in the eyes of the law."

Sylvia felt herself flush. "And in your eyes?"

The agent laughed lightly. "He's got a little growing up to do. He's lucky to have you."

Sylvia smiled. "That's what *he* says."

"Well, I'm sure after all this, he'll really start acting on it, too. I'm sorry, I have no right to judge, I—"

"Yes, you do. You've lived through this with us more than any-one else. You've seen our warts and all. Anyway, thank you for all you've done. And your colleagues, too. Well, goodnight."

"I'll let you know what comes of the Rio bust at that address. Fingers crossed."

"Fingers crossed," said Sylvia.

Sylvia sat on the edge of the bed, with Grace snuggled under the sheets, her daughter's skinny arms tight around her waist.

Grace—her sanctuary. Her peace. Nothing was more important

than family.

It made Sylvia remember LeRoy. If he hadn't drowned, maybe they'd be friends now. Not having him in her life was somehow a blow. To be given something and then instantly lose it again was shocking. She wondered, for a second, if she'd rather not have found that shoebox with the letters at all, yet somehow it made her love her father all the more. His weakness, his pain, the feeling of being torn and, above all, his guilt. She had been there, too, and, thank God, was given a second chance. Her dad's failing made him all the more human to her. And Loretta. Lying to her son to protect him. People usually lied or hid information in order to protect others.

Except in Ruth's case. What was her reason? Who was *she* protecting? Her ego? Sylvia still found it inconceivable that a person like Ruth could function so breezily without remorse.

Grace's eyes were closed but Sylvia sensed she was still awake. Little María was fast asleep on the other bed.

"I love you so much Gracie, you know that?" Sylvia whispered. "I've missed you. Every second of every day. I've missed you and thought about you. All the time. And so has Daddy." Sylvia stroked her tufty hair. "You're like a soft little baby hedgehog." She knew how Grace always likened people to animals. She needed to get her back to being the little girl she had been just a few weeks before. She couldn't imagine her story, but it must have seemed a lifetime to a child her age.

Grace opened her amber-gray eyes and just stared at her mother in response.

"Tell me about your new teddy bear, honey."

"Amarillo."

"That means yellow, doesn't it? Did Ruth buy him for you? And this gold cross around your neck?"

She nodded.

"Was Ruth kind to you?"

Grace lay still. She obviously didn't want to bare her soul.

"Where's Pidgey O Dollars?"

Just then, there was a soft knock on the door. Sylvia got up and unlocked it. "Hi Melinda, come in." All the lights were off except for the bathroom which let off a soft glaze in the room. After all the turmoil, the two children brought an atmosphere of tranquility, as if halos of light were emanating from their beings. Gilded like angels.

"Oh my goodness! Is that the most beautiful little girl in the whole wide world and her name is Grace?" Melinda rushed over to the bed and gave her niece a bear hug. "I could die you're so cute. I've missed you so, so much!" She covered her face with kisses. "I've got you some chocolate! I know it's late and you've probably brushed your teeth, but just for a special treat. "Look," she said unwrapping the foil.

Grace pushed it away. "Nuh-uh."

"You don't want *chocolate*! But you love it usually."

"I think we should wait until tomorrow," Sylvia advised. "She's exhausted. She's been running around that dump with no shoes on." She lowered her voice and said, "Goodness knows what else she's been through. She's hardly speaking. I don't know what happened, but she's not herself at all. Where's Elodie?"

"She got a call. They let Lucho out of the police station. She went to collect him and then they'll either get a room here tonight or go back to the cabin. I gave her a hundred bucks even though she didn't want to take it, but I insisted. Just felt like they might need some help."

"That was nice of you. Thank God he's out."

"Lucho?" Grace said, her eyes wide open.

"Yes, honey . . . Lucho. I imagine you can see him tomorrow, when we go to the beach. To the cabin where you were living."

"And Daddy?"

"Daddy's on his way. He's coming by plane. It might take a

while but he could be here tomorrow night. Or the next day. Thought we'd stay near the cabin for a couple of days before going home to Saginaw. We need to pick up our stuff. Plus, I want get to know the place where you've been living all this time. You can show me around, sweetie." She kissed her on the forehead.

"You can meet Olive Ridley."

"Olive Ridley? Why does that name ring a bell?"

"That's a breed of turtle," Melinda told her.

Grace closed her eyes and, still clutching her mangy yellow teddy, fell immediately asleep, as if somebody had flicked off a switch.

"What about María?" Melinda whispered. "What are we going to do?"

"I don't know."

"Does she have a home?"

"Barely. A shack that's falling apart. Her family doesn't seem to be around. I've got her full name so maybe we can trace them down. Although I think her father's gone AWOL."

"And if not?"

"The priest has been housing children on a makeshift basis."

"Look at her sleeping so peacefully," Melinda said, looking at María. "She's so cute."

"Grace seems to adore her."

"Well, let's try once more tomorrow to find her mom—go to their shack. And if she's not there, we can at least take her to the beach with us for a few days."

Sylvia stretched her arms above her head. "You think we can just do that? I guess we could leave a note saying where she is. You know, I won't feel good about just returning to Saginaw and leaving this place behind. It's not the kind of thing you can just forget. The dump. The faces of those people. The poverty. As you said, whole families living on less money a day than it costs us to buy a cup of coffee. It breaks my heart. I want to *do* something. I'd like to help in some way."

She thought of LeRoy. How he'd wanted to be a soldier when he grew up. To sacrifice his life to help people. She still hadn't told Melinda about him, and wondered if she ever would. Maybe someday. Melinda had a way of unraveling her too much. She wanted LeRoy to be hers.

"I'm going tomorrow," her cousin decided, "to the dump. I want to witness it too. I mean, we've all seen documentaries on TV, but there's nothing like understanding misery with your own eyes."

"And nose. That was the worst. It stank. I mean, it *stinks*."

"To think that Grace was part of it, and yet children live this way their whole lives. Just horrible."

María stirred in her bed. Both women looked over and lowered their whispers.

Melinda shook her head. "Shame really. I mean Nicaragua's got all those amazing national parks which are carefully controlled, and new hotels that are being designed to blend in to their surroundings. Responsible tourism is really beginning to take off. I've read about home-stays and stuff. It sounds as if the government is really trying to get this country going in the right direction. But the poverty factor is so crippling."

"You know, I've been so wrapped up with Grace, I haven't had time to do my homework. I know so little about the history of this country. Kind of shameful, really."

"You mean the war and everything?"

"Yeah. I mean, US soldiers were involved, weren't they?" Sylvia thought of LeRoy again. He could have been one of them if he'd lived. Well, not that war, but Iraq or Afghanistan. Believing he was going in for a good cause. And then getting his heart shattered with the truth.

Melinda said, "Well, I don't know a lot but basically, this family, the Somoza family—a father and two sons—were in power for, I don't know, forty years or more. It was pretty much a dictatorship. From the 1930s right up until about 1979 when the shit hit the fan.

They were supported by the USA. But then the leftist Sandinista party got into power, who, in turn, were supported by the Soviet Union, and that whole Contra War thing broke out—it went on for a good ten years. This is my simplistic explanation. I'm no historian. But I know our country had a lot to answer for at the time. It was pretty brutal. And corrupt, of course. Then, just as Nicaragua was getting back on its feet, Hurricane Mitch struck. They've really had it tough."

Sylvia looked over at María sleeping. "And they still don't seem to have gotten over it."

Melinda also fixed her eyes on María, and said, "Wouldn't it be great if we could help in some way?"

"How?"

"I don't know. Let's sleep on it. Maybe we can come up with a plan."

Sylvia slipped under the sheets beside Grace. It felt so good to be close. To smell her, to wrap her arms around the being she treasured more than her own life. She could feel her heart pumping with love.

IT SEEMED LIKE hours later when the still of the night was jarred, interrupting Sylvia's serenity like a hatchet. Her phone was ringing.

"Yes," she whispered.

"I'm so sorry to wake you, but I thought you'd want to know straight away—"

"Yes?" It was Agent Russo.

"Ruth has out-foxed us again," the detective said bitterly. "She knew exactly what she was doing. The house wasn't empty—she'd been staying there as a kind of paying guest, with a woman and her teenage son. She paid the boy to send those messages to the *Lonely Planet* forum, to do it from different e-mail addresses. She knew we'd be on to that—to make us believe she was still in Rio. In fact, she left several days ago. Bought herself a few days grace—no pun intended. They think she might have got on a ship."

Sylvia felt disappointment rip through her chest. "How can she be so brazen? So confident that she wouldn't get caught? I mean, the port authorities were on the lookout!"

Agent Russo sighed. "I'm sorry, you must have lost all confidence in us. We *will* get her. One day."

One day. When? Although they had Ruth's photo and DNA, neither matched any database to an actual person. They couldn't do a background check because there was *no background*—no old school friends, no family—nothing. Nobody had come forward with information. Ruth was still a mystery—even to the FBI. Without a record to go on and with her blank canvas of a past, there was no chance of preempting where she could go next.

Ruth was still no better than a phantom.

50

Tommy

Tommy sat back in his airplane seat. He could breathe at last. Really breathe. His heart was still racing, not from all the drama that had happened in the last few days, but with fear that Sylvia would not forgive him, or that she might reject him for having been such a jackass. He had pursued her relentlessly when they started dating because he knew how special she was, knew that she was one in a million. Hell, one in a billion. He had never cheated on her during their marriage—not physically, but he had in his mind. He had wandered mentally, had been unfaithful, in a sense. That hurt. How he could have even imagined life without her was an enigma now. She was his everything. His angel. His love. Not to mention Grace. Jesus, to think he had jeopardized that! Thank God some little voice in his head had stopped him from actually going through with any of it—he had overcome temptation with Marie.

He'd win Sylvia back. He'd make her head over heels in love with him again. Failure wasn't an option. He had to have her. Had to make her his again. He dozed off and, with a gentle smile on his

lips he whispered to himself, *I will get my wife back. My life back.*
Wife/life—the words were interchangeable.

                           *

HE STOOD WATCHING Sylvia from afar, sweat beaded on his brow from the long walk. She was lying on her front on a beach towel, the curves of her bottom and thighs making him remember—remember what he could have lost. What he could *still* lose if he didn't play his cards right. Sylvia was still so beautiful, so serene and bronzed; his heart felt as if it could split his chest open. Grace was playing on the sand, making a castle. Her friend was nearby as she ran around, squealing with girlish delight. The scene brought a tear to his eye. His daughter was skinny, her hair short like a boy's—if it hadn't been for her familiar movements, he would not have recognized her. But she was still his girl. Still his All. They both were. Grace and Sylvia. Sylvia and Grace. All this he had gambled with. What a fucking fool.

Grace looked up and screamed, "Daddy, Daddy!" She ran over toward him, flinging her tiny arms around his legs. She buried her face in his jeans. "Daddy, I missed you."

"I missed you too, my angel. So much. He lifted her high in the air and laughed. "Let me see your little pixie face. That's my girl. I could swear you look more grown-up now."

"I have a new friend, María."

"So I've heard," he said.

"She can ride a grownup's bicycle."

"Can she now?" He twizzled Grace about him in a circle and hugged her tight. She smelled so good. Of the ocean and vanilla, or something sweet. She threw her head back and fixed her large amber eyes on his. It felt as if a small bird was flying about inside his ribcage, causing beautiful havoc. Grace's lips quirked into a smile and that smile zapped through to his chest, squeezing his pounding heart so he could hardly breathe.

So much love and wonder packed into such a tiny little girl.

He felt another presence and he saw María standing coyly by them, her long lashes framing her huge brown eyes. Tommy bent down and said hello to the little girl, and Sylvia sat up on her towel. Her faint smirk with a hint of irony told him, *I forgive you.*

Maybe.

She looked down and then up at him again like a flirting schoolgirl. He felt himself shudder, his solar plexus burn, and all he could think of in that second was holding her in his arms and never letting her go.

51

Sylvia

They had been at the guesthouse four days. They were near the quiet fishing village of Aserradores, close to a breezy hillside, just a short walk from the cabin where Lucho and Elodie were still settled. Below the simple hotel was the great sweep of beach that stretched out like a long yawn, and on one side was a wide estuary mouth running into the Pacific Ocean. Behind them was a view over the river's water of the smoking volcano, San Cristóbal, erupting gently every once in a while. It seemed as if it was just a walk away. So high it sat, dominating the horizon, proud, the largest in the country, as if it knew that, one day, it could destroy millions with just one eruption. One day. Maybe not in their lifetime. Maybe never. But who knew?

Every morning, the view looked like it could have been a backdrop for a painted, Hollywood set. The mirrored water of the estuary reflected golden shimmers as the orange sun rose like a child's balloon, and quickly became a glaring ball, too bright to look at without sunglasses.

It was the Garland's first beach vacation outside of the US. Sylvia now understood what holidays overseas could do. The unfamiliar acted as a glue to bond a family together—at least that was how she felt now. All of them as one in their adventure, their moment-by-moment discoveries: a riotously colorful crab, a beautiful shell, the silhouette of banana leaves against a cerise sunset, the river-ribbed patterns rippling in a soft breeze on the estuary. A sailboat drifting by. The mark of a snake on the pristine sand. The rustle of high grass and bamboo at night, the bark of a monkey.

Sylvia felt at peace. Grace was opening up, beginning to chat in her old curious way. Tommy had changed. He was attentive, alert. When Sylvia spoke, it seemed that he eyed her with renewed fascination, even watched her mouth as she spoke, as if each syllable was special. And she laughed. How could she ever have the Ground Dog Look again when all that had passed, had passed? Happiness was something she felt she deserved just a month before. Now she felt she'd earned it and knew that she could never take it for granted again. Happiness was something to be worked at, even in small ways.

SYLVIA AND TOMMY lay side by side in bed. The little girls were in the adjoining room, still fast asleep. Sylvia could feel her husband's eyes on her as if the air around them was shimmering with molecules of love. She nuzzled her head against his warm, wide chest and sighed.

"This is how it should always be," she whispered.

Tommy stroked a tendril of hair away from her face. "It's how it always was in our hearts. I missed you so much."

"I know. Me, too."

"Not just during this whole ordeal, but before that. The distance we had from each other. We let go of what was true. We—"

"I know, Tommy. Sometimes you're not aware of what you have till you've lost it. Things can slip away from you like sand running through your fingers. Or in an egg timer. If you don't flip it around, it can be too late. But we made it, Tommy. We made it." She kissed his arm and breathed in his scent.

"Thank God. I never stopped loving you, Sylvie. Not for one second."

"I know."

"Please forgive me, baby." His eyes shone wet with emotion. "I don't know what came over me. I fucked up. Maybe in some crazy way I was trying to get your attention, but still, no excuse, I—"

Sylvia cut him off, "I know, Tommy, I know." She was sure that he was referring to the Bel Ange but didn't want any of that to sully the moment. He was contrite and that was all that mattered.

Tommy held Sylvia's face in his hands, cupping her cheekbones with his palms so that she was looking at him. He gazed into her eyes. "Christ you're beautiful. I don't deserve you." He rested his lips on hers and gently let his tongue explore her mouth. She moaned quietly and parted her lips. She felt her nipples harden as he plunged his tongue in deeper, running his long fingers down her neck, until they rested on her breast. She could feel herself moisten in between her legs, as desire pumped through her.

"I need you, baby," he said. "Please say you forgive me. Please say you're mine."

"I'm yours," she told him in a whisper. "And yes, of course I forgive you."

"All mine," he said, and kissed her again, his hunger palpable, his desire a raging flame.

Tommy was back. Oh, yes. He wanted to claim her and it felt incredible. She deepened the kiss, letting out whimpers of pleasure. His hand trailed down her stomach as his middle finger dipped into her wetness. This she had been longing for, but had been too closed to even realize it. She opened her legs.

He groaned again. "So beautiful. So ready for me, my beautiful Sylvia."

Sylvia's eyes fluttered as Tommy began to suck one nipple. He let another finger slip deeper inside her. "I need you, too, Tommy. I love you."

He growled like some sort of wild animal, prizing her legs even wider apart, and she arched her back. His mouth sucked greedily at her breasts, her stomach, and then his tongue trailed down to her soft opening. He flickered it around her hard nub and she bucked her hips at him. He swirled his tongue around in tiny circles, teasing her. It was driving her into another realm. He could make her come that way but she needed him inside her. His warm body on top, blanketing her—skin on skin—their psyches entwined; no distance between them. She desired him whole. All of him. Every last inch, every last drop.

"Please, Tommy."

He cupped her buttocks with both hands, pulling her hips closer, bringing her tight against his mouth, devouring her, laying his firm tongue over her quivering core, licking and sucking at her wetness. She clenched her fingers around his head. She'd come any second but she didn't want this to be over so soon. She pulled at him, her fingers walking down to his neck, her nails digging into his biceps, until he eased his way up the bed.

"Please, Tommy." She observed the rising and falling of his solid chest and rippled abdominals as he edged his way closer. He laid himself over her.

"You bet," he murmured, reading her mind. She didn't even need to say the words. He plunged into her and she felt his power. She was his vessel and she loved that. As he drove in deeply, he groaned with each thrust. She couldn't stop herself—it had been so long. She could sense her contractions tight about his erection, and she frantically kissed his mouth, her nipples brushing against his chest each time he came down on her, making her tingle in every part of her body.

"Oh God . . . Tommy . . . oh my God!"

She could feel him harden inside her; he was huge, her desire obviously turning him on like a switch.

"Oh, Sylvia . . . baby."

Her hands were now clawed around his butt, pulling him closer, even deeper inside her. She started coming in a blissful rush. The pulse of her heart was between her legs, and only there in that moment. Every feeling, every emotion was thundering at her center. She could feel him coming too, his climax intense as his hot rush burst inside her. "I love you, Sylvie. I love you so much."

She lay there, weakened. Strengthened. Emotions were circling about her like a wild autumnal wind and she realized that they both needed this release after everything they had been through. Then slowly, she allowed her inner fireworks to cool to a warm plateau of bliss. She could feel her heartbeat again, not only in her groin, but in the place where hearts live. She felt sated and at peace. She opened her eyes and saw the handsome face of the man she knew she wanted to spend the rest of her life with. A man she could forgive. A man who she loved for his weaknesses as well as his strengths. He had come a long way in the last couple of weeks. They both had. They were meant to be together. And she knew that she had no choice but to forgive him, because she couldn't be without him.

Oh yes, Tommy was back, alright. They had gone full circle. She was his again and he was undoubtedly hers. She could feel it in the pattern of his breath, see it in the glimmer of his dark brown eyes. Love lived again. People had warned her that marriages were "work," but this kind of work was worth it for the reward—having him live through her again.

Making love was just one of the bonds that united them as one, but it was an integral ingredient to fulfillment. She had been riding her high horse, she realized, for the last couple of years. So much better to ride Tommy instead, she joked to herself.

She was back down to earth again.

And it felt incredible.

SYLVIA WATCHED HER cousin later at dinner, and was aware that she, too, had been on a spiritual journey—the kind that only unexpected bouts of adversity can offer: the roller coaster ride that is Life. Melinda seemed mesmerized by the wild surf, the trees edging the ocean, the forests, and the clean air. After living with the howling wind of Chicago and the bitterness of the winter cold, the caressing warmth of Nicaragua had obviously wooed her. She was counting her pennies.

"I mean, it's not a crazy idea!" she exclaimed. María was sitting on her lap, toying with fallen wax from the candles that was dripping onto the dinner table. It was after sunset. The sky was swirling in a moody haze of purple. A sluice of dark rain was imminent. But even if it poured, it was warm and the dash of it wouldn't last long. "A plot of land is feasible," she said, "and then I could build something simple in wood. I've been asking around. It's doable, it's not too expensive." Melinda was simultaneously reading a local newspaper, scanning the property ads. "Be careful of that hot wax, María, honey. I don't want to set this paper on fire. Or for you to burn your fingers. *Cuidado.*"

"You'd have to factor in the earthquake possibility," Tommy said in a teasing voice, savoring the flavor of his *Flor de Caña* which he he'd told Sylvia, was the best rum he'd ever tasted. "Although, maybe up here in the north you'd be far enough away from the fault lines."

"Listen, one thing I've learned," Melinda said seriously, "is that disaster can strike at your own front door *wherever* you are—look what happened in nice, safe Wyoming. Ruth came along like a tornado! Oops, sorry."

Nobody had mentioned the R-word for days. They had all, independently, decided on a Thoughts of Ruth Sabbatical.

"Okay, on a different subject, are you going to tell me or do I have to force it out of you?" Melinda glared at Sylvia and then smiled. She had a wicked glint in her eye.

"Me—linda?" Sylvia asked suspiciously.

"Tell me who that photo's of. The one that's sitting at the bottom of your backpack? The curiosity is killing me."

A frisson darted up Sylvia's backbone—LeRoy. Even though she'd never known him, he felt a part of her. She'd brought along one of his pictures as a lucky charm—a mascot. The one of him in a uniform. A little soldier. Grace had also been a soldier. So brave.

"Melinda, have you been snooping through my things?"

"Well not exactly 'snooping,' but with that endless packing and unpacking we've been doing like nomads, it kind of stuck out of your backpack."

"Backpack," repeated María, who was learning new words every day.

"What's in your backpack, Mommy?" Grace asked, her curiosity returned.

"Just a photo of a brave little boy who has brought me lots of luck. Sylvia glanced at Melinda. She never had managed to keep secrets from her prying cousin, no matter how hard she tried. Give it a couple of days and Melinda would pin her down and demand every tiny detail. Oh well.

Melinda burst out, her hand slapping the newspaper, "Oh my God! Oh no!"

"What?" everyone asked. All eyes turned.

"It's here in the paper. That priest, Padre Marco. Oh my God! He was involved in an accident. A bus collision. Hang on, hang on, I'm just trying to translate here. Blah, blah blah, an Italian missionary . . . who spent the past ten years trying to alleviate the problem from the city dump in Chinandega . . . blah, blah, blah . . . it's talking about all the good work he did for the local people, for the children of the dump. Quote, 'One way to successfully reduce poverty and children at risk is through education leading to financial sustainability.' Then the paper talks about the school he started and his extraordinary accomplishments, blah, blah . . . Oh my God! He was on his way back from a three-day visit to Managua. He was riding a motorbike taxi and there was a collision with a bus! His body was thrown into oncoming traffic and then crushed instantly. He was killed, the motorbike driver injured but not grave, not serious. No other deaths."

Grace turned to María and translated, "El Padre está muerto. Un accidente. No tenemos que jugar Pinocchio nunca más." She exhaled heavily as if her body were dispelling some fear that had been locked inside and then said, "No está muerto . . . ES muerto, para *siempre*."

It was a glimmer, a tiny moment that Sylvia was sure nobody else noticed. A Mona Lisa smile, set ever so subtly on her daughter's sweet face, giving little away except serene hope. For the first time since she found her, Sylvia sensed Grace's expression relax. The Padre must have represented homelessness to her, Sylvia reasoned. Or was he less of a good guy than they all supposed? They'd "never have to play Pinocchio again?" Hmm, what did that mean? When Grace was back home—when she was ready—she'd find out more details.

"Isn't fate so bizarre?" Melinda went on. "I mean there are some people doing good and they get their life taken away and others—well we all know who I'm talking about."

"The Padre's school, who's going to run it now?" Sylvia asked.

Melinda laughed. "Oh no! Don't look at me. I wouldn't know the first thing about running a school."

"You'd be great," Tommy said. "You love organizing things, bossing people about—it'll give you something to do while you're getting your house built here."

Melinda took a long swig of beer and said, "You're serious, aren't you?"

María's arms clung to her new protector. Melinda had styled her hair in pigtails and it was heartening to see María as the little girl she was, not a grown-up dressed in a child's body, fending for herself, battling to survive. María wanted, Sylvia noticed, to be part of their family, involved in every moment. Would they find her mom? She knew what Melinda was secretly thinking—with the girl's mother missing she could raise her as her own. Be the parent she had always dreamed of being. The least that would happen would be Melinda's sponsorship for school, and money for clothes and food—María could be certain of that.

And Sylvia, what did she want herself? It was a good question. She'd been mulling over the possibility of raising money and setting up some sort of charity here. There were already plenty, but all seemed to be religiously affiliated—nothing wrong with that—it was what Christianity should be. But there was a gaping hole. Children weren't turning up to school, mothers were not around—everybody was busy scrabbling for a dollar. The word used for wife here was *esposa*, not mujer, the word for woman. *Esposa* also meant handcuff. Something about that resounded with Sylvia. Women here needed help—some sort of network. Finding Grace had been an unforeseen journey, culminating at the dump. A wake-up call, if ever there was one. Sylvia wanted to get back to work, but not soothing actors' woes and insecurities, nor negotiating deals for them, but making transactions on a human scale. Not that actors weren't human, some were the most enlightened people she'd ever met. But she needed to feel *useful.* She'd been searching for years and thought she could find what she was seeking in Wyoming—tapping into her untamed side, the raw core of her nature. Yet it left her feeling isolated.

Was Nicaragua calling her name? They could live in Saginaw, too—in opposite worlds. With her New York contacts, she could fund-raise. Tommy could set up a website. She and Melinda could surely get things moving. They could try, anyway. She'd put the idea to her tomorrow.

Or would it be better to keep Grace away from South America altogether? Perhaps she should leave ambitious schemes alone. After all, she had the best job ever—being Grace's mom.

AS SYLVIA LAY in bed asleep, images of LeRoy sent her head into a spin of dreams. She saw herself with him high up in that tree. She saw them eating ice creams, holding hands and laughing. She was woken, though, by real laughter, and then shouts coming from below: Melinda's whoops of excitement, followed later by an expletive outburst from Tommy.

Sylvia slipped downstairs, thinking she would find a still-starry sky, but it was already light. The two were sitting at the table on the porch, their cell phones placed before them, coffee cups half full. The waves were lapping at the hot beach, the sun already high. Tommy had the magic pen in his hands.

"Shush, you guys, the girls are still asleep. What's all the racket about? What time is it?"

Tommy cut a glance at his watch. "Ten twenty-five. You slept like a log, darling, right through the night."

She yawned. "It feels like dawn. I was really knocked out."

"Your body needed the rest," he said, pulling her onto his lap. "Three things have happened while you've been sleeping. News, both good and bad."

"All concerning Ruth," Melinda added, her face exposing no clues.

Sylvia felt that familiar lurch of her stomach. Just the R-word made her feel sick. "Please don't say she's done something else to hurt us."

"First, I'll tell you something that will make Gracie jump for joy."

Sylvia's heart leapt. Poor Grace had been through the wringer.

Tommy grinned. "Pidgey O Dollars has been found!"

"You're kidding me?"

"He was all over the Internet, after all—the infamous kid-napped teddy, with no legs and only one arm. He is unique, let's face it."

"Where was he?"

"A little girl in El Salvador had him, and a tourist recognized his patched white face. She bribed the child to give up the bear and then contacted the FBI."

A tear trickled down Sylvia's face "That really does make things a whole lot better," she said.

Tommy stroked her knuckles, then wiped away her tear. "I spoke to Agent Russo," he said.

"Doesn't that poor woman ever sleep?"

"She's been sending faxes and making calls all morning. She's a miracle worker." Tommy poured Sylvia some coffee and winked at her.

"You're the one who's the miracle worker," Melinda re-marked—she in turn, winking at Tommy.

He grinned. "Finding it wasn't a miracle. Sylvia must have fast-forwarded over it or something. Easily done."

Sylvia rolled her neck and stretched out her arms. "Fast-forwarded over what? I'm not feeling so on the ball. What's going on?"

"Last night, I listened to the recording pen the whole way through," Tommy told her. "Somehow, you missed a chunk, darling, of the first half. Not only were there Grace's monologues, and the bit where that bitch was belittling her for peeing in her bed, but there were two other recordings when Ruth must have switched the pen on by mistake. Or not. I can't imagine Gracie could have been *that* shrewd."

362

"But Elodie said Grace had the pen hidden in Carrot the whole time. Ruth didn't even know about it."

"Well Ruth must have used it at some point. I mean, look, unless you're clued-up you can't really tell it's a recording pen. It writes just like a biro. Ruth just didn't realize, obviously."

Sylvia took a sip of coffee. "Why, what happened?"

"The stupid cow unwittingly pressed down the recording button on the pocket clip, didn't she? *While* she was on the phone to the bank where she'd stuffed your money! The gadget picked up a good ten minutes worth of Ruth's echoey but clear voice during her telephone conversations."

"No way!"

"Yes way. It's all here, you can listen if you want. She revealed the account number, the name of the person she spoke to and even, can you believe it, mumbled the telephone number to herself—she must have been writing it down."

"Unless Grace pressed—"

"No, I think Ruth finally caught herself out." Tommy was beaming, his white teeth gleaming like a movie star's. Sylvia hadn't seen him look so smug in years.

"Actually, come to think of it," Sylvia said, "you're right. I remember now while we were driving to the airport, she had an obsession with scribbling my instructions in her notebook. Couldn't retain one single thing in her head—even wrote down that she had to run the kitchen tap a long time before the hot water arrived, muttering to herself at the same time. I assumed it was a sign of being a sort of school nerd and attributed all her fancy university degrees to being so diligent."

Tommy punched the air as if he were at a soccer match. "Well thanks to that we've been able to trace the money's whereabouts."

"Oh my God! It's still *there*?"

"Not completely."

Sylvia felt a great talon clawing at her insides. Her money lost.

The beckoning bills: the credit card debts that had mounted during the last few weeks: air fares, food, taxi rides, hotels.

Tommy laughed. "Don't look so terrified, darling. Obviously it's not *all* there. Not all two hundred and forty-seven thousand. She already squandered about thirty grand of it, but still, quite a bonus when we thought the whole lot was lost for good. It's been frozen now. Frozen so Ruth can't get her Ruthless hands on it again. It's right here in a bank in Managua in Knicker Agua," Tommy joked, "where knickerless girls shouldn't climb trees. Ruth can't make off with it now."

"And what about Ruth herself?"

"The money part and Pidgey O Dollars was the good news," Melinda warned with a grimace.

"And the bad?" Sylvia asked, feeling her hackles rise.

Tommy shrugged his shoulders. "Nobody has the foggiest idea where Ruth is. She's simply disappeared into thin air."

EPILOGUE

Sara

Dubai was hotter than Sara expected. Still, the air conditioning in this mansion, with its sealed windows—and the gated, topiary gardens surrounding it—was making her feel claustrophobic. She was like an exotic bird in a gilded cage. How much more of this way of life she could stand, she wasn't sure.

The shopping bags and boxes from their spree were still strewn about the bedroom: Chanel, Prada, Christian Dior, Valentino. Where she was going to wear all these garments, she had no idea. Every time they went out she was expected to wear that goddamn burka. How these poor women had put up with this shit for centuries, she couldn't fathom. *Geez*, she thought, *you'd think they would have staged a revolution by now.*

Sara sat up, and sinking into the luxurious, silk satin cushions, leaned her head against the headboard. She sucked in a long breath and surveyed the bedroom. Everything shone and sparkled. The drapes were pink, the Persian carpet, the paintings on the walls—all glimmered pink. Or gold. She'd have to do something about the tacky decor. He was still snoring. He was like some sort of pig being fattened up for a feast. That's right, not pig, Heaven forbid, not here in Muslim land. She tried to think back to all her encounters over the years with different men. *None* had been so distasteful as last night: finally, she gave in and went down on him. She needed to show good will. Enthusiasm even. Yes, she'd pressed her nose to his naked crotch and nestled her mouth around his walnut—which was topped by shelves of multiple, sweaty bellies—sweat trapped between the hairy, overflowing ridges of his flesh. Never again would she stoop so low. She sniggered at her pun and then bit her lip in disgust. Uh, oh, he was waking up.

Mahmoud opened his dark eyes, turned his head, and smiled at her. The smile was full of devotion. "Good morning, my darling one," he said, taking her hand and kissing it. "Even in my sleep I missed you. Thank you for last night, my precious."

Last night. *Ugh!* She knew what he was referring to but said, "Yesterday was fun, thank *you*," and she squeezed his clammy, jeweled hand. She smiled brightly. "I feel very spoiled. You shouldn't have spent so much money on me, Mahmoud."

"A morning's work, that's all. I earn money when I sleep, you know that."

She tittered. "Two hundred and fifty thousand dollars is a morning's work?"

"Depends on the day. Depends with whom I'm playing ball. Which country, which president. It's usually a lot more than that." He laughed.·

Sara thought of Tommy and Sylvia. Poor things. That sum of money was their *life*. To her now, it was not even a few hours' shopping. She was glad that she'd at least left them their nest egg. Maybe she'd even pay them back someday for what she'd spent— send them some cash, anonymously.

The whole thing had been such a mess. What she'd been thinking, she had no idea, although Tommy was temptingly hot. Still, thank God she was out of it—a narrow escape, for sure. She'd got sloppy—should have been more careful. But she was safe now. Protected. Twenty-four-seven armed guards, a fleet of private jets, helicopters, and a man who would die for her.

"Anyway, I feel spoiled," she told Mahmoud, running her fingers through some strands of his oily black hair.

"I want my future wife to have whatever she wants, whatever her heart desires," he said to her warmly.

"Do you now."

He adjusted the position of his heavy body between the purple, silken sheets and put his arms around his fiancée. "She needed me to pick her up in Rio, so I sent a jet. She wants a cinema in this house, so she shall have a cinema. She wants a chateau in France— her wish is my command. She can have whatever she wants, *whenever* she wants. I promised you that twenty years ago, Sara, but you never believed me. Now, do you believe me, my angel?"

"I did believe you but—"

"I know, I know, you weren't in love with me then."

"I was too young," Sara explained, "I wasn't ready to commit."

"But now you are."

"Yes," she answered, holding up her left hand and inspecting the gleam of her enormous engagement ring. The diamond was blindingly sparkly. She thought of Grace and her Dorothy shoes, also sparkly. Sweet kid, but boy, what a nightmare it had been playing mom. Too much goddamn work! That fantasy was over, for sure. Lucky Mahmoud had been waiting in the wings—*phew* what a close shave. He'd been patiently waiting all these years like an eager spaniel, and it was desperation that had finally caught her in his web of love. Sara had no choice. She had to go with the flow.

"Finally, I got my princess," he said, stroking her cheek.

She grinned, her smile wide and fixed. "I guess you did, honey. Finally, you wound up with me—the object you've been chasing,

Lord knows why, for twenty years."

He laughed. "I don't deserve you, Sara."

Oh yes, you do. She gazed at him, and for a split-second her smile turned to stone, before it set itself into a dazzling grin. "I'm exactly what you deserve, baby. Just you wait and see."

Acknowledgements

I began this novel several years ago and it has been through many different drafts. I would like to thank a few people who helped shape it.

Firstly, Michele Paige Holmes. Thank you for going through my manuscript with a fine toothcomb and suggesting things that I had missed myself, and for questioning my characters. Because of you, *Stolen Grace* evolved into a much better book.

To my beta readers, Nelle l'Amour, Cindy Meyer, Gloria Herrera and Kim Pinard Newsome, who gave me invaluable feedback and mended a few holes in the net. Cheryl Van Horne and Paula Swisher, and Loca Crz for being there with your eagle eyes. Precision Editing for doing a great job. Paul, my formatter at BBebooks, as always, thank you. And to my very early readers who championed me and offered their advice, Betty Kramer, Claire Owen and Lisa Morocco.

And finally, to all my loyal readers. Thank you. Without you, none of this would be possible.

READING GROUP GUIDE

STOLEN GRACE

A novel by
ARIANNE RICHMONDE

An Interview with Arianne Richmonde

(Spoilers ahead—make sure you have read the book before you read this interview!)

What inspired you to write *Stolen Grace*?

I think we often think we know a person when, in fact, we don't. How many of us trust someone who then lets us down? I started asking myself, "What if?" and came up with Ruth. I don't have a child but it was easy to imagine myself as a desperate parent. It was something I wanted to explore. This is every parent's nightmare—something which all of us fear. The What-if question got my imagination ticking.

It is very unusual to read an adult novel written from a five-year-old's point of view. And yet, without that, the book would have been completely different. At what point in your creative process did you decide to tell the story from Grace's perspective?

Right from the beginning, I knew that if the novel wasn't told, at least partly in Grace's voice, then I would only have half a story. The only way this book would work, I decided, was for the reader to experience things through Grace's eyes on a very personal level. I did have an editor warn me that nobody wants to hear a five-year-old's point of view in an adult novel. I disagreed. Readers tell me that Grace is their favorite character so I am glad I followed my instinct.

How did you manage to get so thoroughly into the mindset of such a young child?

I have a great memory, especially long-term. So many of the things that Grace felt and said came directly from my feelings and memories as a child. There is no filter at that small age and kids tend to be honest about their thoughts, until they are conditioned otherwise. I have vivid memories from childhood that seem as if they happened yesterday. The emotions never leave you, both happy and sad. I incorporated all that into Grace's character.

You chose to tell the story from three different points of view, omitting Ruth until the epilogue. Why?

I wanted the reader to feel as if they were in my protagonists' shoes, experience their journey, and ask the question, Why, Why, Why? How does this person's mind work? Why did she do something like this? If I had told the book from Ruth's perspective, it would have been her story. But it was about a family being shattered and the adversity and heartbreak thrown at them, and how each one dealt with a horrific situation. And ultimately how they survived it.

There are a few very strong themes running through the novel: religion, racism and the effects of war and poverty. The book was packed with controversial elements.

The same editor who read the very first draft of **_Stolen Grace_** (who doubted Grace's POV) thought I was being too ambitious—that I should keep it a "light thriller without too much depth" and not introduce these themes, but to me they were an integral part of the story. The battle between good and bad is never black and white. Many religious people believe they are doing the right thing, and that because they believe in God so wholeheartedly, they have some kind of indemnity, because in the end, God is on their side. I also wanted to show how religion can unwittingly close people off—Ruth does not believe animals have souls, for instance. And she talks about Hell, yet somehow she feels she is immune, herself. Children are often taught to become hardened to the world on many levels. Indoctrinated with certain beliefs. Grace is Ruth's antithesis, partly because of her sweet nature, and partly because of how her parents have raised her. Grace believes teddy bears have souls, too. I wanted to give a glimpse into the kind of future Grace would have had with Ruth, and the sort of person Grace may have turned out to be if Ruth had ended up being her mother.

As far as race is concerned, Grace being adopted, and originally from India, made the story more poignant to me. I wanted to show that blood is not necessarily thicker than water and again, how there is no black and white, per se, but many nuanced colors and shades in between. Jacqueline talks about this; that racism takes many guises.

And as for war and the atrocities it brings—well, that's another evil in our world that often starts out as a "noble cause" and escalates into something horrific.

In the beginning of the book, the Garland family are struggling with bills and the recession, but as we find out by the end of the novel, their problems turn out to be nothing in the grand scale of things when compared to the filth and poverty of the trash dumps where so many millions of people are trying to survive in third-world countries. Sylvia feels blessed, not only to be reunited with her family, but for all the small luxuries she has taken for granted throughout her life.

Your descriptions of Nicaragua and South America are so vivid. Did you live there?

No. I visited Peru a couple of years ago and I have backpacked on a budget in many third-world countries, especially South East Asia, so I have seen so much of what is in the book, firsthand.

Padre Marco seems larger than life. Almost a caricature. What inspired you to write a character like him?

Sadly, people like him are all too real. There are a terrifying number of pedophiles globally, especially in positions of authority. I have read about people like Padre Marco, so although he may seem larger than life, he really isn't.

Although the novel is dramatic, it also has a thread of black humor running through it.

Yes, I hope my readers feel free to have a good laugh now and then. Some of the situations are so outrageously awful, that they are funny at the same time. I'm an author who, above all, wants to entertain my readers. I want them to be able to disconnect from their hard day at work and to be able to delve into another world with abandon.

Questions and topics for discussion

1.) In the beginning of the book Sylvia and Tommy's marriage is going through a very rough patch. Who do you think is responsible for this and do you believe that their marriage would have survived had it not been for what happened to Grace? By the end of the book, do you feel they have resolved their problems?

2.) Have you ever been in a position where you have trusted a friend with a member of your family and that person has let you down or deceived you in some way? In Sylvia's case, the decision was catastrophic. Did you identify with Sylvia when she left Grace with Ruth to see her father, or is it something you never would have done under any circumstance?

3.) At what point in the novel did you suspect that Ruth was unhinged?

4.) Would you feel comfortable adopting a child from a foreign country or with skin color different from your own? Do you think there are disadvantages for a mixed race family?

5.) Do you believe Ruth planned everything from the start, or was she an opportunist?

6.) Religion is a theme that runs through **Stolen Grace**. Do you think that being religious hinders people's spirituality or helps them become better human beings?

7.) Of all the characters in the book, who do you think was transformed the most by the events that passed?

8.) Intensive/factory farming is a topic close to Sylvia's heart. And later in the book, Lucho teaches Grace about turtles, and the importance of mangroves and plankton. Do you believe it is the right thing to teach children about ecological issues at a very early age? How do you feel about intensive farming? Did this novel enlighten you to any issues that you didn't already know about?

9.) What role does LeRoy play in the novel? What did he signify to you?

10.) If you had been in Sylvia's shoes, finding out about her father's lies, would you have felt angry or would you have identified with him? Do you think his secretive past and the guilt he bore was the cause of his suicide?

11.) We find out a little history about the involvement of US troops in the Contra War in Nicaragua. How do you feel about the USA involving itself in wars abroad? Vietnam, Iraq, Afghanistan? In each situation, do you believe the government went in for a good cause? Or do you suspect there were ulterior motives?

12.) We get a glimpse of who Ruth/Sara is at the end of the book. Do you sympathize with her at all? What do you believe caused her to be the way she is? And what do you imagine she may get up to next?

13.) If your child were kidnapped and found again, how would it affect you? Would it change the way you parent your child? Would you become extra protective? Or do you believe that fate is going to take its course no matter what you do?

14.) Do you think parents shape a child's personality or are they born a certain way? What are the key elements Tommy and Sylvia teach Grace that make her the person she is? And if Grace had remained with Ruth, what sort of person do you think she would have eventually become?

15.) The Garlands' lives are changed dramatically by circumstance. Have you ever had something happen to you that has turned your life around, for better or worse?

Thank you so much for coming along on this emotional journey with me. I have more books in the pipeline so please go to my website, ariannerichmonde.com and sign up for my future releases..

If you enjoyed this book, please do leave a review on Goodreads or wherever you heard about *Stolen Grace.* This helps authors immensely. If you have any feedback, feel free to write me an email ariannerichmonde@gmail.com or join me on Facebook facebook.com/AuthorArianneRichmonde or Twitter @A_Richmonde or my website www.ariannerichmonde.com. I love hearing from readers.

Many of you are already acquainted with my books from *The Pearl Series,* and some of you will be reading my work for the first time. If I am a new author to you and you are curious about my other work, be advised that the Pearl books are erotic romances and *very* different indeed from *Stolen Grace* in both literary style and content. The Pearl books are for readers 18+ and are not suitable for people who do not appreciate graphic sex scenes and strong, provocative language.

I love having a rapport with my readers and fans so feel free to contact me and thanks again for reading my book—I so hope you enjoyed it.

Arianne.

Made in the USA
San Bernardino, CA
07 May 2014